WEST OF BABYLON

Dawson's Map of the Sierra Blanca
after an old map made by Bernardo de Miera y Pacheco

West of Babylon

A NOVEL

EDUARDO GARRIGUES

TRANSLATED BY
Nasario García

UNIVERSITY OF NEW MEXICO PRESS

✠

ALBUQUERQUE

To my mother,

who supported my

literary vocation.

This edition has been translated with the help of a grant from the
General Administration of the Book, Archives, and Libraries of
the Spanish Ministry of Education, Culture and Recreation.

LIBRARY OF CONGRESS CATALOGING-IN-PUBLICATION DATA

Garrigues, Eduardo.
[Al oeste de Babilonia. English]
West of Babylon : a novel / Eduardo Garrigues ;
translated by Nasario García.—1st ed.
p. cm.
ISBN 0-8263-2340-5 (cloth : alk. paper)
I. García, Nasario. II. Title.
PQ6657.A797 A513 2002
863'.64—dc21
2002007874

DESIGN: MINA YAMASHITA

Contents

Introduction: Gil Gómez is Gilgamesh

Any literary adventure must be preceded by a personal adventure in the author's mind, for only if the author has experienced the emotions and feelings described in a novel can he convey them to the reader. To be able to recount in these pages the journey of the *genízaro* Gil Gómez and his robust companion Decoy over the badlands and sierras of New Mexico, I had to follow the same itinerary, absorbing the human and geographical landscape that I wanted to reflect in my book. The story that I try to re-create here has its origins before the recorded history of the American Southwest, even before the legend of the Navajo Twin Warriors was sung for the first time. When I was still a student in the Diplomatic School in Madrid, a Spanish version of the Sumerian-Babylonian poem of Gilgamesh, one of the oldest tales of humankind, fell into my hands. I had no special knowledge of the historical and literary background of this ancient saga, probably the first yarn in universal literature where men and not gods are the main characters in the story. But in spite of my lack of academic knowledge, or maybe because of it, instead of being overwhelmed by its antiquity or disoriented by the occasional gaps in the text, I reacted simply to the beauty and force of the poem, which vividly evokes universal feelings of friendship, love, jealousy, and ambition.

At the time, the only epic tale I was familiar with was the saga of the American West, which I knew through the novels of Zane Grey and James Fenimore Cooper and through Hollywood films. *Shane* (translated into Spanish as *Raíces Profundas,* since all foreign films were dubbed and different actors like Alan Ladd and Gary Cooper had the same voice) was a favorite, and after seeing it about twenty times, I knew Brandon de Wilde's lines by heart (in Spanish) and could imitate convincingly the snakelike movements of Jack Palance as the bad guy Wilson when he carefully put on his black leather gloves so he could draw his guns even faster.

I read a copy of Gilgamesh which I had covered in manila lest the Prefects in the Diplomatic School figure out that I was not reading the manuals of International Law. As soon as I finished it, I thought that, in order to make this ancient story accessible to the general public, I should write a contemporary version set in the Wild West. But, as the Indian used to say in the movies, many moons had to pass before this thought could become a reality.

After completing my diplomatic studies, I was sent first to Kenya and then to New York, where Macmillan published my novel *The Grass Rains,* set in Africa and later published in Spain. But I had not given up the Gilgamesh project. In a few years, I became a cultural attaché in London, the very city where the first modern versions of the poem of Gilgamesh were published in the late nineteenth century, after the epic had been buried for centuries in the sands of the Mesopotamian desert. In one of the impressive halls of the British Museum, surrounded by the statues of winged bulls and bas-reliefs of Assyrian holocausts, behind the thick glass of a display cabinet, I saw the clay tablet where the story of the Flood, part of the Gilgamesh saga, had been written down by an anonymous scribe several centuries before the same tale was told in the Biblical book of Genesis.

In those same marble-paneled rooms, the self-taught archaeologist George Smith had delivered his famous talk "The Chaldean Account of the Flood." He had managed to decipher the Cuneiform script, which looked like the tracks left by birds running on moist sand. When, thanks to a combination of literary instinct and academic discipline, Smith unveiled the secret scripture, he gave in to an uncontrollable impulse to start taking off his clothes, under the disapproving looks of the Victorian janitors and the stern gaze of the Assyrian stone warriors.

Smith was so eager to complete the part of the Gilgamesh poem dealing with the Flood that he succeeded in having the *London Daily Telegraph* put up £1,000 to sponsor a trip to the digging site in Nineveh, near Baghdad, where, with the luck that seems to reward only the daring, he found among the charred ruins of the palace of the Assyrian King Ashurbanipal, amidst thousands of tablets partly destroyed by the flames and the desert weather, a fragment of the very tablet he was looking for.

Inspired by the successful adventures of the British pioneers of Assyriology, I decided to travel from London to New Mexico, looking for the scenery and the cultural background of the story I wanted to tell. On that first trip, my guide and mentor through the landscapes and historical milestones of the Southwest was the poet Angel González, who at that time taught Spanish literature at the University of New Mexico in Albuquerque. A voluntary exile from Franco's Spain (even though by the time I met González the dictator had been dead for more than a decade), Angel was a typical republican Spanish liberal; he avoided buying gas from Texaco stations because, he said, Texaco had supplied the dictator's troops with fuel during the Civil War. At the time this stance seemed rather quixotic, especially considering how few gas stations one could find along the roads of the

Southwest and how much fuel González's dilapidated '67 Chevrolet devoured. But later I was able to verify, in Gabriel Jackson's history of the Spanish Civil War, that Texaco had supplied Franco' s troops, and I also realized that driving across the wilderness under the constant threat of running out of fuel enabled me to understand the feelings of anxiety and the shortages the first Spanish pioneers must have experienced when crossing such endless deserts as the Jornada del Muerto.

During my first journey in New Mexico I was also introduced to the Hermano Mayor of the Penitente Brotherhood in Santa Cruz. Hilario Martínez and his wife, Ermitas, accompanied me on my visits to the moradas and to the Tinieblas, the Easter week prayers that are still offered in total darkness in the small villages north of Santa Fe. Those little adobe chapels and tin-roofed churches, like the Sanctuario in Chimayó, brought me back to the Spanish religious traditions of my youth, but the New Mexico rituals seemed more authentic, as if distilled through the clean air from the high mountains and the simplicity of the poor people who practiced them.

To get closer to the scene of my story, I asked to be transferred from London to Los Angeles, where I was appointed Consul General, with jurisdiction over several states in the Southwest. This new post allowed me to travel frequently through those vast territories on cultural and diplomatic missions which in most cases were not only compatible but complementary with my historical and literary research. This was close to 1992, the year of the Quincentenary of the Discovery of America by Columbus. I took the opportunity of this commemoration to study in depth the customs and folklore of the native population, as some of the Indian tribes that had kept their traditional ways lived in the Southwestern states. I could write another book of nothing but anecdotes of my trips to the Indian reservations and my encounters with their leaders, in diplomatic missions that sometimes had more in common with the adventures of an Indiana Jones than with traditional diplomacy—but I will save those stories for another occasion.

From the moment I set foot on Southwestern soil, I was convinced that my project of adapting the ancient Babylonian myth to the American West could succeed. But only when I became more proficient in the history and culture of the Southwest did I discover some parallels between the Middle East and the American Southwest that I could hardly have imagined when I started this literary adventure.

Some of the obvious similarities in climate and landscape had been noticed by the first European travelers in the area. The Spanish *"adelantado"*

Francisco Vázquez de Coronado nicknamed one of his native guides "the Turk." Washington Irving, who had visited the palaces of the Alhambra in Granada, called the picturesque rock formations of the Southwest "Arab castles." Journalist Charles F. Lummis, who accompanied the U.S. troops in their pursuit of Geronimo, named the Apache warriors "Bedouins of the desert" because the Chiricahuas, like Arab raiders, came out of nowhere, attacked a caravan, and then disappeared over the dunes, just another mirage in the desert. And to help the American cavalry adapt to the rugged terrain, Secretary of War Jefferson Davis created the U.S. Camel Corps, after persuading the Congress to appropriate funds to import camels from the Near East, and those hardy animals were used successfully in an expedition from Texas to California, though the coming of the Civil War cut this experiment short.

There are deeper similarities between the American Southwest and the Middle East than the use of camels in Indian warfare, as established in Fray Angelico Chavez's book *My Penitente Land.* The Spanish legacy that is still visible in the Western states was influenced by ancient Mediterranean cultures and by eight centuries of Arab domination on the Iberian peninsula. This cultural heritage can be seen in the adobe architecture, in the irrigation system of the acequias, and in folkloric dramas such as the Battle of the Moors and the Christians, still performed in Spain as well as in New Mexico. The colorful pantomime of the Matachines, according to Covarrubias's old Spanish dictionary, has its origin in an ancient war dance in Tracia; and the Oxford Dictionary describes the etymology of the word *Matachines* as coming from the Arab term *mutawajjihin,* meaning "to put on a mask," as the dancers still do in the Southwest.

But it was in the Indian legend of the Twin Warriors that I found the most original key for the adaptation of the Babylonian myth. This story is sung in several Navajo ceremonies, as in the purification ritual performed for warriors after battle known as the Enemy Way. It deals with the deeds of two young brothers, Nayenezgani (the elder, "Slayer of Alien Gods") and Tobadzistsini (the younger, "Born from the Waters"). According to most versions of this myth, the Twins are the children of Changing Woman, and were conceived from a ray of the Sun, which, in the case of the second child, came through the water of a cascade. They came into being for the purpose of freeing humankind from the scourge of monsters who threatened to destroy it. When they were still very young, the Twins set out on a long and dangerous journey, plagued by supernatural obstacles, toward the place where their father, the Sun, lived, to ask him for the magic weapons they needed to be able to destroy the vicious giant Yeitso, who lived in a remote mountain and was protected by flint armor.

Those who are familiar with the Babylonian poem will find obvious similarities between the Twin Warriors' journey and the saga of Gilgamesh and his wild friend Enkidu. After challenging his power in an epic battle, Enkidu becomes Gilgamesh's companion and follows him in a long and hazardous journey through an unknown land, until they reach the Cedar Forest, where the sorcerer Huwawa lives, protected by a set of magic weapons, including a coat of armor with seven layers.

Apart from the main plot, which has resemblances to other universal myths, there are some striking similarities between specific episodes of Gilgamesh and the story of the Twin Warriors. Close to the decisive combat against their gigantic foe, we witness in both tales an inversion of the roles previously played by the main characters: the principal hero in the adventure (Gilgamesh or Nayenezgani) feels a sudden weakness and needs the support and guidance of the younger and until then lesser hero (Enkidu and Tobadzistsini). In both cases, after being subdued, the diehard enemy has to be finished off by the younger hero, as the elder shows some inclination to be merciful.

Another common feature is the ambiguity of the enemy, Huwawa/Yeitso. In the Navajo tale, the gigantic villain who wants to destroy the human race turns out to be half-brother of the Twins, and although their common father, the Sun, allows the young warriors to attack Yeitso, he lets them have the magic weapons only on the condition that they let him shoot first. In Gilgamesh, the villain Huwawa is a witch who creates a thunderstorm and flood in the mountains and will destroy anyone daring to cross the threshold of the sacred forest. But he deserves some sympathy in his role as keeper of the giant cedars and the guardian of the pristine wilderness, which becomes in my novel the Sierra Blanca, the former stronghold of the Mescalero Apache.

In spite of its supernatural elements, the novel has a realistic background, the New Mexico territory in the middle of the nineteenth century. The narrator of the story, Charles Burdette, a dragoon in the U.S. Army of the West, keeps his feet on the ground even in the most unusual situations. Although not always above the prejudices of his times, Burdette has an inquisitive and open mind, and makes the effort to learn Spanish, not only to be able to communicate with the Hispanic population but also with the

Indian tribes who, in times of war and peace, had learned the language of the first colonists.

For the reader who is not familiar with the special vocabulary of the Southwest, we have included a glossary of both Indian and Spanish terms. Some of the Indian expressions needed a detailed explanation, as is the case with the Apache war language, used by the twins to protect themselves in enemy territory. A good number of the Spanish expressions included in the text were commonly used even by Anglos at the time when the novel takes place. Browsing through the pages of Peter Watts's *Dictionary of the Old West,* I discovered that about half the *English* terms referring to agriculture, stock breeding, forest and grazing lands, cattle marking, and many other terms used for material culture originated in Spanish. And a little dictionary published in 1921 by the U.S. Forest Service called *Spanish Terms for Forest Rangers,* which I bought for $3.50 many years ago, covers a good part of the terminology used in open ranges, proving that some knowledge of Spanish was still necessary in the Southwest as soon as the traveler got into a rural area.

I am proud to have been able to complete a literary adventure that in many ways has progressed in parallel to my own life, but this novel is only the latest link in the chain that started with the work of an obscure Sumerian scribe, followed by the first translation by George Smith and numerous later versions of the Gilgamesh poem. A good part of the credit for guidance and advice should go to some of my New Mexican friends, including some Indians like the former Chairman of the All Indian Pueblo Council, James Hena, and such Spanish New Mexicans as Orlando Romero, occasional librarian and enthusiastic fisherman, the genízaro from La Española, Benito Córdova, and many others too numerous to list.

I conclude by expressing my gratitude to Nasario García, who accepted the impossible task of translating into the English language a Spanish version of a myth originated in Iraq, deciphered in London and set in the American West. And to Elizabeth Hadas, who as director and later editor at the University of New Mexico Press, never lost faith in the successful outcome of this long process and has been in many ways the good angel of *West of Babylon.*

—OSLO, 24 MARCH 2002

Allow me to relate the story about

he who descended into the abyss.

I will tell everyone about

he who traveled the earth,

the master of wisdom, Gilgamesh.

He beheld secret things and unlocked

the mysteries, bringing back even word

about what happened before the Flood.

And he journeyed far, returning exhausted,

but satisfied, and had his deeds

engraved on a stone tablet.

POEM OF GILGAMESH
Tablet I, Column i

Prologue

Yesterday evening, while arranging the contents of an old trunk, I ran across a dusty folder that contained the diaries I had written during the years I spent in the Territory of New Mexico, while stationed as a soldier of a corps of dragoons in various frontier garrisons. Since the paper supply from the Quartermaster was not abundant, I became accustomed to writing on the backs of tablets where the company's daily reports or other news items appeared, and which I later bound together in the sheets of brown paper used to wrap dried-up crackers.

I had almost forgotten all about those yellowed pieces of paper, inscribed with a shaky hand by the flickering light of a campfire, and the events of those years seemed so remote in time that it was sometimes difficult for me to come to grips with the fact that I was the protagonist of that story. Protagonist? The term may be an exaggeration, especially during those first few years of service, when all one did was follow the routine and take orders, sometimes spoken, other times sounded on the bugle, from superior officers, although they were not always superior in ethical and cultural upbringing.

I spent several hours reading my faded diaries by the dim light of an oil lamp, sitting on top of the very trunk where I had rediscovered that portion of my life. I even forgot to eat, sending away the poor maid who had come to the attic to remind me that it was suppertime. Sometimes I had to interrupt my reading, because I wasn't able to decipher the hieroglyphics of my own handwriting, which became fainter and fainter as the ink became more watered down to the point of resembling the tracks that birds leave on wet sand.

But by daybreak, when I got to the last sheet of the diary, it dawned on me that this narrative, written with no literary ambition but simply with a concern for accuracy, told the story of a character whose reputation had spread throughout the vast territory along the Río Grande. It was the life of Gil Gómez, the cacique from Cabezón, whom I had occasion to meet more than once during the course of my wanderings in New Mexico. The incidents of my military life in the West—where we frequently changed posts depending on the need for reinforcements in the different frontier areas, or the construction of new garrisons to try to stop the raids of the hostiles—allowed me frequent encounters with that chieftain, hunter, and adventurer.

The time that has elapsed since I first met Gil Gómez allows me to appreciate his deeds—some would call them misdeeds—in a much wider perspective. I believe that of all the notorious people whom I met in that turbulent region, including the trapper Pattie, the cacique Don Anú Baca, and even the guide Kit Carson himself, the one who has left the strongest impression on me is Gil Gómez. If only there had been a Homer on the Río Grande to tell his story!

It is precisely the uncertainty of his origins and the mysterious circumstances regarding his death—if Gil Gómez in fact died—that surround his memory with a romantic halo, like one of those heroes from antiquity whose deeds walk a subtle line between fiction and reality.

Last night when I lay unable to sleep, surrounded by the silence of a dormant house, with a glass of brandy in one hand and a cigar in the other, a smoking habit that I had acquired, as a matter of fact, in New Mexico, the thought crossed my mind that perhaps I should attempt to utilize that personal chronicle to leave a record of Gil Gómez's life. It seemed rather unfair that other characters in the West, because of being white and American, could have become legendary, their exploits embellished to the point of elevation to our national pantheon, while the life of Gil Gómez, because he was a *genízaro,* born of Navajo stock and raised by Spanish people, is barely remembered. His crossing to the Sierra Blanca is as worthy of appearing on library bookshelves as any of the other great odysseys that mankind has seen fit to remember.

In order to fill this gap, I wish humbly to offer the reader this narrative written on the backs of military reports and sewn together with the same cord and awl that we dragoons of the Army of the West used to mend our boots after a long march through the desert. At times I recount events that I witnessed in person; sometimes I relate what others told me, thereby completing the story without making anything up.

I offer my apologies to anyone who is offended by violent or lewd scenes among the following pages, but the period when Gil Gómez lived was a harsh and turbulent one. I can assure you that the Apaches from the Sierra Blanca were not in the habit of asking permission before drawing back the bowstrings and shooting arrows with deadly aim. So just as I saw things, that's the way I have recounted them.

Certainly the desolate desert landscape of New Mexico and the rarefied atmosphere found in its high mountain ranges can create mirages and hallucinations. And certain things that I accepted then as normal seem now, years later, incredible. This is especially true of the Indians' chants and spells and the legend of the Twin Warriors related to me by Tafoya, the Navajo guide, during rest periods between the long walks over the immense wastelands.

Long after my military service, overcome with nostalgia for my youth, I returned to the territory of New Mexico. I found that the village of Cabezón itself had disappeared from the map; it had turned into a ghost town. After traveling in a rented buggy the thirty rock-strewn miles from Bernalillo to Cabezón, I discovered at the end of the path a few adobe houses that erosion had melted almost completely back to earth. The site was recognizable only because of its proximity to the volcanic plug that gave the community its name, meaning *big head.*

A couple of country stores with their rickety food shelves, the remains of a wooden rail where they used to tie the horses, and a church with a tin roof, its door nailed shut to dissuade the vandals who had already desecrated the sepulchers in the cemetery from returning to steal the church bells. That's all that was left of the most famous settlement in the Río Puerco Valley, which in its days of glory had up to four country stores, four saloons, and three dance halls, actually brothels in disguise. The corrals were deserted where once young mustangs, stolen from the Indian settlements, would mill around. The quadrangular plaza, where soldiers from neighboring forts used to strut about looking for a brawl and entertainment, was also abandoned.

The only company for a traveler who ventures to those deserted places is a frigid wind in the winter and a suffocating one in the summer that sends tumbleweeds rolling down dusty wagon tracks. My friend Timothy Baltasar, who was fond of using any excuse to cite passages from the scriptures, would have said:

> *This is that once happy city,*
> *That lived in such self-confidence*
> *And it always said to herself with pride:*
> *It is only I; there is none other!*
> *How bleak and ugly it has become!*

The only thing that remained unchanged in the midst of that desolation was the massive Cabezón Peak, which rose at the eastern bank of the Río

Puerco, impervious to changes in climate and shifts in population. Even Gil Gómez's fortress, constructed on top of the old mission ruins that once rose at the foot of the hill, was now gone, victim to the flood that flattened the valley in a veritable deluge.

If someone should doubt the existence of Gil Gómez, as even I did upon seeing the ruins of his old fiefdom, let him travel to El Morro, where many explorers and adventurers left their names inscribed on the rock. There he can see written with the point of a knife the genízaro's autograph:

> *Paso por aquí Gil Gómez*
> *accompanied by his friend Decoy,*
> *headed for the Sierra Blanca,*
> *to challenge the keeper of the Cedar Forest . . .*

If the traveler looks closely he will also be able to see, to one side of the inscription, the distinctive marks of the Twin Warriors: the taut bow and the hourglass.

Book One

Did you not create this wild bull?

The blow from his weapon is without rival;

at the sound of the drum he awakens his citizens.

He, Gilgamesh, does not allow the son

    to go with his father,

        neither by day nor by night.

Is this really the shepherd of Uruk of the Sheepfold?

Is his shepherd and keeper, strong, shining,

    and compassionate?

Gilgamesh does not allow the young woman

    to go with her mother,

    nor the girl with the warrior,

    nor the bride with her fiancé.

POEM OF GILGAMESH

Tablet I, Column ii

The Natanes from the Río Puerco

I remember as if it were only yesterday the first time I heard of Gil Gómez. One sunny October morning in 1850 a group of Indians, riding their mustangs, headed up the steep, narrow street that stretched from the corrals south of the city to the main plaza of Santa Fe, the capital of the Territory of New Mexico.

The city of Santa Fe was located—and I don't believe it has changed location—on a hill that overlooks the high plateau to the east and south. Above the flat rooftops of the adobe houses looms the silhouette of the Sangre de Cristo mountain range, a name given to it by the Spanish because of the snowcap summit that takes on a reddish glow at sunset resembling blood droplets drawn by the *penitente*'s whip. In the center of the plaza, directly in front of the Palace of the Governors, once the seat of the Spaniards' government and where only a few years back the flag of the Mexican Republic was also raised, the Stars and Stripes of the United States now flew under a blue sky.

At that time I had been at the Fort Marcy military garrison, close to the capital, for a couple of weeks, having spent the better part of a year in small military detachments on the northern frontier, surrounded only by snow, bears, and Indians. My tour of duty at Fort Marcy turned out to be fortunate for me. Although the streets of Santa Fe were as filthy as those in other settlements in the outlying area, it was the closest thing to a city in that uncivilized territory. As I came to the end of my military duties for the day, the nearby town could offer more than enough entertainment with its gambling halls, saloons, and *fandangos*.

It was market day, and vendors were setting up their colorful merchandise under the pine columns. They came from all four points of the compass. *Peones* from ranches near the capital were carrying strings of onions and vegetables; hunters had come down from the mountains to sell sides of deer meat, bear haunches and thighs, and wild turkey strung between the portal columns. Pueblo Indians from the Río Grande basin offered polished black pottery, buckskin tunics decorated with glass beads, and polished silver set with uncut turquoise.

That morning I was to stand guard at the main entrance to the Palace of the Governors, and I must confess that when I saw the band of Indians on horseback come into the plaza, I was startled. At the frontier posts where I had been stationed before, a group of mounted Indian chiefs would have aroused panic among the entire garrison. I knew that these Navajos were not mere traders, especially since their dress was typical of the *natanes,* or heads of the tribes, with their beaded shirts, their rich embroidered blankets, and their rifles sheathed in buckskin scabbards draped across their saddle trees.

Two of the Indian mares were followed by colts, whose muzzles were trying to reach their mothers' belly. Upon seeing the hordes of people gathered for market, the colts were startled, threw back their ears, and reared up a few times, almost knocking over the peddlers' makeshift stands. Without paying much attention to the commotion provoked by their arrival, the eldest of the Navajos, Chief Kiatanito, who wore a leather bonnet adorned with owl feathers, came up to me and, without dismounting, made it clear in correct Spanish that he wished to meet with Colonel Andrew F. Washington.

I ran along the exterior pathway of the palace, stumbling over the knickknacks that the vendors had spread out over their blankets on the floor, and burst into the colonel's office in such a hurry that I forgot about protocol. The commander looked up from the papers that he had been perusing and with his index finger slid his glasses to the tip of his nose, under which his grayish sideburns blended into his red moustache. When I explained why I had broken in on him, the colonel instructed me to have the visitors come into the *zaguán* while he finished reading his dispatches.

A little while later, when the colonel appeared, the Indian leaders were waiting for him wrapped in their blankets, some leaning against the hall columns like caryatids. He was accompanied by Lieutenant Peter F. Stanton, the Navajo interpreter Hilario Tafoya, and me. My presence had been requested because I had devoted myself to learning Spanish ever since my arrival in the territory, and I often acted as an interpreter with Indians who spoke Spanish. After the customary welcoming remarks, and after Lieutenant Stanton offered the visitors a plug of chewing tobacco, the white leader called upon the eldest Navajo, the solemn-looking Chief Kiatanito, to speak.

"Two parts of his body are divine, one part is human," the Indian leader began saying, as if reciting a prayer, and went on, *"Gil Gómez is like a wild young bull from the mountains, his strength is unmatched, the clatter of his armor has no rival, and at the beat of the drum he rallies his companions."*

"The genízaro descends upon our villages with his young chieftains and he abducts our women and forces them to weave blankets on his hacienda or sells them as slaves at the fairs," old man Sandoval, the cacique from the *ranchería* in Cebolleta, said indignantly.

"If he at least left us our horses," added the first to have spoken, Kiatanito, "we could then venture out to find new wives or slaves. But whenever Gil Gómez comes into our villages the first thing he takes with him is our herd of horses, leaving us defenseless against our enemies."

"The tyrant from the Río Puerco has no respect either for the wife of the warrior or the daughter of a prominent person," concluded Chief Barboncito, who showed off the sparse hairs of his beard as though it were flourishing.

The task of interpreting was clumsy since Tafoya—even though he understood some English—preferred to translate from Navajo to Spanish and let me translate his Spanish into English for the officers. Colonel Washington allowed the natanes to vent their anger. "This is not the first time you have come to me with complaints about the behavior of the Río Puerco cacique," said the commander-in-chief in his deep voice. "But with all due respect for the truth, I must say that since Gil Gómez settled in Cabezón, the settlers have gone back to their old farming ways, and as a result they are now using the pastures that since time immemorial had been a bone of contention between your warriors and the Mexicans."

"It is true that Gil Gómez has established his peace in the Río Puerco Valley," responded Barboncito, "but it's a peace based on violence. Besides, we know that many of the horses he steals from our pastures are soon sold to the army."

When he heard this accusation, the colonel's expression tensed, but before answering, he took a pinch of snuff from a little silver box and, after sneezing into a Spanish lace handkerchief that he pulled from his sleeve, he continued. "It may be that the genízaro has sold to the army horses stolen from your rancherías, but it would be worth finding out if some of these animals didn't already have the army's brand. In any case, Gil Gómez's acquaintance with the mountain passes and the watering holes in the desert has served us. In exploring unknown regions, he has been our guide, hence permitting civilization to reach these remote territories."

When Hilario Tafoya had finished translating the speech, Chief Sandoval from Cebolleta raised his hand indicating that he wished to say something. "Of course Gil Gómez knows our lands, for he is one of us. As a child he was a shepherd roaming those valleys. But many moons have come and gone since then and he who once served as our shepherd has become a thorn in our side."

The chiefs didn't look very happy with the colonel's responses. After milling around and chewing tobacco for some time at Uncle Sam's expense, they deemed the conversation ended and left the same way they had come in as the reddish dusk began to fall upon the Sangre de Cristo Mountains.

Seventy Miles from Babylon

A few days after the visit of the natanes to the Palace of the Governors, news reached Fort Marcy that a caravan crossing the southern plains on the way to California had been attacked by a band of Indians that, after killing the men, had taken the women and children captive. Lieutenant Stanton took charge of organizing a column of soldiers to go in pursuit of the bandits, and I was among those lucky ones who would have to hastily pack our equipment, say good-bye to our friends, and depart on the double, headed for an uncertain destination.

To increase our mobility the army tried not to weigh us down. Our field equipment consisted of: 1 cap, 2 flannel shirts, 1 tunic, and 2 pairs of pants. Footwear: 2 pairs of socks, 1 pair of riding boots. Bedding: 1 blanket. Cutlery: 1 tin cup, 1 tablespoon, 1 knife. Toiletry: 1 comb, 1 towel, and 1 bar of soap. As complete as it was compact!

The night before our departure, I had been to a fandango, as they call a party in that part of the world. Anyone who has never traveled to the Southwest territory cannot begin to imagine the wild and jolly atmosphere at these rendezvous. To be sure, they do not correspond to what we in the East refer to as a dance. In a fandango women of all ages and from all social classes participate, in colorful clothing, some with pretty faces (if they weren't covered with a layer of red ochre) and beautiful figures. I must admit that overall they exceeded most American women in grace and charm, although I couldn't say the same for the modesty and good manners of the women who, after a few minutes of getting to know you, treated you with the confidence and ease of a childhood friend.

In the spirit of the dance, customarily a Spanish waltz, some women began by getting rid of their *rebozos,* a kind of fine cloth shawl that is draped over the bare shoulders. Then they would take off their shoes, dancing with great ease on a hard-packed dirt floor, sliding to and fro as though it were the smooth parquet of a ballroom. As the evening progressed, those who were wearing bodices proceeded to unbutton them, giving out a sigh of relief when they freed themselves from the tightness of these garments.

I must confess that this wasn't the first time that I had attended one of these wild parties, which could degenerate into brawls and riots over a trifle. The Mexican gentlemen were easily aggravated, for a typical characteristic of those who are descended from the Spaniards is an inclination toward deceit and violence. At moments like these I was glad that my mother and sisters were far away. I would not have allowed my family to see me in such undesirable company for all the gold in the world!

The day after that binge, my mind still blunted by the effects of alcohol and tobacco, I had to stand in formation in the patio of the garrison next to the other soldiers who would accompany Lieutenant Stanton in the search-and-capture expedition. By two-thirty in the afternoon we were all on horseback with our own equipment and weapons ready and by three o'clock sharp we were on our way out through the large door, in rows of five, singing "Old Friend." As if the heavens were protesting the lack of harmony in our voices, the clouds that had been hovering over the hills of Santa Fe opened up, causing a good-size downpour on the column of soldiers.

Taking advantage of the officer's permission to break formation, Timothy Baltasar came up to me, holding a blanket over his head to protect himself against the rain. He had also been selected for the expedition, which showed how little our superiors knew. He was a living example of how a man of innate abilities in civilian life can turn out to be completely useless in the army.

"I'm glad to see you here, Burdette, to comment on this mad expedition!" said Baltasar, getting his mount so close to mine that the stirrup plates clanked against one another. "I trust that our horses at least have an idea of where we're headed, because I assure you that our officers don't have an inkling."

"Are you joking?" I asked Baltasar, who was prone to exaggeration.

"I can assure you, it's the blind leading the blind. They say the raid was probably the work of the Mescalero Apaches who have their hideout in the Sierra Blanca, but we don't control that region. Our officers don't even know where the Indians who attacked the caravan went, and they certainly don't know the area where we're headed. I got a look at a map that was on the colonel's table and practically the entire region southeast of the Río Grande is marked in red letters as *Terra Incognita*."

"Well, I doubt that we'll be able to find the Indians without knowing their territory; in these badlands locating these elusive bandits is like finding a needle in a haystack," I replied.

"You're right, Burdette. These Indians are like the nomad warriors who used to raid the caravans from the East: they emerge from the desert, attack, and disappear again."

"So to decide our route Lieutenant Stanton will probably toss up the staff of command like the staff of Moses, and wherever it points, that's the way we'll head," said I, taking up Baltasar's metaphor. We had a good laugh in spite of the rain.

Before enlisting in the army, my friend Baltasar, aspiring to become an evangelist minister, had been a student of the Bible, and for him the wide barren plains of the West were a reincarnation of the deserts of the ancient Near East. Timothy liked to compare our posting in that wild territory to the Jews' captivity in Babylon. He was continually drawing parallels to the Holy Scriptures, comparing the Río Grande with the Euphrates River and the Río Puerco with the Tigris. The different savage tribes whom we had to face for him were like the enemy nations of the Jews: the Chaldeans, Assyrians, and Philistines.

I was never able to understand why Baltasar enlisted in the army as a volunteer, for it would be nearly impossible to find anyone whose mentality and disposition were less military. But I knew from my own experience that one does not make the wisest of decisions during times of tribulation. In any case, thanks to his outlandish ideas, Baltasar's conversation never ceased to be stimulating in the midst of that intellectual wasteland.

But Sergeant Sweeny was in a foul mood, and he didn't like our chatter and laughter. All of a sudden we heard his hoarse voice behind our backs, ordering Timothy to return to his place in line. To reassert his authority, the sergeant delivered such a whack with his riding whip to the rump of Baltasar's horse that it reared up and almost dumped its not-so-expert rider. Sweeny was the worst thing that could have happened to our company; he was not a commissioned officer, but he strutted among his soldiers with his fat belly as if he were a brigadier general, speaking to us as if he were God's oracle. He was subservient and flattering with his superiors and mean and bossy with his underlings.

Sergeant Sweeny never got over a quarrel he and Baltasar had when we were still training in the Jefferson Barracks, fresh from the East Coast, and he never lost an opportunity to remind Baltasar of that incident. It was the day they sounded reveille to do exercises on a real horse for the first time, and Baltasar flatly refused to get on his mount, saying that he suffered from vertigo. When Sweeny tried to force him to get on his horse like everyone else, the recruit gave him such a shove with his long arms, strong as the arms of a windmill, that it sent him sailing against the wall and earned Timothy a court-martial.

When he entered the courtroom, all that the accused did was look repeatedly under the tribunal table and around the hall until he caught the eye of the presiding officer, who asked him if he had lost something. Timothy answered yes, that he was "looking for justice." The court made sure he found it! He was sentenced to thirty days' hard labor carrying forty pounds on his back.

That experience taught Baltasar something about discipline. He returned to his place in line without a word, leaving me to my own thoughts while the last light of day fell upon the plains and the mountains faded into the twilight.

As night fell I heard Baltasar singing the old nursery rhyme, one that my mother used to sing us to sleep:

> *How many miles to Babylon?*
> *Three score and ten.*
> *Can I get there by candlelight?*
> *Yes, and back again.*
> *If your heels are nimble and light,*
> *You may get there by candlelight.*

The words to that ballad turned out to be prophetic, for we rode far into the night, taking advantage of a full moon that covered the landscape with its shiny shroud, and we only stopped to camp when the officer in command noticed that some of the animals were about to drop in their tracks. The officers pointed out to us that it wasn't worthwhile setting up tents, since we would only rest for a few hours.

These were the joys of military life: to ride horseback for eight continuous hours in the rain or dark, and when you finally set foot on the ground with swollen knees and a sore posterior, you weren't even offered the feeble protection of a piece of canvas.

I eagerly approached the bonfire where several soldiers were preparing a light repast of a couple of slices of bacon and a piece of dried biscuit. Some of the men had managed to find some water and were preparing a bit of coffee. They gave me some in exchange for a few shots of brandy that I had left from the previous night's binge. I wondered when I would be able to attend a fandango again.

Seated somewhat away from the bonfire was the interpreter and Navajo guide Hilario Tafoya, wrapped in a blanket. After nibbling a piece of biscuit and taking a few sips of coffee, I approached him. Tafoya had been a kind of witch doctor or folk healer in his tribe, and I knew that he liked to tell stories. He spoke Spanish well, and we could communicate in that language. Ever since Colonel Washington had received the delegation of Navajo leaders, I had been interested in knowing a bit more about the life of the cacique from the Río Puerco, and I asked the interpreter about it.

Tafoya told me that, as a child, Gil Gómez had been kidnapped along with his mother from their ranchería near San Mateo Mountain by a group of villagers from Cebolleta. They were both sold at the Taos fair to a rich Chama Valley landowner named Antonio Gil. As was customary with Navajo slaves, the mother, Ninsaba, was assigned the task of carding and spinning wool for weaving, but the *patrón* took a liking to the boy and treated him like his own child, eventually adopting him as his son, since Don Antonio had no male heirs.

Apparently the patrón from the Chama Valley, proud descendant of Spanish *hidalgos,* had always been against American authority. In 1847 he participated along with the Taos Indians in the uprising that cost the life of the first governor of the territory, Charles Bent, whose head was paraded on a pike through the village. After being judged a rebel and traitor—although he had never accepted the yoke of the new government—the adoptive father of Gil Gómez was sentenced to die by hanging and his estate confiscated. The young man retreated to the mountains, fearing the same fate.

For years he roamed the mountains, competing with the wild animals and the hostile tribes to survive. It was then that he became familiar with the mountain trails and the watering holes where the herds of wild horses—or *mesteños,* as the Spanish call them—went to drink. He managed to capture them by making corrals near the watering holes and would sell them later on at fairs or at the garrisons. In this way he was able to gain the confidence of the American army officers, who began to take advantage of his knowledge of the land to use him as a guide on their incursions into Navajo territory.

Later on, Gil Gómez reclaimed some lands in the same valley where as a child he had pastured Navajo sheep. The Río Puerco basin bordered Indian territory, and since the Spanish had had to abandon those lands in the face of continuous Apache and Navajo raids, nobody disputed his right to that land. Gil Gómez reconnoitered the perimeter of the valley, pulling up bunches of weeds and tossing stones to the four cardinal points as he had seen his adoptive father do, since that was how the owners of the lands assigned by the Spanish crown took possession of their grants. And so he had become the Río Puerco cacique.

"It was after Gil Gómez had constructed his fortified hacienda on top of the old mission ruins, and after he had clamped down on the marauding Indians, that the former settlers returned to occupy the town of Cabezón and to bring their livestock to the Río Puerco Valley. And now they were vassals of the genízaro Gil Gómez," concluded Tafoya.

"So," I pondered, "Colonel Washington had a point when he defended Gil Gómez in the presence of the natanes who came to complain of his behavior. But when the colonel referred to him as a *mestizo,* I thought he was the offspring of a relationship of the landowner with the Navajo woman."

"Some thought that he was the son of Don Antonio, especially those who knew how beautiful Ninsaba was, but the truth is that when they were kidnapped, the child was already grown. Gil Gómez's mother is the granddaughter of the great chief Narbona, who during the Mexican period was a leader of the Navajo-Apache alliance that laid siege to Albuquerque."

"And who then is Gil Gómez's father?"

Tafoya made a funny face before answering. "There are those who say that Gil Gómez is the son of an Apache warrior, but in fact no one knows for sure who Gil Gómez's father was. Remember what the old-timer Kiatanito said: *'Two parts of his body are divine, and one part is human.'*"

I could see by the way he was yawning that the Indian wanted to bring the conversation to an end, but before curling up in his blanket, he said, "Tomorrow when we head down toward the Río Grande Valley, from a lookout point not too far from here we'll be able to see the Río Puerco Valley and perhaps even Cabezón Peak, which gave the village its name. We Navajos have referred to it since time immemorial as Tsenajín, which means Black Peak."

Since I couldn't sleep, I started to write in my diary by the bright firelight until my fingers, being outside the blanket, got so cold that they lacked the necessary feeling to guide my pen along. I got up and left the campsite, walking until I came to the edge of a cliff, where I sat down to wait for daybreak.

The expanse of the valley that lay at my feet was saturated with a dark fog until the dawn's first glitter began to break apart the canopy of clouds and reveal portions of the landscape. To the west one could see the reddish shreds of the Jémez Mountains, to the south loomed the snowy peak of San Mateo Mountain, and toward the east spread the endless prairies across which we would have to pursue our enemies.

Soon a cool breeze from the north fanned the valley, separating the mist from the hillsides and leaving the face of the earth looking as if it had just been shaved. Far below the wind had also unveiled the canyon of the Río Puerco, opening up sometimes in meadows and groves of cottonwoods and in other places so boxed in by the red soil that the meager stream disappeared from sight. In a bend of the river I could see a massive volcanic plug, its silhouette stark against the plains.

This had to be the famous Cabezón Peak, the Black Peak Tafoya had mentioned to me, which had given the town its name.

The Scourge of Gil Gómez

A dark fog lay over the village of Cabezón, and one could barely see the Río Puerco. In the deep gorge ran a flow of muddy water, skipping over boulders and tree trunks that had been dragged from the mountains during flash floods.

The light of day was about to break behind Cabezón Peak, projecting its shadow across the small village on the other side of the bank. The morning breeze was trying to dissolve the thick shroud of fog wrapped around the peak's head like a Moorish turban. The same biting wind that was pushing the fog away spread a rhythmic, monotonous rumble that echoed downriver and into the adobe houses built around the plaza.

The people of Cabezón knew the meaning of that ominous sound. It was the beat of the drum inside Gil Gómez's fortified hacienda whose *torreón* loomed out of the fog under the shade of the peak like a young hawk sticking its head out of the nest.

"Gil Gómez takes the children from their parents," whispered the mayor, Bitoriano Montoya, one of the oldest settlers in the village that in olden times was known as the Cabezón of the Montoyas.

"Day and night the genízaro's arrogance knows no bounds," said Juan Lucero, the *hermano mayor* of the Penitente Brotherhood.

"The raising of his weapon has no equal," murmured José de la Luz, the village blacksmith, as he stirred the fire. "The beating of the drum wakes up the townspeople."

"The cacique takes the maiden from her mother's side," Ermitas

Montoya, the mayor's wife, said with a sigh.

"Gil Gómez respects neither the wife of the peon nor the wife of the rich man," said Orlando Romero, who was about to go to the fields. "What a good protector we have found! I believe we were better off when we were at the mercy of the heathen."

"Is there no one who can free us from this scourge?" asked an enraged Arnaulfo Roybal, an old war captain.

As the rhythm of the drum grew stronger, one could hear the creaking of door frames all over the village. The young men were heading for the plaza, some armed with a harquebus, some bearing an iron-tipped lance, and many with cedar bows and a handful of arrows in a buckskin quiver. Leaving the plaza, they crossed the river, whose muddy waters were only ankle deep in spite of last night's downpour in the mountains. When they reached the fortress, the young men knocked on the door, which was made from *reredos* belonging to an old mission destroyed by the Apaches. The *santos* were still riddled with arrowheads from the long-ago raids that had martyred them anew.

As the young men gathered in the courtyard, Gil Gómez appeared at the door, dressed in dark woolen cloth from head to toe and leather moccasins, with gaiters up to his knees. A blue silk serape wrapped around his waist and hanging from a wide silver concha belt was a double-edged axe.

One of his men handed him the reins to a jet-black stallion, and the cacique inspected the troops while another man held a torch high in the air, since daybreak had not yet reached the courtyard. In the torch light, the volunteers were able to make out the cacique's hawk-like profile, his dark hair secured above his forehead with a crimson bandanna, and his gold earring that shone from one ear lobe, the other having been severed, a sign of the servitude of his youth.

The genízaro ordered the large door of the fortress to be opened, and the herd of galloping horses forded the Río Puerco, catching the path that ran along the western bank of the river in the direction of the Jémez Mountains. Running after them on foot, brandishing their lances and harquebuses, were the young men from Cabezón who had abandoned their flocks and fields to accompany the cacique in a raid against the nearby Navajo rancherías.

The galloping echo in the riverbed had hardly faded when the villagers began to exit their homes, and a group of prominent people assembled in a corner of the plaza where they could not be seen by the sentries on the fortress parapet. The battlements of the fortress glittered in the sun as though they were covered with copper, for the adobe was inlaid with sandstone streaked with quartz.

After chatting in low voices, the neighbors returned to their homes and, one after the other, began to leave the village, pulling along their horses and mules by the halters as if they were headed for their fields. But as soon as they were out of sight of the watchmen, they sneaked away along the riverbank and convened at the foot of an old dried-up cottonwood tree. There, still concealed by the steepness of the riverbank, they saddled their horses, put pack saddles on their mules, and headed south.

The villagers were going to Don Anú Baca's hacienda to seek advice and help, hoping that that old patrón still had the courage to oppose the genízaro. For many years Don Anú had been the most powerful cacique in Río Abajo, and his principal hacienda was at the confluence of the Río Puerco and Río Grande, close to a spring called El Ojo de la Parida.

News of the cacique's raid on the Navajos, spread by the echo of his drum, had rapidly reached every corner of the valley, and as the retinue of neighbors continued down the trail, they were joined by other villagers, from Guadalupe and Casa Salazar. It didn't take long for some natanes from nearby Navajo rancherías to join the procession, the same ones who a few days earlier had unsuccessfully sought protection from Colonel Washington.

The colorful attire of the Indians contrasted with the poor clothing of the peones. The natanes wore brightly colored blankets, feathered caps, thick turquoise necklaces, and lances that shone in the noon sun, while the settlers were dressed in sackcloth and coarse *serapes*.

Not far from Cabezón, the road passed between two volcanic peaks, which the local settlers called Los Cuates, after the stories they had heard from the Indians about the hero twins and their fight against the giants who back in antiquity had devastated humanity. As they passed the peaks the old man Juan Lucero commented to his *compadre* Bitoriano Montoya, "If only our young cacique had a rival who was his equal, one who could measure up to him and wear him out."

"But there is not a single man in the valley whose strength can match his own," answered the mayor, Montoya.

"Unfortunately, that is true," commented the blacksmith José de la Luz, who had been listening to the conversation. "The genízaro without a doubt is the most powerful man in all the region."

At that very instant the natán Kiatanito took up the ballad that was either a proverb or a prayer:

"Two parts of his body are divine, one part is human. The gods who created Gil Gómez blessed him with certain faculties: the Sun gave him strength and ardor; Holy Wind gave him cunning and swiftness; and Changing Woman endowed him with wisdom and beauty."

The Río Abajo Cacique

Night was falling when the caravan crossed the Río Grande at a sandy ford, going up the embankment toward the hacienda of El Ojo de la Parida. Seeing in the distance the sun reflecting on the lances of the natanes, foreman Narciso Quintana ordered the servants to shut the main door to the hacienda, but the patrón, who was an experienced Indian fighter, recognized that they were coming in peace and ordered that the doors to the courtyard be opened.

"Since when do you confuse *gente de razón* with hostiles, Quintana?" joked Don Anú Baca with the foreman. "Haven't you noticed that the Indians now always run around wearing shiny new dress coats, with shiny rifles stolen from the Americans?"

The cacique received the Río Puerco delegation in the drawing room, seated in a large leather chair with a high back, dressed in a black woolen vest and patent leather boots, with pants slit on each side from the knees down, held together with a set of silver buttons. The patriarch had his graying hair tied at the nape of his neck with a velvet ribbon, and although his many wrinkles betrayed his age, from between his half-closed lids a pair of flinty eyes still glittered. Behind his bench in a corner of the sitting room the beautiful Esther, Don Anú's only daughter, stood as motionless and silent as a wood carving, observing everything with eyes bright as coals. Her presence was betrayed only when a gust of air ruffled her dark shawl.

In a hospitable gesture with his left hand, Don Anú invited his visitors to sit down on the *jerga* cushions that he had scattered around the drawing room. The creases of his shawl hid his right hand, atrophied as the result of an old injury. While the smoke from his cigar rose toward the ceiling, the patrón waited for his visitors to state their mission. Some didn't dare sit down in the patrón's presence and spoke standing up, nervously turning their wide-rimmed straw hats in their hands.

"Gil Gómez doesn't allow the son to help the father with his chores.

With the help of his men he yanks them away from our harvest fields to go raid the Navajos," said Orlando Romero.

"The genízaro respects neither the wife of the warrior nor the daughter of a prominent person! The maidens from the villages begin by carding the wool in his hacienda and when their eyesight fails, they end up in the brothel in Cabezón," added the mayor, Bitoriano Montoya.

The sonorous voice of the blacksmith José de la Luz echoed in the vault of the hall. "Is there no one who can free us from the scourge of Gil Gómez?"

Once the litany of affronts had been heard, the patrón Don Anú spoke in the well-modulated voice of a man who had never needed to shout to be obeyed. "I'm not unsympathetic to your troubles, but why have you come to me to complain of the genízaro's abuses?"

"Don Anú is the most powerful patrón in Río Abajo," Juan Lucero, the hermano mayor of the Penitentes, said respectfully. "Your lands extend east almost to the Sierra Blanca, and on the other side of the river your grace's pasturelands almost reach the Plains of San Agustín."

"Not without reason have the settlers elected you the *mayordomo* who controls the *acequias* that give life to these lands," echoed the mayor of Cabezón.

Upon hearing those compliments, a slight smile crossed the old cacique's thin lips. "In fact, only with difficulty have I been able to preserve part of the estate that I inherited from my forebears. I have enough to do taking care of it without sticking my nose in somebody else's business. And the authority that my neighbors gave me to oversee the acequias by naming me mayordomo does not permit me to interfere in the troubled waters of the Río Puerco."

With the spirit of youth, Polinio Córdova, who had managed to avoid going out with the other young men from Cabezón by hiding in a secret hovel, raised his hand and spoke. "If Don Anú would like," said the boy, "you could assemble a party of more than a hundred men and teach the Río Puerco tyrant a good lesson."

The patrón smiled at the young man's fiery spirit. "It would be ill-conceived to organize outings to other people's lands when I can barely defend my own from the incursions of the American soldiers," declared the patrón, adding, "But since you were headed for the Río Abajo, instead of sidetracking toward the hills of La Parida, why haven't you sought help from the gringo soldiers who are building a fort below Socorro?"

"The gringo soldiers don't dare confront the Río Puerco cacique. He provides them with the horses that he steals in the rancherías, and he also serves as their guide in their expeditions through the mountain passes," explained the mayor.

"And since not even the gringos are bold enough to make the genízaro behave, you come to this poor old man to bail you out of your troubles?" exclaimed the patrón, with a touch of impatience.

At that moment the hermano mayor of the Penitente brotherhood intervened. "We know that your grace was a relative, on your wife's side, of Don Antonio Gil, Gil Gómez's patrón when the boy was a servant in his hacienda. Perhaps it would suffice to have Don Anú intercede on our behalf with our cacique to have him come to his senses."

"Have you ever tried to reason with a young mustang when it feels the noose around its neck? Haven't you seen how it takes off at a gallop, kicking and bucking the moment it feels the rope tightening? Well, the same thing would happen if I tried to keep a tight rein on the genízaro or asked him to come to his senses."

And, after a short pause, he added: "The truth of the matter is that even if I could, I would have to think twice before taking arms against the adopted son of my compadre."

Upon hearing this, the visitors fell silent. Even among the inscrutable faces of the Indians one could detect traces of disappointment. As he took note of the effect that his words had had, the astute patriarch adopted an almost mournful tone of voice. "It would be useless for me to measure my strength against that wild young bull, for I recognize that my pulse is no longer steady when I fire the rifle, and the arm with which I used to brandish my lance is now atrophied, the result of an old injury." And, taking his right hand out of the creases of his serape, the patrón raised it high in the air, exclaiming: "Do you believe that this crippled arm would be capable of bending the neck of the cacique from Cabezón?"

Nodding their heads in farewell, the Cabezón neighbors and their Indian companions began to rise silently and leave the hall, getting back on their horses out in the courtyard.

But when the last of the visitors headed for the doorway, in this case the young Polinio Córdova, a soft female voice was heard coming from the passage to the vestibule. From behind a pine pillar could be seen the same shining black eyes that had been following the conversation from behind Don Anú Baca's armchair. The young man felt the powerful attraction of the dark pupils as if they had cast an invisible net into the pit of his soul and, separating himself from his partners, he took a few steps in the direction of the shadow.

But Bitoriano Montoya, who noticed Polinio Córdova's hesitation, went after him and, upon seeing in a corner the enticing flutter of a shawl, grabbed him by the neck the way a she-wolf grabs her wandering cub, whispering in his ear as he helped him onto his horse, "Follow me and don't hold back!"

A trifle stunned by the jerking on his neck and still a bit hypnotized by the mesmerizing look that had entered his very soul, young Córdova turned on his horse to contemplate the silhouette of the woman who was watching his departure from the parapet. The movement of the dark shawl fused with the twilight shadows like the fluttering of a night bird. He almost spun around to return to the hacienda, but Montoya sensed his intentions. With the tip of his rope he whipped Polinio's horse on the rump. It took off galloping, frightened by the unexpected punishment, while the old man yelled, "Move on, you wretched thing, and don't look back! For the sake of your father's memory . . ."

"What came over you, mayor?" asked Córdova, once he managed to calm his horse. "You almost made the horse buck me off in front of that beautiful lady!"

"I know you are young, but I didn't think you'd be so stupid," answered Montoya. "Don't you know that that *lady,* as you call her, is Don Anú's daughter who is well known all over the Río Abajo for her sorcery and loose morals? Have you forgotten that the villagers around here tell us she has employed her magical powers to turn her former lovers into animals so that they won't talk about her indiscretions?"

"Who did you say that maiden is?" inquired José Xaramillo, who was riding alongside them but who had joined the conversation late. "From the hacienda's parapet, she resembled the Virgin Mary."

"May God forgive me, dear bailiff, and may He take good care of your eyesight, and pray that it doesn't get any worse," interjected the blacksmith José de la Luz, who spurred on his horse to join the conversation. "If half of what is said concerning the beautiful Esther, who is also called *La Malinche,* is true, then that woman is as likely to be a maiden as I am to have a bachelor's degree in theology."

The hermano mayor of the Penitente brotherhood then joined in the conversation, defending Esther even though deep in his heart he knew that he was doing so more for the sake of her father's reputation than for the daughter:

"I wish you would stop all this talk here and now. Don't kick somebody who's already down. Remember María Magdalena, who repented and washed the Savior's feet with her exquisite perfume."

"May Christ's name be praised forever and ever!" said Montoya. "But I believe that this lady Magdalena would have to tear down the sluice gates of the acequias in order to wash away her sins."

"I had also heard it said," recounted José Xaramillo, "that when La Malinche became pregnant as a result of her misconduct, to cover up the fruit of her sin, she headed for the highest part of the mountains and left her offspring there to the mercy of the wild beasts."

Just then the howl of a coyote could be heard coming from the mountain. The men remained quiet and made the sign of the cross, spurring their horses to join the rest of the retinue, which was crossing the river near a grove of cottonwoods. A cold wind blew down from the mountains, shaking the leaves of the trees. The horses' hooves splashed as they crossed the river.

The Giant's Head

I was watching the sun rise over the Río Grande basin when I heard the sound of a bugle and had to return to the camp, where the soldiers were hurriedly gathering their equipment. During the night a courier had caught up with us from the Albuquerque garrison with more information on the attack on the caravan. It had been confirmed that those responsible for the misdeed were a band of Mescalero Apaches who operated from the Sierra Blanca. We were to attempt to head them off before they arrived back at their mountain sanctuary.

Even at the risk of running our horses to death, the officers were confident that we would be able to intercept the Apaches before they reached their hideout. The column of soldiers took the steep road that had been utilized by caravans of Spanish *carretas* headed to Old Mexico, descending a precipice from which on a clear day you could see sixty miles or more. No wonder the Spaniards had named that cliff La Bajada, and I could imagine the difficulties that the carretas, with their solid wooden wheels, would have had going down that steep hill, for several times our own howitzer was at the point of tumbling over.

As we started going down the cliff, the Navajo Tafoya came up to me, and squinting with his eagle eye, he gestured toward the south of the Jémez

Mountains, where the sun shone upon a winding stream. "That small spring is the Río Puerco, and near the lowest part of the valley is the town of Cabezón. From here you can't make out the village, which lies at a low point, but if you look closely you will be able to make out the top of a peak named Tsenajín, which is one of our sacred mountains."

I asked Tafoya why that peak was sacred to his tribe.

"That history is related to the origins of our people, when some monsters were destroying humanity. To combat them two twin brothers with great power and courage were created. Apparently one of the cruelest giants, named Yeitsó, lived at the top of San Mateo Mountain, and when the Twin Warriors defeated the monster, they cut his head off. It rolled down the side of the mountain until it reached the bottom of the valley, where it turned into a stone. They say that that volcanic plug is the petrified head of the monster Yeitsó."

I would have asked him more, but Sergeant Sweeny passed by and ordered us to rejoin the rest of the formation, which was going down the precipitous hill almost at double time, even though the howitzer was bouncing half a yard in the air.

But when we reached level ground and attempted to cross the Galisteo, which was nothing more than a small arroyo that had turned into a torrent after the rains of the night before, the mules pulling the limber made a false move and the cannon ended up at the bottom of the riverbed. We pulled it out oozing mud, much to the delight of the soldiers and anger of our officers. Sergeant Sweeny did not pass up the opportunity to dole out a few slaps on the head and insults among the soldiers.

To avoid any more delays, Lieutenant Stanton ordered that the cannon be left hidden among some shrubs at the edge of the river, and we continued at a forced march. One of the scouts who had arrived during the night had been at the site where the caravan was assaulted, and he was recounting some horrible things. The travelers, caught by surprise while camping next to an arroyo, had been massacred without mercy. Apparently there were mutilated cadavers everywhere, but the Apaches had also taken with them a white woman and her children.

The scout assured us that if we continued at that pace, we could catch up with the Apaches before dawn. But when two horses fell dead from exhaustion, Lieutenant Stanton ordered us to stop and make camp. It would do us little good to find our enemy if we weren't in condition to fight.

We were not allowed to build a fire lest the Apaches see it, and even though we had something to eat, I was so worn out after going without sleep for almost three days—counting the night of the fandango—that, from sheer exhaustion, I was unable to fall asleep. I got close to the place where Tafoya had rolled up in his blanket. Since he was also awake, I asked him to continue telling me the story of the Twin Warriors.

Tafoya scratched his head and made a clicking sound with his tongue. "That tale is customarily told as part of the Enemy Way ceremony, and it invokes powerful forces that are difficult to control. If I were to tell part of the story incorrectly, the Sacred Beings might be offended and strike me with some kind of punishment."

I took a plug of tobacco out of my pocket and offered some to Tafoya. His hand emerged from underneath his blanket and tore off a piece of my plug, after which he carefully pulled the blanket over himself once again. After chewing silently for a while, and after humming what sounded like a prayer, the Indian began recounting the narrative that I had asked him for.

"The birth of the giant Yeitsó and that of the other monsters is connected to the history of the beginning of the world. In order for you to understand the entire story, I must tell you something about what happened before."

The Birth of the Monsters

It all began after the human race ascended to the Fourth World in order to elude the deluge caused by Water Monster to get back at Coyote for kidnapping his son.

Living beings, including First Man and First Woman, escaped from being drowned in the Third World thanks to the cleverness of Little Wind, who advised them to plant a reed in the ground and to seek refuge in it. When the reed grew tall, it pierced the heavens and appeared in the Fourth World even though some animals, such as Wild Turkey, have mud-colored tails to this day, a remnant of the deluge in the Third World.

With the aid of Blue Crane, First Woman was able to retrieve her bag of magic medicine that in haste had been left behind in the underworld; in her bag she was carrying dirt from the Four Sacred Mountains of the Third World. The benevolent powers of the mountains would enable the people to survive in the new world.

Water Monster, who had provoked the deluge, continued to be upset because of the kidnapping of his son, but Little Wind intervened once again, and managed to have the crafty Coyote return Water Monster's offspring. "From now on," said Water Monster, "whenever someone dies, he will go to the underworld." Then he started running toward the east, cutting a furrow so that the water would follow him, and later a furrow facing south, another in a westward direction, and still another toward the north. In this way, the water ran in all four directions, and thus the oceans were formed.

The ground was still semi-inundated and the tablelands were made of soft mud; so the people sought help from the winds. The winds blew all around and thus dried up the surface of the earth, and people were able to walk.

During all this time, they had been observing how the waters were slowly receding in the distance. Little by little the earth rose, the water disappeared, and the people never saw the water again.

Afterward the living beings tried to start a fire, but they didn't know how to go about it. And then they discovered that one of them had brought with him flint from the underworld. They started a fire using four kinds of wood that they brought with them from the four cardinal points to start that first bonfire: Spanish fir, stone pine, fir, and juniper. They also found the person who had brought corn seeds from the underworld: four white corn seeds, four blue corn seeds, four yellow ones, and four multicolored ones. The seeds that they were going to plant would make the earth swell up; when they grew tall and multiplied, the earth would also expand.

In four days the seeds had sprouted through the earth. And every four days the crop grew, until it was ripe. It was just before the seeds grew that the monsters were conceived. The women had been abusing their bodies, masturbating with different horns and animal hooves that they had found—using a blunt antler's horn, the shaft from a bird's feather, the tendon of a fallow deer's thigh, and even the tip of a round cactus. They were all bad habits that the women had learnt in the underworld.

While the corn was ripening, the women went away so that the men would not find out what they had done, and therefore gave birth to their offspring in remote places, thinking that there they would be devoured by predators. But their progeny was whisked away by the winds, which raised the offspring at the top of the mountains.

The children conceived with the antler's horn turned into Horned Monster, the offspring from the shaft of a bird's feather turned into Giant Eagle, the one who had rubbed herself with the tendon of a fallow deer's thigh engendered Bear That Follows the Trail Without Stopping, and the one who had masturbated with the tip of a cactus gave birth to the Monsters That Slaughter With Their Eyes. Eventually, people found out what happened, and the maidens then confessed. "It is true what we did: we gave birth to them and then abandoned them immediately."

But when people went to inspect those places, they found only the tracks of the wind.

The worst of the monsters turned out to be the one who had been born the last, to the daughter of one of the chiefs. She had gone off into the distance to do her bodily needs in a place where there were many boulders, the type of flint that in the olden days was used to make weapons, and it seems that the girl took with her one of those rocks with which to cleanse herself while she walked toward the rising Sun. After having a bowel movement, the maiden inserted the stone in her genitalia and at that very moment the sun came out, and as the ray of light shone on her private parts, she felt a trembling throughout her entire body.

In this way she was left pregnant and gave birth to a being that was also taken away by the winds. In time, that monstrous creature grew up to be the great Yeitsó known as Lone Traveler, the cruelest and most voracious of the monsters who were on the verge of exterminating the entire human race.

In the meantime, while all this was going on, First Man and First Woman were still living at the foot of the Mountain Around Which the World Had Been Created, and they wondered when Changing Woman would be born. They already knew that she would bring about a solution that would destroy the monsters.

He-Mule Swamp

The light that was breaking through the veil of the horizon made me recall that, however beautiful the Navajo legends, we weren't there to tell stories or to listen to them; rather, we were there to head off a band of fierce

Apache warriors who might be closer than we thought. If we went into battle with the hostiles, it would be my first war action. Previously we had been on the verge of engaging the hostile Indians, but on the northern frontier we were more concerned with trying to dodge Indians than with fighting them. My heart sank, thinking that this day, whose light had yet to break on the vast plains, could well be my last.

We had barely broken camp when one of the scouts came down from the nearby hill at a gallop and in a whisper that could not hide his nervousness, informed us that the Indian camp was just a mile on the other side of the hill. Lieutenant Stanton gave the orders without using the bugle: we would lead the horses by the reins, trying to make as little noise as possible, until we reached the crest, and there we would get on our horses and launch the attack.

When we reached the summit we paused for a moment so the men could tighten the cinches to their saddle, check the bolts on their weapons, loosen the sabres in their sheaths, and perhaps whisper a prayer. I hadn't prayed in a while, perhaps in reaction to the continuous prayers that they made us say at home, but now I searched desperately for the shortest and most effective prayer. I thought of my mother and my sisters who fortunately at that hour were probably in bed in New Rochelle. Thank God!

Timothy Baltasar, who was at my side, whispered in my ear one of his lapidary sentences: *"And when he had opened the Seventh Seal, there was silence in heaven about the space of half an hour."* Baltasar's mocking voice was mixed with the heart-stopping note of the bugle that was sounding the charge along with the rumbling of four hundred hooves going downhill.

In an instant, the silence of the valley was broken by the deafening discharge of guns, shouts of pain, howling, and neighing. The Indians had been taken by surprise, and only a few of their warriors dared to confront the soldiers, whose rifles took a heavy toll. Most of the Apaches dispersed, and the frightened women ran with their babies in their arms, seeking refuge in the riverbed, but the soldiers' sabers cut them down, making no distinction for sex or age in the heat of battle.

Through the cloud of smoke from gunpowder and trampled bonfires, I saw a white woman with her clothes ripped off fighting desperately to free herself from the arms of an old Apache woman who was trying to haul her onto a horse and carry her off as a captive. Seeing that several of us soldiers were coming to her rescue, the white woman redoubled her efforts and managed to escape, running toward us with her arms outstretched.

The scene I was about to witness will never leave my memory if I live to a hundred. When she saw that her prisoner had managed to escape, the old Indian woman reached for a bow that she was carrying behind her back, very deliberately placed her arrow on the string, and took aim for a split second that seemed like an eternity. Afterward I saw the flash of feathers coming from the bow and almost simultaneously I heard the thump of the arrow's impact in the back of the fugitive, who fell flat on her face on the dew-covered grass, almost under my horse's hooves. As I dismounted to assist the wounded woman, I heard a volley of shots: my comrades had fired at the old lady, who paid dearly for her cruelty, falling stone dead.

When I tried to lift the white woman's body, I was struck by the delicacy of her constitution and the many bruises and scratches that could be seen through her torn clothing. The shots and shouts of pain or victory coming from those who were still fighting sounded far away when I turned the delicate body over and straightened her head a little so as to bring my canteen close to her dry lips. The woman's features were of an extraordinary gentleness and her deep blue eyes reflected more bewilderment than fear. Her blood was soaking the hand with which I was supporting her back, and the black tip of the flint arrow protruded an inch between her breasts, like an ugly third nipple. Fortunately the agony lasted only a short time. Her face slackened suddenly, and her clear eyes were covered with a kind of opaque veil.

At that very moment I saw a group of Indians trying to reach a drove of horses that was tied under a small grove of cottonwoods in the arroyo. Abandoning the unknown lady's corpse, I mounted my horse to catch up with them. Among the riders who were fleeing I could identify one of the Apache leaders, a warrior of great size. He was wearing a buffalo-head war bonnet whose horns formed a half moon, and across the horses' withers I was able to make out a human figure with blonde hair hanging next to the stirrup. I thought that it could be one of the white boys that the Indians had kidnapped. But it was a fleeting vision; the Indian rider reached the top of the hill and disappeared from view.

When I returned to the woman's body, I noticed the visible signs of mistreatment to which she had been subjected. Her feet were completely torn up from having walked many miles barefoot through the wilderness, and her naked shoulders were blistered from sunburn. Several soldiers helped me to wrap her body in a blanket, dig a deep hole under the grove of cottonwoods, and bury what was left of the delicate creature as we swore revenge against her executioners.

In spite of the murder of the white lady, the action had been successful, since our troops had not experienced a single casualty. On the other hand, we found nine dead Indian bodies around the combat area, four of them warriors. Three more bodies, all women, were floating among the rushes along the banks of the river, caught while they attempted to cross the river, including the old Indian woman whose arrow had pierced the white lady. As for the children, we didn't count them.

According to the Mexican guide who had taken us there, that lowest part of the valley, cut through by an idyllic arroyo, was named He-Mule Swamp. A bit farther away it widened into a yellowish canebrake. We followed the fugitives' tracks for quite a long while in the vain hope of finding the white child we thought they were holding captive, but as we got to the open range, where we could see the summit of the Sierra Blanca soaring above the haze of the plains, Lieutenant Stanton gave the order to turn back.

It would have been useless to pursue the Indians with our horses exhausted, for they knew we were after them and they had a head start. Besides, our commander had specific orders not to venture beyond the plains, and especially not to enter the Sierra Blanca. These mountains were the Mescalero Apaches' sanctuary, where they could easily lay an ambush and wipe us out.

But Lieutenant Stanton was a soldier through and through, and before asking us to turn back I saw him shake his fist in the direction of the mountains and mutter, "We'll get you Apaches yet!" When we returned to the campsite, he had whiskey and double rations distributed among the troops to celebrate our victory.

As night fell, we heard a moaning sound near the camp. Several of us soldiers went out with our guns drawn thinking that it could be a wild animal or a wounded Apache, but upon checking the willows that were growing next to the arroyo, we found an Indian child a few months old wrapped up on one of those cradle boards that Indian women carry on their backs. The child was crying.

The soldiers went to look for Sergeant Sweeny, who was half drunk, to give him the news. When he saw what all the fuss was about, he asked the men to hand the baby over, and he cuddled him, which seemed to calm the little Indian. Then Sweeny said: "Now you're a fine suckling cub, but soon you'll begin growing up and turning into a big Injun who won't be worth a shit!" And before anybody knew what he was doing, the sergeant took a thick boulder from the riverbank, forced it into the swaddling of the cradle board, and tossed the baby along with the cradle, rock, and all into the middle of the arroyo, where they soon disappeared.

Those of us soldiers who had witnessed this scene were left paralyzed with horror, but the sergeant rounded off his horrible act by commenting, "I'm only sorry not to have others like you on hand so as to treat them in the same way."

The only one who had the guts to reproach him was Timothy Baltasar, who called him a coward and a Herod and grabbed him by the neck with his huge hands. On seeing himself threatened the sergeant took out his pistol and, pointing it at Baltasar's head, threatened to blow out his brains on the grounds of insubordination. Since we were aware that the dirty swine was very much capable of making good on his threats, we whisked our friend away with a profound sense of frustration and injustice.

I got close to the place where the native guides customarily gathered around the bonfire, but I didn't see Tafoya. A while later I found him sitting on a rock, away from the other soldiers, wrapped up in his blanket with his eyes closed, while his lips moved as he muttered one of his prayers or ballads. Whenever the Navajos engaged in combat where deaths occurred, they performed ceremonies to protect themselves against the spirits of the enemies whom they had killed and to purify themselves of the evil effluvia that the dead emitted.

When Tafoya had finished and he saw me, I told him what had just happened with the Apache baby whom the sergeant had tossed to the bottom of the river. He thought for a moment before responding. "The intentions of the Sacred Beings are inscrutable, and it is difficult for men to understand the meaning of these things. If Coyote had not kidnapped Water Monster's son, the human race would not have ascended into the Fourth World fleeing from the deluge; and if the maidens had not given birth to the monsters, surely Changing Woman would not have given birth to the Twin Warriors so as to liberate humanity from that plague: in fact the name of one of those heroes is Born from the Waters.

Then I asked him to tell me the rest of the story.

Born from the Waters

One morning at dawn the First Man and First Woman saw a dark cloud hovering over Gobernador Peak, and they sent a message to the Talking God to tell him what was going on. While the Talking God climbed the mountain from the east, he heard someone crying, but the clouds were so dense that he wasn't able to see anything. He climbed higher, rounding the mountain as he ascended, and from the south he heard a bird sing; from the east there were more birds singing; from the north he heard the corn beetle. By then, he had almost reached the summit. He glanced once again toward the east, where, beside the cloud, there was a rainbow and a light drizzle was falling. He heard someone crying and looked again, and there he saw a newborn baby girl tossed on top of a patch of flowers. She had been born when it was pitch dark, and she was the daughter of dawn.

The First Man and First Woman took the responsibility of raising her, but under the supervision of the Sacred Beings. They nourished her with dust from the sun's rays, cloud dust, pollen from the plants, and dew from the flowers. The little girl stayed in the same place, the Mountain Where the People Moved To, until she became a woman. The name of Changing Woman came about in the same way as the names of the mountains. Since her creation that was her name; others have also called her White Shell Woman, but that name is not as well known.

When the little girl grew up to be a woman, she was given a sacred trousseau that was called Walking in Beauty. The same ceremony is celebrated by all Navajo girls when they reach puberty. The only difference is that in the first ceremony when Changing Woman lay down on top of a pile of blankets she faced west; ever since then girls must face east. Changing Woman said that they had to be facing east in order to see the Earth and the Sky.

One day, Changing Woman felt alone, and she walked away from her cabin. She sat down in a sunny spot and began to play with her hair. It was noon, and the Sun was at its zenith. Then the Woman threw herself down right there and she fell asleep. And when she woke up, she felt tired and sweaty, as if someone had come close to her during her dream. She spotted tracks that came from the east, as if someone had come close to her and then had walked away. She prayed that it hadn't been the giant Yeitsó, since he had come to see her from time to time. She knew that giants sometimes kidnapped maidens.

The Woman got up and was about to head home when someone

held her back, and upon turning around, she saw a stranger with a radiant appearance. She had never seen such a handsome being. "When you return home," the stranger said to her, "you must tidy up around your cabin. Don't leave a single piece of trash around your *hogan*. After four days, I shall come back to visit you." And he disappeared before her eyes.

The Woman remained preoccupied with what the stranger had told her. "I wonder what he has in mind with all of this? I have never in my life seen such a handsome being!" For four days she devoted herself to cleaning around her cabin. And she left her hogan as clean as a whistle. That night she kept on thinking about what all this meant. She couldn't sleep a wink, so she sat up. She remained sitting in the hogan until it was almost daybreak. Just when she thought that nothing else would happen and went back to bed, he arrived and lay beside her. Immediately she fell asleep. Then he lay at her side and had sexual intercourse with her without her realizing it. When he had finished, the Woman all of a sudden woke up and she tried to grab him, but he had already left, so that all her hand grasped was air. She only noticed that the small doormat had moved. And so she stayed awake until dawn.

After these events, she began to feel ill. Two days later she realized that she was going to be a mother, and four days later she gave birth. It was a baby boy. The Woman cried a little, not knowing what she was going to do with the baby. She was afraid of the monsters. She wrapped him up in a piece of bark from a bush, and ever since then that type of bark has been called cradle bark, and she returned with the child to her cabin. The Woman dug a hole, right next to where the fire was, and when she finished digging it up, she dug another one to the side, right behind the first hole, in such a way that if someone should happen to look inside the hole, he wouldn't see anything. She covered the second hole with soft leaves, she nursed the child, and she placed him in the second hole. Afterward she covered him with a flat stone and dirt. In that way the child would be warm with the embers from the fire, and no one could see him or hear him cry.

Then the Woman decided to wash up, and she headed for the edge of the canyon. She didn't see the water, but she heard it dripping. She walked on top of the cliff, along an overhanging rock, until she got to a puddle formed by the dripping of water. She sat down underneath the waterfall and let the water hit her legs and body, including wetting her crotch, until she was clean. It is said that at the moment that the water washed down between her buttocks, a ray of sunshine shone underneath the cascade, and the Woman felt anew a shiver that ran throughout her body as in the act of making love.

From that moment onward that spring water took on the name Water That Falls Like a Long and Stiff Human Object. And the place where the maiden was impregnated by the Sun was named Where the Daylight of the Sun Arrives for the First Time. And we Navajos call our virgin women Those Who Have Never Been Touched by the Light of the Sun.

Then she returned home and picked up the baby and nursed him once again. She didn't feel very well. Two days later she realized that she was going to have another baby, and four days hence she gave birth again. The two babies were born within nine days of each other. Then she made another hole back behind the first one and she put the child inside. The woman was fearful of the crows, owls, and vultures that were the giants' spies and messengers. Within a few days Changing Woman's children had grown enough to run around the cabin with ease.

One fine day Changing Woman made a corn cake and, leaving it on top of the ashes to cook, she left for a stroll close to the hogan. But while she went for a walk, the children escaped from the hole and started to run around outside. At that point the Woman saw the giant Yeitsó headed in her direction; she quickly returned to the cabin and hid the twins in their hole, calmly sitting down close to the fire where the cake was baking.

Yeitsó took a peek at the cabin door just as the Woman was taking the cake out of the ashes. "Have you made that for me?" asked the evildoer. "It smells very appetizing."

"By no means! All I need is to be working to fatten you up, you greedy pig!" responded the Woman.

"Never mind," said the giant. "In reality, I like children better. By the way, where are your kids? I've been told that you have two very beautiful twins and I've come for them."

"There's no child around here," answered the Woman. "You know only too well that a long time ago all the children fell into your clutches and those of your kind."

"So there are no children left?" said the giant. "Could you then explain to me whose small feet belong to these little footprints?"

"Oh, you mean those tracks right there! Well, I drew them to entertain myself," answered the Woman. "Since I'm here all alone, I draw tracks and pretend there are people around me."

"Let's see if you're telling the truth. Draw the tracks in my presence so that I can see how you do it."

"It's very simple. This is the way you do it," said the Woman, pressing her knuckles against the sand with her hand closed and her thumb extended.

The giant compared those tracks with the ones he had seen and he seemed satisfied; he was about to leave when he noticed in one corner of the hogan a piece of cloth stained green from the children's feces, and he asked her again, "If you don't have any children, could you explain to me how that piece of cloth is stained with children's pooh-pooh? I can't imagine that it got stained with that green-colored pooh-pooh by itself," said the clever Yeitsó.

"Perhaps you don't know that there's a plant where the bees make their nest, where they make a kind of honey that is exactly the same color," answered the Woman with great aplomb, adding, "Since there are times when I find myself bored, I play as if I had a baby and I stain the cloth with the honey as if it were the excrement of a baby."

And the Woman showed the monster a shoot from that plant, which in fact had a little bit of greenish substance inside. Fortunately the giant swallowed her lie and took off.

A few days after they were born, Changing Woman's children had grown. Those two babies, born from the Water and the Sun, in time turned into the Twin Warriors. The older one would be called the Monster Slayer and the younger one Born from the Waters. For the Apaches, the principal hero is Born from the Waters.

The Barranca of the Devil

It must have been almost a year after their visit to Don Anú Baca when the people of the Río Puerco Valley had another rendezvous with the natanes from the Navajo rancherías who had accompanied them on their excursion to the Ojo de la Parida. Neither group had succeeded in freeing themselves from Gil Gómez's abuses. As evening fell, they found themselves under a small grove of cottonwoods near the junction of the Río Puerco and the Río Grande. They built a bonfire to ward off the cold air that was blowing down from the Ladrónes Mountains, and they spread out their victuals over a blanket, with a couple of skins of Bernalillo wine.

The Indian chieftains and the Spanish settlers knew each other in peace and in war, and even though the latter boasted about their pure Spanish blood, their copper-colored faces and aquiline noses suggested otherwise. Although the two groups had traditionally stolen each others' livestock and women and burned each others' crops, for the moment they put aside their quarrels to find a way to stop Gil Gómez's tyranny.

The contents of their secret meetings is not known, nor how many goblets of wine were necessary to loosen their tongues so they could come to a meeting of the minds, but when night fell, the retinue remounted their horses to take advantage of the light of the moon that had appeared above the Manzano Mountains. Instead of taking the path that led toward the Río Puerco Valley, they took a shortcut heading for the Ladrones, where the Apache sorcerer Arorú had her hideout at the end of the Devil's Barranca.

The villagers, many of them members of the Holy Brotherhood of the Penitentes, would have let their skin be torn to shreds before confessing that they had consulted an Indian sorcerer in search of a remedy for their troubles. But even the notables who refused to accompany the Indians to the witch's hideout, such as the mayor, Bitoriano Montoya, and Juan Lucero, the hermano mayor of the Holy Brotherhood, contributed money to their compadres to help defray the anticipated costs of exorcism. They were very careful to keep the escapade secret when they returned to the village early in the morning, but as time passes someone's tongue inevitably loosens.

The clouds blocked the moonlight and made the bottom of the ravine look eerie. The trail was so narrow that a slip by a mount would have sent them to meet the one who gave his sinister name to that godforsaken place. The Indian Kiatanito, who was guiding the retinue, was able to locate the entrance to the hideout thanks to the reflection of the bonfire through the mouth of the cave. As if the Indian Arorú had known they were coming, the old woman was seated next to a bluish fire coming from cedar logs, wrapped in her buffalo-skin robe, its shiny hooves crossing her chest. A large, ugly black bird was snoozing toward the back of the grotto, its wings fluttering from time to time in the subterranean breeze that stoked the flames and magnified the shadows on the inside walls of the cave.

"Arorú, you are so old and wise that some people call you Mother of the Human Race," began Barboncito. "People swear that you know how the Twin Warriors acquired their power."

"Since we aren't able to free ourselves from the genízaro," interjected old man Hilario Mestas, "perhaps through her magic she is capable of creating another strapping lad with the same strength as the cacique from the Río Puerco."

"Let's see if she can create a double of Gil Gómez who will act as champion on behalf of the gente de razón," echoed another villager.

"If only they would fight each other; then there would be peace in the valley!" said the villagers and the Indians from the valley, speaking in unison.

The old woman pretended to resist their overtures, claiming that in order to create a double of Gil Gómez she would have to invoke strong and dangerous powers, but the tinkling of the silver coins that suddenly appeared in the visitors' hands was a very inviting melody. Since some of the Spanish visitors were wearing red clothing, which could attract lightning, the old Indian woman asked them to remove any article of red clothing or adornment before she began her spell. The villagers removed their red serapes and hatbands. Those who were wearing crucifixes or scapularies also put them away, so that they would not interfere with the dark powers that Arorú was trying to invoke.

When all the men had complied with these requirements, and after each had deposited a silver coin in a clay pot that the old woman kept in a corner, the witch pulled up her bison robe and went to work. First she sprinkled among the petitioners a few pinches of sacred pollen that she carried in a small buckskin pouch. Then, closing her eyes, her arms stretched out in the form of a cross, holding in each hand between her index finger and her thumb a pinch of dust from the Four Mountains, she sang the same song that the sons of Changing Woman sang when they set out for the Sun:

> *I'm in the Sun, I'm in the Sun.*
> *I'm its armor made of flint,*
> *I'm in the Sun.*

✟

I have my footwear made from flint, I'm in the Sun.
I have my gaiters made from flint, I'm in the Sun.
I have flint in my heart, I'm in the Sun.
I have a bonnet made from flint, I'm in the Sun.
I have two flashing arrows, I'm in the Sun.
I have two flashing arrows with me which add up to four
That spring from my body, I'm in the Sun.

As she finished her canticle, the wizard went to wash her hands in a small puddle of rainwater in a rock depression, and scratching with her fingernails a fist full of mud from the clay ground, she began to mold the statues of two small warriors, each holding a flint sword and a quiver with arrows and a miniature bow.

Without pausing Arorú separated the embers from the fire with her calloused fingers and buried the clay figures in the hot ashes. She spread pollen over the bonfire and sang entreaties so old and powerful that not even the Indians who were witnessing the ceremony could understand them.

All of a sudden a whirlwind developed, starting in the back of the cave and stoking the bonfire until the flames kissed the vault of the grotto and white smoke bounced against the walls. The visitors began coughing, and when the smoke dissipated, the clay figures were consumed, leaving a pungent odor of charred clay. The black bird was no longer in evidence, but one of those present noticed a dark fluttering shadow in the cloud of dazzlingly white smoke that was coming out of the mouth of the cave.

The sorcerer carefully cleaned the residue from her hands where it had stuck to her fingers; when the clay fell onto the embers it crackled fiercely, and out from the particles shot blue smoke through which daylight was beginning to filter. Arorú stood at the mouth of the grotto with her arms stretched out toward the east, and with her bison robe open she received on her wizened flesh the caress of the first ray of sun.

"Oh Sacred Beings, you that gave strength and courage to the Twin Warriors, create a warrior as powerful as Gil Gómez, so that his fiery heart will have a rival! Let us hope that the two of them fight each other and leave the valley in peace!"

The early morning breeze blew away the particles of ashes and clay suspended in the bluish smoke. Crossing the Río Grande basin, it cleared the Manzano Mountains and spread across the plains. The black bird had left Arorú's cave and now glided high above the valley, taking advantage of the pale blue breeze coming off the mountains to let itself be carried off toward the rising sun. It flew over the ruins of the ancient Gran Quivira mission and the lava crust of the *Malpaís,* behind which loomed the Sierra Blanca.

A mountain spring ran twisting and turning down the ravines and embankments, creating in the plains a small marsh scattered with the withered remains of a massacre: skeletons of animals and people chewed on by carrion-eaters and polished by the weather. As the crow flew over a yellowish canebrake, a flock of ducks flew off quacking from the quiet mirror of the swamp, crossing the black bird's path as it descended toward the water in concentric circles.

At the edge of the puddle, half submerged in the rushes and clay, lay the inert body, face up, of a youth of robust proportions. His naked chest, covered with a thick growth of bristle-like hair, was blistered from exposure to the sun; his mouth was half-open, and his powerful chest didn't show the least bit of movement. Around his neck was a rope collar that had left a reddish mark under his chin. His arms, extended in the form of a cross, showed the palms of a pair of wide and calloused hands.

The black bird landed next to the man's outstretched body and with its strong beak it dug into the swamp and deposited a few drops of mud on his swollen tongue and at the corners of his chapped lips. After a few seconds, his nostrils showed signs of life and a breath exhaled from his strong abdomen.

A herd of antelope came close to the edge of the swamp to drink, and upon noticing the shape of a human being at the brink of the water, the cautious animals pricked up their ears and took the scent, not daring either to advance or to step back. Finally, a young female that had recently lost its offspring, showing more of a maternal instinct than fear, got close to the prone body and, after sniffing the extremities, started to lick the blisters on the chest and rub her warm abdomen hard against the boy's numb skin. His parched lips opened upon feeling the warm rubbing, and from the swollen udder of the doe a few drops of liquid shot forth and moistened the dry tongue.

The crow cawed and flew off, its powerful wings flapping across the sun.

Book Two

Father, a man has come down from the hills.

He is without doubt the most robust in the entire region.

He possesses incredible strength.

Like a comet of Anú, he has imposing strength;

 he reconnoiters the hills without stopping,

 he pastures his animals without stopping,

 he heads for the watering holes without stopping,

I do not dare even to get near him.

He blocks up the pits that I dig,

 he springs apart the traps I set,

 and lets the beasts slip through my hands,

 the swift creatures of the wild,

 and does not allow me to work in the wilderness.

POEM OF GILGAMESH
Tablet I, Column iii

Fort Conrad

Barely a year after we were stationed at Fort Marcy, which had the advantage of being close to Santa Fe, my company was sent to build a fort south of a miserable settlement called Socorro, situated at the extreme north of a desert route the Spaniards named the Journey of the Dead Man. I was beginning to learn that the Spaniards had not given those names lightly.

Ever since the colonial period, the area surrounding the fort had the reputation of being inhospitable and unhealthy because of the Río Grande's whims; one moment it could be practically dry, nothing but a sandy gully, and at the next instant it could turn into a roiling torrent whose muddy waters leveled everything in its path and inundated the plains nearby.

By then I had gotten the itch to explore new horizons out of my system, and I had time in the solitude of that desert to assess the grave mistake I had made by enlisting in the army. I still had three years of military duty ahead of me, and I cursed the sudden whim to enlist that had seized me one spring morning in New Rochelle. A few months after my father's death, I found myself strolling down the street in search of work, and as I turned a corner I ran into a soldier who in a few minutes convinced me to enlist, assuring me that these days recruits were destined for California. He also sang the praises of the army, the abundance and variety of the mess and the good medical care. The possibility of going to the land of gold fascinated me, and that same morning I stopped by the recruiting office and swore to serve my country for five years.

Not only was I never sent to California, but in the two years that I had served in the army I had suffered more hunger and deprivation than ever before in my life, including the years of poverty we experienced after the premature death of my poor father. When summer came, the decreased flow of the river caused a scarcity of potable water, and the abundance of miasmas brought on dysentery and fevers that began to take a heavy toll on the soldiers at the fort. Men who only yesterday enjoyed life at work and at play within a few hours became limp rags, tossed into makeshift graves without time even for a whispered prayer.

Some preferred to risk their lives in the desert at the hands of the Apaches rather than chance finding themselves buried in a common grave on the banks of the river. The number of desertions increased. The idea of deserting crossed my mind more than once, and I must confess that if I succeeded in discarding such a thought it wasn't so much out of love for my country, nor because of the ignominy it could bring upon my mother and sisters, but rather because of the fear of falling once again into the hands of the army.

It was terrible to see some of the poor devils who had deserted and been recaptured being herded back to the fort, their feet skinned from walking on the mountain rocks and their clothing torn by the agave plant and bramble patches. The deserters, who were tried by a court martial, invariably were ordered "to forfeit all pay or per diem pending or owed, their heads shaved, branded on the left hip with the letter D an inch and a half long, and flogged and discharged ignominiously from the army to the beat of a drum," in accordance with the laws of the day. I wonder if there is anything more humiliating for a human being than to be displayed with his head completely shaved. Although it was not very pleasant either receiving fifty lashes across your back with a rawhide whip in front of the rest of the company and then being led out of the garrison by a squad with fixed bayonets with the band playing all the while!

In spite of the extremely difficult conditions, or perhaps because of them, in a few months the construction of the fort had gone so fast that we were able to hoist our flag in that remote part of the Territory. It gave us great pleasure to see the fruits of our labor, for we had rescued from the desert a small parcel of civilization. We ourselves had made the adobes, measuring 12 × 24 × 4 inches thick, molded in wooden frames, with dirt and straw taken from the nearby banks of the Río Grande, and dried afterward in the sun. The garrison was baptized Fort Conrad, in honor of a dragoon captain who had drowned nearby in a flood.

Upon reading the word *fort*, you might think it refers to a real military fortress, but the truth is that the new military post was rather modest. The adobe buildings only had one story, and the roof was flat as is customary in that region, with a small parapet protecting the outside wall. In the center was a rectangular plaza where the dragoons exercised their horses and the infantry soldiers drilled every morning. The exterior wall had no windows.

To one side were the officers' quarters; in front was the guardroom, the jail cells, quartermaster, and sick bay. The other two sides of the quadrangle were occupied by the barracks belonging to first infantry soldiers of Company D and Company F of dragoons, which was mine. In the middle of the plaza the Stars and Stripes flew in a wind that was sometimes a pleasant breeze and other times a scorching wind that seemed to blow straight from hell.

As Timothy Baltasar used to say, rather than an American fort, it seemed more like the citadel of an oriental city in an Arabian desert. Even though Timothy had never been to the Orient, he extracted those ideas from pictures in travel books that he guarded jealously in a footlocker under his bed. The normally peaceful Baltasar was capable of killing anybody who dared to poke his nose into that trunk, as if the treasures of the Queen of Sheba were hidden there.

Despite the fact that there was less hustle and bustle in Fort Conrad than in the garrisons of Santa Fe or Albuquerque, since we were on the old Camino Real, which linked that territory with Mexico, there was a certain distraction in the comings and goings of people traveling north and south along the river. Sometimes they came into the fort to barter or to have a drink at the bar.

One evening I happened to bump into a table of Indian traders, and I heard them say that the Apaches talked about a young man with a Herculean build, sporting a long beard and hair, dressed in untanned hides, whom they had seen roaming the prairies surrounded by a herd of antelopes and mustangs. According to the Apaches, the strapping lad didn't belong to any known Indian tribe, but he was neither white nor Mexican. They had run into him close to a watering hole, where he had plunged into the water riding his wild horse. He had drunk along with the herds, frolicking about in the puddle as if he himself were a young mustang.

According to the peddlers' story, even though the Indians on that occasion had had the lad within range of their arrows, they had not dared to fire at him, thinking that he could be the spirit or reincarnation of one of their principal gods, the one who is called Born from the Waters, conceived by a maiden who was touched by a ray of sun while she bathed in spring water. These savage tribes observed some very elaborate traditions, and among the rituals that the war novices practiced, some were related to water, such as swimming during the winter in freezing springs in order to harden their bodies, or retaining a mouthful of water while they ran through the mountains, in order to learn to control their breathing.

The term that the Apaches used to refer to the neophytes who were preparing for war was *dikohé,* and that is what the peddlers called the strapping young savage, although with the white man's limited facility for the indigenous dialects, they pronounced it *Decoy,* a word that in English obviously bears a very different meaning. And as soon as the fame of the mysterious centaur began to spread among the plazas and garrisons along the Río Grande, some soldiers nick-named him Dick for short, as if he were a childhood friend, even though they had never seen him and more than likely never would, for his existence could well have been a mirage caused by the thirst and fatigue of long journeys.

Nevertheless, shortly after having heard the news, when I asked at the *fonda* in Socorro if they had heard of a wild boy who roamed the desert accompanied by his herds, the answer was positive. But even though the Spanish settlers were as superstitious as the natives, they didn't attribute that phenomenon to any prodigious or supernatural origin; they claimed that the lad could well be a white boy who had strayed away from his village or one of the young Indians who oftentimes took to the desert in search of a special power. Since he had adopted the wild life of the untamed horses, the Spanish nicknamed the stranger *Cimarrón*.

A harsh winter in the Río Grande basin was followed by a spring without rain, and that summer's water flow was dreadfully low. All the springs in the area dried up, and where in other years succulent grasses grew in the marshes, now there were only the sharp stalks of cattails, under which a crust of shriveled clay began to appear, resembling a tortoise shell cracked by the scorching sun.

Perhaps the reason Decoy had been seen with his herds near the villages was because thirst and lack of pasture had drawn his flocks closer to the river. At dusk and dawn, one could see from the fort's rooftop herds of wild animals crossing the sandy bed of the Río Grande, headed west toward the Gila Range, in search of pasture high up in the sierras, where water still oozed from the snow-covered peaks.

The Trapper from the Gila

The Apaches must also have felt the effects of the drought, because they intensified their looting and killings in the villages along the river and in isolated garrisons. One of the first places they attacked was a small detachment in the Gila Mountains called Fort Webster, about three days' journey south from our barracks. The hostiles had taken advantage of a lapse in the soldiers' watch to take all the herds of horses in the fort. When a small squad went after them, it was ambushed, and several soldiers were killed or wounded.

The news of that encounter, brought back by one of the few survivors of the squad, coincided with the arrival of Captain Stanton, who was replacing Major Drummond as commander of Fort Conrad. The old man enjoyed the good life and had little desire to die with his boots on. The new commander, however, the same dynamic and courageous officer who had led the expedition to the He-Mule Swamp when he was still a lieutenant, ordered that our company of dragoons be ready to leave on a campaign the following day. That order was received by the troops with a loud round of applause, since we knew that the worst thing for us was to remain in that hole waiting for the ague and cholera to decimate the garrison.

The enthusiasm among the soldiery diminished, however, when we had covered fifty miles in two days of intense heat. We couldn't cool ourselves in the river in spite of its proximity, because it was boxed in between steep slopes. The captain gave the order to dismount to avoid tiring the horses. To travel on foot through rocky terrain is far from pleasant, especially under a scorching sun while pulling on the reins of an exhausted mount. When our thirst became unbearable, we had to slide down to the river to fill up our tin cups with a liquid so filthy that you had to filter it with your teeth. When you shook your cup, algae and tadpoles fell out.

Fortunately, as soon as we moved away from the river and began climbing the hills a cooler breeze started to blow and we found some pasture for our horses. As the evening of the third day fell upon us, we camped in a grove of walnut trees along the banks of the Mimbres River, at the bottom of a deep gorge. In the clear water, one could see large boulders that were blue because of the abundance of copper. Through cracks in the rocks, mountain trout could be seen zigzagging. Using a small willow branch I improvised fishing gear and soon had a couple of good-sized trout flopping around on the grass flashing their beautiful rainbow-hued backs. They took on an even more beautiful color when they started to turn gold in the skillet on the bonfire's live coals.

That night, when the officers had retired to their tents and the soldiers were chit-chatting around the fireplace, an old trapper and his son, who had their cabin in some remote corner of that mountain range, showed up at the camp. The old man turned out to be none other than the famous Jeremiah Pattie, the same one who a few years back had guided Colonel Cook's column of volunteers on his expedition into California during the war with Mexico. He was acquainted with that territory long before it was a part of the United States. The old man was small and sinewy, with a sincere smile and cheerful blue eyes that seemed to pierce the person he was speaking to like two buckshot pellets. A clay pipe that never left his mouth fitted perfectly in the gap it had created between his two incisors. His bony, weather-beaten hands must have taken hundreds of animals' skins, and perhaps more than one human scalp, and a deep scar he bore on his forehead was testimony that at one time someone had attempted to "raise his hair," as the jargon of the mountaineers would have it.

Pattie's son was a bit more corpulent and less seasoned than his father. He was always looking over his shoulder, as if fearful that something bad could happen at any moment. While we conversed next to the fire, a rustling sound came from the thicket that most likely was only an animal, but the young man jumped up and grabbed the butt of his rifle, which brought on laughter among the soldiers.

"My son is a bit nervous these days," old Pattie remarked, taking a drag from his pipe, which he had just lit. "For quite some time now, a stranger has been roaming this mountain range with a herd of wild horses, and he is interfering with our hunting."

Upon hearing that, I pricked up my ears like a horse that sees a snake on the road, and I asked young Pattie to tell us what he had seen, which he did without having to be asked twice.

"For several weeks now I have noticed that someone has been destroying the traps and covering the pits that I dug, allowing the beasts to slip through my hands. At first I thought it was a wild animal, but I didn't find bear or lion tracks. The fact is that someone was breaking my traps and setting free the animals that I had caught. So I began to scour the mountains and before long I found large human footprints. They were not prints from Indian moccasins or the footprints of a white man; they were barefoot tracks, but those of enormously big feet.

"Every time I saw the man's footprints, they were surrounded by antelope tracks or those of unshod horses. So I lay in wait, well hidden in the bushes with my father's flintlock with a double powder charge, close to a watering hole that wild horses like. I didn't have to wait long. I had begun to stand guard at noon, and at dusk I heard the thundering of the mountain under the hooves of the mustangs that were coming down to drink at the spring."

Young Pattie paused for a moment to take a sip of coffee; his father was listening to him attentively, although surely he had heard him tell this story before.

"When the cloud of dust raised by the wild herd around the watering hole had settled, I saw at the very edge of the water a strapping lad dressed in untanned animal hides, with hair down to his shoulders. Believe me, I have never seen a stronger-looking man: he had broad, square shoulders, and his neck was like that of a wild bull. He looked like a picture of Samson from the Bible. In addition to his mane of long hair, his chest and forearms were also covered with short, thick hair, like wild boar bristles. I have to admit that when I saw him, the blood in my veins froze, and the rifle shook so much in my hands that I didn't dare to fire. If I had missed the target, he could have torn me to pieces with his bare hands!"

Since his voice was trembling, the young man had to pause.

"What did you do then?" I asked him, eager to hear the end of the story.

"I sneaked off through the thicket once again, and I called my dogs, which I had left tied not too far away. Then I dashed out of there with my tail between my legs and didn't stop until I reached the cabin where I live with my father."

"For sure, when I saw him coming back," the old man agreed, exhaling a mouthful of smoke between his teeth, "I thought the boy must have run into a wild animal or perhaps a band of Apaches. His face was ashen and his hands were shaking, and he looked as if he'd been to hell and back. He was paralyzed with fear."

"I can assure you," said the young man, "that stranger is fiercer than a mountain lion; I'd rather have it out with half a dozen Apaches than fight that stallion."

Old Pattie shook his head, like someone who has been trying to talk sense into a child. He said to me, "I have already told the boy that in order to tame this wild stallion one of the first things you have to do is separate him from his herd. In the Río Puerco Valley lives Gil Gómez, who is the craftiest mustanger in all the region and knows every trick in the book. What you have to do, I've told the boy, is go see Gil Gómez and ask him to lend you one of the prostitutes from the fonda of Cabezón, so you can bring the woman to the wilderness and show her to the young stallion."

"But father," interjected his son, "what do you want me to do with a whore in the wilderness?"

"Listen to the voice of experience and heed my advice," answered the father. "If you ask Gil Gómez for advice, he will tell you: 'Take a prostitute from the fonda to the wilderness, a woman with firm flesh and a large bosom. When the stranger comes down from the mountain for water for himself and his herds, have the woman stand in full view of him, have her undress and show the young savage her abundant charms. When the young buck sees her naked, he will want her, and as soon as he comes close to the prostitute, the animals will desert him.' You will use the whore as bait to catch him!"

Following this dialogue intently was my friend Timothy Baltasar, he of the biblical background, who whispered in my ear. "Of course, the old man is right. What needs to be done to control that Samson is to find a Delilah who can cut his hair!"

Everything seemed to confirm that Decoy was not just a mirage. That night I spent a good while recording all this in my diary after everyone else had hit the sack, including Pattie's son, who fell asleep hugging his flintlock as if it were his fiancée.

The following day we left before dawn, and at sunrise we reached the old site of the Copper Mines, abandoned on account of the raids of the Mimbres Apaches. Old Pattie explained to us that for some time now the situation had deteriorated in these mountains, although according to him the fault did not lie entirely with the Indians. He explained to us that when the first American explorers and trappers started to arrive in these mountains, the Apaches respected them and were on good terms with the Americans, allowing them to trap beaver in these idyllic streams. At that time the Indians made a distinction in their treatment of the Americans and the Mexicans, as they considered the latter their ancestral enemies. Even after the price of beaver pelts had plummeted, the trappers did well selling hides and meat to the miners and merchants at the Copper Mines, a thriving operation in those days.

But everything changed immediately after an incident with the Mimbres Apache tribe of chief Juan Compá, which occurred close to the mines. An American scalp hunter named Mathias Johnson enticed the Compá's band to the village near the mines, inviting them to a party of corn gruel and *mescal.* When the men and women of the tribe were gathered around the village plaza enjoying the banquet, the peddler took them to a place where he had set out a huge pile of corn flour, inviting them to help themselves, and then he lit the wick to a cannon loaded with shrapnel and nails, concealed under some blankets.

When the powerful discharge reached those wretched souls, most of the tribe's women and children soaked the flour with their blood. Johnson and his henchmen dispatched the warriors one by one to get their scalps, which would be sold to the Mexican governor of Chihuahua. The only Apache who survived was the chief, Juan Compá, who managed to escape the slaughter although he was seriously injured. Old Pattie thought that he was still roaming the wilderness thirsting for vengeance. Apparently the Indians called him the Lone Traveler, because the shrapnel had left part of his face disfigured and he shied away from people, covering his face with a mask made from animal hide.

According to old Pattie, many of the trappers and miners who in years past roamed those mountains ranges in peace had paid with their lives for the treachery of Johnson, the scalp hunter. Few ventured there in search of minerals, and the copper mines were abandoned since the threat of Apache attack made transporting the ore too dangerous. The few remaining miners and hunters in the area had to be constantly on the alert, and at night they couldn't build a bonfire or play the harmonica in camp lest they attract the attention of the vengeful Mimbres Apaches.

Old Pattie thought it was those very Mimbres Apaches who had attacked Fort Webster, leaving the entire garrison without horses and decimating the troops who had gone after them. At mid-morning when we came within sight of the barracks from the crest of the mountain, we saw that the survivors had placed a barricade of old carretas, used barrels, tree trunks, and other odds and ends around the main entrance. They were so fearful of a new attack from the Apaches that upon seeing our column looming behind the hill, they trained in our direction the cannon that they had on the rooftop of the fort and before we could tell them who we were, fired a projectile, which fortunately went over our heads.

Captain Stanton immediately gave orders to unfurl the banner and play the bugle, so that our own companions would know we weren't a band of hostiles. When the troops at the fort finally understood that we were soldiers, they started to shout with joy and dance at the edge of the parapet. I could understand how those men felt, remembering what my life was like in the northern forts, where we, too, always felt besieged by men and wild animals. When we camped out in the mountains, there were times when we would be surrounded by packs of hungry wolves. I recall on more than one occasion being at the point of firing a shot at a mule because I saw its reddish eyes shining in the dark and took the poor animal for a predator.

The captain ordered the men to remove the items they had stacked up against the entrance, after convincing the old major who had been left in command of the fort that if they were attacked, the barricade would serve more as a hindrance than as protection. And if by chance a fire broke out in the barracks, everyone would be burned to a crisp. We remained three days camped close to the fort so that the soldiers could regain their confidence and look for firewood and fodder for the few horses they had left.

Little by little life for the detachment returned to normal, and a few prospectors began to approach the barracks, as well as hunters who had been hiding out in the mountains. Even small bands of Apaches came in peace, bringing with them women and children. But old Pattie, who was an old hand in these matters, claimed that the Indians only came to spy.

The night before undertaking the return trip, old Pattie asked me if his son could make the first part of his trip to Cabezón under the soldiers' protection. I told him that I didn't think this would be an inconvenience, provided that he didn't tell Captain Stanton the peculiar nature of his mission with the Río Puerco cacique. Our commander was a man of puritanical morality who didn't even allow his soldiers to swear in his presence.

After seeking permission from Stanton, Pattie Junior retrieved from his cache in the stables the bales of tanned hides that he planned to sell in the Río Grande settlements, on the way to Cabezón, so he would have money to buy the services of a prostitute. And when, at dawn of the following day, our column left Fort Webster, the trapper followed us on a black and white mule that he called Caprichos (Whims), in honor of its unpredictable and obstinate temperament.

The sun had still not risen, but Timothy Baltasar's voice could be heard in the hollow of the valley singing his childhood ballad:

> *How many miles to Babylon?*
> *Three score and ten.*
> *Can I get there by candlelight?*
> *Yes, and back again . . .*

The Taming of Cimarrón

Young Pattie left the dragoon column near Fort Conrad, where he was advised not to follow the Camino Real because a band of young Navajos was said to be prowling around the Sierra de los Ladrones, wanting to prove themselves by attacking unescorted travelers.

Making a detour due northwest, Pattie ended up at Laguna Pueblo, where he was lucky enough to find a fair going on and was able to sell almost all his merchandise—pelts and jerky. From there he went down the Cebolleta Canyon headed for the Río Puerco, and by the end of the third day he could see Cabezón Peak, the point of reference that his father had given him to find the village. The reddish sunset reflecting on the angles and bulges of the peak gave it the facial features of a monster.

When he reached the village they were about to close the gate to the plaza, and at the fonda they had begun to light the candles. This made Pattie think of a line from the ballad he had heard a soldier sing while he traveled through the Gila mountain range: "Can I get there by candlelight?" He was told that he could find Gil Gómez in the back room, where the cacique normally took care of business and received tribute from his vassals. And indeed, upon opening the wicker partition, he found the genízaro with his elbows resting on a table made of rough-cut lumber. The black mane on the back of his neck was folded under a wide red bandanna from which protruded the edge of his severed earlobe.

The cacique stared intensely at the trapper from under his thick eyebrows; the rest of his face remained expressionless. "What brings you to these parts, stranger?" he asked. The way he invited the trapper to sit across the table from him was not welcoming. It seemed more like a great cat stretching its paws with its claws retracted.

The cacique listened attentively to Young Pattie's account of his encounter with Decoy at the watering hole. Gil Gómez was particularly interested in the detailed description of the young savage's stature and his build. It was not the first time that the genízaro had heard talk of the young giant, but up to now he had not spoken with anyone who had seen him face to face. When the young man, staring at the floor and blushing, talked of the assignment that his father had given him, to contract with a harlot in order to tame the wild young man, suddenly Gil Gómez's face lit up with a wide smile, showing a set of teeth as white and sharp as those of a mountain lion.

"You can tell that your father is an old hand!" said the cacique. "You'll see—as soon as the stallion bites the nipples of a woman he'll forget all about antelope milk! You'll find that here in the fonda we have the best women in the region."

When Gómez took him up to the main floor where the women were, so the trapper could choose the one he liked best, Young Pattie saw a small notice board that was hanging above the staircase:

In the Fonda de la Reunión
Men's destiny is fixed.
The woman who is chosen through luck
Is quickly impregnated, and then . . . comes death!

Crossing the threshold of the brothel, the trapper was met by a stench like a grizzly's den. When his eyes adjusted to the twilight, the young man saw scantily clad women of different shapes and colors lying in every corner of the room. Overcoming his embarrassment, he tried to figure out which one would be likeliest to seduce the wild man, knowing full well that his choice could determine the success of the ploy.

The Spanish girls looked at him impudently, halfway reclined on huge rough serge pillows, with small cigars dangling from their mouths and their cheeks covered with a thick layer of ochre. There were several Navajo girls; among the American soldiers, Navajos had the reputation of being submissive and voluptuous. A couple of young Apaches in the corner of the room, captured only recently, kept a watchful eye on the stranger. They looked like trapped animals, capable of responding to a caress by lashing out with their claws. The trapper noticed a white woman called Maggie Smith whose family had been wiped out on the Santa Fe Trail by Comanches. Her horrible memories caused her to be in a perpetual trance-like state, but that didn't decrease the number of her clients, who didn't care to waste time on conversation anyway.

The young man turned down the Apache girls, realizing that given the opportunity they might stab him in the back to return to their ranchería. But it was not advisable to pick one of the Spanish girls either; probably they would repel the mustangs with their cigar smell. And Maggie Smith's fragile nerves would not be up to the sexual onslaught of a young stud.

So as not to rush his enjoyable decision, the trapper weighed carefully the merits of each candidate, and finally selected a white woman with reddish hair and freckles on her turned-up nose, whom they called Sam Hat. The girl was wearing a wide-brimmed hat, which she apparently never removed, not even while making love, and her ample bosom was spilling over the top of her whalebone corset. A knife scar left by a drunkard did not improve her looks, but her calves and ankles were nicely rounded, and her tiny feet in red satin slippers seemed to the trapper the height of elegance. According to Gil Gómez, who considered his choice a wise one, in spite of certain setbacks in life, Sam Hat had held on to certain principles that she had learned from her father, an evangelist minister who had also presented her with a Bible. She read aloud from it whenever she felt inspired, which meant that her customers left her bedroom satisfied both carnally and spiritually.

When the trapper asked Sam Hat if she would be willing, for a reasonable fee, to accompany him to the wilderness to show a wild strapping lad the ways of a woman, the redhead responded that for five silver dollars she was capable of taking the breath away from Beelzebub himself. When the first ray of sun came over Cabezón Peak, the shadow of the mule could be seen along the Río Puerco with the trapper in the saddle and the prostitute behind him, heading south at a slow trot.

Unfortunately, as they reached the Sierra de los Ladrones, a group of young Navajos in war paint, armed to the teeth, blocked their path defiantly; they were the same ones whom the trapper had tried to avoid by taking a roundabout route to Cabezón. Pattie allowed the young warriors to take the remaining animal skins in exchange for saving his own, and by bribing them with a small carafe of brandy, he persuaded them not to take the woman with them.

Riding at a good pace and resting only during the heat of the day, the trapper and the harlot arrived at the Gila without further incident and lay in wait near the watering hole where Pattie had seen the young stud for the first time. On the third day at sunset, just when they were beginning to get tired of waiting, they felt the ground trembling and heard the thundering hooves of the antelopes and mustangs tearing through the bushes in search of water. Among them was the wild man, who rushed to drink and frolic about in the clear water just like one more colt from the herd.

Hiding behind the branches of a thick shrub, the trapper whispered instructions from the bushes: "Here comes Decoy! Expose your breasts, lift your skirts, and open your legs! As soon as he sees you, he'll come close to you. Take off your dress so that he can mount you, and show that savage what a woman is really like!"

The woman was flabbergasted when she saw the human beast panting and coming toward her with water running down his long mane and his chest covered with hair, but she stood her ground. She opened her bodice, showing off her breasts, and as soon as the strapping lad sensed the smell of the woman's body, he pounced on her. For once, she took off her hat, knowing that this was going to be an exceptional job. She removed her dress and spread it on the grass. And when Decoy came close to her, the woman guided his vessel to a safe haven, where he dropped his anchor in deep waters. For six days and nights, the young savage had sexual relations with the whore, and not for a single moment did he lose his strength. The man from the plains even forgot the prairies where he came from.

Only when he awoke on the seventh day after having his fill of her charms did the strapping lad remember his herds, which were in a nearby *potrero*. But as he approached them, the antelopes were put off by his human scent and bolted; the young mustangs began to stampede and scattered at full speed throughout the wilderness, as if lightning had suddenly struck the middle of the herd.

Decoy took off running after them, but he felt as though his limbs were paralyzed. Before he realized it, his herds had deserted him, suddenly shying away from him.

The trapper, having witnessed the scene from his hiding place at the edge of the waterhole, astounded at the stallion's sexual stamina, eventually fell asleep; but misfortune struck him. The branch of the shrub where he was resting broke, sending his body into the icy water, whence he emerged with his powder horn and spirits equally damp. His firing cap was also rendered useless. He had no choice but to sneak away once again through the underbrush and return to the camp, where his father, who was waiting for him, listened to the details of his adventure while he smoked his pipe. A mocking twinkle, which was not just a reflection of the campfire's flames, lit up his eyes.

After the stampede, the young lad returned to the spring where he had been with the whore and, hiding his face between his hands, began to sob bitterly. When her caresses failed to console him, Sam Hat began to stroke his tangled hair, talking to him softly, as if he were a child, though she was unsure if he could understand what she was saying. She remembered what the soldiers who frequented the fonda in Cabezón had named the young savage, and she decided to use that name too, since she didn't know how else to address him.

"Come now, Decoy, you're not as wild as you appear to be!" she said to herself. "It's a pity that you spend your time roaming the mountains with wild horses, because you have the body of a prince."

The savage kept staring at her. He seemed to be trying to repeat some of the sounds that he was hearing. As patiently as she could, the woman proceeded to teach him a few words. As he began to form sentences, Sam Hat had the impression that at one time he had known how to speak.

One day the woman was caressing the savage while he was sound asleep. She discovered a spot where his beard didn't grow and where the skin had a deep crimson mark. Sam Hat wondered whether his mysterious past could be explained by that scar, but her instinct told her not to mention it. She vowed never to ask him about the mark on his neck.

As time went on, Decoy could understand enough to have a conversation—that is, whenever he wasn't swimming in the spring or frolicking on the grass with the courtesan. One afternoon while Sam was seated next to him reading her Bible, she ran across a passage she thought was interesting, and after reading it to Decoy, she applied her own catechesis:

"And when the woman saw that the tree was good for food, and that it was pleasant to the eyes, and a tree to be desired to make one wise, she took of the fruit thereof, and did eat, and gave also unto her husband with her; and he did eat. . . . and they knew that they were naked; and they sewed fig leaves together, and made themselves aprons . . . ," to which Sam added: "My father, who was a wise man, used to say that sex kills innocence, but that it stimulates intelligence; that is why Jews used the word *to know* to mean *to fuck.* And for you the doors of understanding opened up after you *'got to know me,'* like what happened to Adam and Eve, whose knowledge improved after eating the forbidden fruit from the tree of pleasure."

But when the leaves of the cottonwood began to turn yellow, and the breeze in the ravine turned cool, Sam Hat started to miss the hustle and bustle of the settlements. The woman had tired of the peace and tranquility in that Eden, and she tempted the man once again with the forbidden fruit:

"Let's go, Decoy, on your feet! Don't lie there on the ground like an animal!" she scolded him one day while he was taking a siesta under a bush. "I'll guide you to the village of Cabezón, where there are always fandangos and entertainment and where the cacique Gil Gómez has fun day and night without ever resting. Now there's a strong man! He controls the people of the valley the way a stallion dominates his herd! For sure you two will make a good pair, because you're chips off the same block!"

The strapping lad immediately jumped to his feet, saying with a mixture of clumsiness and arrogance, "Let's go, woman! Lead me to this Gil Gómez, for I wish to challenge him to see if he can measure up to me. When I get to that village, I shall begin shouting: I am the strongest man around! I can change the world! Because he who is raised on the plains is stronger than anyone."

And reaching for the branch of a shrub, he split it in two effortlessly. But Sam warned him, "Don't you believe it! You may be stronger, but Gil Gómez has the advantage when it comes to experience and shrewdness. He's already heard of you and no doubt will be looking forward to making your acquaintance. If you rub him the wrong way you may regret it! Up! I don't want to see you lying on the ground any longer; the ground is for sheepherders."

Peeling off part of her dress, she covered the man's nakedness. She took him by the hand, and they headed for Cabezón.

The Dreams of Gil Gómez

Sam Hat was not mistaken when she said that Gil Gómez had anticipated Decoy's arrival, but what she could not have guessed was that the cacique was waiting for the arrival of the stranger with a mixture of curiosity and fear. Although in front of his young chieftains the genízaro made fun of the youth's prodigious strength, pretending there was nothing to the stories they had heard, down deep in his heart he wondered if behind those tall tales there might not be a kernel of truth.

For two consecutive nights Gil Gómez had suffered nightmares, waking up in cold sweats, and on the third night, unable to sleep, he abandoned the arms of the woman who had been sharing his bed and, without telling his servants, saddled his horse and slipped out the back door.

The new moon shone brightly over Cabezón Peak, and the genízaro recalled the stories that he had been told as a child about the giant Yeitsó and the Twin Warriors. Although he bragged about his skepticism, he had not forgotten Navajo tradition. At times of trouble he would usually go to his mother, the divine Ninsaba, who lived in a Navajo ranchería on the other side of Chivato Mesa, and ask her to recite one of the sacred chants that her people used to create man's harmony with the surrounding world.

Traveling mountain trails that he knew almost better than the wild animals did, the genízaro reached his mother's cabin at dawn. She had already come out of her hogan and was seated at a wooden loom that hung from the low branches of a dry cottonwood tree. She was weaving a blanket with wool from her own sheep. Even though she had her back to him, Ninsaba recognized her son's footsteps as he walked on the sand still crusted with frost.

"My son, is that you?" she asked without stopping her weaving and added, "Tell me what storm lies ahead, because you only come to see me when you have problems."

The genízaro remained speechless for a moment, but Ninsaba stood up and called him. "Come in the house. I know you must be famished, because the evil women you associate with don't take care of you."

Gil Gómez followed his mother into the hogan, which was octagonal, built from pine logs chinked with mud. It had a dirt floor and from the walls hung cooking utensils and bags of dried plants and seeds. With his huge body stooped over, he went into the room, walking in a sunwise circle, according to Navajo custom. He sat down before a fire of cedar wood where a lamb stew was bubbling, crossing his long legs, remaining for a moment with his head bowed like a huge dog that lies down at its master's feet.

The smoke from the fire was going out through a hole in the cabin's roof, and Ninsaba sat on a sheepskin on the other side of the fire, her body upright. On her strong and well-rounded shoulders rested two shiny black braids. Her unlined face was oval, her nose slender. Underneath a wide and convex forehead her black eyes stared at her son with a hint of reproach.

"My people always tell me that you're up to no good and they come to me complaining of your misdeeds," said Ninsaba, continuing to stir the stew with a willow stick. "If they haven't tossed me out of this village I believe that it's because of the respect grandfather Narbona inspires in them."

"Mother, lately I've had some strange dreams," said Gil Gómez. "The other night I dreamt that I was seeing a sky full of stars right over my head when one of them became detached from the firmament and landed near me like a meteorite. I tried to lift the rock, but it weighed too much; I wanted to move it but I couldn't. The villagers from Cabezón milled around the comet, the notables left their houses to view the miracle, and even my men paid homage to it. The weird thing is that I felt attracted to that piece of rock as though it were a woman, and I placed the rock before you so that you could compare it to me."

Gil Gómez's mother pondered for a few moments before responding, and then she began to speak with her eyes fixed on the fire. "The star in your dreams is a powerful fighter, who appears next to you as if he had dropped from the sky; that is why you were trying to lift him but were unsuccessful. You attempted to turn him over but you couldn't even move him. That rock represents a good friend, a loyal and true companion, someone whom you will be able to trust. That's how I interpret this dream."

"Wait, because last night I had another dream; this time I saw an axe falling into the patio of my fortress. Everyone was running to see it; all of my men gathered around the axe. I presented it to you and you placed it by my side."

"The axe in your dream represents a man who has come from faraway lands. He may appear hard and sharp like a flint axe, and you may even fight against him as if he were a rival, but later on you will embrace him as though he were your brother. He will be like that weapon that you always carry at your side. He will accompany you in the most difficult adventures, and he will cover your back in the most perilous episodes."

Gil Gómez let out a sigh of relief. "I hope what you say is true, and that your prophecy is fulfilled. I would like nothing more than to encounter a strong and courageous friend so that we could undertake new adventures together."

"Don't worry," Ninsaba said to him. "I don't see anything bad in that dream."

Before taking off, Gil Gómez looked straight into his mother's eyes and asked her the same thing he had asked since he was a child, even though he always got the same answer. "Mother, some day, are you going to tell me who my father is?"

"Son, you know very well that I cannot answer that. Remember what Changing Woman told her son when he asked her the same question."

"Yes, I already know," responded Gil Gómez. *"Round cactus, elongated cactus, that is your father.'* But I'm not a child anymore, and I need to know who my father is. Couldn't you at least tell me where I might be able to find him?"

"You are still as impulsive and reckless as when you used to play around the village with the cedar bow. No matter how much time goes by, I think most people remain the same."

Knowing that he would not get a satisfactory answer, the genízaro did not want to press the issue, but he ate only a couple of bites of the lamb stew that his mother offered him. As she did not want to let him go in a bad mood, Ninsaba smiled and said to him, "Surely you want me to tell you one of the stories that I used to share with you when you were a child. Stay a while and listen."

Through the Sun Path

A few weeks after they were born, the sons of Changing Woman had grown a lot and were able to run around the cabin and outside it as they pleased, something that worried the Woman, who feared that one day the giant Yeitsó or his friends might discover them.

Coyote was one of Yeitsó's spies. Crow, Magpie, and Vulture also aided the giant, and they were always snooping around so as to tell the giant later what they had seen.

When the children grew even bigger, the Woman made a crude bow from a Rocky Mountain cedar, leaving the needles at the tip of the bow. She also made arrows from reeds that she gathered at a place called Big Planted Reed. Nowadays, the rattle stick used during the Girls' Dance in the Enemyway symbolizes the bow that Changing Woman made for her sons from the cedar branches. And the reeds that she utilized for making the arrows are the same ones that are used in the Arrowway, among other objects, for the ceremony.

The boys would run hither and thither, and during one of their runs, they happened to go by the cabin where their grandparents lived, First Man and First Woman. They heard the old folks talking about the extraordinary way in which Changing Woman had conceived the Two Warriors, thanks to the Sun's intervention. Even though the two children were still too young to understand it completely, what they heard caused a certain restlessness in their young hearts.

So, when they got back to their mother's hogan, they asked her: "Mother, you never talked to us about our father. Can you tell us now who our father is?" Changing Woman was so surprised by the question that she didn't know what to answer, and so the boys persisted: "Mother, could you tell us who our father is?" "You wish to know who your father is?" the Woman finally responded. "Well, it is best for you to know that you don't have a father, and you will never get to know him!" When the children insisted, Changing Woman got even more nervous, and she said the first thing that came into her head: "Very well then, you want to know who your father is—the round cactus, the elongated cactus, those are your fathers!"

In order to keep the boys busy, this time the Woman gave the older one a black bow and arrow with a feather from the tail of the Eagle and to the smaller one she gave a bow made from mahogany with an arrow from Yellow Feather, and she said to them: "Go and play with them, but don't go far from the cabin and, above all, don't even think about going east!" (She knew that the monsters roamed the East). Of course the boys went some distance away from the cabin and headed east until they ran across a big ugly black bird resting on a tree. The two boys got ready to shoot their arrows at it, but just as they were about to fire, the big ugly black bird flapped its wings and flew away.

When they got back to the hogan, the boys told their mother: "Mother, today we went toward the East and over there we saw a big ugly black bird, which we tried to shoot; but just when we were going to, it got up and flew off." "You scoundrels! What you saw was the Crow!" exclaimed Changing Woman. "He's one of the giant Yeitsó's spies, and as soon as the Crow tells the giant he has seen you, he'll come to devour you just as he consumed a great portion of humanity before you two came into this world."

One fine day when the Woman was busier than usual, the boys left the cabin without being seen and headed for the summit of a mountain in the East. When the Woman noticed their absence and went out to look for them, she couldn't find them no matter where she searched. Fearful that they might have fallen into the hands of some monster, she followed their tracks to the top of the mountain, but when she reached the summit she saw that the twins' tracks ended there. Then she imagined that the young boys had taken a magic path, surely asking the rainbow to serve as a bridge for them so they could get close to the Sun's dwelling place.

Realizing that she couldn't do anything to recover her sons, she returned to her hogan and sat down on the ground and began crying.

Meanwhile, the twins had taken the path that leads to the Sun, and as dawn broke, they were singing this song:

> *I have emerged from under her;*
> *I, who am the son of the Changing Woman,*
> *I have emerged from under her.*
> *I have emerged from the blue twilight;*
> *I walk between the sons of the blue twilight;*
> *I salute the sons of the blue twilight;*
> *I salute the sons of Sahanahray Bekay Hozoní;*
> *Through the twilight, I have emerged from there.*

The Molting of the Snake

Walking and walking down narrow paths and mountain trails, Decoy and the woman ran into a group of shepherds who were coming from the Ojo de la Parida and had crossed the river with their flocks in search of pasture. Upon seeing the wild man and the courtesan both half-naked, the shepherds' eyes immediately focused on the prostitute's tattered clothing and the shapely figure that it revealed, but as soon as they noticed the youth and his imposing physique—the width of his chest and the thick hair that covered his forearms—they guessed that he must be the famous Cimarrón.

"He must be the same one who roamed the plains with his wild herd," said the head shepherd, Boleslo Romero, a middle-aged man with even facial features framed by a full beard.

"Word has it that he used to eat grass alongside the mustangs and that he was raised on antelope milk," added Pedro Chávez.

"Well, if it is true," commented Elisario Ortiz, "the milk from the wild herds has served him well."

"He will match up very well in size and girth to the cacique from Cabezón," observed Nepomuceno Muñoz. "It could be that the genízaro has the advantage in height, but it appears to me that this one has stronger limbs."

"Perhaps you're right," concurred Elisario. "Can't you just see them in a fight?"

Since night was falling, the shepherds invited the travelers to take shelter in the sheepfold and share their supper, which consisted of pieces of jerky, dried cornbread, and fists full of dried fruit, all of it washed down with generous portions of El Paso wine passed around in a goatskin.

Everything was going along just fine until Cimarrón tried to drink from the wineskin, imitating what everyone else was doing. Part of the wine dripped down his beard and hairy chest, and what he managed to swallow went down the wrong pipe, making him cough noisily. And when he tried to gulp down a piece of cornbread, it got stuck in his windpipe and wouldn't go either up or down. The strapping lad thought he was choking to death, and Sam Hat had to come to his rescue. She gave him a good swat on the back, and soon he regained his color.

"Come on, Decoy! Be a man!" said the whore. "Take a piece of bread and drink wine—it's the custom of the country!"

"Yes—no need to stand on ceremony among us. He can eat and drink until he's stuffed!" echoed the shepherds.

Although at first he made faces and gasped for air, he soon took a liking to the bread and wine, and when a shepherd offered him a tin cup so he could drink the wine without spilling it, he drank the whole cup without blinking an eye, and then another and another, until he had drunk seven cups. Cimarrón felt a pleasant warmth in his stomach, and a blissful new feeling reached his brain.

When the shepherds saw him so peaceful and relaxed, they couldn't resist touching the muscles of his arms and thighs, and one of the shepherds even dared to feel the size of his penis, which was in direct proportion to the rest of his body. In the midst of all the excitement, someone came up with the bright idea that Cimarrón would look better if he were cleaned up, and that some of his hair should be cut and his hairy forearms trimmed. And without thinking twice, with everyone pitching in, they removed the untanned piece of hide that he had wrapped around his loins and stuck him in a huge tub where they kept water from the nearby arroyo. They scrubbed his body with suds from the maguey plant. They cut his crop of hair and trimmed his beard and forearms using the same knives they used for shearing sheep. Afterward they rubbed oil over his body to soothe whatever scrapes had been caused by a slip of the knife.

Once he was washed, shaven, and sweet smelling, they dressed him up in a brand-new linen shirt and wool pants, and the strapping lad looked like a new man, as handsome and clean as a groom. As if it were all happening to somebody else, he saw someone toss the long locks of hair and beard trimmings into the fire. They sparked for a moment and were consumed by the flames, just as the snakeskin left in the brambles is consumed under the scourge of the sun. When Cimarrón touched his neck and noticed that his old scar was exposed, he asked the woman for a handkerchief and used it to cover his neck.

One of the sheepherders brought a guitar from the *jacal,* and the head shepherd, Romero, who had a deep and harmonious voice, began singing a ballad about the love affairs of a rich patrón's daughter who used secret spells to seduce the peones in the hacienda. At the end of each stanza the rest of the shepherds repeated the refrain.

Because of your love, your ungrateful love.

You were dazzled by the mauve-colored bird,
Who follows the flocks of sheep, breaking its wing.
It still can be heard in the forest shouting:
"Ouch, my wing! Ouch, my wing!"

Because of your love, your ungrateful love.

You fell in love with the shepherd,
The flock's head shepherd,
Who always offered you curdled milk,
And who always brought you kids.

Because of your love, your ungrateful love.

At first you bewitched him,
Turning him into a wolf.
Now his own young shepherds are running him off,
His very own dogs nip at his flanks.

✝

Because of your love, your ungrateful love.

As they sang, the shepherds winked and smiled at each other. The strangers couldn't understand the meaning of it all, but Decoy was fascinated by the sound of the guitar and the beat of the song. Afterward, they invited the courtesan to dance a few *seguidillas,* which she did with more energy than grace, although the shepherds responded to the wriggling of her rotund bosom and hips with enthusiastic applause.

About this time, a furious bleating erupted from the direction of the sheepfold, along with a frightful growling. Taking advantage of the shepherds' inattention, a pair of wolves had jumped into the fold and were slaughtering the sheep. When he heard the noise, Cimarrón grabbed a firebrand and headed for the sheep pen, hopped over the fence, and trapped the wolves in a corner while they growled and showed their teeth.

With incredible dexterity and speed, the strapping lad grabbed one of the beasts by the scruff of the neck and lifted it up in the air as though it were a kitten, then tossed it out of the sheepfold with such force that it broke its back upon landing. The other wolf did not wait to suffer the same fate; it leapt over the fence, disappearing into the darkness and howling with fear like a cub.

The shepherds let out several cheers for Cimarrón. He and Sam Hat enjoyed the shepherds' hospitality for several days, and Cimarrón became the protector of the flock, scaring away the wolves and mountain lions that prowled around the sheepfold.

Duel in Cabezón

Many different stories have been told in the Río Abajo about the famous fight between the Río Puerco cacique and the strapping lad who came down from the mountains accompanied by Sam Hat. Perhaps some of these tales exaggerate the strength of the champions or the destruction caused during the fight in Cabezón. The fact is that the event had been so anticipated by the inhabitants of the valley that it would be difficult to tell it impartially. What is known for sure is that the immediate cause of the fight was a misdeed that Gil Gómez's henchmen committed the night before Decoy arrived in the valley.

The whore and the wild man had stopped to rest under the shade of a cottonwood tree near the Río Puerco when, along the tracks that ran parallel to the river, they saw coming toward them a motley convoy, preceded by the screeching wails of the poorly greased axles of a carreta, the type that was used by the peones of that territory. Over that plaintive sound could be heard the moaning of a family riding on the carreta, which was drawn by two oxen with a rough wooden yoke. Walking in front of the vehicle was a man who appeared to be the head of the family, right behind him were a couple of young boys, and on top of the carreta were seated five women of different ages, some of them wearing brightly colored rebozos.

What surprised Sam Hat as the retinue came closer was that the outfits the peasants wore and the cart decorations resembled those used for a popular fiesta, with flowers and wreaths on the necks of the oxen. Yet the looks on the people's faces and the moaning suggested that they were returning from a funeral. The contrast was so apparent that it piqued Decoy's curiosity. He asked Sam to approach the carreta and ask what was going on. "Ask those people what's wrong with them," he demanded, "and tell the man who's crying to shut up because it's making me feel bad!"

The whore went up to the driver and asked him to come close to the grove where they had stopped; and when he did, Cimarrón asked him, in his awkward way, "My dear fellow, I would like to know the reason for your crying and where you're headed on your painful journey."

Noting Decoy's distinguished bearing, the peon respectfully removed his straw hat, mistaking him for a rich patrón. "I would like very much to answer you, your grace, but I could hardly say where it is that I'm headed, since need and shame don't have a clear destination; rather, they follow the urge to leave behind this accursed valley where for several generations my hardworking ancestors withstood the terrible Indian raids as well as the inclemency of the heavens and the earth. I must admit that I'm abandoning these abodes with sadness, and that is the reason for our wailing, since I'm leaving several generations of Montoyas buried in the Cabezón cemetery; but, on the other hand, I'm happy to get away from the yoke of tyranny and injustice that Gil Gómez has imposed on these lands. And I have given up both my home and hacienda—no matter how much I have gone into debt with the genízaro—so as to save those two young girls, traveling on the back of the wagon, from the perverted habits that this man and his henchmen have started in the valley. That degenerate respects neither the daughter of a peón nor the wife of a prominent citizen, and very few of the girls are still virgins when they marry."

Cimarrón had listened attentively to the litany of misfortunes, without grasping the meaning of all the speaker's words.

"Excuse me, but I haven't really understood what you're saying. But if it's Gil Gómez who has offended you, I'm prepared to ask him for an explanation, because there's no match for the power of a man who grew up on the plains!"

The driver glanced at Decoy again, and as he observed the size of his chest and the strength of his neck, a glimmer of hope flashed across his face and his rhetoric flowed more profusely than ever.

"We were celebrating the wedding of Josefa Montoya, my niece, to a young man from the settlement of Sandoval, when the henchmen of Gil Gómez went right inside the church and ruined the ceremony. Ignoring the pleas and threats of the bride and groom's families, the leaders took the bride away so that Gil Gómez, that tyrant, could enjoy her charms before her fiancé."

"I still cannot understand you," said Cimarrón, scratching his head. "Why did they want to take her to Gil Gómez if she wasn't his wife? Didn't you say that your niece was going to marry a young man from Sandoval?"

"That's the law that Gil Gómez has imposed on the region: he takes his turn first and then the husband can taste her afterward! As if it were his God-given right ever since he was taken from his mother's womb . . ."

Embarrassed that this evidence of abuse and injustice should be Cimarron's first exposure to civilization, Sam Hat was attempting to interrupt the verbose peasant. She attempted to pull Cimarrón away and cut the conversation short. But once the Demosthenes of the Río Puerco got started, his speech flowed in an unstoppable flood. "Gil Gómez's henchmen tore the bride from the arms of her fiancé, whose pleas and threats were of no avail. And imagine what it cost us to bring the priest Don Matías Luján all the way from Bernalillo! Now the priest has left the village, without even wanting to look back. He says God should unleash the plagues of Egypt on these lands because of the conduct of the genízaro! As if we hadn't already been punished enough by droughts, floods, and the attacks of heathens even before the scourge of Gil Gómez!"

Finally Decoy seemed to understand the message. His face turned white with indignation. Closing his Herculean fists, without even turning his head to see if the woman was following him, he strode forth confidently along the path that led to the village. As he went past the carreta, the women's heads emerged from under their rebozos. When they saw the fierce expression and determined step of the stranger, they could somehow guess his intentions. The girls made the sign of the cross, and the grandmother, who, wrapped up in her dark rebozo, was the very image of *Doña Sebastiana,* said a brief prayer.

Sam Hat was running by fits and starts down the uneven trail, holding onto her hat with one hand to avoid losing it in the evening breeze and trying in vain to catch up with Decoy, who had gotten way ahead of her. In her red satin slippers, stumbling over every clod of dirt, and catching her flaring dress on bushes and thistles, the woman embodied the Spanish expression of running "like a whore through the wilderness."

As he reached the last steep slope on the path, Decoy saw Cabezón Peak, lit up by the sunset, dominating the Río Puerco Valley. A gale-force wind made the tumbleweeds roll along the tracks on the road, and over the mountains in the background storm clouds were forming and the changes in light created strange shapes on the rugged face of the peak. In the village plaza, the locals and the peones from the surrounding area who had come to the wedding of Rumaldo Montoya's niece were still upset, raving about the cacique's behavior, and upon seeing the robust stranger come through the huge main door, they surrounded him, almost stopping him in his tracks.

"He's the spitting image of Gil Gómez!" exclaimed young Polinio Córdova.

"If I didn't know the genízaro so well, I'd swear they were twins," said a Navajo chieftain who had come all the way from his ranchería to take part in the aborted party.

"The stranger may be shorter, but his bones are much stronger," commented a peón from Casa Salazar.

"This young man is for sure the one who roamed the plains with the wild mustangs, the one the soldiers nicknamed Decoy," said Trinidad Armijo. "Word has it that he ate prairie grass and even nursed on antelope milk!"

The village noteworthies, the same ones who had accompanied the Indians to the cave of Arorú, reacted to the appearance of Cimarrón with a mixture of hope and incredulity. Some pinched themselves to make sure they were not dreaming. Seeing their most secret desires become a reality, they said to themselves that perhaps the witch's spell had borne fruit.

"I believe that this man is now the strongest in all the Río Abajo," whispered the mayor, Bitoriano Montoya, as if he could hardly believe his own eyes. "It seems as though the genízaro has finally met his match!"

The blacksmith, José de la Luz, dared to express his feelings without the slightest restraint. "I bet we're going to have a good fight!" he shouted loudly in the middle of the plaza. "The clashing of arms is going to be heard all over the Puerco Valley!"

"It's about time that we gente de razón had a champion after tolerating so many abuses and injustices!" said Hilario Mestas.

"Let us hope that from this day forward the decent women of Cabezón are able to live in peace!" said the mayor, who was a close relative of the abducted bride.

Decoy lost no time in asking for Gil Gómez's whereabouts, since he wanted to challenge him without delay. The villagers, who were gathered around him just as the mob pursues the matador before he enters the bull ring, informed him that the cacique was still resting in his fortress, preparing to come down to the village at dusk to enjoy his undeserved reward. When Sam Hat reached the plaza, almost out of breath, shoving her way through throngs of people, she told Decoy what she had just heard from the villagers. Apparently, after having been kidnapped in the church, the bride had been able to elude Gil Gómez's henchmen and had locked herself up in one of the rooms on the fonda's upper floor, vowing to stab herself with a dagger that she had hidden in her bodice if a man other than her husband stepped across the threshold.

Decoy decided to wait for the genízaro to come down to the village. He situated himself in the inn, at the landing of the stairs, knowing that Gil Gómez had no choice but to go through there to reach the room where the offended bride had barricaded herself.

One of his henchmen notified Gil Gómez of the arrival of the powerful stranger while the genízaro was taking a bath in a copper tub that he had had hauled on the back of a mule all the way from Albuquerque. The genízaro kept on soaping and grooming himself, showing not the slightest fear. After finishing his bath, he dressed himself in his finest clothing as if his only worry were to dazzle the bride.

In order not to have an obvious advantage over Cimarrón who he had been told used no weapons other than his strong arms, Gil Gómez wanted to give the appearance of being unarmed, but he had concealed a pistol in his silk sash and slipped a hunting knife in the cuff of his moccasin. He ordered his jet-black horse to be saddled with his best riding saddle, covered with the hide of a mountain lion with small silver bells on the bridle and martingale. Preceded by the happy tinkling of his horse trappings, he crossed the Río Puerco, which the drought had reduced to a river of sand where frogs croaked in the few remaining puddles. The storm clouds that had gathered at sunset on the Jémez Mountains had moved south and hung over Cabezón Peak, accentuating the darkness.

While Gil Gómez was crossing the river, the first big drops of rain began to fall, but they were absorbed by the dry air almost before they touched the ground. In spite of the late hour and the rain, groups of villagers were still milling around the plaza, gossiping about the arrival of Cimarrón and speculating how everything would turn out. A few Indians from the neighboring rancherías, wrapped in their blankets, had been attracted by the wedding party and lingered at the prospect of a good fight.

As Gil Gómez crossed the plaza, preceded by the tinkling of his horse trappings, silence fell, but the whispers increased again after he went by. The crowd's murmur of expectation seemed to be part of the rumbling of the storm. The genízaro left his horse tied at the main entrance to the fonda. Climbing up the stairs with his pistol in his hand he headed toward the landing that gave access to the upstairs rooms. Thinking that Cimarrón could well be waiting for him, he was careful not to make the wooden steps creak as he went up. He felt a chill run up and down his spine upon noticing the board that told of the harmony between love and death, and for the first time it struck him as being a jinx:

> *In the Fonda de la Reunión*
> *Men's destiny is fixed.*
> *The woman who is chosen through luck*
> *Is quickly impregnated, and then . . . comes death!*

As he reached the last step without incident, the genízaro thought that perhaps the stranger had gotten tired of waiting and had left, so he put his pistol back into his sash. But as he started to cross the landing, he tripped over Decoy, who had fallen asleep with his legs sticking out, blocking the landing.

Gil Gómez fell forward the length of his body and cracked open the locked door of the bedroom with his head. In the back of the room he saw a woman in a wedding dress. She was holding a candle in one hand and a shiny dagger in the other, as tense and composed as a virgin ready for sacrifice. Horrified, the bride cried out the holy name of Mary; Cimarrón, barely awake, let out a deep grunt; and the genízaro, who had gotten up from the floor with his forehead bleeding, uttered a loud curse.

For a few seconds, the two thugs stared at each other—as if some witch had placed a huge mirror on that landing where both of them could observe the same image—without believing what they were seeing. Then they grabbed each other, tumbling down the stairs, making the wooden bars of the banisters fly off as if they were matchsticks, smashing to smithereens the hall tables in their savage struggle. Even the lintel of the door gave way, and the hall columns wobbled with the action of the fighters, who were rolling on the floor hugging each other and eventually landed right in the center of the plaza, which the rain was turning into a muddy mess.

The mob that was waiting for the fighters to appear let out a raucous ovation, like a crowd at a cockfight. Some of the villagers had made torches from juniper branches so as to follow the battle in the dark. Those who have never witnessed a battle between two wild stallions fighting for possession of their mares, standing high up on their hind legs, jabbing at each other with their sharp hooves, taking ferocious bites at one another's necks, foaming at the mouth in their fury, would find it very difficult to imagine the violence of the struggle between the two champions. With every blow, chest bones and jaws cracked, and at times the huge body of one of the combatants ended up in the mud until he jumped up to continue wrestling.

The hurricane wind was hurling huge drops of rain with such force that they were snuffing out the villagers' torches one by one. The onlookers began to go home to seek refuge from the downpour, and finally the two bullies were left to fight each other in the dark.

The rivals rolled on the muddy ground until they ended up at the very edge of the Río Puerco. Before they knew it, there was no more ground for their bodies to roll over and, still intertwined, they fell straight down the steep slope to the bottom of the river, which in no time had turned into a torrential flow, dragging along broken bushes and rocks. The fall seemed to favor Cimarrón, who gained an advantage from the force of the water and managed to get a grip on his opponent's neck, keeping his head under water until he noticed that the genízaro's arms were beginning to loosen their grip on his waist.

At that moment, the wind tore the dark mantle of the clouds and a moonbeam lit up the face of Cabezón Peak, whose rocky features seemed to contract into a diabolical grin. The sight momentarily paralyzed Cimarrón's heart, and his hands loosened their pressure on the genízaro's neck. Gil Gómez's mouth emerged from the current spitting water and mud.

Turning his back on the victor, the cacique climbed like an otter up the slippery bank. Pulling himself up with great difficulty, he headed for the fortress with an unsteady gait and the downcast head of a loser.

But Cimarrón called him and, approaching his rival with his hand stretched out, said, "I've never met another fighter like you! You truly deserve to be the cacique of these environs! You're strong as a wild bull and you must continue as the leader of the herd."

The genízaro turned back and accepted the hand that was extended to him. And so, embracing each other tightly, Gil Gómez and Decoy sealed their friendship.

Book Three

Let us go, then, so that you may see each other

 face to face.

I know well all there is to know; believe me.

Come with me to Uruk of the Sheepfold,

 where people are radiant in their wide belts,

 and where there's festivity everyday,

 where string instruments and drums are played,

 and the holy courtesans show off their beauty,

 glowing with sexual grace and boasting sensuality.

At night they drag the caciques into their beds.

Enkidu, you who like to evoke pleasure from life,

 will enjoy meeting Gilgamesh, the king

 of good times.

POEM OF GILGAMESH
Tablet I, Column v

The New Babylon

The day after the famous fight, the villagers of Cabezón were dismayed to see Gil Gómez and the stranger walking around the plaza arm in arm. Particularly disturbed were those who had accompanied the Indians to Old Lady Arorú's hideout so that the witch could model a second Gil Gómez, and had even spent a silver dollar to pay for the exorcism. After all their trouble and expense, it seemed that the one who was supposed to rein in the tyrant from the Río Puerco was about to become his partner in bingeing and brawling.

The new compadres—the *cuates,* as they were now being called in the Río Puerco Valley—shared the same fondness for merrymaking and fornication, exacerbated in the case of Cimarrón because of years of abstinence in the desert. For a time the village turned into the most depraved Babylon that a prophet ever denounced to Jehovah. Don Matías Luján, parish priest of Bernalillo, whose spiritual jurisdiction included Cabezón, didn't dare to invoke either excommunication or anathema against those two sinners, fearing he might become a victim of their reprisals. Instead the priest decided never to set foot again in the Río Puerco Valley, as in the past when it was considered to be heathen territory.

After a while, the hermano mayor of the Penitentes, Juan Lucero, convened a meeting of the Holy Brotherhood in the adobe *morada* on the hill, where the Brothers usually met to carry out their prayers and rituals. After kneeling down in front of the image of Jesus on the cross—whose face showed a look of anguish more because of the knots that gnarled the olive wood than because of the skills of the *santero* who had carved it—and saying an Our Father, the brothers sat down on the wooden benches. The whitewashed walls still sparkled with the splashes of blood from the *disciplinas* that the brothers applied to themselves to cleanse their sins.

"You already know why I have summoned you here," said the hermano mayor. "We all thought that if another man as big and strong as Gil Gómez came to the valley, they would fight between themselves and leave us in peace. But it doesn't seem as though the arrival of Cimarrón has solved our problems; rather it has aggravated them."

"It seems as if the savage wants to make up for the time he spent alone in the desert by causing even more mischief than the genízaro himself," commented Trinidad Armijo. "We would have been better off if he had never come down from the wilderness!"

"What a good champion we have found! I don't know how it ever crossed our minds to beg that another braggart show up around these parts," said Hilario Mestas.

"He who refuses a spoonful of medicine gets the full bottle!" declared the blacksmith José de la Luz.

"We already had to hide our daughters in our *trasteros* before the stranger arrived, so that the cacique wouldn't take them away. What will we have to do now to free ourselves from the cuates' scourge?" asked Bitoriano Montoya.

"We are going to have to hide in the mountains, in the company of snakes and other vermin!" concluded Trinidad Armijo.

"The one to blame for all this is that woman they call Sam Hat, who, with her evil ways, attracted the savage to our village," said Hilario Mestas. "It would have been better for her to stick a red iron up her private parts than to start screwing the stallion!"

"Pardon me, *abuelo,* but I know that redhead and I don't believe that she's a bad woman; I have often seen her with the Holy Scriptures in her hand," interjected the young Polinio Córdova. "And to tell the truth, it doesn't surprise me that the savage has fallen victim to temptation. With those buttocks and such firm breasts she would be capable of arousing even the chaste Joseph!"

Everyone made the sign of the cross upon hearing that irreverent suggestion, and the hermano mayor ordered that an *alabado* be sung before leaving the morada:

> *Wake up if you're asleep,*
> *Stop living recklessly*
> *Because to live only having fun,*
> *Friend, you have forgotten about God.*

✜

> *Just as you deceived yourself*
> *Wake up and warn others*
> *As time goes by*

✜

> *You're closer and closer to death.*

As the villagers passed by Gil Gómez's fortress, the cacique's henchmen standing guard on the parapet did not miss the opportunity to crack jokes about the Penitentes:

> *Penitente, sinner that you are,*
> *Why are you whipping yourself?*
> *Because of a cow that I stole*
> *And here I am making amends.*

The Orchid of Fort Conrad

The heavy rains in the Río Puerco Valley had swollen the Río Grande with a foaming, turbulent rush, cleaning out the stagnant pools that had formed during the drought. The leaves of the cottonwoods changed color, and the air in Fort Conrad was easier to breathe.

Coinciding with the change of seasons, a rare and delicate flower appeared on the riverbank: the beautiful Eleanor, wife of our commander. Captain Stanton had met her in St. Louis a few months before, when he had gone to Missouri to bring back the last group of recruits, and they had been married by proxy. The arrival at the fort of that fair lady of great beauty and distinction caused an indescribable commotion among the troops. Although some cracked dirty jokes behind her back as anyone who knows the vulgarity of army troops can imagine, others made her an object of unbounded platonic devotion.

I was among those who would have been ready to give my life to get a simple glance from our fair madonna. And I must admit that I even wrote a poem on the sly in which with clumsy rhymes I praised her exquisite beauty as much as the gentleness of her behavior, virtues which were as rare in those wastelands as an orchid in the wilderness.

Even now, when I think about it, I have trouble understanding why Captain Stanton risked bringing that fragile and delicate being, accustomed to the refinements of civilization, to such a godforsaken place. Even compared to other parts of untamed New Mexico, it was a remote outpost in hostile territory. Perhaps part of the tenderness that I felt toward the wife of my captain was because the bearing of Eleanor Stanton reminded me of my sixteen-year-old sister, María, who had the same glowing skin. The last time I had seen her was when she came to bid me farewell at the train station in New York. I was already carrying the rifle and knapsack of a soldier, and she appeared with her blond school braids and her freckled cheeks covered with tears, which she tried to hold back.

Unfortunately, the captain didn't have much time to enjoy his honeymoon with the beautiful Eleanor, since the same autumn rains that refilled the Río Grande had also refreshed the waterholes of the plains. This gave greater mobility to the Apaches, who until then had stayed close to the springs in the Sierra Blanca. We soon had word of new attacks, possibly by the same band of Mescalero Apaches whom we had fought in the He-Mule Swamp—the ones who had fled toward the mountain range. Captain Stanton, who still vividly remembered their escape, burned with the desire to have a second chance at those bandits, who posed a grave threat to the caravans that crossed the plains on the southern route to California. So he sent a courier to Santa Fe, asking for authorization to undertake a search-and-destroy mission to the eastern mountains.

Permission was slow in coming, given that the region east of the Río Grande was still considered Terra Incognita and headquarters had reservations about sending a detachment there, fearing it would be wiped out. But when a dispatch finally arrived from Santa Fe with authorization, the captain encountered another problem: he couldn't find native scouts willing to accompany us on the expedition. Their help was an absolute necessity since we knew nothing at all about the region.

We soldiers saw a parade of native auxiliaries—the ones who usually served as scouts on those missions—going in and out of the officers' barracks without appearing to have reached an agreement with our superiors. And money didn't seem to be the problem, for on many occasions Indians of warring tribes were willing to serve as scouts in return for a pack of tobacco or a handful of bullets.

Once we found out that the mission had been authorized, we began to prepare ourselves to go on the campaign, and under the officers' supervision, we set about oiling our firearms, undertaking target practice on the parapet that faced the river, and fighting mock battles every morning on horseback until our detachment could perform with the precision of a circus troop.

Eventually we had to abandon our target practice because we were running out of ammunition. The rifle barrels shone like medallions, and even the horses seemed impatient to go into the field after so much training. But for some reason unknown to us, we didn't receive our marching orders, and I noticed that the officers became more and more nervous, reprimanding us for the slightest fault. Of course, Sergeant Sweeny was the most unbearable.

Finally, one of the native guides whose services they had tried to contract let slip the real reason for the delay, which then spread by word of mouth throughout the garrison: those who knew the territory were unwilling to accompany us because they believed that the Sierra Blanca was inhabited by the spirits of their ancestors. In particular there was a place called the Cedar Forest where a chieftain or sorcerer with supernatural powers didn't tolerate any trespassers.

It was then that the tall, unkempt figure of Aaron Dawson made his appearance. From the time he crossed through the main gate of the fort with his ungainly stride and his weasel-like nose, I was reminded of drawings that I had seen in children's stories about the Pied Piper of Hamlin. One look at him and the man gave me a feeling of apprehension that later events would eventually confirm. It wasn't that I had any special foresight but rather that Dawson was one of those people whose apparently amiable manner and persuasive talk could not hide his innate cunning and ambition.

Dawson was a typical frontiersman; he had spent time as a trapper, gold prospector, scalp hunter, and volunteer in the war against Mexico, and finally he had established himself in Rincón, a small village where he married a local woman who gave him a horde of mestizo kids. After asking for an appointment to see the captain, he offered his services as guide to take us to the Sierra Blanca, saying that he was in possession of an old Spanish map which clearly indicated the desert waterholes and the locations of the rivers and mountains. What he didn't tell us then was how he had acquired the map. Some time later I learned that he had seized it from another man, one Isaac Larson, after a fatal fight. In addition, he didn't tell us that the map also showed the location of some old gold deposits mined during Spanish colonial times, which had later been blocked so that no one could discover them.

I hadn't been mistaken in my first impression of this rascal, whose ability did not consist in charming the rats with his flute to drown them in the river but in luring stupid people like us into the mountains in search of hidden *placers* and treasures.

For our superiors the most important thing at the moment was that Dawson knew the area and was willing to accompany us to the Sierra Blanca without worrying about haunted forests or the spirits of dead Apaches. In fact, he had been to that remote mountain range before, as some of us soldiers found out the night before we left on the expedition. When the guide had had one too many to drink he told us the story of his first trip to the Sierra Blanca. After hearing his story in the cantina, we understood better why the native guides who usually accompanied us on other missions had refused to come with us this time.

Dawson's Story

"It happened not long after we returned from the campaign in Mexico. A few of us volunteers who had nothing left to do got together with the idea of exploring the mountains where the natives claimed that the Spaniards had discovered rich gold deposits that they later blocked when the Apaches expelled them from the area. The Apaches have a god named Usen who is a kind of sun god; because the color of gold reminds them of his shining rays, they consider it sacrilegious to mine that particular mineral.

"There were about a dozen of us, including two Mexicans and a Negro slave. We left El Paso with a drove of mules, which were heavily laden with stores and weapons. Back then, those mountains weren't as perilous as now, and the Indians even looked upon the Americans, who had just defeated their ancestral enemy, the Mexicans, with a certain sympathy. Even so, we still kept our eyes peeled, always sending one man ahead in the narrow canyons and keeping night watches at the campsite.

"We crossed the first mountain ranges through the narrow pass between the San Andrés Mountains and the Organ Mountains, which is the same road that we'll take tomorrow. Skirting White Dunes Desert, we camped near a small village called La Luz, which I believe was later abandoned. The Sierra Blanca range lay more to the north, but the map that one of my companions had showed a canyon that figured in the map as the Quebrada de los Mesteños (Wild Horse Ravine) whose upper end, close to a stream called the Ruidoso, was reputed to contain gold.

"After replenishing some of our supplies in La Luz, we began to climb through the bottom of the canyon, where we didn't encounter a single herd of wild horses. It would have been difficult to imagine mustangs willing to enter that cul-de-sac; on some sides the walls were more than three hundred feet high. As we climbed the canyon, we came to a hollow where a small brook ran down from the mountain, the current forming tiny cascades that at times produced a soothing singsong sound; at other times, however, when the terrain was uneven and the water pounded against the rocks, the sound was deafening. That stream was in fact the Ruidoso River, whose headwaters were on the eastern slope of the Sierra Blanca.

"We chose a still pool where the water flowed quietly and where there was plenty of pasture for the horses, and there we set up camp. Not far away, at the foot of a cliff, we found a heap of animal bones, possibly those of horses, and the Mexican guide told us that that was the place where the former denizens of those mountain ranges would drive the wild horses to their death after cornering them; that is why it was called Wild Horse Ravine. Later on it was known as Dog Canyon.

"Next morning, when one of us went down to the river to pan for gold, he had barely started washing the sand when a shout boomed through the canyon. In the bottom of his pan shone gold nuggets the size of lima beans! In less than ten days, we had filled up our saddlebags with the ore from that rich spring. To avoid thefts or fights over the division of the treasure, we decided to put it all into one common bag. We buried it on a hillock protected from the rain and floods by an overhanging ledge, which we marked with a pile of rocks.

"The problems started when we had cleaned all the gold out of that part of the arroyo. My companions thought that if they built a wooden drag line that fit the mouth of the spring, they could channel all the gold that was dragged by the current. Others thought of blowing up the rock from which the gold itself was coming, hoping to find the mother lode. The problem was in reaching the mouth of the spring since at the bottom of the steep cliff, the Ruidoso River cascaded over a rock wall, which was difficult to climb. And to build the wooden channel we would need the right tree trunks, which did not grow at the bottom of the canyon.

"Someone had seen treetops emerging from the top of the ravine, but we had to take a roundabout route to climb up the canyon with the mules and the tools to reach the tree grove. When we got to the top, we saw that the higher plateau was covered with large cedars in a forest that extended as far as the eye could see. The trunks were as tall as ponderosa pine, and they were too thick for our purpose. Dismounting, axes in hand, we headed through a path that crossed the forest, where we soon lost the light of day. In addition to the ominous twilight, a heavy silence fell over the place, which none of us dared to break. The only thing we could hear was the murmur of the mules' hooves, muffled by the undergrowth of the forest as we led them by the halter.

"All of a sudden, as we emerged into a small clearing, we encountered a group of Apache warriors on horseback, their eyes shining above their red ochre-painted faces. They were so motionless and silent that we could have walked right under their horses' hooves without realizing it. They already had their arrows ready on their bowstrings, and none of us thought of going for our guns, knowing that the Apaches could have riddled us with arrows at the least movement. For a few instants that seemed like centuries, the two groups just stared at each other silently. Then one of the Apaches spoke to us in his language, which one of the Mexican guides understood.

"The message that the interpreter communicated to us was extremely clear: for them that forest was sacred, and besides it was the refuge of a sorcerer with supernatural powers. A stranger who entered the sanctuary and cut even one limb from those cedars must die. Since it was the first time we had entered the sacred forest, the Apaches would let us go this once; but if we were to reenter their sanctuary, we would be annihilated and our bodies strung from the forks of the cedars to placate the mountain spirits.

"While the Mexican was translating the Indian's speech, I noticed another rider on a jet-black horse, half-hidden in the trees, who was observing the parley from a distance. Even in the semi-darkness, I saw that the warrior was wearing a mask in the shape of a buffalo head that covered his face.

"We knew there was no use arguing. The Apaches outnumbered us, and who knows how many more were hidden behind the trees like that evil being with a mask and horns. After instructing the interpreter to assure the Indians that we had entered the forest by mistake and that we would never again take that path, we hightailed it out without daring to look back, fearful of hearing the hiss of an arrow at our backs.

"That night, back at the camp, we held a spirited powwow that quickly turned into a war council. When the heat from the fire and a demijohn of brandy managed to erase the memory of the Apache faces, the men regained their courage. They felt ashamed to have been intimidated by a group of painted savages who, pretending to defend their spirits and their witches, were simply trying to drive us away from the rich gold mine at the headwaters of the Ruidoso, of which so far we had only enjoyed a few pebbles.

"My companions thought that to offer an adequate response to the savages we needed a good supply of ammunition and a few sticks of dynamite to blow up the rocks of the narrow gorge and reach the mother lode. Perhaps because they noticed that I was the one in the group least eager to fight, they sent me with two mules to the village of La Luz to look for ammunition and explosives, while the others worked at fortifying our camp and reconnoitering the bottom of the canyon to see if there were other ways of reaching the headwaters of the spring.

"When I returned from the village with my delicate cargo, it got dark at the bottom of the ravine before I was able to reach camp, which surely saved my life. As I walked—very cautiously lest the mules take a false step—I saw the embers of a fire glowing at the bottom of the canyon, and I first thought that it had to be the glow of our campfire. But as I got closer I realized that I was looking at the remains of a fire in which the whole camp had burnt. By the faint light of the live coals I was able to identify broken lances and cartridges, the signs of a fight. I searched the immediate surroundings for the bodies of my companions, but to no avail.

"I spent the night hiding among some rocks, shaking from fear and cold, and before dawn, I started to climb the canyon wall in the hope of finding some sign as to what had happened to the miners. Building up courage, I sneaked through the trees, whose trunks seemed to emit a somber glow. The silence was even more oppressive than the first time I was there. I was constantly afraid of seeing one of those devils with his face painted red and his axe ready to cut off my head. I was particularly obsessed with the memory of the warrior with his buffalo mask, and on several occasions my blood froze when I thought I saw the tips of buffalo horns in the dim light of dawn. They turned out to be nothing more than the ends of a fork in a tree.

"I don't know how long I wandered around that forest, sneaking from tree to tree to avoid being seen, but I ended up going out through the same tiny clearing where the Apaches had stopped us.

Daylight barely penetrated a thick mantle of fog that floated above the foliage. All of a sudden something prompted me to look up. There they were, hanging from the tallest cedars, the bodies of my companions, with their joints cracked and their bellies split open. With the cutting edges of the same axes that they were going to use for cutting down the cedars, the Apaches had nailed them to the trees."

Wild Horse Ravine

That expedition was jinxed from the first day. When, only a few miles from the fort, we tried to cross the river, we lost two horses and three mules that were swept away by the current. And two soldiers were saved from the same fate by a hair's breadth, literally pulled out by their hair. Two boxes of ammunition and several bundles of supplies sank in the turbulent water.

Next we undertook the crossing of the Jornada del Muerto, a stretch of about eighty miles without a good drinking point, as could be reckoned by the large number of animal skeletons and crosses marking travelers' graves. Leaving behind to the east a mountain chain called the Sierra Oscura, we descended toward Soledad Mountain, avoiding a valley of volcanic rock that the Spaniards called malpaís, where a horse could scarcely walk without breaking a leg. According to our guide, those frightful wastelands formed a kind of protective circle around the Sierra Blanca, so it was necessary to detour more than seventy miles to the south. This we succeeded in doing in only three days thanks to the determination of our commander and our intense preparation.

Finally, we came out onto the eastern plains after crossing a pass between two mountain ranges, one of which, the Organ Mountains, was named after some curious formations of basaltic rock that looked like organ pipes. On the fourth day we camped in what was left of the village called La Luz, which Dawson had mentioned in his account; it had been abandoned for some time, and its adobe houses were mostly in ruins. Only the stone church was still standing, and its bells rang lugubriously in the evening breeze amid the impressive silence of the plains. Before the sun set I could make out toward the west, above the hot vibration of the desert sand dunes, the snow-covered peak of Sierra Blanca, and I remembered the first time I saw that mountain hovering like a mirage above the horizon.

Although we had only the ruins of the adobe houses as protection from the mountain wind, spending the night within walls even without roofs seemed an eastern luxury after having camped out for four consecutive nights in the middle of the desert. We had to wrap our blankets carefully around us so as not to awake in the company of the snakes and scorpions that had taken over the homes of the previous inhabitants.

While I was writing in my diary, taking advantage of the last embers of the fire, I heard from the other side of the wall the voice of Timothy Baltasar, reading some verses from the Bible:

> *I shall leave Nineveh by herself,*
> *Arid as a desert,*
> *In her bosom will remain a heap of all kinds of animals;*
> *Including swift and vicious bulls.*
> *They will live on their columns and sing at their windows,*
> *And at their thresholds destruction shall prevail.*

The following morning we set off before dawn, and after the sun came up we could observe on our right almost vertical slopes, which, according to our guide, were the spurs of the Sacramento Mountains, a southern extension of the Sierra Blanca. It occurred to me then that traveling through territory explored and colonized by Spaniards, you end up familiarizing yourself with the saints and rituals of the Roman Catholic pantheon: Sacramento, Sangre de Cristo, San Mateo, San Andrés, and so forth.

Perhaps for that reason I was relieved when, at dusk, we arrived at a narrow gorge that the guide called Dog Canyon, a more prosaic name but perhaps more colorful. Access to the pass was so hidden amongst the numerous rock crevasses and so protected by a wall of cactus that our detachment could have gone by the entrance a hundred times without finding it. From that moment on we were in Apache territory.

Apart from the profusion of different species of cacti and the *palo verde* which grew right on the sides of the ravine, there was an abundance of century plants, whose long straight stalks can reach a height of several feet (probably it's because of that upright shoot that we call it *Spanish bayonet*). The Mexicans use the fiber from the wide leaves that grow on the base to make cord and burlap, and the Indians eat the meaty pulp of those same leaves, cooking them in an oven dug into the ground. They also ferment the juice of this plant to make mescal, which is a powerful liquor. According to Dawson, the name *Mescaleros* was given by the Spaniards to the Apaches of that region because of their use of the century plant.

Speaking of the devil . . . upon penetrating that narrow pass we saw several silhouettes of Indians on horseback riding along the upper edge of the ravine, and they made gestures as though inviting us to penetrate further into the canyon. And so we did, but with the necessary precautions. Before nightfall the captain ordered us to dismount and set up camp with sentries everywhere; if the Indians decided to attack us, at least we would not be taken by surprise.

It was difficult for me to fall asleep seeing the dozens of small fires the savages had made on the rim of the canyon; from time to time against the glow of the fire one could make out the tiny silhouettes of the warriors, writhing about in some ritual dance, although neither the beating of the drums nor the chanting reached the bottom of the ravine. The officers didn't allow us to light a fire, so that the Apaches wouldn't be able to spy on us; consequently, that night I slept stiff from the cold and couldn't write in my diary.

On the other hand, our awakening was pretty hot: a number of rifles cracked in the dark and dozens of arrows came flying over us; at the same time, some Apaches succeeded in lighting the dry grass around the encampment, provoking a general stampede of our horses. The remainder of the night we spent trying to dodge arrows, which were shot from above with little accuracy but a lot of momentum, and trying at the same time to round up our horses, which was almost impossible in the dark.

Although the attackers had only managed to wound a couple of men and steal some horses, Captain Stanton was indignant that the Apaches had succeeded in surprising us in spite of all our precautions. At daybreak he left with a squad to pursue a group of Apaches who had been seen riding toward the bottom of the canyon, leaving the rest of the company under the command of Lieutenant Dick Ewin. That's exactly what the Indians wanted, for they had set an ambush a mile from the camp where the bed of the ravine dropped into a deep gully so that you couldn't see what was on the other side.

When Captain Stanton and his squad arrived at that bend and crossed the arroyo at full gallop, a massive discharge rang out, echoing along the rock formations. We immediately realized that the advance party had fallen into an ambush, for the shots were fired not from the top of the cliff but on our level, very close and deadly. The first to fall was Captain Stanton, with a bullet through the forehead, and Sergeant Peters also fell under the first volley. My heart was in my mouth when I heard the firing, because my friend Timothy Baltasar had gone with the reconnaissance squad.

I was told later that the dragoons had tried to repel the attack, but not being able to see who was shooting or from where, the second in command had sounded retreat. By the sound of the bugle we knew that the group was running back to the camp, although we were not able to help them because the rocky terrain concealed the enemy sharpshooters. One private, his horse having been wounded by a bullet, and falling under his rider, was immediately surrounded by the Apaches, who pierced him with their lances like a swarm of bees. But Timothy Baltasar, who had been hit in the thigh by an arrow, miraculously escaped from the skirmish by protecting himself between two riderless horses. Holding onto the stirrup straps with both hands without his feet touching the ground, he managed to return to the camp, more than a mile away.

Lieutenant Ewin ordered us to deploy our forces with great caution to the spot where the captain had fallen. We retrieved his body and those of the other two soldiers near the arroyo and made camp right there, placing lookouts everywhere. We had easy access to the spring water, so we might be able to hold out if the Apaches besieged us.

On one side of the ravine, an overhanging rock provided excellent protection, and in that natural cavity we placed the wounded, the provisions, the ammunition, and all the most valuable things in the camp, including a demijohn of whiskey. From that position, which was slightly elevated, we had a fine view of the stream surrounded by walnut trees and wild grapevines. It would have been an enchanting panorama if it hadn't been for the spectacle of the buzzards circling over the bodies of three of our horses, which had fallen to Apache arrows, their bellies swollen in the heat of the sun.

According to Dawson, the spring that could be seen from the promontory was the source of the Ruidoso, and at the back of the ravine you could make out a huge pile of jawbones and animal skeletons, which had given the place its name, the Quebrada de los Mesteños. It was disturbing to think that it was precisely at this idyllic location where the party of prospectors had been massacred by the Apaches—not to mention what Dawson had told us about the way he found them hanging like scarecrows in the forbidden forest.

Trying not to offer too easy a target to the sharpshooters, we dug a grave for the bodies of the captain and the two other comrades under a canopy of walnut trees beside the stream. Since our company had no chaplain, Lieutenant Ewin borrowed Timothy Baltasar's Bible and, after reading some verses which seemed appropriate for the occasion by way of a funeral speech, he added: "Here lies a good soldier!" There was no gun salute as is customary for those fallen in battle, for fear of alerting the Apaches; besides, we had to save our powder and ammunition.

The rest of the day passed without incident, but with a growing sense of claustrophobia as dark clouds gathered at the head of the ravine. That afternoon we didn't see any more Apaches, but we all knew that our problems hadn't ended. The ominous silence was worse for us than the yelling of a visible enemy. The horizon was so overcast that you didn't need to be a witch doctor to predict that there would be a downpour that night.

When I arrived at the hillock protected by the overhanging ledge where we had installed the wounded and provisions, Timothy Baltasar gave me a detailed account of his escape hanging onto the stirrups. And he admitted that from now on he was going to have more respect for horses, which until then had seemed to him stupid and untrustworthy creatures. I reminded him of his first quarrel with Sweeny, when he refused to get on a horse, saying he would get vertigo. Sweeny had been lucky enough to come down with a fever the day before our departure—or maybe he had pretended to be ill, sensing the danger of the expedition. In any case, Timothy Baltasar must have had nine lives like a cat, because just a few hours after his accident he had made some rudimentary crutches with palo verde branches, and he was already hopping about the camp and telling anyone who would listen about his miraculous ride. But after the death of our captain, and being trapped by the Apaches at the bottom of the canyon, no one was in the mood for his stories, and he finally shut up.

In the hollow of the canyon an oppressive silence spread, disturbed only by the murmur of water from the arroyo and by the sound of thunder, still distant, from the storm that hovered over the Sierra Blanca.

The Night of the Deluge

That night two soldiers sheltered under the rocky ledge found the demijohn of whiskey among the provisions and decided to drown their worries in it. But when their companions discovered that their source of fleeting well-being was about to run out, they demanded to participate in the party. Near midnight we were awakened by the drunken soldiers brawling so desperately over the last drops of liquor that they ended up breaking the demijohn into a thousand pieces against the rocks.

I went to tell Lieutenant Ewin, who put on his boots and went where the shouts and blows of the quarrel were heard, sabre drawn, prepared to put an end to the fracas at any cost. As we got closer to the ledge in the middle of the most complete darkness, a bolt of lightning flashed with great intensity and projected the silhouettes of the soldiers involved in the fight against the wall of the ravine like a scene in Chinese theater. At the same time, the walls of the canyon resounded with a clap of thunder like a cannon shot.

The scene that unfolded next remains as clear in my mind as a nightmare from which I have just awakened. As if the zigzag of the lightning had ripped open the womb of the clouds, the floodgates of the heavens burst open, unleashing a heavy downpour on the valley floor. The raindrops were blown by a hurricane-like wind that seemed sent from hell, since moments before not even a breath of air ran through the narrow pass. The small arroyo at the bottom of the canyon filled suddenly, and the springs that came out of the wall of the ravine turned all at once into powerful waterfalls.

In the blink of an eye the camp equipment was first flooded and then swept away by the current, and we lost everything we couldn't hurriedly catch splashing about in the dark. Frightened by the thunder, the horses had scattered in all directions, and no one could catch them because each man was trying to keep his possessions from being carried away by the flood. In their anxiety to flee from that trap the poor beasts stumbled and broke their legs or fell into the middle of the torrent where they were rapidly swept away. When a flash of lightning illuminated the bottom of the ravine, the scene was one of such chaos that we would have preferred to stay in the dark.

I began to offer prayers not only to the God of Israel, who saved Noah from the flood, but to the pagan gods who seemed to reign in those mountains and to the Water Monster who had saved the Navajos from a deluge. I succeeded in rescuing my weapons and saddle from the flood, and I curled up shivering in a crevice, waiting for the storm to calm and dawn to break.

When the light of dawn finally spilled over the edge of the ravine, we could see that our field equipment had been dragged by the current to the most unbelievable places: canvas tents had been ripped on the rocks and were hanging from bushes; kitchen utensils and personal toiletries adorned the arms of cacti; and a dragoon's cap appeared on the top of a Spanish bayonet like a Dantesque greased pole. The Ruidoso made good its name, falling to the bottom of the ravine in a loud cascade and raising a cloud of foam.

When the sun succeeded in dissipating the mist, the soldiers began to emerge from the cracks in the rocks like snakes slithering out of their holes, their uniforms soaked and their boots oozing water . . . that is, those who had been lucky enough to sleep with their boots on, since many others had lost them in the flood and walked on tip-toe over the rocks, swearing when they stepped on a sharp point.

Under orders from Lieutenant Ewin, we did a count, which confirmed that we had lost ninety percent of the weapons and provisions, fifty percent of the horse herd, some of them drowned in the torrent and others disappeared during the stampede and perhaps by now in the hands of the Apaches. The only equipment that had been saved were the provisions and ammunition placed under the rocky ledge in the upper part of the ravine . . . except the whiskey, of course. And if we hadn't been farsighted enough to place the wounded there, they too would have been swept away. We could hear their laments, since the gusts of wind had blown water under the ledge and they were soaked to the bone.

The only one who seemed to keep his sense of humor was the wounded Timothy Baltasar, who, as soon as it stopped raining, climbed to the top of a rock with the aid of his crutches, Bible in hand, and began to read some verses that seemed appropriate under the circumstances: *The fountains also of the deep and the windows of heaven were stopped, and the rain from heaven was restrained.*

The thin layer of earth that we had put over the graves of Captain Stanton and the two other soldiers had been removed by the current, and their shattered bodies now lay under the walnut trees, their faces showing the pain of having been tortured twice, first by Apache arrows and then by the violence of the flood. So that they wouldn't fall into the hands of the hostiles, Lieutenant Ewin had us make a mound out of the saddles of those left without horses along with other belongings that we couldn't transport; underneath and on the sides of the pile we put cedar branches and other bushes that had been torn out by the flood, and when the pyre was burning, we placed the dead bodies on it until all but the bones were consumed. We kept those relics in leather sacks, tagged with the names we presumed belonged to the remains of each one.

While the fire continued crackling, emitting black smoke and a strange odor of smoked leather mixed with the pleasant aroma of cedar branches, Timothy Baltasar continued reading the Bible from his rock pulpit. I thought that at least those soldiers had had a suitable funeral oration.

And the Lord smelled a sweet savor; and the Lord said in his heart, I will not again curse the ground any more for man's sake; for the imagination of man's heart is evil from his youth; neither will I again smite any more every thing living, as I have done.

When I saw a rainbow spanning the canyon over the cascade of the Ruidoso River, I felt tears rolling down my cheeks.

When the lieutenant ordered the company to form up on the sandy bank that was left after the current subsided, we had as much of a military aspect as a pack of wet dogs. Many of the soldiers had lost their rifles and boots, and we all had uniforms so muddy and dusty that any trace of blue on the tunics or red trim had disappeared. And still we could thank God that we had not sustained a single casualty during the flood, although more than one had come close to drowning.

But when we were ready to leave, we noticed our guide, Dawson, was missing. Someone had seen him the night before, trying to cross the flooded arroyo to save a mule that carried on its saddle-tree two leather saddlebags. Dawson had always kept them closed, and I had often wondered what the devil he carried inside. After forming a small search party and dragging the arroyo we soon shed our doubts.

I myself found the scout's body, half buried in the mud, with his left hand still clutching the leather saddlebags. Before stopping to think I reached and found a small pistol and a knife with a mother-of-pearl handle, several old silver coins, and a piece of parchment folded and protected by an oilskin wrapper. Just then I heard the voice of the officer asking me what I was doing bent over the mud since from where he was he couldn't see Dawson's drowned body.

Fearing that I might have been caught red-handed, I instinctively concealed the oilskin bundle inside my shirt. When I realized what I had done, it was too late to admit it, because if the officer had seen me, he could have had me court-martialed on the spot, for stealing from a dead person on a battlefield is considered a serious offense. I handed the saddlebags to the sergeant, and, after inspecting them, he murmured, "Just imagine, Burdette, the dirty tricks that life plays: after having saved his ass years ago in this very place, this poor soul has returned to meet his fate in Dog Canyon."

It took us almost two weeks to return to the fort, slowed down as much by the lack of horses and provisions as the absence of the guide who had oriented us on the way out. As soon as I had the chance, when my companions were asleep around the campfire, I took the oilskin bundle that I had removed from Dawson's saddlebags to a quiet spot, drew out the parchment, and unfolded it on the sand. By the light of a firebrand I confirmed that it was an old Spanish map, with an inscription written in small characters in the lower left corner and signed in 1776 by Miera and Pacheco. It was pretty well preserved except for the borders, where pieces of leather were missing because it had been passed from hand to hand so many times. You could also see that on top of the original ink there were other, more recent signs and annotations in different characters, some of them in English.

The map described the lower basin of the Río Grande—although calling it *Río del Norte*—including the same arroyos, mountains, and villages we had seen on our journey toward the Sierra Blanca, drawn in detail. On the west slope of the mountain symbols of forests covered a large portion, with the caption *Bosque de los Cedros;* and on the eastern side, little Indian huts were painted with the note *Avitaciones de Apaches* near the head of an arroyo called *Ojo del Ruidoso.* There was also the ravine where the Apaches had ambushed us, marked as *Quebrada de los Mesteños,* just as Dawson had mentioned.

Among the recent annotations, you could see a large circle around the Sierra Blanca made with ink of a different color from that used for the original printing of the map. And on the inside of that circle was a series of lines with points and crosses in red with the caption *Placer.* Suddenly I understood that the parchment I held in my hands wasn't just a geographical map but one used by treasure hunters, showing the locations of mines for whose possession people were willing to die or kill. This map had already provoked the violent death of the miners who had accompanied Dawson on his first expedition. And surely that Pied Piper had guided us there thinking that under the protection of the army he could recover the gold buried in the ravine. If that was true, his ambition had cost him his life. And unfortunately one also had to add the names of Captain Stanton and the two other comrades to the list of those who had fallen victim to the curse of that mountain range.

I was on the point of setting fire to the blood-stained parchment. But the map seemed to emit some magnetism or special force that had saved it so far from destruction; so I carefully folded the parchment again to keep it in its oilskin pouch, which I slipped into my tunic. It wouldn't be long before I regretted not having thrown it in the fire.

Between the animals that we lost in the flood, the ones lost in the desert for lack of pasture and water, and the ones we killed for food, our detachment of dragoons returned to Fort Conrad converted almost into an infantry brigade. We marched through the fort gate, many of us barefoot, our feet cut from the desert stones, and so emaciated that our own barracks comrades could hardly recognize us.

When Mrs. Stanton saw the column draw near, she believed she recognized her husband in the silhouette of one of the officers who was riding in the glare of sunset. She ran toward the horseman with such an expression of happiness in her beautiful blue eyes that the officer turned his face, not having the courage to tell her what had happened to her husband. That first officer's reaction became contagious and as she went from one rider to the next, clutching the metal stirrups with her delicate hands, no one dared tell her the truth.

When all the company had paraded past her, Mrs. Stanton finally understood what was happening. She remained seated for a long time on a rock, the tears rolling down her rosy cheeks. Then one of the officers approached her and handed her the leather bag with the charred remains of the captain.

The poor lady cradled that relic in her arms for a while the way you rock a newborn baby. It occurred to me that if one of those rude soldiers still had an ounce of pity in his heart, this would have been a good time to show it.

Market Day at Bernalillo

When we returned from our disastrous expedition, we heard about the arrival of Decoy in Cabezón and about his fight with the Río Puerco cacique, reputed to be the most spectacular ever witnessed in the entire region. Since there was no clear winner in the fight, evidently the two champions had decided to become friends. And the people of the valley, who had hoped that the arrival of the powerful stranger might rein in the abuses of their patrón, were suddenly confronted with not one but two tyrants hungry for adventure.

In spite of the bad reputation it had acquired—or rather because of it— the village of Cabezón was frequented more and more not only by shepherds and peddlers, but also by soldiers from the small fort at Cebolleta, recently constructed on the slope of San Mateo Mountain in Navajo Territory. And La Fonda de la Reunión had turned into a famous place because of the historic fight between the two strongest men in the Río Abajo. If any stranger had money or goods to trade for alcohol, gambling, or women, he was welcome at the fonda where he could see the magnificent Gil Gómez and the imposing Decoy, now inseparable friends or cuates, as the peones of the area called them.

The first months after the encounter confirmed the gloomy predictions of the villagers. The two leaders devoted themselves to competing over their amatory endurance or over who could drink the most jugs of wine without falling under the table—competitions that Decoy usually lost, not being as practiced as Gil Gómez in the sciences of vice and fornication, although no less eager than his friend.

But with the passing of time the desires of the cuates were satiated, and the villagers of Cabezón began to recall the Spanish proverb *God sometimes squeezes us but never chokes us.* Cimarrón began to miss the plains and mountains, and he started to leave the village on excursions that lasted days and sometimes weeks. The genízaro, who had become Cimarrón's shadow, usually accompanied him on these expeditions.

The cuates would return to the wilderness with nothing but a horse *remuda* and perhaps a couple of dogs to help them to follow the track of a mountain lion or lead them into a grizzly's den. Once they had located a wild beast they would fight it with a spear or hunting knife, sometimes with their bare hands, in order to prove their bravery and strength, competing against each other to provoke the most difficult and hair-raising situations. Sometimes they went to the northern plains to hunt buffalo with spears, according to the traditional technique that the genízaro had learned from his adoptive father, Antonio Gil, who used to call those quadrupeds *cíbolos,* so named when the first Spanish adelantado ventured into the sea of grass in search of the legendary Cities of Cíbola.

What Cimarrón and the genízaro didn't share was the latter's passion for chasing and lassoing the mustangs that roamed free on the plains and in the mountains. Gil Gómez had earned a reputation as a mustanger and had built up a small fortune selling the animals both to American soldiers and to Spanish ranchers. His friend Decoy, in contrast, who had shared his life with the wild herds, didn't permit anyone to pen them up and deprive them of their freedom.

Once, they say, when the genízaro returned to the hunting camp leading a beautiful stallion by a rope from which it was trying to free itself, the strapping lad hurried to meet his friend and with his powerful hands tore the rope in two, letting the wild horse gallop in freedom again. The story goes that Decoy was able to communicate with those animals in a special language, and certainly seeing him gallop bareback on an unbroken stallion you were reminded of the legend of the centaur, for man and horse seemed to be the same animal.

I have kept with my diaries a drawing from that period, published by
Mercurio Volante in Bernalillo, showing a robust hunter suffocating two
half-grown mountain lions, their heads sticking out from under his
powerful forearms. Some thought this was a likeness of Gil Gómez, but by
the size of the shoulders and the thickness of the arms, more likely the artist
had tried to portray the strong body of Cimarrón. In fact, the clothing of
the hunter was not in the style of dress of either one: he was wearing a kind
of shiny armor or breastplate, and over his shoulder you could see a golden
bow and quiver, as if he were a mythological hero.

While the cuates were away, the people of Cabezón could breathe easy,
or as those who work on the acequias used to say, the flow of abuses to
which they were subjected by the young caciques finally opened their sluice
gates. And for a few days or weeks the villagers could enjoy peace . . . or
what passed for peace in that wild territory.

And yet even though the two young chieftains had become a living
legend throughout the region; in spite of the fact that they had at their
disposal all the pleasures that civilization offers, after a time Decoy began
to miss the freedom of his old life on the plains, and he felt his strength
waning with the softness of life in town. And even Gil Gómez started to
be bored with his comfortable existence, and his restless heart began to
conceive the idea of some wild venture that would put his courage and
endurance to the test.

A few days after returning to the barracks I had an opportunity to
get rid of the cursed parchment that I had acquired in such peculiar
circumstances. If by some twist of fate my superiors found out how that
map had fallen into my hands, I would be severely punished. And it
wouldn't be the first time that nosy Sergeant Sweeny had snooped in the
belongings of some soldier.

One afternoon after drills, Pat Dixon came up to me. He was aware of
my devotion to the wife of the deceased Stanton, and told me he had
found a silver medallion with the likeness of the beautiful Eleanor close to
the place where the captain had fallen. He proposed trading it to me in
exchange for the map, which he had heard about thanks to an indiscretion
by Timothy Baltasar. When he furtively showed me his treasure, I verified
that on the inside of the locket the face of my platonic love was painted in
exquisite enamel and next to it a date that had to commemorate her
wedding or engagement to the captain.

I didn't worry too much about whether he had *found* it on the banks of the Ruidoso River, or swiped it from the dead officer's belongings as I had swiped the map, and I didn't hesitate for an instant to make the exchange. I valued the medallion infinitely more than the map, which I wanted to get rid of anyway. We celebrated the exchange with a glass of brandy and that night I slept peacefully, thinking I would never see that damned parchment again.

But the destiny of some objects seems to be linked to certain people, and perhaps the parchment had become accustomed to the warmth of my body on the long journey across the desert, because in very little time it crossed my path again, and in circumstances that would be difficult to forget.

Only a week after returning from our disastrous expedition I was sent to Albuquerque, escorting some wagons that were going to replace the supplies we had lost during the Dog Canyon tempest and the subsequent retreat across the desert. Since the officers of the quartermaster's store took a long time completing the paperwork necessary for the transfer of provisions, I asked permission to go to a fair in the nearby settlement of Bernalillo, located on the east bank of the Río Grande.

The streets of the village were very lively since traders, landowners, and ranchers from the surrounding settlements came there to sell their products. There were also Indians and Comancheros offering human merchandise. For a few dollars you could buy a Navajo slave or ransom a white woman who had been held by the hostiles. As long as the transaction was not completed under the nose of an officer, the American authorities looked the other way, and some soldiers were even said to profit from this commerce.

As proof of origin was not required to sell cattle or horses, notorious rustlers and mustangers brought their herds to market and were cheeky enough to sell back to American army officers their own horses with the brand barely altered. Among the famous people who wandered about the fair I recognized Kit Carson, the trapper and military scout who lived in a small settlement north of Santa Fe, and old Pattie and his son who had come up from the Gila to sell hides. Suddenly, the rumor spread that Gil Gómez had arrived at the market with a herd of cattle that he had just stolen during one of his raids through the Indian rancherías close to the Río Puerco Valley. It goes without saying that, with everything I had heard about the cuates, I had a tremendous curiosity to meet the chieftain from the Río Puerco and his new friend.

Among the strangers who had come to the fair, I noticed an American officer with an aristocratic bearing who was observing the haggling of the merchants with the curiosity of a newcomer. He stood out like a sore thumb in that motley crowd of shabby peones and seasoned horse thieves. He was dressed in a dark frock coat of impeccable cut and wore a silk cravat, as if he were attending a gala in a New York social club.

As I later learned, army engineer Lieutenant Peter Loring came from a rich New England family and had just arrived in New Mexico, having graduated from the military academy at West Point. I wondered by what twist of fate such a distinguished person had ended up in this hole, where we rarely had the chance to rub elbows with the cream of eastern society. Apparently he had been sent west to survey uncharted areas, and in spite of his delicate appearance, with his gold-rimmed spectacles and his locks of blond hair, Loring was an efficient professional who had graduated with honors from West Point.

At the end of the market day, many of the dealers went to the Bernalillo fonda to have a card game. Those same merchants and ranchers who half an hour earlier had been haggling over the price of a nag down to the last penny now lost all their hard-won profits at the gambling table. The rich patrones as well as the most miserable peones were betting their fortunes, abundant or meager, without thinking twice. In the game of monte one could see rich haciendas changing hands, and even poor peasants would offer up their wives or sons "in bondage"—a euphemism for slavery—in order to continue playing. Although it may seem to contradict the well-known Spanish lust for gold, I had observed in their descendants in New Mexico a certain stoicism about their changing fortunes.

American citizens sometimes indulged in the gambling vice, and in spite of his distinguished appearance, even Lieutenant Loring was ready to sit down at that filthy card table and shuffle the monte cards. Soon the game was joined by two landowners from Bernalillo, a Mexican muleteer named Ordovás, and old Pattie, who spit into the palms of his hands before taking the cards as though he might be about to skin a deer.

At that point the door of the fonda opened wide and the silhouette of Gil Gómez appeared on the threshold. He almost had to bend double to fit his body under the lintel. He was followed by his inseparable companion Decoy, who had the advantage in bulk but not in height. The tremor that ran through the tables when the cuates entered that place, crammed with people and poisoned by the smell of cheap liquor and cigars, was like the flutter produced by a fox poking through the henhouse windows. And the Cyclopean build and swaggering airs of the cuates lived up their reputation.

When the Río Puerco cacique headed to the gambling table, even though the monte cards had already been dealt, the two villagers from Bernalillo immediately got up and relinquished their places. Gil Gómez sat at the table while his friend sat in a corner guarding the cacique's back and enjoying a jug of Taos lightning.

When the vacant place in the game was taken by the soldier Pat Dixon, a shiver ran down my spine. Having in the same game the soldier to whom I'd traded Dawson's map, the young officer from Boston, and Gil Gómez did not bode well. Unfortunately, my misgivings proved well founded.

As experienced players usually do, Gil Gómez let several hands go by without showing his skills. Then when the other players had relaxed, he began to bet heavily and to win almost all the pots, with surprising luck or ability. If the genízaro was cheating, he must have done so with great skill, for I could detect nothing amiss. Soon the coins and bills of other players were piled up in front of him. Although Lieutenant Loring lost quite a sum of money, he did not show his annoyance; he behaved like a proper gentleman. But suddenly Pat Dixon, who had been left without a cent but couldn't leave well enough alone, took from his pocket a bundle I immediately recognized: it was the famous parchment, wrapped in its oilskin pouch. Seeing him unfold the Spanish map on the table knocked the breath out of me.

"Gil Gómez, I'd like you to give me one more chance before I leave," said Dixon. "In order to stay in the game, for a hundred dollars I am offering you this old map that marks the location of some gold placers in the Sierra Blanca."

That offer attracted the attention of the rest of the clientele, who got up from their tables and came to peer at the map on the plank table. The owner of the establishment, an Irishman with red mustaches named MacMikin, brought a tallow candle closer to the table so that everyone could examine the document. When I noticed that Lieutenant Loring was looking at the map with great interest, my anxiety increased.

"I've heard of this map," said MacMikin, observing the map under the candlelight, "and I wouldn't want it even as a gift. It has brought bad luck to everyone who has had it in his possession."

"The Irishman is right," declared old Pattie, sniffing at the parchment as if it smelled bad. "I don't know of anyone who has entered the sanctuary of the Mescalero Apaches and returned to tell about it."

"I've heard it said that in that mountain range there's a forest of giant cedars where a witch doctor who controls lightning and storms has his lair," said a trapper wearing a badger-skin hat.

"A couple of years ago I tried to cross the Sierra Blanca with a caravan going west. But we had to make a big detour to the south. We couldn't find a single native guide who would enter those mountains," said the muleteer Ordovás, who until then hadn't opened his mouth except to curse when he lost a hand.

"I have also heard of an Apache chieftain who controls those mountains and destroys anyone who dares to set foot in the haunted forest," added old Pattie. "His face is covered by a buffalo-skin mask, but I know they call him Huwawa or Humbaba . . ."

At that moment the coarse voice of Decoy was heard coming from the back of the room. "The guardian of the Cedar Forest is the ferocious Humbaba. His voice is as powerful as thunder, his mouth spits fire, and his breath is death . . . Humbaba hears the step of the deer at the threshold of the forest and does not tolerate anyone approaching his sacred trees."

As if the mention of the witch's name had brought on some powerful magic spell, a hush descended on the room; the guitars playing at the back of the shack became quiet and even the gay women with their ochre-painted faces stopped flirting. The only one who dared break the spell was Gil Gómez himself, who in a mocking tone said to the soldier who had offered him the map, "So you want to sell me the map of a mine near a haunted forest surrounded by Apaches. Would you dare go with me to exploit this treasure?"

"I've already been there, and I wouldn't want to go back for all the gold in the world," declared the soldier.

"There must be some truth to those stories, since when we neared the headwaters of the Ruidoso River a tremendous cloudburst swept away the camp and half the horses," said another soldier, who had been with the column at Dog Canyon.

Gil Gómez extended his right hand toward the parchment, while with the left hand he counted out some coins from the pile in front of him. "Fortunately, I don't believe those lies, and to prove it I'm going to buy your map for twenty dollars." He extended a handful of coins to Dixon.

The dragoon already had his hand out to take the coins when Decoy's voice was heard again. "Anyone who ventures into the forest is attacked by a strange weakness. . . . And those who dare to desecrate that sanctuary end up hanging from the branches of the sacred trees."

This threat sounded so terrible that not even Gil Gómez knew how to respond. Lieutenant Loring took advantage of the silence to try a new tack. "On behalf of the United States Army I want to take possession of this document since it may have military significance," said the officer, extending his hand.

"Just a moment. No one can have that map because I have just bought it from this soldier," said Gil Gómez in a clear voice, adding in a defiant tone: "If someone wants it, it will be on my terms."

And before the officer could react, the genízaro had grabbed the parchment with a swift gesture and set about folding it back into its oilskin wrapper.

I could tell by the look on Loring's face that he had taken Gil Gómez's words as a provocation; the officer got up from the table with a tense, resolute expression and opened his jacket, under which a pearl-handled revolver was sticking out of a satin holster. When he saw the exquisitely carved firearm, Gil Gómez let out a guffaw, as if Loring had just shown him a delicate piece of lady's underclothing, and the crowd echoed his jeer. But Decoy slipped stealthily from his corner and placed himself behind the lieutenant, ready to defend his friend.

I realized that something had be done soon, and going quickly to Loring, I whispered in his ear, "Maybe this is none of my business, Lieutenant, but I am acquainted with that map, and I can assure you it's not worth risking your life for." And I added, praying to God that the others couldn't hear me, "Believe me, these rogues aren't worth wasting gunpowder on."

Loring turned toward me blankly, since he had never seen me before. But he stuck to his guns. "Thanks for that information, soldier, but I believe this half-breed needs a lesson."

"I promise you, the map is a fake, good only to cheat gullible fools," I insisted, in the most persuasive tone I could muster. "We found it buried in the mud, and since then it has been passing from hand to hand because no one wants it."

With the help of other solders, I eventually convinced the lieutenant that he should avoid fighting with Gil Gómez, and finally we were able to drag Loring out of the fonda. When the fresh breeze in the street had calmed his nerves, Loring said to me, "I'm glad you stepped in, soldier.

That stupid piece of paper wasn't worth a fight, even though I was ready to teach those two bullies a good lesson!"

I thought that he would never know what a close call he had had. The genízaro and his robust companion could have torn him apart with their bare hands.

Book Four

Enkidu opened his mouth, addressing Gilgamesh:

"I found while roaming the hills with wild animals,

    that the forest covers ten thousand leagues.

Who could possibly dare to go into it?

The howl of Huwawa is like the Flood,

    fire comes out his mouth and his breath is deadly.

Why do you wish to do that?

Trying to come face to face with the

    invincible Huwawa,

    will prove to be an unequal match."

POEM OF GILGAMESH
Tablet II, Column v

The Thunderstorm on the Plains

Leaving Bernalillo in the last light of day, the cuates headed back to Cabezón across the plateau toward the Río Puerco basin. Even though the sky was still clear, storm clouds were beginning to form above the Jémez Mountains; the riders spurred their horses to reach their destination before they were caught by the weather.

They rode for a good while without saying a word, but when they slowed down to cross a gully, Gil Gómez asked his friend the question that had been eating away at him since they had left the fonda.

"When the story of the Sierra Blanca came up, you already seemed to know about that enchanted forest and its fierce guardian. Who told you those stories?"

Decoy took a few moments to answer while they finished climbing the steep slope; as they reached the top a gust of wind blew sand in their faces.

"Everything I said is true: Humbaba has the strength of a mountain flood and his hearing is capable of detecting even the slightest rustling of leaves in the most remote corners of the forest."

"They say that no one who has entered that enchanted forest has ever come out alive to tell about it. So how can you be so familiar with it?"

"I once became lost in the Cedar Forest," said Decoy after another pause.

The wind created dust devils in the twilight and the thunderstorm was already above their heads, but Cimarrón continued talking, protecting his head with his blanket from the drizzle that was beginning to fall.

With his voice still hoarse from the brandy he had consumed at the fonda, he began to tell his story.

"It happened when I was roaming the plains with my herds south of Sierra Blanca. Suddenly, the horizon turned purple and a big thunderstorm hit the desert; a bolt of lightning ripped through a black cloud and struck close to my herd, scaring the mustangs. I was riding on the strongest stallion, and I let it run while there was open space ahead.

"But the rain and lightning increased, and the wind pushed the storm toward the mountains, where the herd, gone mad, was also headed, until we reached the mouth of a deep ravine where the mustangs sought refuge. But the gorge narrowed as it went up the mountain, and soon we found ourselves in a forest of huge cedars. As I entered the dense grove, all of a sudden I felt weak, as if I were running out of breath."

Farther up the Puerco, a thunder bolt struck, and the horses staggered, pricking their ears; to hear better, Gil Gómez came closer to Decoy, who continued his story.

"I ran back and forth from one end of the forest to the other, but it was getting darker and darker, and I couldn't find my way out. Just when an opening seemed to appear, I found myself at the very edge of a huge cliff. I didn't fall off thanks to a streak of lightning that lit the precipice almost under my stallion's hooves. It looked as though the forest was surrounded on all sides by deep ravines, and when it got dark, I noticed that a strange radiance was emanating from the trunks of the giant cedars as if they were will-o'-the-wisps.

"I tried to lead the horses out of that labyrinth, but several of them, frightened by a terrifying howl as the wind whistled between the trees, ended up plunging headlong into the darkness. I'll never forget the way those poor animals neighed in terror and the cracking sound of bones as they fell over the precipice, mixed in with the echoing of thunder at the end of the barranca.

"Finally, following a night of fear during which strange lights could be seen and echoes that sounded like the voices of grieving souls, at dawn I managed to find a path down the mountain. I rounded up the remaining animals to lead them back to the plains.

"Now you know how I'm acquainted with the Cedar Forest, and why I believe that it is bewitched. I guarantee you that someone with a special power controlled the elements there, sending a tempest to punish those who dared to venture into the forest!" Decoy's voice broke from anxiety.

For a few moments, Gil Gómez remained quiet, respecting Decoy's emotions; but after a brief pause he asked, "My friend, do you think you'll ever be able to find your way back to the Cedar Forest?"

"Do you by chance wish to go there?"

"We could go together to the Sierra Blanca and kill the guardian of the forest before the Apaches from the Ruidoso found out we were there."

"And why do you wish to do that?"

"Because up to now no one has been able to overcome the curse that haunts that wilderness. You just told me what happened to you when the thunderstorm took you to that forest, and not long ago a column of American soldiers suffered an ambush in that very place. They had to retreat, leaving their provisions and weapons scattered around the desert.

But two determined men can succeed where a battalion would fail."

"If you want my advice, you should never try to enter the haunted forest. No matter how much cunning and endurance you may have, you'll never be able to defeat the spirits that dwell in the mountain range. If you value your life, never go to the Sierra Blanca."

"Since when are you afraid of death, brother? I can't believe that the person talking to me is the same one I've seen fight the most dangerous beasts with his bare hands! If we join forces, we can be invincible."

"It's true that we have overcome many dangers together, but I also know that it's useless to try to go against the powers of Humbaba . . ."

The cuates had reached the edge of the mesa that overlooked the Río Puerco. The moon was shining on Cabezón Peak amid large black clouds. "Did you know that the Navajos believe that that rock is the petrified head of the giant Yeitsó?" said Gil Gómez, pointing to the peak.

"No, I don't know that story."

"Well, people say that many years ago when the monsters destroyed the Earth, two young men who would later be called the Twin Warriors followed the path up to the high mountain, to the lair of the cruelest and most voracious of all monsters. This was Yeitsó. And after killing him, they cut off his head, which came rolling down the hillside to the valley and then turned into that rock."

"Do you think the two of us are capable of defeating a supernatural enemy? Those things only happen in legends."

"Who knows? Maybe my mother could help us obtain special powers. Don't forget that some of those old legends really did happen."

"Well, since you have told me the story of Yeitsó, I'm going to tell you another one about the monster's head. Do you remember the night of our fight, when we ended up fighting at the bottom of the river?"

"How could I forget it? I thought I was going to swallow all the water in the Río Puerco when you stuck my head under water."

"And has it ever occurred to you why I turned you loose right at that moment when I had you at my mercy?"

"I thought you didn't want to finish me off, and that you were satisfied with having taught me a lesson."

"Actually at that moment I was blinded by hate, and I could have held you under water until you stopped breathing. But remember, it was also a stormy night, and every once in a while the clouds overshadowed the moon."

The genízaro agreed, and Decoy went on.

"The fact is that just as I had you under water, the clouds that covered Cabezón Peak broke up and under the moonlight I saw a monstrous face in the mountain, with a kind of diabolic grin. It was the shock of that vision that made me turn you loose."

"So it was the monster Yeitsó who saved my life? Well, when I was a child my mother used to scare me, warning me that if I didn't behave, the giant would come and eat me alive." Just then the storm got so bad that the cuates had to spur their horses to reach the house before getting soaked. At the main gate, they had to beat the oak planks with their rifle butts to let the sentries know they were waiting outside.

The Light from Terra Incognita

Even before Gil Gómez had convinced his friend to accompany him on his journey, news that the cuates were preparing an expedition to the Sierra Blanca had spread throughout the Río Puerco Valley. The very idea stimulated the imagination of the poor villagers. After all, these peones were descendants of the Spanish explorers who had left testimony of their explorations into Apachería on the sandstone of El Morro: *Por aquí paso* . . . I pass by here. . . . People like Don Francisco Vázquez de Coronado, who abandoned his privileged position in Mexico in search of the fabulous Seven Cities of Cíbola only to lose his bearings in the vast badlands. Or like Don Juan de Oñate, who searched in vain for the famous straits of Anián on the road to California. And although those quixotic journeys may have broken the health and fortunes of those hidalgos, their adventures were still remembered by the fireside among the poor peones who still harbored a secret fascination for impossible dreams. Some even kept old helmets and rusty spears, which they used only for the traditional drama of *Los Comanches,* immortalizing the victory of a Spanish governor against the powerful Chief Green Horn.

In order to stop the rumors and conjectures that were spreading through the village, the hermano mayor of the Penitente brotherhood, Juan Lucero, saw fit to convene a meeting of the villagers and peones in the Cabezón morada.

"I have brought you to this holy place to be able to discuss the cuates' expedition to the Sierra Blanca," said Lucero, after having everyone kneel down before the image of the suffering Nazarene carved in olive wood to pray an Our Father. "Although no one knows exactly the purpose or the route of this journey, for several days now that's the only thing you hear all over the Río Puerco Valley. And as a result of those rumors, the birthing of sheep is neglected, water is allowed to spill over in the acequias, and even husbands forget their most sacred duties, all because their minds are distracted with what the cuates are up to."

When they heard the hermano mayor refer to conjugal duties, a murmur spread and even a few muffled laughs could be heard in the morada. But Lucero continued without batting an eye.

"For the good of our community, and in my capacity as hermano mayor of the Holy Brotherhood, I want you to forget a matter that is of no concern to you, and which is jeopardizing your work and wasting your time."

José de la Luz, the blacksmith and barber, who on account of his line of work was usually well informed, interjected, "There are those who say that the cuates are going in search of gold placers that have been found in the Sierra Blanca; others say that they're only looking for a fight with the Ruidoso Apaches. Regardless, I believe that Compadre Lucero is right: what the genízaro and Cimarrón want to do with their bodies and souls is none of our business."

The convincing tone and the booming voice of the blacksmith persuaded a good portion of those in attendance, who responded in unison, "If the cuates want to lose their lives in Apachería, to find treasures or to right wrongs, it doesn't concern us."

But several arms went up in the nave, trying to voice other opinions. Lucero allowed the former bailiff of Cabezón, José Xaramillo, to speak. "Our hermano mayor is right in saying that it is better for us to tend to our lands and sheep than to listen to gossips and gossipmongers. But on the other hand, I do not agree with Lucero nor with those who have said that the fate of the cuates is none of our business; whether we like it or not, anything that happens to our cacique and his friend is bound to have an influence in our lives."

"Xaramillo is right!" agreed the fiery young Polinio Córdova, without waiting to be allowed to speak. "All of the villagers in the environs, from the peones who cultivate the lands of the patrón to the shepherds who look after his flock, and even those of us who work in the fonda, as I do, we rely on Gil Gómez for our support. Therefore, we cannot remain indifferent if he and his friend seek adventures in distant lands and perhaps lose their lives in the process."

"May God be praised, I can hardly believe what I'm hearing!" exclaimed the blacksmith José de la Luz, without hiding his indignation. "I wonder how many Our Fathers I've prayed before this very same Christ on the cross so that we might see ourselves free of the yoke of those two chieftains! If they now want to lose their lives among the Apaches, I wish them the best of luck. I only hope they never come around here again!"

"I understand very well the blacksmith's feelings and others that have been expressed here," agreed Xaramillo, who was well respected among the villagers for his wisdom. "But has anyone stopped to think what will happen to us if the cuates don't return from their journey to the Sierra Blanca?"

An eloquent silence fell on the crowd, which was finally broken up by Juan Lucero. "Our compadre, Bailiff Xaramillo, has asked a question that nobody has answered and that I'm going to repeat in case someone in the back of the morada has not heard it. What would happen in the valley if Gil Gómez and his friend were to die in the course of their dangerous journey?"

Upon seeing that no one dared to respond, the mayor, Bitoriano Montoya, a descendant of the old settlers who was considered the historical conscience of the place, broke the silence. "I will try to answer that question since, more because of my old age than my limited wisdom, I think I can guess what the bailiff is hinting at. Although it is indeed true that the yoke of our patrón has been heavy, it is also fair to recognize that when he arrived in the valley he offered us protection from the Indians and now he protects us from the arrogance of the Americans, who in other parts of this territory have established themselves as if they were in a conquered land. If it weren't for the respect that the genízaro inspires in them, in no time the new invaders would have robbed us of what little we have left from our ancestors."

"Abuelo Montoya has accurately interpreted what I was thinking," observed Xaramillo, adding, "No matter how much we have suffered from the genízaro's abuses, and lately from his companion, when I see them about to embark on this uncertain journey, the old proverb comes to mind: 'Better the devil you know than the one you don't.'"

That commentary provoked an avalanche of contrasting opinions, some in support of what the mayor and Xaramillo were saying, others against it. Finally, unable to control the uproar in that place of meditation and penance, the hermano mayor had to impose order with his *vara,* and the meeting was dissolved without an agreement.

Meanwhile, Gil Gómez was still trying to convince Decoy to accompany him on his expedition to the eastern mountains. One night when he was up studying the map by lamplight, he heard behind him a sound like an animal's moan. In the semi-darkness he caught a glimpse of his friend crouched in a corner near the fireplace.

He approached his friend, carrying the oil lamp in his outstretched arm, and noticed that Cimarrón was hiding his face between his hands to conceal the tears that were running down his cheeks.

"What's wrong, brother? Don't you feel well? I thought you had gone to bed a long time ago."

"For several days now I've felt as if I had a weight on my chest and sighs bursting from my throat," said the strapping lad, barely able to hold back his sobs. "Can't you see that my arms hang down weakly and that I have lost the energy I once had?"

"I don't see that you have symptoms of illness of any kind, nor have I noticed that you have lost strength. Could it be that you have overindulged in lovemaking and drinking?"

"I haven't gone to bed with Sam Hat for several nights, and the only thing that good woman does at night is cover me up with a blanket when I get the chills. Believe me, the energy I used to have is leaving me, and I'm no longer the person I once was. When I lived on the plains with my animals, I'd go days and nights without eating or drinking, but I felt strong, just like one more horse from the herd; now I eat more than what I need and I drink until I'm sick, and each day I feel weaker."

The genízaro knelt next to him and tapped him affectionately on his wide back. "Cheer up, brother! I don't think you're sick or weak; if anything you have more energy than you need. Not even our easy raids on Navajo rancherías or our hunting excursions are enough. At times I also feel a kind of laziness because of the soft life we lead; what we both need is a challenge! Only a difficult mission will bring back our vitality and stamina. The journey to the Sierra Blanca will get us in shape and will give us the chance to have an adventure that everyone will remember!"

"Why do you need to be remembered?" asked Decoy, wiping away his tears with the back of his hand. "Don't you think you're already famous enough?"

"Brother, you're never famous enough, even if it's bad fame. Do you believe that I'll go down in history as the chieftain who controlled a fistful of peaceful villagers and sacked a couple of Navajo rancherías to get women for the bordello in Cabezón?"

"Why do you wish to be remembered? Let the American soldiers subdue the Apaches in the Sierra Blanca and be recorded in history! I was never happier than when nobody knew who I was except the wild horses and the antelopes on the plains."

"You know as well as I do that the Americans will never be able to subdue the Apaches of the Ruidoso. They are not used to the harsh wastelands nor do they know how to find the mountain passes; we, on the other hand, are capable of finding the best-hidden waterhole in the wilderness and crawling through the underbrush where not even a snake could go."

"If you're so eager to go, you'll have to manage alone, because I'll never go back to that godforsaken mountain; I already told you that the other day. And if I can't keep you from risking your life, at the very least don't ask me to go with you to die there."

"Who among us lives forever? Don't you know that fame is the only thing left after we die? But I'm beginning to think you really have changed, that the easy life has softened your spirit and weakened your courage."

"If that were true, it would be your fault! It was you who sent the woman who made me forsake my life in the mountain, and brought me to Cabezón, where I feel that I'm wasting away one day at a time."

Gil Gómez grabbed his friend's head between his powerful forearms as if trying to shake the somber thoughts out of him.

"On the way to Sierra Blanca, we'll go by El Morro rock, where others before us have inscribed their deeds. And many years after we have departed this earth, we'll be remembered for having inscribed our own names on the rock: 'Gil Gómez passed by here, accompanied by his friend Decoy, headed for the Sierra Blanca to challenge the Keeper of the Cedar Forest.'"

"What if we fail? Our bones will be left bleaching in the forks of the cedars and the wind will play the flute on our ribs. Do you want to be remembered that way?"

"On the contrary! If we should fall in defeat against Humbaba, when people see our names inscribed on the rock, someone will say, 'These were the brave ones who dared to challenge the ferocious Humbaba!'"

One morning the villagers of Cabezón, worried about what could become of them if the genízaro did not return from his journey to the Sierra Blanca, traveled to Los Altos de la Parida, once again seeking Don Anú Baca's advice. Some peones from the neighboring haciendas began to join them, and a few Navajos who shared the Spaniards' fears, so the party that went before the old patrón was almost the same group who had been received in the hacienda a couple of years before, when they wanted to complain about Gil Gómez's abuses. But this time their speech was quite different.

"The cacique is leaving with his friend bound for the Sierra Blanca, allegedly in search of a gold mine marked on an old Spanish map," said José Xaramillo. "But we were told that that mountain range is cursed, and we are afraid that our cacique and his friend may not come out alive."

"According to my uncle Belisario," commented Polinio Córdova, "who as a young man joined the *conducta* from Santa Fe to Chihuahua, there's no way of reaching the Sierra Blanca without crossing the rocky malpaís and the treacherous White Sands, where the horses sink to their chests. And he also believes that the Ruidoso Apaches' sanctuary is impregnable, as the defeat of a detachment of American soldiers has just proved."

"They say that the Indian Humbaba who protects the Cedar Forest is endowed with diabolic powers, and that he is capable of unleashing thunderstorms at will," said a peón from Casa Salazar.

"People claim that a party of prospectors who dared to enter the sacred forest were chopped into quarters by the guardian of the forest, and their corpses strung from the trees," added the blacksmith José de la Luz.

Don Anú listened silently to all the arguments, and with his thin lips pursed into a mocking smile, observed, "It's barely been two years since you asked me if I could help rid you of the yoke of Gil Gómez and now you seem to be concerned that he may lose his life in the sierra!"

"If our cacique doesn't come back from the journey," explained Mayor Montoya to the patrón, "the Americans will take away what little land that we have left, the Indians will steal our livestock, and the soldiers from Fort Cebolleta will rape our wives and daughters. At least the cacique makes them pay to use the women of the fonda!"

This time the patrón burst out laughing, at the same time exhaling cigar smoke.

"Only yesterday you wanted me to help you fight Gil Gómez's tyranny, and now you're asking me to help keep your shackles! And in both cases my answer must be the same. Knowing the genízaro's character, if I were to attempt to discourage him from undertaking that journey I would only be adding fuel to the fire. I am convinced that what drives him is the danger and the difficulty of the adventure."

"The patrón Don Anú knows well the hearts of those two young daredevils," acknowledged Mayor Montoya. "As I've already commented to some of my compadres, the best way to dissuade the genízaro and his companion from going to the eastern sierras would be to encourage them, even offering them weapons and provisions for the trip."

"If the cacique has any sense left at all, he will turn back when he encounters the obstacles of the *despoblado*," corroborated Xaramillo.

The old patrón nodded his head in agreement. "The Indians used to do the same when our forefathers came here from Old Mexico looking for gold and riches. Instead of telling them the truth about their pipe dreams, to get rid of the strangers they encouraged them to go on by pretending that what they were looking for was always farther ahead, beyond the horizon. And so the Spaniards followed a mirage that kept moving farther away the more they pursued it, attracted by the lure of the unknown."

Don Anú Baca's advice was respected, as he knew the Indians well, and had used to his advantage the right combination of flattery and intimidation with the most dangerous tribes in the region. It was even rumored that he had an understanding with the Ruidoso Apaches, who rarely bothered his livestock even though at times the shepherds from the Ojo de la Parida pastured their flocks at the very foot of the Sierra Blanca.

And so, forced to accept the old man's wisdom, the villagers from Cabezón took to the road, even though they had achieved little, and went back to the Río Puerco Valley.

The Land of the Deluge

With all the talk the cuates' trip had stirred up before it had started, it was no surprise that one of the soldiers found out about it at the Fonda de la Reunión. And since the devil never rests, the news reached the ears of an officer in Santa Fe, who in turn relayed it to Colonel Washington, who was preparing for a campaign in Navajo territory and had made his temporary headquarters on the banks of the Río Grande.

The very day we were about to return to Fort Conrad, having loaded the wagons with supplies and ammunition in Albuquerque, I saw a horseman on an elegant chestnut mount approaching our caravan. It was none other than Lieutenant Loring, the same officer who almost fought a duel with the genízaro of Cabezón. I regretted having been fool enough to tell him what I knew about the map; when I saw him coming a proverb that I had often heard from the Mexican *arrieros* came to mind: "From the chief and the mule, the farther you are, the safer."

Loring spoke with Sergeant Sweeny and by the happy smile that appeared on the face of that ruffian when he came to find me, I knew what was in store for me.

"They want you to go before the staff of Colonel Washington," Sweeny told me, adding, with a malicious wink, "I don't know what you've done this time, Burdette, but I'll bet they haven't sent for you to give you a medal."

The commander's camp was set up some miles north of Bernalillo, on the west bank of the river, across from the Indian pueblo of Santo Domingo, whose reddish adobes could be seen on the opposite bank. On fording the river we saw smoke coming from the roof of one of the kivas, and we assumed that the members of one of their religious clans were meeting there to prepare a ceremony.

When I reached the camp, Lieutenant Loring explained to me that the colonel had learned that the map of the Sierra Blanca had ended up in the hands of Gil Gómez and wanted me to tell him what I knew about the damned parchment. When they took me into his presence, Washington must have noticed that I was trembling like a leaf, because he offered me a glass of brandy, which I didn't refuse. Although I had known our commander in chief from the time when I served at Fort Marcy, I discovered that bringing a cup of coffee to the colonel's office was quite different from being debriefed by five high-ranking officers, who looked at me as if I were a lemon from which they were planning to squeeze the last drop of information.

"They tell me that at one time you had in your possession a map that could be of interest to the United States Army," said the colonel, using his finger to slide his spectacles down to the end of his nose, a gesture I had seen before. He cleared his throat before going on. "For now, we have no interest in investigating the circumstances by which this map arrived in your hands, as long as you can recall the details of that map, in order to complete the information included in our charts."

They had placed on the table an American military map, which certainly needed to be updated, since it showed all the eastern part of the Río Grande basin as Terra Incognita, just as Timothy Baltasar had told me the night we rode together in the rain. An aide-de-camp with curly mustaches handed me a finely sharpened pencil as though he were presenting me with a dueling foil. That polite invitation—together with the glass of brandy—had the effect of loosening my tongue and my hand. Between what I remembered of Dawson's map and what I had seen during the expedition to Dog Canyon, I succeeded in filling in enough of the blank spaces; and when I couldn't recall some detail, I invented one.

Come to think of it, I may have laid it on too thick when it came to putting the names of Roman Catholic saints on every mountain and range whose name I was unsure of. So if, years hence, someone rummaging through a drawer in the Department of War finds a military map whose topography reminds him somewhat of a prayerbook, he'll know the reason for it. The area of the map that had been almost blank was by then a lot more complete, and with the second glass of brandy they had to remove the pencil from my hands, because I was almost ready to reproduce in an empty corner of the paper the portrait of the beautiful Eleanor Stanton that I had received from Pat Dixon in exchange for that cursed map.

When suppertime came, instead of sending me to share the lousy mess with my peers, they took a campaign table out of the officers' tent, and one of the colonel's orderlies was put in charge of serving me the same wines and foods as the officers. I should have wondered why they didn't let me join my companions, but between the excitement of having performed in front of that group of officers like the young Jesus before the High Priests and the euphoria produced by two glasses of French brandy, it didn't occur to me that the privilege could have a meaning comparable to the treatment given to the victims of sacrifice in Old Mexico, who were showered with attention before losing their lives to an obsidian machete.

Fortunately, the fresh breeze that came down the banks of the Río Grande, whose willows were beginning to vanish into the mauve halo of dusk, soon dissipated the alcoholic vapors. And since I was so close to the colonel's tent, I could scarcely avoid following the conversation the officers were having on the other side of the canvas. At first they were speaking in low voices, and the breeze carried away some snatches of their sentences, but as they finished eating, they began to get excited and speak louder, and I could hear every word of their conversation.

"Considering that we're talking about a strategic point that dominates the southern basin of the Río Grande as well as the southern caravan route to California, it seems obvious that we must rid the Sierra Blanca of the bands of Apaches who operate from the area," one of the officers was saying.

"The same way we built Fort Defiance in the very heart of Navajo Territory," said Major McAlister, who had long red sideburns like an Irish bandit and a high-pitched voice. "The best thing would be to build another fort at the headwaters of the Ruidoso River, which seems to be the sanctuary from which these bandits operate."

The colonel agreed with such vehemence that I thought I detected in his hoarse voice the effects of alcohol. "Hear, hear! With the very trees that grow in the Sierra Blanca we'll build a fort in the heart of the sacred forest, and we'll call it Fort Stanton, in memory of the captain who died on the expedition to the Dog Canyon."

At that moment the voice of Lieutenant Loring was heard. "In my opinion, the first thing we should do is recover the map which is in the hands of that braggart called Gil Gómez. Although Burdette might seem to recall some details, those who go on the expedition should have the original."

"According to what the soldiers at Fort Cebolleta have told us, the Río Puerco cacique is ready to leave for the Sierra Blanca on his sole initiative and responsibility, and I'm afraid that this improvised expedition could alert the Apaches and jeopardize the army's plans," said another officer.

I recognized again the voice of McAlister, who was saying, "And not only that, I think we would be left in an awkward position if that mestizo chieftain and his savage companion succeeded in getting to the heart of the Sierra Blanca when a company of United States dragoons has failed in the attempt."

"On the other hand," observed Warrant Officer Richardson, who was an experienced Indian fighter, "it is true that a handful of volunteers with a good knowledge of the mountains could succeed in getting where it would be difficult for a conventional detachment to go."

"Perhaps we could convince the mestizo Gil Gómez and his friend to serve as guides for an army column going to the Sierra Blanca," the colonel then suggested, "besides which we would also have their map at our disposal."

"I regret not having taken advantage of the opportunity that I had to get the map, but I didn't wish to use force for it. In retrospect, perhaps it would have been better to put a bullet through the chest of that braggart," said Lieutenant Loring, whose voice was beginning to show the effects of alcohol.

"I believe you were right in not challenging the Río Puerco cacique," said the colonel. "Thanks to the authority which he wields in the Río Puerco basin, that valley is no longer at the mercy of Apache and Navajo bandits."

"Since when has the United States Army needed renegades to rule our territory?" replied the lieutenant in a tone that didn't seem proper in addressing a superior. "From what I've been told, that rogue has imposed his tyranny on all the people of the area, and he and his henchmen subject the people of Cabezón and other settlements to all sorts of abuses and injustices."

Even from behind the tent, I could clearly make out the irritated tone of the colonel's response. "Lieutenant, you should know that at the moment Gil Gómez is our ally and I will do my best to keep him one. And I'll tell you another thing: if we ever succeed in controlling the Ruidoso Apaches, it will be because of the cunning and experience of the mestizo and his friend, not because of the efficiency of our dragoons, who scare off the Indians with the noise of their cannons and the creaking of their overloaded supply wagons."

After a moment of silence, the colonel added, this time with a certain sarcasm, "Come to think of it, lieutenant, I believe I'm going to entrust you with the delicate mission of going to the village of Cabezón and convincing its cacique to serve as our guide and accompany us on our next expedition to the Sierra Blanca."

I had liked the courage with which Loring had been able to defend his ideas before a superior. But this time there was no answer.

Later I learned that between Colonel Washington and the engineer lieutenant there were frequent disagreements, the kinds of differences of opinion that could easily exist between people of diverse social backgrounds and different education. Because he belonged to an influential family from Boston, Loring had been accepted at West Point and had been commissioned effortlessly; the colonel, on the other hand, had had to earn his stripes with spurs and sabre during the Mexico campaign, where he had been promoted for his bravery in the taking of Cerro Gordo. Loring did not have the colonel's leathery complexion or bow-leggedness from long hours spent in the saddle, but in spite of his aristocratic demeanor, he also was a good soldier.

Loring wasn't capable of remaining silent when he thought he was right, and he proved it again later that night. After the other officers had left and Colonel Washington and Loring were left alone smoking cigars next to the fire, the lieutenant returned to the point that he had failed to clarify before, probably because he did not want to contradict the colonel in front of the other officers. I remained seated on a tree trunk, in a place where the light of the fire didn't reach me, so they were not aware of my presence and I could listen to all they said.

"Forgive me, colonel, if maybe I have expressed my opinion on the Río Puerco cacique too frankly," said the lieutenant. "Perhaps I am still new in this territory, but I thought we came west to bring civilization, not to tolerate the misbehavior of the former rulers."

"I agree that you are indeed new, and not only in this territory. We Americans are in a hostile region, and the only way to be able to control the savage tribes is by allying ourselves with the local people, who know their way of fighting, and share their skills and craftiness . . . among other things, because they are all half Indian, like the Río Puerco cacique and his wild friend."

"At the price of their continuing to tyrannize the Indians as well as the Spanish?" asked Loring.

The colonel stretched his hand toward the bottle of liquor that the aide-de-camp had put beside him and poured a glass of brandy before he answered.

"If we are too intolerant and try to impose our way of life, the only thing we'll accomplish is that the Indians and the Spanish will form an alliance and try to expel us from here, as happened only a few years ago in Taos, when they paraded the head of Governor Bent on the point of a lance."

From the other side of the river the wind brought the sound of a ritual chant from Santo Domingo Pueblo, together with the smell of burning cedar. Stretching his arm out, Colonel Washington took in the curve of the sky, the profile of the mountains and the river basin, where the singing of the Indians resonated.

"Lieutenant, look at that sky filled with stars, breathe the delicate smell of the wild roses and reed beds, listen to that ancestral melody that puts us in contact with past generations of humanity . . . isn't it wonderful?" And, suddenly, with a dramatic change in his voice, the colonel exploded, "Why, all that forms part of the magic trick, the consummate fraud of this damned territory!"

"Forgive me colonel," said the lieutenant, "but I don't understood what you're referring to."

"Surely someone must have warned you not to trust human beings, but here you cannot even trust inanimate things, like the water in the rivers, the silence of the night, or the profile of the mountain ranges." And again the gesture of the colonel's arms took in the wide sky. "This night that seems so clear can be suddenly filled with huge dark clouds, and you could go to sleep under the bright stars and wake up with two feet of water under your cot. That silly little stream, which does not look 'grand' in spite of its name, can suddenly flow with as much force as the Tigris and

Euphrates combined, and carry away our entire camp during the night, like a true deluge."

The colonel remained quiet, and soon, the glass that he had in his hand rolled to the ground. He had fallen asleep, lulled by his own rhetoric. Before retiring to his tent, Lieutenant Loring called the aide-de-camp for a blanket to cover the colonel, since a cold evening breeze was blowing from the river.

A short while later I also had to seek shelter in a tent because it had begun to rain quite hard. I rolled up in my blanket thinking that my friend Timothy Baltasar would have enjoyed that conversation tremendously, since the colonel seemed to share some of his theories on the captivity of Babylon.

The Fiestas of Cabezón

Two days after that conversation on the banks of the Río Grande, Lieutenant Loring and I were leaving the encampment at dawn, headed for Cabezón. The Indian Tafoya was coming with us as guide and interpreter. I hadn't seen him since my company was assigned to Fort Conrad. Since he didn't speak English well, if we had a conversation with the Navajos, Tafoya would translate from their language to Spanish and I from that language to English, so that the officer could understand it. Loring had reluctantly accepted the assignment with which Colonel Washington had entrusted him: to try to persuade Gil Gómez to accompany us to the Sierra Blanca or at least sell us his map at a reasonable price.

I was proud to serve as the interpreter to the interpreter, and to be able to travel with the distinguished lieutenant. The assignment proved that the senior officers hadn't lost confidence in me, despite the mess around Dawson's map. Tafoya didn't seem displeased either. He was returning to his native land; and I also think he had taken a certain liking to me, from the times when he told me the stories of his people's origins during our long fireside chats. Of course, he disguised his soft spot for me behind the closed mask of his face, which was furrowed with deep wrinkles. But at times I noticed in the depths of his intense eyes a trace of affection or at least condescension, especially when I gave him the chance to teach me a lesson or prove that I was wrong in some respect, something that happened frequently during the course of our conversations.

When the sun came up over the Mesa Prieta, sparsely dotted with cedar bushes and *chamiza,* it revealed a motley group. Engineer Loring wore an elegant civilian jacket and was using an English saddle. The Navajo's voluminous silhouette was wrapped in a blanket with black and ochre stripes that fluttered up and down with the trot of his tiny mustang pony, saddled only with an Indian blanket. The shadow of my dragoon hat was projected over the ears of my horse, which carried me on a large Spanish saddle, the kind from which it was almost impossible to fall, even if you were drunk. Too bad that in that wilderness the only spectators of our retinue were the lizards and rabbits that had come out of their holes to sun themselves and stayed a few moments to watch us pass before scurrying behind a rock or bush.

Leaving the Jémez Mountains to the north, before noon we arrived in sight of the monolith of Cabezón Peak, which rose over the flat horizon of the mesa.

"How far is the village of Cabezón from that peak?" Lieutenant Loring asked Tafoya, using me as interpreter.

"You can't see the village because it lies in the river valley, but it's at the very foot of the promontory; we still have a couple of leagues to go to reach the Río Puerco Valley," said Tafoya in his perfect Spanish, which I translated.

"Will we arrive there before nightfall?" asked the lieutenant.

"Of course, and we'd better get to the village before dark because at night Gil Gómez's men close the plaza gate, and after sunset they might welcome us with bullets."

Without being aware of it I began humming Timothy Baltasar's favorite ballad.

> *How many miles to Babylon?*
> *Three score and ten.*
> *Can I get there by candlelight?*
> *Yes, and back again.*

As Tafoya had predicted, about two in the afternoon we crossed the Río Puerco, whose current carried more mud and silt than water, in accordance with its not very elegant name in English: the Dirty River. On entering Cabezón we saw a crowd gathering in the village, probably bigger than the total population of Cabezón. We soon learned that the people were celebrating the fiesta of their patron saint, Saint Joseph, and visitors from other settlements in the valley had come to join in the festivities.

Also present were Indians from the surrounding area, among them some Navajos, who stood out with their rich and colorful attire: feathered war bonnets, velvet tunics, and wide belts with silver conchas.

In the church that faced the plaza a Mass was being celebrated, and out of curiosity I went in to look at the sanctuary, entering a large door of old cottonwood boards whose jambs squeaked on their hinges from lack of use. In the reredos one could see the influence of the Indian tribes: on each side of a Holy Virgin covered with a purple mantle were painted images of the sun and the moon and a giant stalk of corn, the same symbols that were found on the walls of a Pueblo kiva.

The most distinguished architectural features were the thick pine *vigas* that supported the roof, and the hand-carved lintels with their exotic native designs. Trees of that size didn't grow on the bare hillsides of the valley. Those cruel Roman Catholic priests must have had the heavy trunks brought from the San Mateo Mountains on the shoulders of their Indian parishioners.

When I entered the church, the Mass was coming to an end. The Latin phrases were continually interrupted by the crying of children, the mumbling of old women who prayed their own litanies, and the occasional alabado recited by some Penitente brother who sang with his outstretched arms forming a cross. Only when the priest turned toward the congregation to give the benediction was there silence in the nave. Even a stray dog that had until then been sprawled at the foot of the altar must have guessed that this was not a proper place for an animal, or perhaps it interpreted the gesture of the raised pastoral arm as a threat, because it chose that moment to run toward the exit down the central aisle as though pursued by the devil.

While those who had attended Mass gathered in the church doorway to join a procession presided over by a wooden figure carving the saint, the lieutenant and I went for a stroll around the village, sending Tafoya to Gil Gómez's fortress to request an audience with the cacique. Turning into one of the dusty back alleys we found ourselves in front of the shop of a blacksmith who was hammering a tool of great size on the anvil.

Loring was curious to know how important this work order could be to have the blacksmith sweating while the whole village was at the fiesta. Absorbed in his work, the smith was molding a two-sided axe that must have weighed ten or twelve pounds. I approached, but the blacksmith didn't utter a word to me until he had set the metal in a pine handle as thick as my forearm, afterward letting the red-hot axe fall into a bucket of water, where the incandescent metal sizzled like a rattlesnake.

"I am a soldier in the United States Army visiting Cabezón," I said when I judged that the right moment had arrived. "Excuse me for asking, but could you tell me what that colossal hatchet is used for?"

The man wiped the sweat from his brow with hands smudged with soot and sighed deeply before answering. "I'm the village blacksmith, although at times I'm also a barber and I pull the teeth of those who allow me to do so. I'd be happy to answer your question but all I know is that our cacique ordered it made because he leaves soon on an excursion to faraway lands." And after a few moments of silence, and looking Loring and me up and down, the blacksmith added, "Don't they say that the trees of the Sierra Blanca are giant cedars? Well, here you have a giant axe, so the genízaro will need fewer blows to cut them down."

At that moment Tafoya came to find us to tell us that Gil Gómez would receive us immediately and to accompany us to the other side of the Río Puerco where the genízaro's fortress rose at the base of the volcanic plug. The solid oak doors with images of saints carved in the panels were soon opened. We entered a spacious patio where some servants armed like brigands escorted us to the main room.

While they went to tell the cacique we had arrived, they left us in a large, well-appointed room with a serge rug, several large cushions, and even a French-style divan. An Indian servant girl with regular features placed in front of us a jug of steaming chocolate next to a platter of *bizcochitos,* which are very tasty local cookies. That snack went down like unexpected rainfall in my dry throat, which hadn't seen a mouthful since we had left Bernalillo. Tafoya refused to eat or drink anything, and remained half-crouched next to a corner fireplace where a cedar log burned.

After a long while Gil Gómez appeared in the room, as clean and fragrant as if he had just gotten out of a bath, and, after inviting us to make ourselves comfortable on the divan, he sat on a large satin-covered cushion in cross-legged oriental style. With his dark mane caught in a crimson bandanna, his gold earring in the right ear, his satin sash securing his flared linen trousers, and his Apache-style moccasins, which looked like Arab slippers, the genízaro had the demeanor of an eastern pasha, as my friend Baltasar would certainly have noticed had he been there.

Lieutenant Loring had accepted his mission like a soldier, for deep down he thought that the best treatment one could give that braggart was to make him dance at the end of a rope, but I must say that the engineer fulfilled his assignment with exemplary diplomacy. Although the cacique spoke English reasonably well, he asked me to interpret, pretending that he could express his thoughts better in Spanish.

The lieutenant began. "Colonel Washington has charged me to ask you if you and your friend, the one called Decoy, would accompany us as guides on an expedition which the army is organizing to punish the Ruidoso Apaches and build a fort in the Sierra Blanca."

Once I had translated for the lieutenant, the cacique took a few moments before answering. "Tell the colonel that I am very honored by his offer, but my friend and I don't need the help of the army to enter Apache territory."

"Do you truly believe that you and your friend can confront the Ruidoso Apaches by yourselves?" responded Loring. "I suppose you are aware of what happened to Captain Stanton, who fell into an ambush on the way to the Sierra Blanca. Private Burdette, who is accompanying me, was there and could give you more details."

Again I translated for Gil Gómez, although I was certain that he understood perfectly. He answered, "I don't need more information about the Sierra Blanca; remember that I have a map that describes how to get there."

"Yes, but I also remind you that the man who owned that map died during the expedition."

"Who's foolish enough to take a company of soldiers into a box canyon?"

I noticed that the lieutenant had to bite his lip in order not to respond to that insolence the way it deserved, but he continued trying to persuade the cacique. "In any case, I have instructions from the colonel to offer you a good sum of money to come with us, and to double that if you hand over the Spanish map; we want to build a bastion in the heart of Mescalero territory, the same as we did at Fort Defiance in Navajo territory."

In spite of my mediation, the conversation between Loring and the cacique soon turned into a meaningless exchange since neither was ready to listen to the other's point of view. Finally, probably so that we would leave him alone, the cacique promised to advise the army when he was about to start his expedition into the Sierra Blanca, and said that he would be willing to help build the fort. With this vague promise, we said good-bye, but the lieutenant, with good reason, didn't trust Gil Gómez's word one bit and decided to remain for the moment in Cabezón to be able to monitor his activities.

The Drama of *Los Comanches*

As we went back across the Río Puerco, we saw a retinue of horsemen with lances and swords leaving the village and gathering at a nearby esplanade with a band of Indians who seemed to be painted for war. We were told that these men were preparing for a performance of a play the Spanish called *Los Comanches,* which I had heard about but never seen before.

According to the villagers the play celebrated the victory of Spanish troops over the warriors of Comanche chief Cuerno Verde (Green Horn), who at one time was their principal enemy. This was the great attraction of the fiesta, not the religious celebrations or the processions. This war drama had a deep significance to people who for generations had lived with the threat of Indian attacks.

Loring, Tafoya, and I followed the crowd up the riverbank, which offered a splendid natural grandstand above the spacious *cañada* where the spectacle unfolded.

The horsemen separated into two groups: the "Spanish" and the "Comanche." While the "Spanish" horsemen congregated on the other side of the river, below Gil Gómez's fortress, the armies of the "Comanches" retreated to the bottom of the esplanade, leaving an empty space in between. The scenery was perfect for this drama, for Gil Gómez's fortress, with its Moorish parapet, provided a convincing replica of the bastion that the colonial troops pretended to defend. To give it greater realism and color they had decorated the *torreón* with red and yellow banners, the colors of the Spanish flag.

Those playing the roles of conquistadors wore armor and carried lances from the viceroyalty period that the villagers must have kept hidden in some secret cache, and those who assumed the role of Comanche warriors wore feather bonnets and buckskin robes embroidered with beads and carried sharp lances and maces. According to Tafoya, some of the Comanches were actual Indians from the nearby rancherías who participated with great enthusiasm. There was also some musical accompaniment. When the Spanish soldiers took their turn, the village band played military marches, and when attention was on the Comanches, a group of Pueblo Indians from Cochití played the drums. A blunderbuss shot by the master of ceremonies was the signal to start the battle.

The chief Cuerno Verde, mounted on a handsome, spirited pinto horse, galloped across the field to where the Spanish forces were situated and still prancing and brandishing his sharp lance, he began to harangue his opponents, extolling his heroics in battle and belittling the courage and strength of his enemies:

> *From East to West,*
> *From South to the cold North,*
> *The shiny bugle sounds,*
> *And my sword sparkles!*

The Spanish captain, portrayed by a notable from Cabezón wearing a breastplate and helmet, emerged from among his troops brandishing his sword and responded to the Indian's challenge, saying:

> *Hold on, hold it, wait;*
> *For I am of such noble mettle*
> *That I come without your summons*
> *To watch over this castle.*

After the exchange of challenges, the Indians performed a colorful war display on horseback and then charged at a full gallop, shouting war whoops that sounded completely authentic to those of us who in real life had been in similar situations. And when they saw the enemy arrive with lances and axes at the ready, the Spaniards also gave their traditional war cry, while the trumpets played and the volleys from flintlock guns resounded:

> *And thus, courageous lions,*
> *Take up arms, warriors.*
> *Let the drum beat and war begin*
> *In the name of Santiago*
> *And the Blessed Virgin Mary!*

The battle unfolded with such realism that children cried and some of the women covered their faces with their rebozos. At the edge of the embankment where we were seated, the smell of sweat from the horses and their riders reached us, mixed with the pungent odor of gunpowder and the noise of spears striking armor. At one point I thought I recognized Gil Gómez riding his spirited jet black stallion, his chest covered with shiny brass armor, as well as the enormous body of Decoy, dressed in a leather tunic with brass buttons, the kind used by the soldiers guarding the Spanish *presidios*. But the horses' maneuvers and the riders' feints raised so much dust that it was difficult to make out the contenders.

The end came pretty quickly. The Comanche forces were promptly defeated by the Spanish horsemen, who continued to chase the enemy beyond the esplanade, even pursuing them behind Cabezón Peak. Finally, the captain for the Spaniards appeared in the middle of the riverbed raising in the air the feather bonnet belonging to Cuerno Verde, who supposedly had died in the fight, and with that everybody applauded and the fiesta ended.

The sun was beginning to set behind the village, lighting up the face of the promontory with a reddish splendor. Lieutenant Loring decided to spend that night in Cabezón in order to meet again with Gil Gómez the following day, when things would have quieted down.

It was not easy for us to find lodging at La Fonda de la Reunión. They stuck the lieutenant and me in a filthy hole in the attic, where we were kept awake by the cackling of whores and guitar and violin music. The Indian Tafoya was sent to the horse stables. We heard the fandango music from the floor below us till the wee hours of the morning, but finally the fatigue of the long journey overcame us, and we fell into the arms of Morpheus.

Power against the Enemy

At dawn the following day the noise of the tapping heels, which the night before had rocked me to sleep, seemed to have blended with the noise of Tafoya's knuckles knocking on the door. He had learned that Gil Gómez and his powerful friend had left the village the night before, taking advantage of the confusion of the fiesta. Although no one knew for sure which direction they had taken, based on what our guide had heard about the load of arms and provisions that the cuates were carrying, one could guess that they had set out on their journey to the Sierra Blanca.

Upon hearing this news, the lieutenant leaped from his rough bed like a shot and ordered us to saddle the horses to go immediately in pursuit of the fugitives. But we made the officer realize the difficulty of catching up with the travelers without knowing which way they were headed. The sun had already risen behind Cabezón Peak when we drew near a group of villagers who were sitting and chatting on the stone steps of the church. After cursory greetings, and after slipping some copper coins into their calloused hands, we discovered that each one of those compadres had a different notion of where the cuates had gone.

Some thought the young chieftains had taken off to the south by the trail that ran parallel to the Río Puerco, which seemed the best route to the mountains east of the Río Grande. Others, however, were sure Gil Gómez wanted to go to El Morro to carve his mark on that stone where other explorers had left inscriptions on their way to fame. But the village *alcalde,* Bitoriano Montoya, who seemed to know a lot about the cacique, said that surely Gil Gómez would not go on his dangerous journey without asking for his mother's blessing and undergoing some tribal ritual that might give him what they called *power against enemy.* But if he wanted to go by the ranchería of Ninsaba, Gil Gómez had to go toward the northwest, the opposite direction from the Sierra Blanca.

Not being able to get any reliable advice from the crafty villagers, who seemed to enjoy our confusion after having collected our coins, Lieutenant Loring decided that he would return to the encampment on the Río Grande to inform Colonel Washington of the situation, leaving us there trying to follow the trail of the cuates. Assuming that the colonel would give him permission to form a detail to reach the Sierra Blanca before the two adventurers, after five days Loring would rejoin us at Fort Conrad, which was halfway to the eastern sierras.

After jumping his horse over the Río Puerco at full gallop at the risk of breaking his neck, Lieutenant Loring disappeared on the horizon in a cloud of dust. I tried to get Tafoya to hurry out of the village, but he took his time, tightening the cinch on his horse and even lighting a cigar while he adjusted the packs on our mule. When I called attention to his lack of diligence, the Indian looked at me with that expression he adopted whenever he received useless and inopportune orders from white men. He said to me, "The cacique and his friend have many hours on us, and no matter how fast we go it will be difficult to catch up to them. If we hurry, we will only put them on alert. If we leave them in peace, after a while they will think that we are not following them and perhaps we will be able to catch them while they rest."

"You must understand," I replied, "that I'm ashamed that we two are here marking time while poor Lieutenant Loring has left for the garrison as though pursued by the devil. I'd like to get going in search of those rogues as soon as possible."

Again the Indian looked at me blankly, and after exhaling a mouthful of smoke and watching it ascend toward the blue morning sky, he added with the same indifference, "When one is hunting and wounds a deer in the wilderness, it isn't good to go in pursuit when the wound is still warm and the animal still has all its strength. It's better to stop and smoke a cigar in a place where he cannot catch your scent and wait until the wound cools and the deer lies down to rest under a shrub where the hunter will be able to sneak up on him if he knows how to follow the track patiently."

In fact, not only was the trail of Gil Gómez and his friend cold, but because the rush of hooves the night before had trampled all the pathways around Cabezón, we weren't even able to distinguish the hoof prints of their mounts. When we came near the ravine where they had celebrated the battle of Los Comanches, the air was still full of the smell of smoke and sweat.

In the end, the Indian decided to trust what old Montoya had said, since he took neither the path south that ran parallel to the Río Puerco nor the path that went due southwest. He directed his horse straight to the San Mateo Mountains, due northwest, toward Ninsaba's village.

It was a clear day, and the sun blazed on the mountainside, so as soon as we started riding uphill we no longer needed either a blanket or a tunic, and our horses started oozing sweat through every pore. We stopped to rest at the top of a hillock. From there the cone of Cabezón Peak looked like a thimble, and on the other side of the river the houses of the village seemed like the little dwellings of a crèche.

I remembered then to ask the Indian the meaning of what old Montoya had mentioned about *power against the enemy.* Tafoya stared at me with a certain air of satisfaction; I think he appreciated my interest in things few whites noticed.

After remaining silent some moments to whet my interest, the Indian explained to me, "Our people, the *dinéh,* we believe that our strengths come from the land where we were born and raised, and when we leave the borders of our territory and go into enemy land, we lose part of that power. For that reason we have to counteract that disadvantage with a special protection. That protection, that power, is what Gil Gómez is looking for in his mother's ranchería, before embarking on the path of the enemy and leaving behind the territory of his ancestors."

On the other side of the mountain ridge we could see a deep gorge, where a sparkling spring was surrounded by a patch of green. I suggested to Tafoya that we go down to the spring to fill our canteens with fresh water and lie down a bit in the shade. The Indian again adopted the condescending expression with which the natives show the white man that, although we may consider our culture superior to theirs, we cannot grasp some concepts that to them are obvious. "When we prepare the young men of our tribe to go on the warpath, the first thing they are taught is that when the sun beats fiercely, it is not advisable to rest in a place where there is a lot of shade, since it's the first place an enemy from another tribe will go looking for you, and also a wild animal could be lying in wait there. It is wiser to stay in the open on a hill next to some small bushes, the way we are, where we can see without being seen."

The sun was in fact at its zenith, and its rays beat straight down on the summit of the hill, where only sparse grass and a few juniper shrubs grew, not tall enough to give shade.

"Another piece of advice they give the war novices," continued Tafoya, who didn't seem bothered by the blistering sun, "is don't go down from the mountains during the day to look for water in an arroyo, no matter how thirsty you are; it is better to wait until nightfall to go down to the watering hole, to drink water then and fill your canteen for next day's journey. Those are things that our young men learn almost from childhood. It is strange that in the army of the whites the chiefs or elders don't teach you these things."

While he was talking, Tafoya had been smoothing with his hands a small pile of sand. When the sand was completely level, he buried his open hand in it and, with a swift movement, turned his wrist so that the imprint of his hand in the sand was pointing in the opposite direction from the one we had been following.

Just at that moment I spotted a small cloud of dust on the slope opposite the ravine. I looked through my spyglass and saw two riders climbing with a pair of pack mules. When they were on the point of going over the crest of the ravine, the sun struck the metal breastplate one of them wore; the other wore a leather tunic riveted with brass buttons, which also sparkled under the midday sun. I pointed my index finger in the direction of the convoy, which had just crossed the hill headed northwest.

"Hey, Tafoya! Look, those have to be the cuates. They're still wearing the armor that they used for *Los Comanches!*" I was shouting excitedly, but I noticed that the Indian barely turned his head in that direction, as if he had expected the cuates to appear at that exact spot.

"Quiet, calm down," said Tafoya, detaining me with a gesture of his hand when I made as if to rise. "It's better if they don't know we're following them."

"It's funny that the one of them is still wearing a breastplate under this blistering sun," I remarked.

"Perhaps he wants to use it as protection, although they know they're going to face an enemy more dangerous than those make-believe Comanche warriors." The Indian paused. "I imagine that if they are going to ask for help from Gil Gómez's mother, it will be for more powerful arms." He stared at me with a mysterious expression, knowing that that phrase would intrigue me. But for once I didn't take the bait. When Tafoya dropped one of those enigmatic sentences, if you asked him for an explanation immediately, he closed up like an armadillo.

Keeping a distance, we followed the trail of the cuates until they arrived, as evening approached, at the valley where Ninsaba lived. We could see people entering and leaving a hogan somewhat apart from the other cabins, from which a very dense white smoke was emanating. Tafoya told me that in that cabin a *kináalda* was taking place, the ceremony the Navajos practiced when the girls reached puberty. He did not want to enter the settlement in the middle of that ritual.

We prepared a frugal meal without building a fire so as not to draw attention, and spread our blankets under some bushes. It occurred to me that in those remote valleys, whether inhabited by Indian or Spanish people, despite poverty and the harshness of the environment, there always seemed to be fiestas and celebrations. On the other hand, if a stranger looked in the evening at the streets of a big city of the civilized world, like New York or Boston, with all their wealth and security, he would see people returning home after work with their heads down and in a somber mood, and he would think they were coming back from a funeral.

All night we heard the drums and chants of the healers, and at daybreak we saw the four novices who had participated in the ritual leave the cabin where the ceremony was taking place, dressed in robes of spotless buckskin, their faces painted white. One after the other the young maidens left running toward the east, in the direction of the rising sun, and they didn't stop until they were about a mile and a half from the settlement; then turned around and ran at full speed back to the settlement. When the novices returned from their run toward the sun, the celebrants removed from the earth oven a corncake, which they dished out first to the novices and then to the rest of those present.

Tafoya told me that this ceremony was related to the history of the origins of mankind and the struggle of the Navajo ancestors against the destructive monsters.

Running to the Sun

You will recall that First Man and First Woman had raised Changing Woman in the hope that she would help them free themselves from the monsters who were on the brink of annihilating the entire human race. But as it turned out, the lonely giant Yeitsó was the son of the Sun, and since that monster was the leader of all the devourers of men, there was absolutely nothing that could be done to control them.

Nevertheless, the Sun possessed an arrow called Zigzag Lightning Arrow, and another one called Straight Lightning Arrow, and another with the name Sunray Arrow, and another Rainbow Arrow. And it is said that First Man and First Woman were plotting precisely how to obtain those weapons, and planning how things were to occur in the future. Evidently there existed, in addition to the weapons of the Sun mentioned previously, a mace of black flint, another mace of blue flint, another one of yellow flint and another flint with a serrated edge that First Man and First Woman wanted to obtain to free themselves from the monsters.

They began to discuss the first menstruation of Changing Woman. First Man and First Woman gave her the following instructions: "As soon as you see your blood flowing, you must tell us immediately. Don't keep it to yourself!"

And so when this occurred, she said: "Mother, my period has started; Father, my period has started." Immediately the news was spread by the Talking God, who passed along instructions from First Man saying that all of the people should present themselves to sing the songs that they had been assigned. When the clan members came together on the third day, First Man gave Changing Woman these instructions: "You must run several times in the direction of the rising sun, and return here again. You must turn after each time sunwise according to tradition." That's the way he instructed her. All this was done in honor of the Sun.

Changing Woman complied with what she was told. When she had completed the third run, she returned, saying: "Take notice that a ray of sun spoke to me, telling me: 'You must know that the Sun calls you White Shell Woman.' That's what he said to me," so she related. "My dear daughter, why do you think we wanted you to run?" said the two of them, happy with the result.

"Sit down here, my daughter," said First Woman. Then she extended the buckskin of an unwounded deer adorned with white beads, another adorned with turquoise, another with concha shells, and another with jet. The woman held out four capes in total. Then she put white bead moccasins on Changing Woman, gave her white bead leggings, a white skirt with white beads, wrapped a white bead belt around her waist, adorned the fringes on her sleeves with white beads, and made wrist straps with white beads. Afterward she draped a necklace around her neck with all kinds of beads: white ones, turquoise, concha shells, and some jet. She also gave her earrings and, from her forehead toward her back, she ran her hand all along her head, smoothing her hair, thinking about everything that was going to happen next. And, giving her a feathered headdress decorated with white beads, she referred to her for the first time by that name: White Shell Woman.

Toward the east, the indigo bunting gave forth its song, toward the south the black and white bird gave forth its song, toward the west the wild canary gave forth its song, toward the north the black corn beetle gave forth its song. First Man as well as First Woman felt satisfied. "That's the way I like it! This is the sound of the groups that are approaching," said he. And just when the sun was peeking over the horizon, people started to arrive. There were many people, and they formed four lines, one behind the other.

"Listen to me. Now Changing Woman is called White Shell Woman," said First Man, "because she has dressed in white shells. Therefore, tonight you can only call her White Shell Woman," he warned. But some objected immediately, saying, "I shall call her Changing Woman." While others said, "I shall call her White Shell Woman." Also during that same occasion a pastry was baked and offered to the Sun, after which it was shared among those present.

Blessingway

When Gil Gómez and Decoy arrived at Ninsaba's ranchería, most of the adults and old people from the neighborhood were gathered around the hogan where the puberty ceremony was being celebrated, so only the dogs and some of the young boys were there to welcome the strangers. The dogs started barking at the horses, and the boys greeted the strangers with a volley of rocks that resounded as they struck the breastplate and the leather jacket that the cuates still had on.

When they went to notify Ninsaba—who was acting as godmother for one of the novices of the Kináalda—that a strapping lad wearing a breastplate had appeared in the village and that he was asking for her, she knew that her son had gotten into trouble again. She did not hide her annoyance.

"Tell me what's wrong, my son, but please make it short because I have to return immediately to take my place in the ceremony."

Gil Gómez dismounted and kept his head bowed with his eyes on the ground, the submissive attitude that he always assumed in the presence of his mother.

"My friend Decoy and I have decided to undertake the journey to the Sierra Blanca to challenge the powerful Humbaba, the keeper of the Cedar Forest."

"Are you saying that you want to go to the Sierra Blanca and fight Huwawa? If you wish to die, you need not go that far."

"My good friend and I wish to prove that together we are invincible. We wish to free the region from Humbaba's yoke. But to be able to reach that remote territory and succeed in our undertaking, we have come to ask for your blessing and for the strength that we need against the power of the enemy."

"When I was told that you were here, I already knew you had come up with some crazy idea," answered Ninsaba, without hiding her impatience. "Besides, you've caught me while I am very busy, because we're right in the middle of the Kináalda ceremony. Couldn't you come some other time?"

"We can't lose even a minute, because the chief of the American soldiers has ordered us followed since he doesn't wish us to reach the Sierra Blanca. As we were headed here, a couple of spies were on our tail."

Ninsaba's impatient expression changed upon noticing the anxiety in her son's voice. "Very well, if that's the way it is, I will attend to you right away, while the maidens are getting ready for the night ceremony; but as soon as the sun sets, I'll have to rejoin the ritual."

Ninsaba went into her cabin. First she washed her hair with an emulsion of aromatic plants. She then undressed, put on a white buckskin tunic like the ones that the novices wore when they headed for the Sun, a white bead necklace, and a headband made of white beads. Dressed and adorned in this fashion, she came out of her tent with a little bag of pollen and two small freshly cut cedar branches, which were used in the maidens' ceremony, and she headed for the high point of the promontory that overlooked the valley.

As she reached the top of a rock ledge halfway up the slope, illuminated by the oblique rays of the sun that was about to sink behind the narrow gorge, she sprinkled the pollen toward the four cardinal points and with the cedar shoots in her hands she raised them toward the sunset, while she whispered this prayer:

> *Why did you give our son*
> *Such a restless heart?*
> *Now you urge him to take*
> *The long path that will take him*
> *Up to Huwawa's dwelling.*

✠

> *So that he may face up to*
> *Such a dangerous enemy*
> *And for him to triumph in this rash undertaking,*
> *Until he reaches and returns from the Cedar Forest*
> *Until he slaughters the ferocious Huwawa,*
> *Erasing from the face of the earth*
> *That scourge of humanity,*
> *Just as the Twin Warriors*
> *Destroyed the monsters,*
> *I beg you to guide and protect,*
> *These two bold fingerlings.*

✠

> *And while they're on the road*
> *During the day and night*
> *May you commend over them the protection*
> *Of the stars and morning star*
> *Watchmen of the night and messenger of the day.*

The orange disk sent its last light to the edge of the mesa, and the woman's silhouette remained for a moment enveloped in that reddish halo. Ninsaba then descended the promontory and invited Gil Gómez and Decoy to come into her ceremonial hogan where the maidens who had participated in the puberty rite all day long were asleep, curled on top of the white buckskin that covered the floor.

Ninsaba told the cuates to undress and to sit down at one end of the hogan, and she sprinkled sacred pollen over both of them, beginning with their feet, knees, hands, chest, back, shoulders, cheeks, and lastly she spread some pollen on their tongues and the crowns of their heads.

Afterward she sprinkled their limbs with the aromatic emulsion and, with the help of two novices, rubbed their legs and forearms with some plants that oozed a sticky liquid. Then the woman tossed into the fire the cedar branches that she had offered to the Sun. They sparkled for a few moments while they burned, leaving a resin odor in the atmosphere.

Ninsaba addressed Decoy.

> *Oh powerful Cimarrón*
> *Even though you're not the child of my womb!*
> *I hereby adopt you as though I had conceived you*
> *Underneath the water,*
> *the same way as the Sun created*
> *Tobascistiní under the waterfall.*
> *And I hereby give you my blessing.*
> *The same way in which the earth welcomes the seed*
> *And these maidens welcome the germ*
> *From the man who shall impregnate them,*
> *On behalf of these novices who tomorrow*
> *Shall run toward the Sun,*

> *I beg you to assist and welcome*
> *My son into your strong arms.*

> *And that you may guide my son*
> *Down a sure road*
> *And for you to take him through the deep*
> *Ravines and narrow pathways.*

She approached Decoy and put her arms around his shoulders and neck, while the two novices who had assisted her rubbed his body with the sap from the sticky plants to give him strength and resistance during his trip.

At that moment, from outside the hogan they could hear the voice of a man singing.

Here I start walking!
I am the son of Changing Woman and go on walking.
I am the son of Sun whenever I take off walking,
Beyond the Mountain of Dawn I go on walking!
Beyond the mountain range of a long life I go on walking
Beyond the frontier of happiness I go on walking.
The Sun is watching me walk and he sees one of my footsteps;
I walk down the Path of Beauty, and he sees all of my
footsteps.

Hearing this chant, Ninsaba stood up as though propelled by an invisible spring and addressed the cuates. "The moment has come for you to leave, because the sun has set and we must proceed with the Kináalda ceremony. I have already given you my blessing and you may be on your way."

But Gil Gómez was not ready to leave. He replied, "I remember that when the young warriors from the tribe were going into enemy territory for the first time, an old man with war experience would give them his advice and recite a prayer over them, and he even made them follow a ritual that enabled them to combat the power of the enemy."

"Yes, I know, but unfortunately, there's no time for that. You always come at the worst possible moment with some urgent problem, so I can't help you the way I would like. The ritual you want requires some time to prepare, and as you can see we're already celebrating another ceremony. We can't be in two places at once!"

"If it can't be done here, tell me where I must go, since I don't want to start this long journey without the teachings and prayers of an instructor."

"How do you expect me to know where you must go? We would have to speak with an old man from the tribe, and they're all busy with the maidens' puberty ceremony."

Gil Gómez remained silent, but in the expression of his eyes one could read his anxiety and dismay. Finally his mother said, "Don't look at me with that pathetic expression! I shall look for a singer who can recite a war chant over both of you and give you the advice you need to survive in enemy territory. The day after tomorrow at dusk we shall meet near the Ojo del Oso, and I shall lead you to a place where you will find what you've been looking for. But now you must leave here. The novices are beginning to wake up, and we must prepare them for the night ritual and for their run toward the Sun."

On the Trail of Gil Gómez

While Tafoya was telling me the origin of the girl's puberty ceremony, the wind from the valley brought the aroma of the corncake made in honor of the girls who were becoming women. That smell whetted our appetites so much that it wasn't difficult to convince the Indian that the time had come to forget our anonymity and participate in the banquet.

We weren't the only strangers attending the celebration, and we mingled with the other visitors extending their hands toward the women who handed out the freshly baked cake. It tasted divine, especially after our frugal supper the night before, which had consisted of a few handfuls of jerky and a piece of moldy biscuit.

I thought it was strange that the Navajos didn't seem bothered by our presence, considering that their ranchería was so isolated in the mountains and too far away from any military post to be visited often by soldiers. And the presence of Tafoya couldn't go unnoticed, since his ordnance Springfield rifle and his cartridge belt with ammunition and the buckle of the dragoon corps identified him clearly as an Indian auxiliary; in other words, as a renegade who served the American army against his own people. But the only notice of us was taken by some of the young warriors, who were glancing at us out of the corners of their eyes.

It was well known that Indians could change their behavior according to the occasion. A person whom they ordinarily considered an enemy, in certain other situations might be treated with respect and even friendliness. I had noticed this peculiar behavior when I was serving in the northern garrisons and had gone down to the Indian pueblo of Taos, where they celebrated annually a fair that was known as a rendezvous of mountain trappers, Indians of different tribes, and Spanish peones and villagers. There they traded all kinds of articles, from hides, firearms, brandy—the famous Taos Lightning—to human beings, mostly captive women and children whom the Apaches, Utes, and Comanches came to sell.

In Taos you could see how the chiefs of rival and archenemy tribes, who would have tried to lift each other's scalp if they found one another in the wilderness, here treated each other with deference and exquisite urbanity while they bartered arms that might be used a few days later to cut their enemies' throats. This was the case as long as their behavior was not altered by the demon called alcohol, which both Indians and whites abused without limit during the fair. When people had been drinking, the opposite could happen: blood brothers and members of the same tribe or clan might rip open each others' bellies for a trifle, and that peaceful rendezvous turned into a true battleground.

In any case, at Ninsaba's ranchería that day a hospitable and cosmopolitan ambience prevailed—which didn't rule out the possibility that some of those young warriors who looked askance at us might not already be plotting to steal our arms and horses. Everything was fine until it occurred to me to ask one of the old men who spoke Spanish if they had by any chance seen Gil Gómez, the son of Ninsaba, pass that way. Immediately I felt a wall of reserve rise between us, and the penetrating look of Tafoya bored into me for my imprudence. The Navajos, who one minute before had been chatting and laughing with us, clammed up, answering our questions evasively if at all. And little by little the people moved away from us, as if we were infected with the plague.

Before the situation deteriorated even further, we decided it would be better to make a strategic retreat, which we did without drawing attention to ourselves, taking advantage of the confusion of the fiesta. We tried in vain to find the track of the cuates' horses. Since part of the gully that surrounded the settlement was of basalt rock, scarcely any sign would be left even by a whole cavalry regiment. So Tafoya started back up San Mateo Mountain, following his instinct again since we hadn't the least indication of where the two elusive travelers were headed.

When we reached the top, we were able to behold the panorama that spread out to the other side of the valley. To the north was Chivato Mesa, which opened into deep potreros in the shape of a fan; to the west extended the San José River basin whose meanders marked the western plains like the iron brand on the rump of a young bull; and almost at our feet erupted a flow of volcanic rock that went down to the southwest, forming the stony and fragmented layer that the Spanish called el malpaís.

Pointing to the wide bed of solidified lava, Tafoya said, "That is the trail of blood that the giant Yeitsó shed after being defeated by the Twin Warriors. When the younger brother cut off his head, that black flow began to go down the mountain, but a spy called Big Bottlefly warned them that if the giant's blood reached the Ojo de Oso, the monster would come back to life. Then the older brother started running down the slope and with his flint axe cut a deep ravine to stop the flow. That is the rocky outcrop you are seeing."

Along the sides of the lava trail, rocky outcrops stuck out crosswise;

They did seem to have served as retaining walls against the flow. We stopped on the way behind a spur of basaltic rock so the horses could rest and we could protect ourselves from the icy wind that was coming down from the top of the mountain.

"Where do you think the cuates are headed now?" I asked Tafoya, who took advantage of the pause to light a cigar, throwing the blanket over his head to protect himself from the wind. "Now that they have already obtained the power against the enemy, they can go directly to the Sierra Blanca, unless they first want to pass by El Morro rock, as some villagers in Cabezón said."

Tafoya shook his head and stared at me with an expression of perplexity that in this case was not feigned. "I'm not so sure that the cuates have gotten from Ninsaba all that they wanted. Because the old ones were at the Kináalda ceremony they couldn't sing the war ritual for them, because the two ceremonies are very distinct, and are not even recited by the same singers. Gil Gómez may have left the settlement without having obtained the power or the weapons he will need to confront his enemy."

"What weapons are you referring to? The cuates have two mules loaded with weapons and provisions—a veritable arsenal!"

"Those weapons will not be good enough to confront the powers of Huwawa. If they wish to succeed, they need more powerful arms."

"Like those that the Sun loaned the Twin Warriors to combat the giant of the San Mateo Mountain? The Zigzag Lightning Arrow, the Straight Lightning Arrow, the Sunray Arrow, and the Rainbow Arrow . . ."

"I see that you don't forget the things I tell you. If you were a young Navajo, you could become a singer, since the most important thing to be a good singer is to remember exactly all the stories that correspond to each ritual. From the time they are very young, the singer apprentices usually start learning with a veteran chanter the way in which the stories are told, which pass orally from generation to generation."

"You still haven't told me in detail the episode of the battle of the Twin Warriors against the giant Yeitsó."

"I've already forgotten which episodes I have told you and which I have not, but if you close your eyes, you will be able to imagine how this land was; but hundreds, thousands of years ago, at the beginning of time. Imagine how this slope would be without the lava bed, and a little lower down, halfway down the hillside, imagine the lake where the giant Yeitsó used to drink."

The San Mateo Mountain Combat

It happened right after the Twin Warriors had been in the home of their father, after having finished a long journey filled with obstacles and dangers, and after having received from their father the weapons they needed in order to confront their gigantic rival. Their Father, the Sun, had given them his powerful weapons, knowing that they would use them against Yeitsó. But before they left he warned them that the giant was also his son, and this is why they should let him shoot his arrows first, and when the moment arrived to kill the monster, he himself, the Sun, would be in charge of delivering the first mortal blow.

When the twins arrived at Tsótsil (San Mateo Mountain), they met in a cave in the mountain several of the Sacred Beings, who told them that the giant usually went down from the top of the mountain to a small lake called Tósato. When he knelt down on the shore to drink, one of his hands rested on top of the mountain, the other leaned on a high hill on the other side of the valley, while his feet were stretched out as far as the distance that a man can walk between dawn and midday.

The twins soon heard the sound of powerful footsteps and saw the giant's head peek over a hill toward the east. He disappeared immediately. A short while later, the monster stuck his head and chest out over a hill toward the south, and he stayed somewhat longer than when he leaned out from the east. Later he showed his body to the waist over a hill toward the west, and finally he showed himself to the knees, over Tsótsil toward the north. Then he came down from the mountain, arrived at the edge of the lake, and deposited there a basket, which he usually carried with him.

Without noticing that he was being observed, the giant knelt and immediately began to drink, making a great deal of noise while sucking up the water (k-ol, k-ol, k-ol, is the way it sounded), and the level of the lake began to drop. He raised his head again and then buried it in the water again. The twins had been struck dumb when they saw the size and strength of the giant, and they didn't do anything until a messenger from the gods, the Bottlefly, whispered in their ears: "Move forward so the giant can see you." And the two came out of a black cloud where they had been hidden and neared the same lake's edge, right in the open, until Yeitsó could see their reflection in the water.

For a moment the giant didn't react, thinking that what he was seeing was a shadow in the bottom of the lake. But upon raising his head he saw the twins were standing at the edge of the water and in his turn he rose. "Well, what a pretty thing comes walking around here! I ask myself, Where can I have been hunting?"

Then the younger brother said to the older, "Answer him immediately in the same manner, make him eat his words!" And the older one answered right away, "Well now, what huge thing is crawling around here! I ask myself, Where can I have been hunting?" When the monster heard that answer, he ground his teeth, indignant. "Oh, little round eyes! Oh, little round eyes!" he repeated again and again, unable to control his indignation.

The three rivals exchanged challenges simultaneously, repeating the same words four times, and on the fourth, the twins heard the Bottlefly whisper in their ears, "Aké! Aké! Beware! He is already aiming at you, and you will have to be ready to duck when he shoots." He had barely finished saying it when a shining war club whistled past their heads. With the speed of a lightning bolt, the giant threw four incandescent projectiles at the twins, but the twins dodged the weapons, jumping on a magic feather that Spider Woman had given them during their journey to the Sun. When the incandescent mace passed beneath their feet, twirling vertiginously, it flattened plants and rocks in its path, leaving a barren firebreak behind. When it passed over their heads, it disappeared in the clouds with a terrible bang, similar to thunder. And after throwing the fourth projectile, the giant was left without weapons and at their mercy.

"Remember that our father said he would be the first to act against the giant," the older brother said to the younger one. At that moment a dark cloud whirled about in the center of the sky, with a tumultuous roar. Heavy drops of water began to fall, splashing everywhere, and a zigzagging bolt of lightning burst out of the sky. For a few seconds the giant was illuminated by the lightning. Soon the twins could hear the rattle of the flakes of flint that formed his armor. Another bolt of lightning struck the immense body of Yeitsó, enveloping it in a bright halo, and the flakes of flint vibrated harder. A third and fourth bolt struck the giant, shaking the flint of his armor; and when the shiny shield dissipated, the flint armor was also gone, leaving him unprotected.

"Let's go now; it's your turn! What are you waiting for?" It was the voice of the Bottlefly, whispering in the ears of the twins. "Point at the soles of his feet!" The older one then shot his zigzag arrow with the bow he had received from the Sun, and the giant felt the impact and staggered to the east, but managed to stay on his feet. Then he shot his straight incandescent arrow aiming at the waist; the giant received the impact again twisting to the south and this time almost fell to his knees, but not completely. He shot another zigzag arrow to the small of the back, and this time the giant fell on his knees to the west but got up again. At the fourth arrow the twin shot, aiming at the nape of the neck, the giant fell to the north, tried to get up again, fell again with his face on the ground, stretched out his arms and legs, and did not move any more.

The twins then approached the fallen enemy, and the younger one scalped him. Until then the younger had been called Born from the Waters (Tobadzístsíni), but from that moment on, his brother called him Naidikísi (The One Who Cuts Around). Also after that the older brother was called Nayénézgani (Slayer of Alien Monsters).

Afterward they cut off the giant's head and threw it down the other side of the mountain, and it rolled east to the bottom of the valley. But then the blood of the monster began to pour out in torrents, forming a spring so powerful that it spilled over the Tósato Lake and broke the rock barrier that held it back, and began to run down the mountain in two cascades of thick liquid running parallel to each other.

"What are you thinking now?" whispered the Bottlefly in the ears of the twins. "Don't you see that if those two torrents meet the monster will come back to life? You must mark a line between them!" The older one rushed then and marked a zigzag line with his stone machete, dividing the two blood flows; the younger also ran down and marked a straight line with his flint mace, parting the two rivers. Between the two they had formed a deep ditch where the blood flow was contained. Then the liquid coagulated rapidly and the blood turned into petrified lava.

They say that then the earth trembled and the sky rumbled, and only when those quakes faded away did the giant's body stop moving. The twins went to look for their weapons and the scalp, and put them in the basket that the giant carried, to take them as trophies. The vapors of the monster's blood were too strong for them, and they became dizzy and began to stagger. They clung to each other's hands then so as not to fall and together came to a cedar bush, under which they crawled. And tearing some cedar branches, they sucked some buds, and breathing the aroma of the resin they recovered their strength and set off with the spoils of the giant to the dwelling of their mother.

Book Five

Friend, who is capable of scaling heaven?

Only the gods live in perpetuity under the sun,

    but for us mortals our days are numbered,

    and our accomplishments are like a puff of wind.

How can you possibly fear death,

    and what about your great strength?

Let me walk ahead of you and listen to your voice say:

"Go on, go on, do not be afraid of anything!"

And if I failed, at least I will have

    made a name for myself,

    and people would then say:

"Gilgamesh went to fight Huwawa and perished."

Then they'll recall the son my mother gave birth to.

POEM OF GILGAMESH
Tablet II, Column vi

The Teachings of Narbona

Upon arriving at Ojo del Oso, which was a dry gully between two walls of volcanic rock, the cuates unsaddled their horses and hid themselves among the palo verde bushes, waiting for Ninsaba to show up for the rendezvous they had agreed upon. As the sun set they heard the hooves of two horses in the sandy ravine, but since shreds of mist were floating at the bottom, they couldn't recognize the riders, and Gil Gómez waited in the bushes with his pistol cocked.

"Wait, don't shoot! It's Ninsaba! The last thing you need to do is kill your poor mother after all the trouble I've had getting here!" As she came close, Gil Gómez recognized his mother's silhouette, and saw that the other horse she had behind her was without a rider.

"Mother, you scared me! For a moment I thought you were a pair of American soldiers who have been following our trail from Cabezón!" said the genízaro, as he eased up on the hammer.

"If you don't want to be caught unaware, you shouldn't leave such clear tracks on the sandy ravine," answered Ninsaba, dismounting. "That's what the white soldiers do, not a Navajo warrior on the enemy way."

After drinking a swallow of water from the canteen that Gil Gómez offered her, Ninsaba remounted and told the cuates to follow her. All night they rode through the maze of that mountain wilderness behind the woman, who oriented herself by following the position of the stars. With the first signs of daylight, Gil Gómez noticed that they had crossed the San Mateo Mountains and were entering the San José River valley.

A dense mantle of fog prolonged the darkness, but they could already hear ducks and other birds stirring about in the cane thicket near the river. The sun was going to rise soon over the mountains, and the milky clarity of dawn already projected the shadows of the horses and their riders over the mist.

When he looked back into the shadows, Gil Gómez suddenly realized that there was one more rider at the rear of the retinue, riding the spare horse that Ninsaba had brought with her the night before. The genízaro doubled back beside his mother's pony. "Who is that man and where has he come from?" he whispered in Ninsaba's ear without trying to hide his surprise.

"This is the singer who will perform the Enemyway ritual for you. Why did you think I brought a spare horse?"

"He looks very old and his tunic and bonnet are worn out. Why haven't I noticed him until now?"

"Well, he's been with us since we left Ojo del Oso. Don't you recognize him? It's grandfather Narbona, the one who used to make bows for you and who taught you how to hunt birds when you were a child."

Gil Gómez recalled that the old man Narbona had disappeared during one of the first skirmishes between the Navajos and the white soldiers, when the American army tried to enter Navajo Territory. He was almost positive that the man had been given up for dead, but the memories from his childhood were very vague, and they became confused in his mind with the legends about his tribe that he had heard when he was part of Don Antonio Gil's household.

When sunlight reached the bottom of the ravine, Gil Gómez began to watch the old man out of the corner of his eye. Narbona rode staring off into the distance; his pupils were covered with a veil as dense as the fog covering the canebrake. From his wrinkled neck hung a necklace with an oversized solid turquoise, the type that only the most important natanes wore; the cut of his buckskin pants and the shape of his moccasins were old-fashioned. His thick leather robe was also the type worn by Navajo warriors of old to protect themselves from enemy arrows.

Ninsaba continued riding until she found an appropriate place to dismount and make the necessary introductions, beside a pool of clear water in the shade of a stone monolith.

"Gil Gómez, this is Chief Narbona. Many things have happened since you last saw him."

The old man dismounted without looking at the ground and sized up his footing with the staff that he was carrying in his hand, confirming Gil Gómez's impression that Narbona was blind. Once he had regained his balance with the help of his cane, the natán walked on the rocky arroyo with the firm stride of a much younger man, and he approached the genízaro with his arms extended. The bony hands of the old-timer first grabbed him by the shoulders, next they touched his chest, still covered with the brass breastplate, and finally they touched his face, pausing for a few moments as the old man felt the severed earlobe, the mark of servitude.

"Many moons have passed since I used to make you a bow of mountain cedar so that you could go out and hunt rabbits and birds, and since the white thieves stole you, you have lived many years away from the dinéh," said the old man. "I have been told that you now want to make an expedition to the Sierra Blanca, and you need to have a prayer sung over you that will offer protection to travel in enemy territory."

"That's how it is, Chief Narbona. My friend Decoy and I want to reach the heart of the mountain range, where no one has been before, and challenge the powerful Humbaba, the guardian of the Cedar Forest."

As he felt the armor's metal, the old man's knuckles tapped on the brass breastplate, which produced a hollow sound. "You can begin by taking off that armor, because the enemy you're going to face will pierce that plate with his darts as if it were a dry pumpkin," said the old man. "I hope that you will be able to obtain more powerful weapons to defend yourself against him."

"Grandfather, I also want you to extend your protection to my friend Decoy, who will be my companion on this journey."

The old man stretched his hands toward the genízaro's companion, going over his strong limbs with his bony fingers and embracing with his thin arms the perimeter of his broad chest.

"Another well-fed young bull!" proclaimed Narbona. "You have a neck as strong as a wild horse, and I can barely close my hands around your forearm, but I am not sure that underneath those strong muscles there's a steel soul capable of withstanding fatigue and deprivation."

The old man shook his head disapprovingly and pointed at the cuates with the tip of his cane. "Before I can recite my prayers over you, you will have to cleanse your bodies and burn the fat that you have accumulated eating too much lamb and drinking the white man's strong liquors. Take notice that it is one thing to sack a ranchería of peaceful Indians and to take a few women captive; it is quite another to enter the Sierra Blanca and challenge the keeper of the Cedar Forest in his sanctuary."

"We are prepared to do what you tell us to obtain the power necessary to defeat our enemy."

"Well, to begin with, you're going to take off running to the bottom of this ravine and return running, without stopping. Let's see if we can turn the fat into muscles of iron! But before that I want you to take off that breastplate and that leather jacket and also your moccasins. You have to learn to run barefoot to go light like the wind."

Naked and shoeless, the cuates took off running through the rocky riverbed to the bottom of the ravine, at times stepping on a sharp-edged rock or a thistle that made them swear.

Meanwhile, Narbona sat down in the shade of the stone monolith and was singing this song:

My son, you must run.
You were born to destroy the wicked monsters.
My son, you must run.
You have black flint shoes, you must run.
You have black flint leggings, you must run.
You have a black flint breastplate, you must run.
You have a black flint heart inside of you, you must run.
My son, you must run.

When the cuates returned breathless, their bodies covered with dust and sweat, he took them to the edge of the pond filled with the icy spring waters coming from the edge of the cliff. Since the pool fell to the north of the rock, where the sun didn't reach, the puddle was still covered with a thin layer of ice.

"What are you waiting for?" asked the old man, and pointing to the pool with his staff, he commanded, "Jump!"

The cuates jumped without thinking twice, breaking the ice, and splashed in the cold pool until their teeth started chattering. When they could barely feel their extremities, the old man let them come out and shake their limbs like wet puppies. But as soon as they had rested for a few minutes, Narbona ordered them to take a mouthful of water and, without spitting it out, to run again to the bottom of the ravine and back without stopping until they reached the stone monolith. "That's how you'll learn to breathe through your nose while running, and you'll increase the capacity of your lungs; when the enemy comes behind you, you won't have time to catch your breath," said Narbona.

At last, when they got back to the monolith, the old man allowed them to spit out the water and lie down on a small sandy beach, where they dried themselves by rolling in the dirt.

While the twins did these exercises, Ninsaba prepared breakfast in a clay pot near the bonfire; upon smelling the lamb stew, the cuates seemed to revive, and as they got close they looked at the bubbling pot with greedy eyes.

"You need not eat a lot while you're on a trip; remember that on a full stomach one thinks poorly and runs worse," Narbona warned them. "You will be able to eat till you're stuffed when you return to your village with the spoils of the enemy and celebrate your victory."

While they listened attentively to the advice of their mentor, the cuates' mouths were watering, since they had gone almost two days without eating. Decoy especially felt a great emptiness in his stomach, because he needed an abundant amount of food to feed his husky body.

Narbona looked at him. "This stocky young man must follow a very strict discipline," he said. "I have heard that they call him Decoy, but that is wrong, since his name must be Dikohé, which is what the Apaches call the war novice who is preparing himself to go out into enemy territory. In his first excursion, Dikohé has to respect several special rules: you cannot eat the food while it's still warm; rather, you have to wait till it gets cold because otherwise your teeth might fall out. You also cannot eat the delicate parts of an animal, such as the head and the entrails; instead, you must select the toughest and most rubbery, such as the meat from the neck."

Barely able to control his hunger, the novice had to wait until the food cooled down before coming close to the cooking pot and beginning to chew the toughest spoils. Meanwhile Gil Gómez ate to his heart's content, pulling a mocking face at Decoy.

When he had finished eating the leftovers and was going to get a drink from the spring, Narbona called Dikohé over and showed him two objects that he had in his hand, tied by a cord: one was a hollow cane tube about three inches long and a half inch in diameter and the other a piece of cedar wood approximately the same size, whose tip had the shape of a horse's hoof.

"Dikohé, this is a tube for drinking and this other one a stick to scratch yourself with," said the old man. "While your journey in enemy territory lasts, be careful not to scratch yourself with your fingernails, because that would soften your skin tissue and weaken your muscles: always use this scratcher. Also, as you drink, don't let the water touch your lips, because your mustache will grow excessively long and your life will be shortened. Always use this cane to drink with."

The utensils were tied together with a long leather cord that Narbona draped around the novice's neck. They had different marks carved by a knife along the length of the wood. One looked like an hourglass and the other a taut bow with an arrow.

Decoy was going to ask the old man what the symbols meant, but at that moment Ninsaba approached to help the old man mount his horse, interlacing her hands to make a stirrup. The natán sat up straight in the saddle and as he dug his heels into the colt's flanks, he told his pupil, "While we are on the road I'll be explaining other things that you must know; now we have to ride again, because we still have a long way to go."

The Apache War Language

They continued riding along the San José River, which in certain places opened out into a marshland where the horses sank up to their hocks. Narbona told Decoy to go in front so he could continue teaching him what he must do and what he must avoid as a novice on a war expedition.

"Dikohé, while you are riding in enemy territory, try always to be looking toward the points of the ears of the steed; try not to look toward the horse's hooves, nor backwards nor to the sides, because that draws the enemy to you. If you have to look back, you must not turn suddenly; rather, look first over your right shoulder and then slowly turn your head sunwise. And avoid, by all means, lifting your eyes toward the sky, because you could unleash a heavy cloudburst or even a storm with lightning and thunder."

Decoy listened silently to all those instructions, and tried to memorize them, while Gil Gómez, who was also listening from behind, could hardly hold back his mocking smile.

"While you are on a war expedition it is very important that you always behave well, because as a novice you must set an example for the other members of the group. You must not laugh your head off, no matter how funny the situation might be, Dikohé, because you would lose the power of concentration necessary to fight. Never make fun of someone, and be respectful to women; avoid saying any obscenities in front of them. For sure, and your friend should hear this also . . ." the old man called the genízaro to come near and then proceeded. "Listen to this, Gil Gómez. I was telling Dikohé that you must be respectful to females. While you are in enemy territory, you cannot have sexual relations with any woman; don't even think about going near a female either on the way out or on your way back, because sexual intercourse would weaken your body and contaminate your soul. According to what they've told me, so far you have wasted your energy more in binges and brothel brawls than on proper fights, but from now on you will have to be chaste and disciplined."

Upon arriving at the junction of the San José and San Juan rivers, Ninsaba headed in the direction of the Colorado Mountains. When Decoy saw that they were leaving the bed of the arroyo, he asked the old man for permission to drink. "Grandfather, I am thirsty and I would like to go fill my canteen before we move away from the water."

"Very well, Dikohé, you can dismount, but before you drink I want to explain something important to you. The dinéh, as well as our cousins the Apaches, use a special language when we go on the warpath: we call it *warpath language* or *not talking plainly,* because one must say things in a different way when one is on the warpath. As you cross Apache territory, I believe that it will give you more strength against the enemy if you use the war language of the Apache, which is what I am going to teach you now."

The cuates had drawn near Narbona and listened attentively. Directing himself to Decoy, he began. "Dikohé, when an Apache is in enemy territory he doesn't say *I want to drink water,* as you have just said; rather, *I begin to swim the specular iron ore.* Because in the altered language a river is known as *a rope-like object of specular iron ore lies.* Do you understand?"

They continued riding toward the west, while the old man taught them the war language of the Apaches: a horse was *that which has its nose to the ground;* a saddle *that which prevents the horse from being hurt.* The heart was called *that by means of which one lives;* the pollen that was sprinkled in the ceremonies *that which is becoming life;* an eagle or a crow was *he who spreads his wings* and an owl, *he who wanders about at night.* The fire was *that which tells a story* and the blanket *that by means of which one becomes warm.*

"Although at first this way of talking may seem strange to you, most of the expressions are easy to memorize." And when he saw the cuates' bewildered expressions, he added, "You must remember to use these expressions when dangerous situations arise, which is when they are most difficult to recall. For example, if you encounter the tracks of the enemy you don't say *These are the tracks of the enemy!* but instead, *The enemy's horses have been here.* But you must only use that language when you find yourselves in enemy territory: if you use these expressions while you're in your own territory, you could draw the attack of the enemy even in your own land."

By evening they reached the foothills of the Colorado Mountains, and they came through a deep canyon from which arroyos forked off in different directions, like a labyrinth. Ninsaba moved with ease through the maze, and soon they arrived at a narrow canyon at whose bottom ran a spring. At the edge of the stream grew abundant grass, and when he sensed the freshness of the potrero Narbona removed the bridle from his steed, jumped down to the ground, and set off walking without the help of his stick.

Giving the reins to Decoy to loosen the cinch and lead the horse to water, the old man headed toward a point of the canyon where there was a deep crevice in the rock wall; groping the wall of the canyon with his hand until he found the opening, the old man entered the cave and came out again in a moment with a bunch of dry branches and utensils to build a fire. Turning a round stick on a piece of wood with a hole, he got a spark, lit the firewood, and soon had a fire reddening the walls of the gorge.

Afterward the old man had Decoy prepare the camp and lay out the blankets for sleeping, warning him that, in his role as novice, he must be the last to go to bed in order to be available for any service or task. From a bag he had stored in the back of the cave Narbona took out several handfuls of dry yucca, wild seeds, and a few balls of jerked deer meat crushed and mixed with fat, which he distributed among Ninsaba and the cuates. He gave very little to the boys, telling them, "A warrior with a belly too full can hardly move and cannot fight with proper agility. If in the middle of a journey you feel hungry, all you have to do is to tighten your belt. When you have worn out your moccasins, don't throw them away. Put them on your stomach when you lie down to rest; they say that's a remedy for your hunger pangs. Remember that if you wish to succeed in your adventure, you have to be ready to endure privation. And to prepare yourself mentally, I want you to repeat this invocation with me." And he made them stand up and answer these questions: "Are you strong in body and soul and prepared to suffer hunger and cold?"

"Yes, we are!"

"Do you know you can go sometimes five or six night without sleeping?"

"Yes, we know it!"

"Do you feel prepared to follow the path of the enemy day and night?"

"We are prepared!"

"Will you be capable of not missing your land when you are in enemy territory and not trembling with fear when the hour of combat nears?"

"Yes, we are capable!"

The cuates responded in unison to the old warrior's questions, and their bare chests throbbed with the force of their invocation. The mentor finally permitted them to go to bed and rest, but seeing that they fell face up on their blankets with their bodies and limbs stretched out, he told them, "Try not to sleep on your stomach or back; rest on your side. That way, it will be easier to sleep without spreading out your arms and legs, but with them tucked in. If your limbs are stretched out, you can attract the enemy."

He also advised them, "While you are in enemy territory, you must have your weapons where you can grab them. You always have your knife and your bow right beside you. Don't spend much time resting or sleeping:

always be alert. And always sleep with your moccasins right beside you, in case you have to leave running. Watch for the morning star; don't let it get up before you."

As an answer, the old man heard the deep breathing of the cuates, who had fallen asleep while he was talking.

"Rest, rest, for tomorrow the day will be harder than today. I won't sing the ritual of The Two Go To the Father until you are physically and spiritually ready for it."

Where the Gods Come and Go

The following day Narbona awakened the cuates before dawn and gave them instructions on preparing the sweat lodge so they could purify their bodies before the ceremony that would give them the necessary strength to enter enemy territory. He told them to look for firewood for the sweathouse, but not just any kind of wood; they must take the wood from a tree trunk struck by lightning. Also, the stones that would be used in the fire to heat the sweat lodge couldn't be ordinary stones, but rather rocks that had been displaced by the foot of a bear or mossy rocks with the outline of a snake.

After much walking around, the cuates found on the north slope of the canyon the trunk of a pine with the bark scorched by lightning, and going toward the head of the arroyo, they found heavy stones that had recently been displaced by some large animal. Some of the rocks had on their lower part a zigzag outline, like the back of a rattlesnake.

When the novices returned loaded with the firewood and the stones, the natán gave Gil Gómez instructions to build the sweat hut against the canyon wall with cedar branches and chamisa. When they had made a hut out of the branches, they covered it with several blankets so that the heat wouldn't escape. Inside they placed the hot stones, which had been under the coals of the fire. The old man ordered the cuates to undress and stay in the hut until he summoned them. They obeyed without a word.

While the novices were in the sweat lodge, Narbona called Ninsaba to accompany him inside the cave where they would perform the initiation ceremony. The grotto had the necessary features: the entrance faced east, it had an oval interior, and in the rock ceiling there was a hole through which the smoke from the fire could escape, as in the ceremonial hogans that were used for these purposes in the Navajo rancherías.

Sitting down on the white sand that covered the floor of the cave,

Narbona began to remove from a purse made from the skin of a young deer other smaller leather bags, placing them in a pair of willow baskets that Ninsaba had set at his feet. With special care, the old man took out a small leather bag decorated with tiny mother-of-pearl shells, in which he carried sand from the Four Sacred Mountains.

While the woman finished preparing the ritual objects, Narbona called the cuates out of the sweat lodge. Gil Gómez and Decoy came out of the hut dripping sweat and stumbling, dizzy from the intense heat that had accumulated inside, but the old man didn't let them rest. He asked them to show him the firearms they had brought. After examining with his calloused hands the butts and barrels of the weapons, he put them aside with a scornful expression, exclaiming, "The powers against which you have to fight are not vulnerable to powder or bullets. These weapons will be useless against the guardian of the Cedar Forest, because he is protected by seven shining layers that not even a cannon ball can pierce; using those weapons you will only succeed in scaring away the protection of the Sacred Beings, and we call them *that which discharges wind.* But if you use a bow and the appropriate arrows, the Supreme Wind will make your arrows fly to the heart of your enemy. I recommend that you make a good bow of mountain cedar with a bowstring from deer tendon."

Narbona sent the cuates to the mountain to find some cedar for a bow, telling them to leave some leaves on the ends of the branches, the way they were left on the first bow that Changing Woman gave to the older of the Twin Warriors. The old man chose the branch that seemed most appropriate and shaved the bark from the middle part with a bone scraper. He gave it the required curvature, passing it through the embers of the fire, and took a bowstring of deer tendon out of the buckskin bag.

"They say that at the beginning of time, when the maidens abused their bodies with various objects, among them was a deer thigh, including its tendon. Let's hope that this tendon can help you vanquish the guardian of the Cedar Forest, who has powers similar to those of the first monsters!"

When the cuates asked what arrows they would shoot, the old man remained silent a moment, and then said, "It isn't up to me to give you the arrows to fight your enemy; farther ahead, along the way, you will meet someone stronger than I whom you can ask for the arrows you will need for your battle. Remember that in the war language, for *bow* you say *that which is good for one* and arrows are known as *those with which one throws first.*"

After leaving the cuates to get their weapons ready, Narbona went back to the cave to make the final preparations for the ceremony. The ritual song that Narbona would sing over the cuates would be the one called The Two Go To The Father. It would begin at sunset, would last three nights and two days, and would include the creation of a sand painting that would be erased at dawn on the third day. The symbolic design and the bright colors of the painting would be like a lure for the Sacred Beings, who would be attracted by their own portraits in the sand painting as if they were looking in a mirror and would hence transmit their powers and blessing to the cuates through the singer of the ceremony. This is why sand paintings in Navajo are called *iikááh*, which means *where the gods come and go*.

Before initiating the ritual, the old man began placing on the ground, around the patch of smooth white sand, the abalone shells where he arranged the mineral and vegetable pigments that would be used to color the design that would invite the gods to that place. Yellow, white, and red were obtained by pulverizing colored rocks. Black was obtained by mixing charcoal with red pigment and sand, to give it consistency. Blue was made mixing white sand and charcoal.

Ninsaba had prepared other plant pigments in little vessels of bark from the wild olive tree. She had gathered sagebrush pollen and seeds from bushes of diverse colors, and she had mixed petals of crushed dried flowers with sacred cornmeal that she carried in a small bag.

When all the colors were ready, Narbona directed Ninsaba while she drew the forms and lines of the dry painting, keeping the pigments between her index and middle fingers, letting the colors flow delicately on the sand, guiding them with the thumb, sunwise. Although he couldn't see, the old man indicated to his assistant the dimension that the design must have and the exact proportion of the pigments to obtain the appropriate mix in each color. Soon the sand painting began taking shape.

Two elongated figures, the warriors, were framed with an outline of the Rainbow, the divinity protecting the dry painting. Their feet rested on the skin of a buffalo, symbol of strength and bravery, and both were covered in flint armor from head to foot. One of the suits of armor was of black flint and the other blue flint. In the right hand the warriors carried a bow and lightning arrows, and in the left, one brandished a hatchet and the other a flint machete. Lightning also came out of the palms of the hands and the joints of the arms and legs. And both wore flint caps and gaiters. These were the Twin Warriors: the older, Nayénézgani (Slayer of Alien Monsters), was the one in black armor; the younger, Tobadzístsíni (Born From the

Waters), the one in blue armor.

When the painting was finished, and the sun had set behind the walls of the ravine, the cuates were allowed to go inside the cave. They walked on a path of dry flowers and pollen that led to a platform on which they set a basket of tarred willow full of soapy water. The singer, who had put on a cap of owl feathers and a collar with amulets, sprinkled the novices with a spray of medicinal plants and soapsuds made with yucca plant. Narbona dried their bodies with sacred cornmeal and, putting saliva on his hands, began pressing his palms on parts of the sacred painting and applying the sand that stuck to his hands to the same parts of the novices' bodies; this way the power of the twin warriors would be transferred to the cuates. Thereafter he made the novices sit on the figures painted in the sand, Gil Gómez on that of Nayénézgani and Decoy on that of Tobadzístsíni, both with their feet facing the entrance of the cave, toward the east.

The ceremony lasted all that night and the following day, and after a brief rest they began again on nightfall of the second day, when Narbona painted snakes on the chests of the cuates to give them the lethal power of the reptile and bear claws on their forearms so that they might have the bravery of the bear. Later he tied a small bunch of eagle feathers to a lock on each of their foreheads, and on the crowns of their heads he put pieces of turquoise, which would give power and determination to their thoughts.

And lastly, he gave to each one a small bag with earth from the Four Sacred Mountains.

The Cuates Go to the Father

On the beginning of the third day, just when the first ray of the sun was breaking over the ridge of the ravine, Narbona took the cuates out of the cave to breathe the fresh dawn air. And he made them take a few steps, still unsteady because of the long fast and the vigil, toward the brightness that was filling the valley, while he sang this song:

> *I walk out.*
> *I am the child of Changing Woman as I walk out.*
> *I am the child of the Sun as I walk out.*
> *Beyond the range of Dawn Mountain I walk out.*
> *Beyond the range of long life I walk out,*
> *Beyond the range of happiness I walk out.*

With that chant and the breathing of the morning air, the ceremony of the iikááh had concluded and Narbona went back into the cave to erase what remained of the sand painting. Ninsaba had to leave the cavern, since a woman could not witness that part of the ritual. The old man started erasing the figures of the design in the reverse order of how they had been painted, beginning by destroying the rainbow that had served as a protective frame for the images of the Twin Warriors.

After completely erasing the painting he called the cuates so that they could pick up in their blankets the sand mixed with pigment that he had made into a pile. Since it had absorbed the negative effluvia and the weakness of the novices during the ritual, it could contaminate other people, so Narbona instructed the cuates to throw it far away, on the northern slope of the canyon.

Then he permitted them to drink water from the nearby spring—although he reminded Decoy to use the cane tube so that the liquid would not touch his lips—and afterward to rest at the entrance of the cave. Before letting them sleep, the old man warned them, "Before making camp, when you are in enemy territory, you must find a place with water and trees, but don't go near there until it's night. Before drinking you will have to make an offering of sacred pollen and libations to the Sun. Before closing your eyes, ask the mountains to bring you a favorable dream. But you must not worry if you have a bad dream, because a nightmare can have positive results if you know how to interpret it. If you dream that they kill you, however, the next day you must kill one of your horses or another range animal, in order for that animal to take your place in destiny. Do you have any questions?"

But the cuates were already snoring.

They were awakened by the impatient voice of Ninsaba. "Come on, wake up, it's getting late and soon it will be dawn! Remember what Narbona told you: don't let the morning star catch you sleeping!"

"But how can it be morning? Is night already gone?" asked Gil Gómez, still dreaming.

"What do you mean is night already gone? You have slept straight through all of yesterday and part of tonight. Is that the way you follow the instructions of your mentor?"

Groping about, the cuates hurriedly gathered their things in the half-light of the cave and saddled their mounts. When they were ready to leave and wanted to say good-bye to the old man, Narbona had disappeared.

"Where can we find Narbona, to thank him for his advice and prayers?" Gil Gómez asked his mother.

"It isn't necessary to take your leave of grandfather: the spirit of Narbona will accompany you while you act according to his recommendations. The best way to thank him for his troubles will be to follow his advice exactly. Come on, follow me. I will show you the way out of the ravine."

The cuates followed Ninsaba's horse in the milky half-light. Its shoeless hooves scarcely made a sound on the sandy riverbed. Her spare pony, which once again had an empty saddle, followed behind. The morning breeze through the tall stalks of century plants was the only sound.

But after a short while, Gil Gómez began to talk to Ninsaba. "Mother, Narbona has sung the ritual over us that will let us overcome the negative power of the enemy territory. But we are missing something important."

"And you're going to ask for it, aren't you?" said Ninsaba. "What is it this time?"

"When the Twin Warriors went out to fight the monsters, they asked their father for special weapons to conquer their powerful rivals. But it would be very difficult for me to ask my father for help in this situation, since I don't even know who my father is."

The mother remained silent a moment before answering, "Do you know what Changing Woman said to her son when he asked who his father was?"

"*The round cactus, the long cactus, that's who your father is!* That's what you always told me, ever since I asked as a child who my father was . . . but this time I ask by all that is holy that you tell me the truth!"

"And why do you think I know the whereabouts of your father? I have not seen him in many, many years. The only thing I know is that the road that takes you to his dwelling is full of dangers and bristling with obstacles."

"Although the road may be long and filled with great obstacles, I will find him if you will at least tell me in which direction I must go."

Ninsaba paused again. Finally her lips contracted in a grimace of contained fury. "Very well, I will tell you where you can find your father! But if you don't find him or he gives you a good beating when you meet him, don't say I didn't warn you . . ."

She prodded her pony with reins and heels, climbing up a trail where a wild *berrendo* would have difficulty going. In the semi-darkness the horses had trouble following the Indian pony on that hazardous path, and more than once the pack mules were on the verge of falling off the side of the mountain. Just when the horizon was beginning to light up, the group arrived at the top of a hill overlooking the plains to the east.

They dismounted and set about rubbing down the rumps and bellies of the horses with their blankets to prevent the morning dew and sweat from cooling on their hides. Still half-groping, they spent some time tightening the cinches on the mules and adjusting the straps that had loosened during the difficult climb.

When the sun finally came up, Ninsaba pointed to the red ball as it began to burst on the far edge of the eastern horizon, beyond the malpaís and the Ladrones Mountains, whose silhouette was a faint blue line over the green patch of the Río Grande Valley:

"Your father is somewhere over there! Following the route of the sun you will find his dwelling, although it's as difficult to get there as to the Sierra Blanca. From here I can't give you more precise directions, but when you have crossed the Río Grande, northeast of the Sierra Oscura, you will find a tableland called the Chupadera Mesa, and nearby are the ruins of an old mission called Gran Quivira. Somewhere in those ruins an old woman lives alone, hidden in a crevice full of spider webs. She knows all that region well and will be able to guide you toward the lair of your father. If she wants, she can help you overcome the obstacles that you are going to encounter on the way."

Jumping on her horse again, Ninsaba started galloping toward the top of the slope, followed by the pony, but before disappearing, she turned and once more warned the cuates, "But you can't blame me if he doesn't want to see you!"

The Path of the Rainbow

After taking a roundabout route to avoid crossing the malpaís, Tafoya and I went down the western slope of the San Mateos and spent a whole day milling about at the foot of the mountain range without finding a trace of the cuates.

I was beginning to wonder if the Indian was putting his whole heart into catching up with the fugitives, or whether in fact he was keeping an intentional distance behind them. When I urged Tafoya to put more effort into getting back on the trail, the Indian responded, "Remember that when the Twin Warriors undertook their route toward the Sun, Changing Woman followed her sons' tracks to the top of a mountain. But upon arriving at the summit, the tracks vanished, because they had gotten on a rainbow path in order to reach the dwelling of the Sun rapidly."

In these mountains one felt overwhelmed indeed with their grandeur and very much removed from the concerns of the civilized world. Was it really that important for us to catch up with that pair of rogues before they reached the Sierra Blanca? Was it crucial for the army's honor? I thought both parties were equally insane, my superiors and the fugitives.

At dusk Tafoya managed to recover the cuates' tracks in the environs of the Ojo del Oso at the bottom of the canyon. He found the horse tracks of the wanderers and those of their two mules, and then they were joined by the tracks of two unshod ponies, the kind used by Indians. With the expertise characteristic of the native trackers, who could detect the trace of a snake on a bare rock, he decided that one of the ponies was being ridden by a woman while the other was without a rider.

After following the tracks all night through the rugged mountains, at dawn we were rewarded by the sight of the shiny armor of Gil Gómez below us in the San José River basin. The rising sun behind our backs illuminated the riverbed covered by a thick layer of mist. Down below, half enveloped in that white shroud, the silhouettes of three riders were followed by two mules and the spare pony as they traveled along the edge of the arroyo.

After waiting for a while so they wouldn't suspect they were being followed, we went down to the edge of the river. Tafoya dismounted to reexamine the tracks at his leisure. He seemed to be paying peculiarly close attention to the unshod horses' spoor. The horses' hooves marked the muddy ground so clearly that even I could have followed that trail, but the Indian stooped over them for a long time, sticking his finger in the mud, which was still fresh. Finally he turned to ask me, "When we saw the cuates' group from the top of the ravine, how many people were on horseback, three or four?"

"I only saw three: the two men on their horses and the woman on the Indian pony. The mules and the other pony were without riders," I answered without hesitation.

"That's what I saw, but what the tracks tell me is different; here it seems as though the second pony also had a rider, because of the way the hoof prints are marked in the mud. Although it is not absolutely clear, because the marks are not very deep, as if the fourth rider were not very heavy, possibly a child or an older person."

We followed the trail to a sandy ravine. The retinue had stopped near a huge stone monolith whose shadow fell over a pool of clear water fed by a mountain spring.

"Here the tracks are a lot clearer," said Tafoya. "You can see the marks of other Indian moccasins besides those of Gil Gómez's mother. I believe it is the footprint of a little old man, because they are not very deep and he walks with a stick," said Tafoya, snooping around the sand in the immediate area of the rock. Shaking his head, the Indian added, "It appears that Ninsaba has found a singer for her son's ceremony."

Bare footprints could be seen in all directions, including some along the edge of the pool, which was brimming with ice-cold water. Tafoya laughed as he saw those tracks.

"The old man, whoever he may be, forced the cuates to bathe in the frozen water of the pond. Look! You can see the marks of their bodies as they rolled in the sand to get themselves dry! And these stronger footprints are those of the cuates running barefoot on the bed of the canyon."

The bare footprints went all the way to the bottom of the canyon and back, and we could also see the marks of the two long husky bodies where they had lain down on the sand.

"These exercises are part of the preparation of novices who are to go on a war expedition. I wouldn't want to be in the cuates' shoes, for I believe that these greenhorns are going to have to break their backs and sweat blood to obtain power against the enemy."

"Once they have submitted themselves to these purification rituals, what does the ceremony consist of?" I asked the Indian.

"Not all the singers practice the same prayers, but a sand painting is customarily done to attract the benevolence of the Sacred Beings, who can see their images painted on the sand just as you can see the reflection of your body in that pond."

While Tafoya spoke, using a stick he began to draw in the sand, around the spot where I was seated, the silhouette of a thick, coiled snake with a head, hands, and feet. Afterward he pulled out of his chest a small bag, which he said held earth from the Four Sacred Mountains, and he sprinkled a few grains around the design on the sand. The Indian told me not to move from where I was sitting, occupying the center of the coiled snake, and said I should close my eyes and extend the palms of my hands toward the heavens to absorb the powerful vibrations that would emanate from that design. I obediently closed my eyes, while Tafoya sang one of his ritual songs, which went like this:

I am in the Sun.
Lightning comes out of my toes, I am in the Sun.
Lightning comes out of my palms, I am in the Sun.
Four lightning arrows come out of my body,
> *I am in the Sun.*
When the lightning strikes from these places,
the enemy cries and falls back,
> *I am in the Sun, I am in the Sun.*

At that moment I felt a strong vibration throughout my body, from the tip of my toes, through my abdomen, my neck and head, to the palms of my open hands, as if a flow of energy shot forth from each of my fingers.

That feeling of vertigo lasted only a few seconds, and when I reopened my eyes I saw that the incandescent disc of the sun had peeked over the stone monolith, illuminating the patch of sand where I was seated, which only a few moments earlier was in the shade.

"Don't get up right away," said Tafoya, when he saw that I was preparing to move. "Because if you leave the circle of power before I finish erasing the painting, it could bring you bad vapors."

I actually felt quite dizzy, so it didn't bother me to stay in the same position while the Indian erased with utmost care the drawing that he had sketched in the sand, reversing the way he had painted it, until the tail of the snake disappeared and the surface of the sandy ravine was completely smooth.

I then noticed a couple of marks incised with a sharp object on the monolith. One was like two triangles linked at the points like an hourglass, and the other one seemed to represent a taut bow. I would have asked Tafoya the significance of those symbols, but I still felt dizzy, and he, on the other hand, wanted to talk.

"The full rituals require much greater preparation. The history of the Twin Warriors is sung, the tale of how they undertook their journey to the dwelling of their father, the Sun, to ask him for the magical weapons to defeat their enemies."

Enjoying the pleasant breeze that had started to blow across the ravine, I went to the shade and asked Tafoya to recount the part of the story I still didn't know.

In the Home of the Father

The House of the Sun was made of turquoise; it was square like a Pueblo Indian house, and it was built on the edge of a large pond. When the twins entered it around twelve noon, seated in the west was a very beautiful woman, and in the north and south, respectively, there were two young maidens of exceptional beauty. The women saw the strangers arrive and lowered their gaze.

Eventually, the woman said to them, "From where have you come and how is it that you got here?" "Well, the matter is very simple: someone told us that the Sun was our father, and we have come to greet him." "By all that's holy, how did you dare do this! I can assure you that he will not have pity on you!" the woman warned them. But then the two young maidens got up saying: "Wait, don't leave. Since we don't know what our father will do with you, it's better if you wait for him here." They took out a dawn blanket and wrapped them in it; after that they took out a sky-blue blanket and wrapped them in it; then they wrapped them in a twilight blanket and finally in a darkness blanket. And they put the rolls of blankets in a hidden place, out of sight.

At dusk, the light of the Sun was falling, making a great racket, at the same time that the sunset rays were bursting from behind the horizon in the west with a deafening echo. One of the young maidens, who had sat down again in the south, commented aloud, obviously so that the twins who were rolled up in the blankets could hear, "That is the noise my father makes when he returns home." The same racket was heard three more times and, after the fourth time, the second maiden, who was seated in the north, commented, "It seems that the noise is getting near; my father must be about to arrive."

And right at the moment in which the last flash of the Sun set in the neighboring lake, one could hear the typical noise that light makes as it enters the water—something like *sheel, sheel, sheel*—and the father appeared on the threshold of the house with a few sun rays still stuck to his braids. The first thing he did was to hang his shield, which had a resplendent sun painted on it, from a peg in the wall, where it remained vibrating and radiating light a good while, making the typical deep sound that hot metal makes when cooling: *tla, tla, tla,* or something like that . . .

The one who had just entered the house was none other than Tsóhaloai, the so-called Sun Bearer, but he entered scolding his family the way most fathers do upon returning home: "Let's see if someone can explain to me what's going on here! Around noon I saw a dark shadow entering this house, but now I don't see anyone here. What am I saying: one dark shadow? Two dark shadows! But now you would say that they have vanished. Would someone have the courtesy to tell me where they went?"

As usually happens in these cases, no one answered, so the Sun asked again, impatiently: "How is it possible that I am talking and no one answers me? I tell you someone came in here at noon, more specifically, two young men, and now it seems that no one has seen them. Do you by chance believe that when I am away I don't know what happens around here?" Again he was met with complete silence, which made the Sun red with anger: "Very well, I demand an explanation! It's intolerable that I have asked the same question four times! This is like talking to a stone! Am I to believe that you are accomplices with the young men who have entered here in my absence?" asked the Sun, incensed.

"If I were you," the woman finally answered, "I would keep quiet. A certain person is in the habit of boasting that he does nothing wrong on his journeys and that he has never been with a woman other than myself. Can you then explain to me how it is possible that this morning these two young men have arrived asking for their father? Those two greenhorns have presented themselves here saying, 'Well, the thing is very simple: someone told us that the Sun was our father, and we have come to greet him.'"

"And now," added the woman, "I am the one who would like to have someone give me an explanation about what is going on here, because according to what you say, you have never done anything bad, but here we have two young men who come asking, 'Where is my father?'"

Once again the Sun blushed, but this time with embarrassment. Without daring to say a word, he looked in all the corners of the house, until he noticed the roll of blankets where they had hidden the twins. When he jerked open the first blanket that was the color of darkness, the second that was twilight, the third that was sky blue, and the fourth that was the color of dawn, the twins fell on the floor twirling like tops.

The Sun saw them then, and tying them with a ray of light, he lifted them from the floor and threw them against one of the walls in the house that was covered with flint points. But the live feathers that Spider Woman had given them raised them in the air, preventing them from crashing against the wall bristling with points, and placed them again where they had landed after the blankets unrolled.

Upon seeing what had happened, and that they had not been injured by the flint points, the Sun stared at them and said to himself: "Look at these twins! Maybe you really are my sons!" Changing his attitude, he helped them get up from the floor and brush off a little of the dust from the blankets, and he said to them: "Forgive me if I have received you in a somewhat brusque manner, but the truth is that I'm not used to receiving visits from strangers in this house!" He remained pensive for a moment and then said, as though talking to himself: "I ask myself, Where could these strangers spend the night? Having two young maidens in the house, it would not look right for them to sleep under the same roof."

And he sent them to spend the night outside on the edge of the lake, whose surface usually froze at night, thinking that in the morning he would find them frozen stiff, not being able to endure the cold without blankets. But when the father was asleep, and outside an intense cold was creeping, the two maidens went out on the sly and went near where the twins were shivering. The maidens gave them two buffalo robes to keep them warm, so they spent the rest of the night very comfortably.

The following day when the father went out expecting to find them like two icicles, the two maidens had already brought the robes back, and the father found the twins breathing deeply the air of the mountains, as if nothing had happened. Again the Sun murmured to himself: "Well, well. What a thing if it turns out that the two twins really are my sons!"

Just in case, he decided to subject them to other tests, and calling his daughters, he ordered them to make a sweat hut and to be heating some stones: "Prepare for the sweat house the hardest rocks you can find; heat a white one, a blue one, a yellow one, and a black one." The maidens found quartz rocks of all those colors, and put them to heat, after building a sweat hut against the slope of a ravine.

But one of the girls, the youngest, called the older twin aside and said to him: "Truly your father has no mercy for you: now he intends to burn you to a crisp inside this hut, but I am willing to save you. I have made a hole in the wall of the slope, so that you can get in there and cover the opening with a flat rock. When he asks you if you are already hot, don't answer right away, because he will pour water through the roof and it will make the hot rocks explode. Only answer when he has asked the same question four times. Then you can answer yes and leave your hole."

Everything happened the way the maiden had warned. The Sun prepared a basin of cold water near the sweat hut, and once the twins got in, he asked them, "Are you hot yet?" But they slipped into the hole and covered it with a flat rock, so that when the father poured the water on the hot stones and they exploded into a thousand fragments, none of the quartz splinters reached the twins.

They waited until the stones stopped emitting a whistling noise, like when a hot metal is put in a bucket of water, and then they came out from their hiding place. Meanwhile, the father asked two more times. "Are you very hot yet?" but they didn't answer, as if they were dead. Finally, the father exclaimed in a triumphant voice, "But what is happening to you? Is it that you're still not hot enough?" The twins answered calmly, "Yes, now we are hot enough!" and they left the sweat lodge completely relaxed, leaving their father with his mouth open. "Well, well, let's see if you are really going to be my sons," he said to himself again.

He decided to submit them to one last test. "Truly, you are two very resilient young men. You deserve to come with me to smoke a pipe of special tobacco," he said to the twins. What he wanted was to kill them with a poisonous tobacco that he had in a pipe made of turquoise. But then the young men heard the voice of the Big Bottlefly whom Spider Woman had given them to protect them from danger. "Aké, aké, what your father now wants to do is kill you with a very powerful tobacco that only he can resist! Remember that, on coming here, you met a Giant Caterpillar who gave you a gift of a blue secretion that she spit out; put that in your throats before taking the first puff."

That's what the Big Bottlefly said in their ears, and the twins put the liquid under their tongues before taking the pipe. At the first puff, they noticed a very strong flavor, but as the pipe went from hand to hand, they took a liking to the tobacco, and before the surprised eyes of their father, they inhaled smoke four consecutive times without exhaling it from their lungs. "This tobacco is excellent. Don't you have more?" the older brother asked, returning the pipe completely empty to his father.

"Now you have convinced me, and I truly believe you are my sons. Tell me, what I can do for you?" said the father, taking them to a very large cave where he had all his valuable things. First he showed them a cavity full of white glass beads and precious stones. "Is this what you have come looking for?" he asked them. But the Big Bottlefly whispered in their ears: "Answer him that in no way is that what interests you." The twins answered their father in the negative. "Then can it be that you have come for this?" and he showed them a side cave where all kinds of wild animals and some ponies were running freely. "You may take whichever ones please you most." Again the Big Bottlefly and the twins answered that it was not for that reason they had come.

The father then began to become impatient. "If you haven't come looking for gems or animals or horses, do you want to tell me once and for all what interests you?" he exclaimed. Again the Big Bottlefly whispered the answer they must give him. "Very simple: we have come looking for the Zigzag Lightning Arrow, the Straight Lightning Arrow, the Sunray Arrow, and the Rainbow Arrow; that's what we came looking for. That is the reason why we made this long trip to visit you."

That's what the older brother said, the one who later would be called Slayer of Alien Monsters. And the younger one, who would be called Born From The Waters, said: "We also need a flint breastplate, some flint wristbands, a flint knife, a flint mace, flint gaiters, flint shoes, and a flint cap."

"You don't ask for much, do you? Have you lost your minds? Under no circumstances will I let you take all those arms!" answered the father furiously. "Could I ask you what you want to use all those arms for?" When the twins answered that they would need them to kill Yeitsó and the other monsters who were devouring mankind, the Sun became very sad, because it seems that all those monsters were his sons, and he had fathered them copulating in secret with the first maidens who had abused their bodies.

At last the twins convinced him to loan them all those arms, promising him that they would return them once they had killed all the monsters. The Sun even agreed that the first to die would be the giant Yeitsó, the so-called Lone Traveler, but on the condition that they let him shoot first. "Remember that he is your brother, and don't shoot him in a treacherous way. When the moment comes I will be there, and I myself will hit him with the first arrow. After that, you can destroy him."

And the twins agreed not to be the first to shoot.

The Taut Bow and the Hourglass

We followed the trail of Gil Gómez and his retinue until we reached the junction of the San José and San Juan rivers. But when he went into the canyons of the Colorado Mountains, I noticed my guide's enthusiasm was beginning to wane, and he started to slacken his pace, to avoid following the tracks of the fugitives. When we found ourselves facing a deep sandy ravine where a spring ran, Tafoya stopped his mount in its tracks and said that he wouldn't go any farther.

"This is Dead Man's Canyon, where many years ago a battle took place between men from my tribe and the white soldiers, and the spirits of those who died in this fight still haunt the walls of this barranca. The American army pays me to fight against the live ones but not to follow the dead to their domains, and these places are haunted by the spirits of deceased chiefs."

It was useless trying to convince Tafoya that if others had passed through there, including a woman and an old man, we should also be able to do so without any problem. When a Navajo makes up his mind, he can be stubborner than an old mule. The Indian had said that he wouldn't go through there and that was that, even if I threatened to blow his brains out with my revolver. The Navajos have a true fear of anything that has to do with dead people, to the point of not ever wearing garments of a deceased relative. They even abandon and burn the cabins on their rancherías where a death has taken place.

There was nothing to do but turn back and wait for the cuates to retrace their steps—if in fact they were still planning to go to the Sierra Blanca. I then had the brilliant idea that we could intercept them at El Morro. Gil Gómez and his friend Decoy had said that they would pass by there to inscribe their names on the rock, and it was on the way southwest, the direction that the cuates would have to take to reach the eastern sierras.

Leaving to our left the river of petrified lava below San Mateo Mountain, we crossed a high tableland covered with juniper and ponderosa pine. Rising in the background were the Zuñi Mountains. As the afternoon wore on, we came within view of El Morro. The majestic ponderosa pines growing at its foot looked tiny next to the rock. It resembled a ship, whose bow cut through an ocean of sagebrush and cedar. My heart beat with excitement as I got close to the sandstone wall where the travelers who had crossed those barren plains more than three hundred years ago had signed their names. As a child, I had had an album of signatures in which I kept the autographs of local celebrities, such as the mayor of New Rochelle, the famous Commodore Reginald Coperton, and the great whaler Lewis Sidney, but I had to abandon that interest when my father died. In any case, how could a schoolboy's notebook compare with the stone tablets of that Babylon of the West?

In one of the recesses of the cliff, we found the spring that had drawn travelers from time immemorial. There we gathered wood to build a fire. While the Indian prepared something to eat, I couldn't resist the temptation of looking at some of the inscriptions, making use of the last of the daylight.

A sandy path went around the base of the rock, and although the light was fading rapidly, I succeeded in locating several signatures, including some of the old Spanish inscriptions, like that of the first colonizer of that territory, Don Juan de Oñate:

The Governor Don Juan de Oñate passed by here on the way to discover the southern ocean on April 16, 1605.

And another one of Don Diego de Vargas, the Spanish soldier who reconquered the province after the Pueblo Indians expelled the colonists of the Río Grande basin in 1680.

Here was General Don Diego de Vargas, who conquered for our Holy Faith and the Royal Crown all of New Mexico at his expense in the year of 1692.

I was also able to locate other, more recent inscriptions with signatures of United States army soldiers who had passed by there on reconnaissance missions. Lieutenant Simpson, an engineer, left his signature on the 17th and 18th of September, 1849, when he was accompanying the expedition of Colonel Washington in Navajo Territory. He made sketches of the rock and its inscriptions that I had seen later collected in a War Department report.

When I returned to the campsite I told Tafoya that I had seen

Simpson's inscription. I remembered Tafoya telling me that he had been present at that first meeting between the American army and his tribe. The Indian nodded his head affirmatively without stopping his chewing on a strip of jerky.

"In fact, that was the first time that the Americans went into the heart of the dinéh territory, and a skirmish took place between our warriors and American soldiers because of a tragic confusion. A soldier thought he recognized among the Indians' ponies a stolen horse, and when he tried to recover it, the Navajos drew their weapons, but without firing. Feeling himself threatened, a greenhorn American soldier lost his nerve and made use of his revolver; in the clash which followed, Chief Narbona, who was trying to stop the fight, was shot in the back. To prevent a full-blown battle, the American officers hid Narbona's body in a rock crevice, a place which since then is called Dead Man's Canyon, close to where we were this morning."

Now I understood better why the guide had refused to enter that narrow pass, but I said nothing. Tafoya continued, "Narbona was one of the most respected chiefs of our tribe, and it was a pity that after having survived so many battles, he lost his life because of a stupid discussion over a stolen horse. There are those who think that had he lived, he might have obtained a treaty with the white man favorable to our people, because besides being a great warrior, he was also a wise man."

I let a few moments pass, out of respect for the dead chief, before proceeding. "Do you believe the cuates will pass by here to carve their names in the rock before continuing on the way to the Sierra Blanca?" I asked the Indian.

"Gil Gómez was raised by a descendant of the Spanish, and it matters to them that others remember their exploits, more so than earning a victory or getting the spoils of the enemy," answered Tafoya, who had finished the jerky and had rolled up some tobacco in a cornhusk.

"But the Spanish were looking for gold and riches, not just to leave their names written on the rock."

"The Spaniards came here disoriented and misguided, the same way you Americans have arrived; but it seems that the whites, whenever they make a mistake, don't know how to return the same way they came." The Indian paused to inhale a puff of tobacco smoke, and then went on. "You already see that the Spaniards were especially concerned that people know they had 'passed by here,' and the genízaro from Cabezón has inherited some of that pride."

"Don't you think it's strange that, after being blessed by a shaman of your tribe, the cacique has to come here and carve his name in the rock?" I asked him then.

"Remember what Chief Kiatanito said: *'Two thirds of his body are divine, and one-third is human. . . .'* Gil Gómez at times behaves like a white and other times like an Indian." He added, "I saw up there the same signs that I saw in the stone monolith near the Dead Man's Canyon, engraved in the rock. One was a small bow with its arrow and the cord pulled back, and the other had a design like two triangles joined at the apex." Tafoya blew a puff of smoke toward the sky, and with a certain solemnity explained, "The taut bow is the symbol of the older of the Twin Warriors, the one called Nayénézgani, the one who shot the arrows that killed the giant Yeitsó."

"And the hourglass?"

A condescending smile appeared on the guide's lips. "That sign represents the ponytail the warriors wear to keep their hair out of their eyes; that's where you grab the enemy to scalp him. And that's where the younger of the two brothers grabbed Yeitsó in order to cut off his head after bringing him down. That reason is why it's used to represent Born from the Water, who is also called Naidikísi, which means *the one who cuts around.*" The Indian paused briefly before adding, "I bet that's not the last time you'll find those marks, as long as we are on the trail of the cuates."

Book Six

They stood gazing at the forest,

noticing how tall the cedars were,

as well as the forest's threshold.

Where Humbaba strolled, he left a path.

The trail was straight, and road was good.

They looked at the cedar mountain, sanctuary

of the gods,

the pedestal throne of Irnini.

At the foot of the mountain, the cedar

had lifted its seed,

its foliage was thick, and it provided

ample shade.

POEM OF GILGAMESH
Tablet V, Column i

The Head Shepherd

The cuates passed by El Morro shortly after Tafoya and Burdette had departed. On the sandstone they left written the following inscription: *Gil Gómez passed through here, accompanied by his friend Decoy, headed for the Sierra Blanca, to challenge the keeper of the Cedar Forest,* with their initials next to the date.

Following the advice of Narbona, to avoid being seen, they kept from crossing open spaces during the day and traveled mainly by night. But they reached the Plains of San Agustín on a very hot afternoon, and instead of waiting for nightfall to fill their canteens at the watering hole, they went down to a ravine while there was still daylight. They were unaware that a group of shepherds who had arrived there before them were hiding in the bushes, ready to ambush them.

When the cuates had dismounted and were face down drinking from the arroyo, Decoy using the cane tube that Narbona had given him and the genízaro with his head stuck in the water, the shepherds pounced on them, those who had flintlocks pointing them at the cuates and the others brandishing their machetes and clubs.

"If you move, you are dead Indians!" said Nepomuceno Muñoz, pressing the barrel of his blunderbuss up against Cimarrón's chest.

"Wait till I bring a rope, and it won't be long before these scoundrels know what's good for them," said Pedro Chávez. "These damned Apaches are going to pay dearly for the many times they've stolen our sheep and stampeded our horses."

"Let them pray before we kill them, because they may be Christian Indians!" said one the younger shepherds, who had never seen a man hanged.

"Do you hear the lad wondering whether the Indians may be Christians?" marveled one of the shepherds. "You should see how these so-called Christians work a boy like you—after they burn his brains and castrate him like a pig."

"One can tell that you still have your mother's milk on your lips, but at the very least you ought to be able to notice how these devils are painted with their heathen witchcraft!" added Pedro Chávez.

The cuates had put their weapons down before approaching the watering hole, but their torsos and powerful forearms painted with snake symbols and bear claws gave them a warlike appearance. With the barrels of the old flintlocks pointed at their chests, they saw that the shepherds were making nooses at the ends of some sturdy rope, and the headman, Hilario García, seemed to be picking out a suitable branch on a thick wild olive tree at the edge of the arroyo.

Decoy could feel the hemp rope being lowered over his head when he suddenly recognized the face of one of the men who was tightening the slipknot around his neck. It was one of the shepherds from the Ojo de la Parida whom he had seen before at the same spot when he and Sam Hat were traveling from the Gila wilderness toward Cabezón.

"Wait. I know you . . ." said Decoy, stammering because the pressure of the rope barely allowed him to speak. "You're the one who cut my mane with the knife whose sharp edge left scars on the back of my neck. Your name is Pedro Chávez!"

Chávez was stunned to hear his name pronounced. He made the sign of the cross, thinking that it must be the devil talking through the mouth of that savage. But the stoutness of his prisoner did remind him of the powerful build of the man from the plains. "Why, it's Cimarrón!" the shepherd finally exclaimed.

"It's the same young man that we shaved and dressed when he arrived half naked to the sheepfold, with that woman with a good ass and a big bosom," added another shepherd.

"But why on earth are you crossing the mountain disguised as Indians?" said Elisario Ortiz, moving the barrel of his rifle to one side.

Upon seeing that his companions recognized the renegade, the headman García loosened the rope around Decoy's neck and with his knife cut the end with which he had tied his hands behind his back, although he didn't seem too happy to have to set them free. "You should be grateful that Chávez recognized you," he growled, "because otherwise by now you'd be dancing at the end of the hemp rope."

"To tell you the truth, I did wonder how we managed to catch you so easily," mused Nepomuceno Muñoz as he released the hammer of his blunderbuss. "Real Apaches are as shrewd as the devil himself."

"Well, in fact we are after a Mescalero Apache chieftain who has his lair in the eastern mountains," said Cimarrón, swallowing saliva, since his mouth had gone completely dry. "And my friend, here, is Gil Gómez, the cacique from Cabezón."

As the famous chieftains from the Río Puerco and their expedition to the Sierra Blanca were the talk of all the rancherías of the Río Abajo, the shepherds, proud to have such distinguished visitors, offered the hospitality of the sheepfold to the cuates, inviting them to share their supper. After filling several goatskins with fresh water, they set out for the sheep camp, where they soon gathered around the bonfire. Over it was roasting a young lamb's leg, while under the embers several loaves of cornbread were baking, their aroma perfuming the camp.

The shepherds went out of their way to offer their best hospitality, and soon a skin of El Paso wine was making the rounds, but somehow they could not achieve the cordial atmosphere Cimarrón remembered from his first visit. The old head shepherd, a handsome man with a flourishing beard, was gone, and García, the new headman, didn't have the same warmth as his predecessor.

The shepherds, in turn, noticed that the cuates followed a peculiar ritual when it came to eating and drinking, especially Cimarrón, who chose the worst parts of the lamb and let the strips of meat cool at the end of his knife before touching them. They noticed also that the cuates used a strange language among themselves.

"Seems to me that Cimarrón used to have more of an appetite when he roamed the mountains free," said Pedro Chávez to another shepherd.

"Maybe he has gotten soft now that he lives in town," added his companion.

"Well, the first time we gave him shelter in the despoblado, I remember he didn't turn up his nose at food or drink," commented Elisario Ortiz.

"Although at first he choked on bread, he soon ate everything and drank his fill of wine," agreed Nepomuceno Muñoz.

There was something heavy in the atmosphere, and it grew heavier when Decoy, having finished the toughest pieces of meat, asked for guitar music. "The last time I was here, one of you sang a ballad, and everyone joined in on the refrain," he said, trying to sing what he remembered of the song.

The shepherds remained silent, some stuffing their mouths with the last pieces of bread, others staring into their tin cups or diverting their eyes toward the dancing flames to avoid answering. Finally, Elisario Ortiz tried to steer the conversation in a different direction. "Where are your worships headed with so much equipment?"

"We're heading for the Ruidoso River in the Sierra Blanca," said Gil Gómez, "and we're trying to get to the sanctuary of the Mescalero Apaches."

"Well, you better be careful! Word has it that those mountains are home to a famous Apache witch doctor," warned Nepomuceno Muñoz.

"I just now remembered the name of the head shepherd," Decoy interjected. "His name was Boleslo Romero!"

At the name of the head shepherd, a hush fell once again, and even though the fire had just been piled high with dry sagebrush, it looked as if someone had poured a shovel of sand on it instead. The only one who had the courage to answer Decoy was Pedro Chávez. "Boleslo Romero is no longer with us; and although I don't have a well-tuned voice like his, in order to please our guests, I'm going to sing 'The Ballad of Ungrateful Love.'" And retrieving a guitar from a nook, Chávez started singing.

> *Because of your love, your ungrateful love.*

> *Then you fell in love with the shepherd,*
> *With the head shepherd,*
> *Who always offered you curd,*
> *And always brought you tender billy goats.*

> *Because of your love, your ungrateful love.*

> *Soon you bewitched him,*
> *Turning him into a wolf.*
> *Now his own young shepherds run him off,*
> *His own dogs bite his loins.*

> *Because of your love, your ungrateful love.*

As he got to the end of the stanza, the shepherd broke down, and the strumming of the guitar melted into his sobbing. Afterward, one after another, the shepherds began getting ready to wrap themselves in their blankets and lie down near the fire. The cuates spread their blankets farther away from the fire.

But no one was sleeping. Pedro Chávez came over to where the twins had spread their bedrolls and whispered to Decoy, "Because of the beautiful

Esther, the daughter of Don Anú Baca, 'The Ballad of Ungrateful Love,' in which the head shepherd was transformed into a wolf, has come true. The unfortunate Boleslo Romero now finds himself roaming the mountains without a home because he made the mistake of falling in love with the patrón's daughter." After making sure that no one was listening, the shepherd continued, "In fact, that woman, who is called La Malinche, became infatuated with the head shepherd and, as she's done with other lovers, when she got tired of him, she accused him in front of her father of having seduced her. Romero had to flee the hacienda like a rat. Just as the ballad says, his own shepherds are after him, and their mastiffs are biting his flanks."

"And what does the patrón Baca think about all this?" asked Gil Gómez.

"The patrón is an honest man, but some say that this sorceress has bewitched him, so that he's not aware of her misdeeds and flirtations. But I pray you by all that's holy not to tell anyone what I have just confided. The patrón's daughter has spies everywhere, and I'm afraid of ending up roaming the mountains like a wolf or a coyote."

As if to confirm what the shepherd had just said, the mournful howl of a wild animal was heard at the top of the mountain.

"Listen to *he who customarily howls at the dawn!*" said Gil Gómez to Cimarrón. "It's getting late, and we'd better get to sleep right away. Remember to watch for the morning star; don't let it get up before you do."

"You're right. I'm going to wrap myself in *that by means of which one becomes warm*. Tomorrow we'll have to leave before *that which customarily blows against it* arrives," answered Decoy.

Even though the shepherd didn't understand any of their jargon, before taking off, he told the cuates, "Don't think that I'm poking my nose into your business, but if I were you, I wouldn't stay here till dawn. If the patrón's daughter finds you trespassing on her land, she won't hesitate to sending a posse of her peones after you."

Before they fell asleep, Decoy said to the genízaro, "Do you believe what the shepherd has just told us about the patron's daughter?"

"I knew Esther's father, who was a compadre of my adoptive father, Don Antonio Gil, but a lot of water has flowed under the bridge since then."

"According to what the shepherd tells us, she must be a real witch."

"*She by reason of whom one is not permitted to live,*" Gil Gómez reminded him.

They had hardly fallen asleep when Pedro Chávez came to wake them up, pulling at their blankets in the pitch darkness. "Wake up, Cimarrón and company, wake up! Hilario García has sneaked out of camp; for sure he's on his way to the hacienda to tell Mistress Esther that he has seen you here. Wake the genízaro up, load your mules, and saddle up your horses without delay. Can't you hear the galloping of a horse in the distance?"

No sooner said than done, the twins had saddled their horses and loaded their mules. And, before the first morning star appeared, they had left the camp unnoticed.

Those by Reason of Whom
One Is Not Permitted to Live

According to the legends about the origins of the Navajo people, Coyote was one of the giant Yeitsó's spies. Also Crow, Magpie, and Vulture used to go snooping about the countryside back then to tell the monster everything they saw. But the daughter of Don Anú Baca didn't need to use animals to find out what was happening on her properties since she had confidantes in every group of shepherds and peones who served in her vast hacienda. The head shepherd, who had left the sheepfold the night before, arrived at La Parida as dawn was breaking. He entered the courtyard at full gallop, and went immediately to wake up the patron's daughter, who was still in the arms of Morpheus, for lack of better company. As soon as she heard the news that the twins were going to cross the Río Grande on the way to the Sierra Blanca, Esther had her horse Estrellado saddled, the fastest in her stables, and went galloping down the cliffs that ended in the river.

Although the water gushed down in a torrent, upon arriving at the edge she dug her spurs into the flanks of her steed, who leapt into the water, and, dodging the tree trunks dragged by the flood and the whirlpools that the water formed over the depths, she succeeded in reaching the other side. The woman hiked up her skirt to the waist and, with her bare thighs dripping water, she began to drive her horse up the slope of the Sierra de los Ladrones.

At the top she took the narrow pass that led to the Devil's Ravine, dismounting to relieve the steed of her weight, since its chest and belly were covered with foam. And after carefully following the narrow trail along the edge of the cliff, Esther arrived at the entrance of the cave where Arorú lived. The old woman was preparing a concoction in a clay pot, and although she had been alerted to the arrival of the young woman by the cawing of the crow that served as her spy and sentry, she acted as if she were surprised to see her.

"To what do I owe the honor of a visit by the daughter of the Río Abajo patrón to my humble little cave?" said the old woman.

Esther came near the fire to dry her dripping clothes. "You know I avoid coming up here unless something grave happens, but this time we have a serious problem."

"What do you mean *we have?*"

"I have learned that last night, the genízaro Gil Gómez and his powerful friend arrived at the San Agustín plains and they're headed this way to cross the river on their way to the Sierra Blanca."

"For all I care the cuates can pass by here on their way to hell, as long as they don't bother me in my cave."

"My men were about to send them to hell, but they lacked determination. They are now on their way, and if we don't do something about it, they're likely to get to the Sierra Blanca and kill the guardian of the Cedar Forest."

"Bah, the Ruidoso Apaches will give them a warm reception, and even if they reach the sacred forest, I don't believe those two greenhorns have the guts to overcome the power of the Lone Traveler."

"You haven't seen these men! The shepherd who saw them told me they had their faces and chests painted with ritual designs and from what they have told me, I believe the cuates were speaking to each other in a language that the others could not understand. Who could have taught them the war talk of the Apaches?"

On hearing that, the old woman stopped stirring the stew and stared at Esther, who was squatting next to the fire, spreading out her skirts on the ground so that the heat from the embers would dry them and wringing her hair with both hands to squeeze the water out.

"The Río del Norte must be rushing fiercely! I know there have been storms in the Río Puerco Valley because these past nights my joints have been hurting, keeping me awake." The old woman straightened up, and putting down the stick she had been using to stir the stew, she brushed her braids away from her face and went on, "To tell you the truth, it hasn't been only the bad weather that has kept me awake; I actually had a bad dream last night. I was seeing the ghost of old Narbona wandering through the Colorado Mountains with two youngsters and a woman on horseback. Then I saw them again in a grotto, where a war ritual was being performed. In the dream I didn't see the faces of the novices, but while they were riding I saw that one of them had a shiny breastplate and the other had a leather jacket with metal studs, the kind the Spaniards used long ago."

"You are right! Because those whom you saw in the dream are none other than Gil Gómez and Decoy, who left Cabezón costumed for the fiesta of Los Comanches, and they have continued riding in that attire . . . that's exactly the way my shepherds found them!"

"Well, if that's the way it is, make no mistake, Chief Narbona's ghost must have summoned up powerful forces to protect them," said the old woman. "I wish the old natán had stayed in the cave where the American soldiers buried him!"

"The dead should stay where they are, and not interfere in the affairs of the living; otherwise I don't know where we will end up," agreed Esther. "Do you think he has also given them special weapons to fight the guardian of the Cedar Forest?"

"Let's not get discouraged yet. The road to the Sierra Blanca is difficult, and now they will meet obstacles that will delay or impede their way. Rest assured that their journey is going to be full of surprises! Right now I'm going to send Little Wind to keep an eye on the mountains and rivers, so it can tell us of their presence and which way they are headed."

"What Little Wind? Are you referring to that ugly black bird I've seen flying around here?" asked Esther. "Is that the best you can do to delay the progress of those rascals?"

"That ugly black bird, as you call it, is a more powerful ally than you can imagine. Who do you think told the Lone Traveler where to find the Twin Warriors? The same Little Wind will advise Huwawa at the right time of the arrival of the twins to the Cedar Forest. Have no fear!"

The bird, which was smoothing its feathers in its niche, emitted a caw and fluffed itself out arrogantly, as if it knew they were talking about it.

"I hope we can find them!" Esther exclaimed. "I will send a party of armed peones along the river. Unfortunately, I have to hide all this from my father, because the old man is soft-hearted. Apparently the Cabezón cacique was an adopted son of Don Antonio Gil . . . who has now gone to heaven!"

"Only after having gone through hell first!" said old Arorú. "Remember, he died hanged by the Americans and cursing the soldiers who hanged him."

In spite of the many ugly words that had just come from her sinful mouth, the beautiful Esther had the nerve to cross herself on hearing hell mentioned, and even dared to kiss with her blasphemous lips a scapulary that she wore hanging on her breast—with the saint turned upside down, of course.

He Who Spreads His Wings

After riding all night, the cuates went over the ridge of the sierra just before dawn. They could barely make out the Río Grande basin below, its leafy groves still covered with mist and its waters swollen by the flood in the Río Puerco basin.

"It seems to have rained a lot upstream," commented Cimarrón as he went down toward the bank. "We'll have to find a place to ford the river."

"Remember that for river you must say *a rope-like object of specular iron ore lies.* When we have gotten to the other side we'll already be in enemy territory!" Gil Gómez warned him.

"All right, all right," said Decoy, who was still in a foul mood. "How does one say *fog?*"

"*That on the surface of which nothing is visible.*"

"And how do you say *morning, dawn?*"

"*That which customarily blows against it.* Why do you ask?"

"I wanted to say that it seems the wind is parting the mist and that finally the light of day will break through; but it isn't easy to express yourself in this damned gibberish."

"I don't think it's so difficult; all you have to say is: it seems to me the wind is parting *that on the surface of which nothing is visible* and that soon will break *that which customarily blows against it.*"

"Do you really think we are going to have to talk this rot all the way?" Decoy asked impatiently.

"After all the time we have spent in preparing for this journey, it would be silly not to take advantage of Narbona's teachings," answered the genízaro in a tone that bore no argument.

"As long as it helps us get through this damned trip alive, I'm prepared to speak the Apache war language until we return to Cabezón. By the way, have you noticed that big ugly black bird that is flying above *a rope-like object of specular iron ore lies?* I would swear it has followed us since we began to descend the Sierra de los Ladrones. Don't you think that a black bird can bring us bad luck?"

"For sure it will if you don't use the war language correctly: remember that in the secret talk bird is *he who spreads his wings.* But I do think it has been following us," acknowledged the genízaro.

What was spreading its wings in the half-light of dawn was none other than old Arorú's pet crow; from her lair at the top of the ravine she had spotted the shiny armor of the cuates coming down the mountain and had sent her watchbird to keep track of the strangers' whereabouts.

"I wish the bird could serve as our guide the rest of our journey, because it can fly over mountain ranges and show us the shortest and safest path," Decoy said.

The cuates had to go back upstream until they found a place where a pile of tree trunks and mud carried by the flood had formed a kind of natural dam, slowing the current. The black bird went on ahead flying over the horses—so low that the shine of its black feathers was reflected on the warriors' armor. The riders thought it was showing them the best place to cross the river, but its trajectory was misleading: Gil Gómez's horse sank to its hindquarters in a treacherous pool, and the mule following behind came close to losing its load in the turbulent waters.

"Well, it seems as though *he who spread his wings* isn't much of a guide! Following it has only gotten us into this damned pool!" exclaimed Gil Gómez, spurring the animals to try to get out of the flooded river.

"Look out for the mule or it's going to fall into the same trap!" Decoy warned him.

"Remember that the mule is *he who drags its tail* and the horse *nose to the ground,*" the genízaro shouted as he was about to be sucked into a whirlpool.

"If we manage not to drown ourselves, I promise you that I will learn this cursed language better, but now pull the halter of *he who drags his tail* if you don't want the current to carry it away."

Upon getting to the other side and crossing the hills that overlooked the river, the cuates saw the hacienda of Ojo de la Parida, whose solid torreones shone under the morning sun, surrounded by a green belt of orchards and cultivated fields. Impressed by the size and solid appearance of the main house, Decoy asked Gil Gómez, using the secret language, "Do you know who owns that *mud mass* on top of the hill?"

"It's the hacienda of Don Anú Baca, who owns all these lands up to the plains of San Agustín on the west bank of the Río Grande and on the other side almost to the foothills of the Sierra Blanca. They say that he is the wealthiest patrón in the Río Abajo, and it is in fact his daughter, Esther, about whom the shepherd told us all those bad things."

"Aren't you tempted to go over there and pay your respects to that woman, to see if she is as beautiful and as evil as they say?"

"Remember, as long as we are in enemy territory we are not allowed even to smell the scent of a woman—especially you, the novice of this expedition."

"I was only joking. I have no desire to see any woman, much less the way we look now!" said Decoy. "Perhaps we should detour and not go anywhere near the hacienda because remember, the shepherd warned us against the peones of the beautiful Esther."

The cuates went through the Pinos Mountains where the vegetation of firs and chaparral was very dense; from that hilltop they noticed that below, on the riverbank, a group of men was seated under the cottonwoods that grew beside the river, while a boy cared for the horses that were grazing nearby. It seemed strange to them that those peones were idle, as if they were waiting for something or someone. But they soon found out what the men were doing. The black bird, which had taken off again and had reached the hills that overlooked the basin, suddenly dove down to where the men were sitting. Circling overhead, it woke them with its raucous cawing, drawing the attention of the peones to the cuates, who had almost crossed over the brow of the mountain.

One of the men spotted them and began to shout. All the men went to their horses and took off at a full gallop in pursuit of the cuates, who spurred their horses down the mountain.

"Have you seen what *he who spreads his wings* has done to call their attention to us?" said Gil Gómez. "Those men were waiting for us, and I'm sure it was Esther who sent them!"

"If it weren't for the bird and its caws, we would have passed unnoticed," agreed Decoy, "but spur *nose to the ground* and whip *he who drags his tail* if you don't want them to catch us!"

Thanks to the time the peones had lost gathering and saddling their horses, the cuates succeeded in getting far enough ahead. But the shrewd black bird, as if having betrayed their presence to the peones was not enough, had flown off again and went ahead of the cuates, signaling with its flapping wings and caws the way they had taken. Fortunately, a short distance ahead, the fugitives found a gully covered with thick growth where they were able to shake off the riders from Ojo de la Parida, who passed by without noticing that the crow circled and cawed desperately over the gate to the potrero.

The Hospitality of Don Anú

For two days and two nights we waited for the cuates to arrive at the foot of El Morro, and at dawn of the third day I ordered Tafoya to saddle up the horses. I was so influenced by the stories Tafoya had told me that I began to think the cuates had learned to ride on the back of the rainbow, in which case surely they would have gained an unstoppable lead and might already have crossed the Río Grande.

Taking a short detour so as not to go through the Ladrones Mountains, which bands of Indian renegades and other outlaws were said to use as a hideout, Tafoya and I reached the Río Grande Valley. When I saw from a distance the tiny village of San Acacia, surrounded by cultivated fields and vineyards, I felt as if I were looking at a family orchard, since it was only a few miles from Fort Conrad, which in the midst of that inhospitable desert had become my second home.

Neither Tafoya nor I felt any special urgency about getting back to the garrison to admit our failure to catch up with the fugitives; so we stopped at La Fonda del Güero in San Acacia to quench our thirst with a couple of drinks of brandy before continuing downriver.

Any explanation that I could have offered at the fort about the erratic itinerary of the adventurers would have included the concepts of Power Against the Enemy and the rituals of sand paintings and the Blessingway, which my officers could hardly be expected to understand. Most probably they would have sent me straight to the infirmary, thinking I had suffered a sunstroke crossing the desert. It would all sound like drivel to them.

We bumped into Lieutenant Loring as we were entering the fonda at San Acacia, and that brought us back to reality with a jolt. Although meeting him there was totally fortuitous, it seemed as though the officer had been waiting for us in that corner since the beginning of time. We must have looked so pathetic that the lieutenant didn't even ask about the mission he had entrusted us with in Cabezón.

On his way back to Fort Conrad from Santa Fe, Loring had found out that the cuates had already crossed the Río Grande, and he had stopped at the village to try to find out what direction the fugitives had taken. Once he had that information, he was confident that the military detachment he would recruit at the fort would be able to catch up with them while they were still crossing the desert, before they reached the Sierra Blanca.

Despite the fact that Loring had more imagination and culture than the rest of the officers, there was no point trying to persuade him that a Navajo ritual had lent the cuates special powers that enabled them to overcome natural and supernatural obstacles.

When the lieutenant learned that the twins had crossed Don Anú Baca's lands and that he had sent a posse of peones after them, he decided to stop by El Ojo de la Parida, which was practically on the way to Fort Conrad, hoping to get more information from the Río Abajo cacique. Privately I thought that the old hidalgos of the territory were more likely to offer a fresh horse to a fleeing renegade than to turn him over to American justice, but I refused to disappoint the officer. In fact, I was dying of curiosity to meet the rich landowner and his beautiful daughter.

The patrón Don Anú Baca, like many of the proud descendants of the Spanish conquistadores, harbored little sympathy toward the government in Washington and probably had certain doubts regarding the legitimacy of the American presence in that territory. If these people did not approve of the manner in which we took possession of those lands during the war, they liked even less the recent acquisition from Mexico of Arizona and California thanks to the good offices of Minister Gadsden.

Nevertheless, any such misgivings were belied by the hospitable way in which the rich patrón received us in his imposing hacienda, which was built on top of the hills that overlooked the river. Between the main house and outlying buildings, it occupied more than double the entire perimeter of Fort Conrad. Don Anú received us in a drawing room with a dais draped in red satin tapestries, covered with huge cushions of the same color, fit for the beautiful houris of an oriental harem; and for those of us who weren't used to sitting on the floor, in another corner of the room was a pair of European-style armchairs and a French divan.

The paintings hanging on the walls—a touch of distinction uncommon in the homes of the area—represented the ancestors of the Baca family. The men were proudly posed, with stern expressions, and the women bore a certain nun-like, dried-up appearance. Several of the pictures had black crêpe still stuck on the frame, which made me think that the funerals of those family members were celebrated in that same salon. When we entered, the room was in semi-darkness, and it seemed to me that funeral canticles still echoed between those carefully whitewashed adobe walls.

The patrón had ceremoniously invited us to dinner, "if such distinguished gentlemen would deign to share with the owners of this house our simple food." While Tafoya tended to our horses in the corrals, Don Anú's servants took us to a guestroom close to the torreón, where we could refresh ourselves with a jug of water and a porcelain dish with soap. To dry ourselves, we used pure linen towels exquisitely embroidered with an A and a B, without doubt by the delicate hands of the beautiful Esther. I changed my drilling coat for a new tunic I had tucked among my belongings. The clothing that

I had worn to cross the desert had lost its blue color, fading into the ochre, yellowish, and purplish shades of the dust accumulated during our journey, and the pants' red stripes had withered to the sandy color of a dry arroyo.

After we had made ourselves presentable, we went downstairs for dinner. Don Anú and his daughter were waiting for us. In my case it was difficult to know whether I was more anxious to sit down to eat at a beautifully set table or to finally meet the famous daughter of the patrón. And I wasn't disappointed either by the appearance of the food displayed on the table with plates and silver cutlery or by the beauty of Esther, who stayed discreetly in one corner ready to serve us, as only the men sat down at the table.

The daughter of the patrón was dressed in a white silk blouse and a flaring skirt of the same color that contrasted with the dark mauve silk shawl covering her bare shoulders. The low neckline of her blouse offered a glimpse of her shapely bosom and slender neck without compromising her decency. It seemed as though the flare of her dark rebozo had a life of its own, and when its owner moved to pick up a plate or help serve the wine, the fringe of the shawl moved like the ominous fluttering of a night bird.

Don Anú had the courtesy to lead the conversation in English, a language that he handled quite well although with a strong Spanish accent, from the days when he had been involved in trade with St. Louis on the famous Santa Fe Trail. Our host was pleased to hear Lieutenant Loring's compliments regarding the quality of the food and drinks—served in silver chalices, which gave the vintage wine from El Paso a certain sacrilegious taste—and returned the compliments of the officer by ceremoniously toasting the health of his guests. Following these flowery exchanges, Loring went directly to the topic that was of interest to him.

"It is my understanding that Gil Gómez and his friend Decoy came through your lands recently. Do you know by any chance which way they went?"

"Has the genízaro done something wrong, for you to be looking for him?" asked the patriarch, with an innocent smile on his thin lips.

The lieutenant also smiled, probably remembering what I had told him about the craftiness of those old Spanish, who frequently didn't answer a question directly but rather responded with another query. "You probably know better than I," he began, "the good and bad things that Gil Gómez has done. Nevertheless, for his own good we are trying to find him and stop him in his journey. The United States Army wishes to make an expedition to the Sierra Blanca to teach the Mescalero Apaches a good lesson, but the mestizo and his friend think that they should be the first ones to penetrate the Apache sanctuary; if we don't head these two off in time I am fearful that both of them may perish at the hands of those red devils."

"And if the genízaro and his friend want to leave their scalps hanging high on those cliffs, what business is it of the United States if they die in that dangerous journey?"

"Their death would only serve to put those devils on guard," replied the lieutenant, "and that would make the army's entry into Apache territory even more difficult."

"Don't you think that your superiors may be afraid that those adventurers will succeed in their undertaking and thus triumph where a company of American dragoons failed recently?"

The astute patriarch had hit the nail on the head; but the engineer wouldn't let him have the last word. "If up to now no one has succeeded in controlling the Apaches from the Sierra Blanca," said Loring, "do you sincerely believe that two daredevils with two rifles and four mounts between them are going to defeat a band of hostile Indians in their own territory?"

"I would say, with all due respect to the American army, that two men who know how to sneak through the rocks and spring a sudden attack have a better chance for success in that mission than a military battalion." The patriarch paused to light up a long, thin cigar, offering one to the lieutenant and me, although I had to decline because it would not have been proper for me to smoke in front of an officer.

From time to time I would look over my shoulder toward the corner where the beautiful Esther remained standing motionless behind me. Throughout dinner, I had the impression that the patrón's daughter was riveting her eyes on the back of my neck; but when I dared to look back, I could see that it wasn't me she was looking at but the lieutenant, who was in front of me, on the other side of the table. Up until then I had never thought of Lieutenant Loring as a handsome man, but I had to admit that with his golden epaulettes and his crimson sash, the officer was looking much better than usual.

When I realized that I wasn't the object of Esther's attentions, I was struck with an irrational pang of jealousy. The rumors about her love life that traveled through all the villages of the Río Abajo came to my head then, gossip that until then I thought I could blame on the peones' resentment of the local aristocracy. But the brazen look that I had caught in her beautiful eyes was enough to confirm the tales of her lack of modesty and the power of her passions.

"You Americans," continued the patriarch, blowing cigar smoke toward the ceiling, "still have a lot to learn about the manner in which one must deal with the Indians. Those of us who have been in these valleys for many years have learned to coexist with them; we have learned from them how to hunt with the bow and arrow, which are quieter than rifles, how to tan buckskin, and to follow a spoor in dense cover. They have learned from us how to raise sheep and horses, to card wool, and to work with metal. Yet today, when the Mescaleros come down from the Sierra Blanca, I prefer to have my corrals full of livestock and let them take a few head, to keep them happy, rather than get involved in a fight which would not benefit either one of the parties."

"Listening to your arguments, it seems as if a peaceful relationship between you and the savage Indians has always existed, but the truth is that you Spaniards have also been at war with the hostile tribes since you set foot on this territory."

"Perhaps, but it has never been a war of annihilation. In fact, there were times when they were stronger and could have destroyed us, but they preferred to let us continue raising our livestock and harvesting our crops so that they could steal them when the right time came. There were also other situations in which our military force was stronger than some of the tribes, but we refused to squash the heathens because if we did, where were we going to get maids to weave our wool or women for our peones?"

"I thought that to keep someone in bondage was contrary to your Catholic faith," said the lieutenant.

"Go ask Gil Gómez and his mother how they ended up at the hacienda of my compadre, Don Antonio Gil. May he rest in peace! Until only a few years ago, in all of the Río Grande basin, the customary wedding gift for his fiancée, for any suitor who wanted to show off his bravery, was a couple of Navajo maids, whom he had to abduct at the risk of losing his own hide in the undertaking. I myself did it, when I was courting my wife, Doña Leonor. May she rest in peace."

The lieutenant thought it was about time to change the subject to avoid saying something that might offend his host. "I understand you were a great Indian fighter," he said.

"No one is great against those devils, but I confess that I am acquainted with the bravery and endurance of the Apaches. During colonial days, when the Spaniards used to fight the Mescalero Apaches, at times they would take their prisoners in chains in a caravan all the way to Mexico City, some three hundred leagues from here. But often the Apache warriors and their women escaped and succeeded in returning to their mountains, walking barefoot and unarmed for hundreds of miles in hostile territory. Even when the Apache captives were deported to the island of Cuba for forced labor in remote mountain plantations, they managed to break their shackles and, allying themselves with runaway black slaves, fought the colonists from the jungle of the Sierra Madre."

"So you don't believe that the Americans can get the Sierra Blanca Apaches under control?"

"If the Mescaleros were capable of defending themselves against the Spanish soldiers, who nicknamed them *pharaohs,* even though the Spanish knew their customs and territory to a tee, don't you think they will fight to preserve their last stronghold against you greenhorn soldiers?"

Suddenly I became aware that Lieutenant Loring was responding to the burning looks of our host's daughter. He started to sit up straight at the table, to smooth his long locks, and to glance out of the corner of his eye in her direction, while paying less attention to the discussion with Don Anú. I had to bite my tongue at certain moments in order not to answer in place of the officer, as our host, in his gentlemanly way, was accusing the American soldiers of being clumsy and incompetent in dealing with the Indians of this territory.

But the officer's mind was already absorbed in other battles.

The Memoirs of the Patriarch

As soon as we got up from the table, Lieutenant Loring approached the patrón's daughter to compliment her on the food and service in a few words of broken Spanish, since the beautiful Esther spoke little English. On the other hand, as far as the language of love was concerned, she knew every expression; with a few passionate glances and a couple of sighs, she succeeded in infatuating the officer, who started flirting with her among the cushions in the drawing room's dais. Meanwhile Don Anú and I drew near a fireplace in the corner where a big oak stump was blazing. Although it had been hot during the day, in the heights where Don Anú's hacienda was, it turned cool at nightfall. My host offered me a glass of brandy that I did not refuse.

"I noted that you have followed with interest my conversation with the lieutenant," the patriarch said to me, observing that he had lost the previous interlocutor. "And I have noted with satisfaction that you speak our language correctly. Unfortunately, many of your soldiers don't bother to learn Spanish, because they consider themselves in conquered territory but they're mistaken. The first thing that conquerors must do is learn the language of the vanquished, the way the Romans did with the Greeks and the Spanish soldiers and missionaries did with the natives in America."

After he lit another cigar and had a little more brandy, I noticed that the patriarch's eyes sparkled with an idea that he immediately shared with me. "I perceive in your alert expression the thirst for knowledge, and I'm sure that you will be interested in the diary that I began on the very day the American army entered the New Mexico Territory. Just imagine: I found myself at that time hunting *cíbolo* in the northern plains, with other hunters! And right there among them was the genízaro Gil Gómez, when he was still a little brat, with his adoptive father, Don Antonio Gil."

I could not refuse this kind of offer, but while the old man was reading me his memoirs—written in a flowery calligraphy in a notebook bound in fine Cordovan leather—I followed out of the corner of my eye the billing and cooing of the lovebirds. They had made themselves comfortable on the large cushions of the dais in the drawing room with so much intimacy that it was difficult to know where the flowing skirts of Esther ended and the red stripe of the engineering lieutenant's pants began.

The patriarch started to read us his diary:

August 15, 1846, General Stephen Watts Kearny, Commander of the Army of the West, who had left Independence, on the banks of the Missouri River, the end of June and during six weeks crossed the great prairies by the same route as the caravans that went to Santa Fe, arrived at the New Mexican village of Las Vegas at eight sharp in the morning. General Kearny entered the plaza of the settlement on horseback, accompanied by his general staff and a squadron of dragoons, whose metal shakos shone under the fierce sun, and was received by the mayor, Don Juan de Díos Maes, and two officers of the New Mexican militia. They were soon surrounded by a multitude of villagers and peones who had congregated on the plaza upon learning of the approach of the Union Army.

The general invited the mayor and his entourage, more by gestures than by words, since he spoke no Spanish nor did the Mexican speak English, to go up on the roof of a building on the plaza. From there they could be seen and heard—although perhaps not understood, because the majority of the population didn't understand the language of the invaders, except for the few words necessary to do business with the North American merchants who for some time had come down the Santa Fe Trail.

"Mr. Alcalde and people of New Mexico," the general began, in English, of course: *"I have come amongst you by the orders of my government, to take possession of your country and extend over it the laws of the United States. We consider it, and have done so for some time, a part of the territory of the United States. We come amongst you as friends, not as enemies; as protectors, not as conquerors."*

While the American general continued reading his speech from the roof, a rider dressed as a *cibolero* on a richly harnessed chestnut horse cut through the crowd without any consideration for that audience of peasants, who seemed mesmerized, not so much by the eloquence of the orator as by the authoritative tone and the shiny weapons and uniforms of the foreign troops. The horseman wore a hat with a broad brim and golden band, a serape of lively colors, pants open from the knee down with silver buttons along the side. Supported on the tip of the stirrup was a long lance with an iron point that stood higher than the American banners. He was followed by an Indian boy on a pinto pony; the lad was so small that his moccasin-clad feet barely reached the edge of the stirrups. He carried a bow and arrows on his back and a skinning knife at his belt, and he controlled as best he could the rearing of the mustang pony, which pricked its ears with fear, prancing in the midst of the silent crowd.

Upon arriving at that point, the old man raised his eyes from his notebook, directing at me a wink of complicity, and whispered in my ear, "I was one of the ciboleros on that expedition, and as you have probably already guessed, the two horsemen I have just described were none other than Don Antonio Gil and his adopted son, the Cabezón genízaro." Then he proceeded with General Kearny's harangue.

". . . now I tell you, that those who remain peaceably at home, attending to their crops, and their herds, shall be protected by me in their property, their persons and their religion; and not a pepper, not an

onion, shall be disturbed or taken by my troops without pay, or by the
consent of the owner. But listen! He who promises to be quiet and is
found in arms against me, I will hang."

You didn't have to know much English to understand that behind
the civilized speech of the general lay a serious threat, and the audience
of Spanish villagers and peones perceived it that way. Behind the
adobe houses of the plaza one could see some stubble fields where
normally only flocks of sheep were grazing; but that day those gentle
rolling hills were bristling with the rifles of the invading army.
As the heat of the sun burned away the mist, a huge encampment
with tents and wagons could be seen over the hills, and here and
there the somber shine of a bronze cannon stood out over an artillery
limber.

"From the Mexican government, you have never received protection,"
continued the general. *"The Apaches and the Navajos come down*
from the mountains and carry off your sheep, and even your women,
whenever they please. My government will correct all this. It will keep
off the Indians, protect you in your persons and property; and, I repeat,
will protect you in your religion. I know you are all great Catholics;
that some of your priests have told you all sorts of stories; that we would
ill-treat your women and brand them on the cheek, as you do your
mules on the hip. It is all false . . ."

When General Kearny got to that point in his speech, the cibolero
turned his horse around, and as soon as he managed to clear some
space in the crowd, he dug his silver spurs into the flanks of the
chestnut and galloped away, followed by his young companion, whose
pony tried to bolt when it felt the reins let loose.

The two riders met the rest of the buffalo hunters on the top
of a hill where they were waiting with the horse remuda and
several carretas loaded with meat and buffalo hides. There they could
contemplate the maneuvers of the gringo army, whose main body
was on the crest of the nearby hills awaiting the outcome of their
commander's negotiations with the mayor of Las Vegas.

After clearing his throat with one last sip of brandy, the old man
finished the last page from that chapter of his diary.

A short while later General Kearny and his entourage were leaving the village galloping with regimental pennants unfurled and the blue tunics of the officers, with the red stripe, making a vivid contrast with the dry grass of the fields behind them. When the troops arrived at the crest of the hill, the order was given to sound, *mount up!* And the sound of the bugles echoed a long time in the valley, while on the hill opposite the caravan of buffalo hunters also pulled out, accompanied by the squeaking melody of the carretas, onto the Santa Fe Trail.

Apparently the patriarch could stay awake exactly the length of an episode of his memoirs. As he got to the last line, Don Anú's head rested on his chest and he fell sound asleep, the leather notebook still open in his hands. Two seconds later, his half-closed mouth emitted a powerful snore, loud enough to startle the two love birds, who were deep in conversation without knowing one another's language, not unlike General Kearny and the mayor of Las Vegas.

But people of opposite sexes have a more effective universal language. Once when I glanced over in that direction, I thought I saw the lieutenant's hand graze the waist of the beautiful Esther. No doubt lying on satin-covered cushions could lead to the promiscuity of an eastern seraglio.

In any case, after covering her father's legs with a blanket as soon as she noticed he had fallen asleep next to the fire, the beautiful Esther returned to say good-bye to her new flame, but before retiring to her room she furtively slipped a folded note between the trembling fingers of Lieutenant Loring. Since the note was written in Spanish, no sooner did we return to our room than the officer handed me the paper, and with an authoritative voice that could not conceal his embarrassment, he said, "Burdette, tell me what this note says and immediately forget its contents. That's an order!"

By the light of the oil lamp that had been left in our room, I promptly read and translated the note into English: "At twelve sharp tonight I'll wait for you alone in the torreón gallery. Signed: Yours Forever, Esther."

No sooner had I read the note than there passed through my mind in rapid sequence fragments of the stories I had heard about the beautiful Esther. I had discarded them before as ghastly fables, but suddenly they didn't seem so improbable. According to the gossip, the patrón's daughter used love potions to bewitch her lovers, and when she had tired of them she would turn them into strange birds and animals.

And when I noticed the expression of rapture that shone through the officer's spectacles, I knew that I had to think fast if I wanted to save the day. I couldn't have cared less if the officer had a love affair with the beautiful minx—after all, Loring was certainly old enough to know what he was getting into—but I was afraid the encounter might be only the first episode in a more dangerous adventure, where he could end up being the victim of some spell. What if the things they said were true: could Esther really turn her men into animals? Although I had had some quite extraordinary experiences in the army, I still hadn't had to suffer the humiliation of receiving orders from an owl or a coyote.

Something had to be done to prevent the gullible officer from throwing himself into the arms of that witch; and I did it. In La Fonda del Güero at San Acacia I had had time to buy a little bottle of brandy. So while the officer spruced up his hair in front of the mirror, carefully polished his spectacles, and brushed his uniform as though going to a dress parade, I sat down on my cot on the other side of the room and uncorked the demijohn as loudly as possible.

I knew that Loring would need a couple of swigs to boost his self-assurance for a first rendezvous of that kind; and half a minute later, the officer had crossed the room and was beside me, asking me if I would let him try a sip of that liquor. I also knew that the generous wine at supper had affected the lieutenant, whose cheeks had turned red, and not just from amorous excitement.

A couple of brimming cups of that powerful brandy on top of the alcohol that he had drunk before had such a calming effect that, when midnight, the time of the meeting, arrived, the officer was sleeping like a log on his bed. I carefully loosened some of his buttons and removed his boots so that he would be more comfortable. Also—since so much time has gone by, why not admit it?—I had guaranteed the efficacy of the drink by adding to the brandy a couple of spoonfuls of bromide from the bottle that I carried in my pack, from when I had been a nurse at the fort's sick bay.

For good measure I placed a heavy bar against the cottonwood door and seated myself on a chair in front of the only entrance to the room, with my pistol cocked and my sabre unsheathed on my knees. Anyone who might want to disturb the lieutenant's sleep would have to kill me to get to him.

At midnight sharp, when the silver watch that Loring had left open on the table struck the hour ("in case I take a nap," as the officer had said . . . it would have taken at least the firing of an artillery round to wake him from that sleep!), I heard footsteps in the corridor that led to the torreón.

Getting up from my guard post, I approached the door and peeked through one of the many cracks that the rough carpentry had left between the wood planks.

The first thing I saw was a wavering light that was approaching from the back of the hallway. Then a woman's shadow was projected on the whitewashed wall—and I knew she was wearing few clothes, if any, because her breasts made long, pointed shadows on the wall, like the horns of a young bull. Finally the beautiful Esther appeared, covered only by the long dark shawl that seemed molded to the curves of her body, creating fleeting mysteries with the folds of the veil and revealing the unmentionable by the light of a candle that she carried in her hand. It impressed me that the witch would carry a candle without a candlestick; she seemed not to mind if the hot wax melted over her fingers and arm!

For a few moments Esther stood in front of the door as though hoping that its crude leather hinges might loosen with the mere heat of her desire; and seeing that the door didn't open, she drew near the wood and began to rub herself against it, all the while emitting a throaty moan, like the guttural cry of an animal in heat. To keep the witch from detecting my presence, I stayed glued to the wood, motionless, in the same position as when I came to the door to spy through the crack. God forgive me, but I swear that in that moment I sensed through the cottonwood planks the odor of that female body! And I felt in my loins the spur of the dark poppy that was her crotch and the nipples that I could sense driving themselves into the wood like copper rivets. Through the dry cottonwood, I seemed to feel the moisture of her skin, and if I hadn't taken the precaution of bolting the door, I swear that at that moment I too would have given in to the frenzy of sin. Thank God the officer was lying on the cot like a new Ulysses tied to the mast lest he succumb to the singing of the sirens.

I let a long time pass, to be sure the witch had gotten tired of waiting, and when I was sure she was gone, and that Loring had rested enough, I poured a washbasin of cold water on his face and shirtfront.

When the officer opened his eyes, he looked at me as though from a great distance. Then he tried to get up to look at the watch he had left next to the bed, but as if his head were full of lead, it fell back on the straw pillow.

"Easy, easy," I murmured. "The rendezvous was called off. Shortly after you fell asleep a maid came with the message that her mistress had to postpone your meeting, as she was afraid of being caught by her father. I didn't want to wake you . . ."

Later, when he was more fully awake, I told Loring that the same maid had warned us to leave the hacienda before daybreak, since unbeknownst to Don Anú, some of his men were preparing for us a farewell a lot less pleasant than our reception. It was difficult to convince the officer that he must go without saying good-bye to his passionate—and yet unconsummated—conquest, but I explained that there was no time to lose if we wanted to reduce the advantage that the cuates had on us. Upon returning from our expedition, I suggested, there would be time to see the beautiful Esther again, and to thank the patriarch for his courtesy, if he wanted to.

Trying to make as little noise as possible, I sent Tafoya to prepare the horses, and we left the hacienda on the sly, asking the shepherd Narciso Quintana to pay our respects to the patrón, who was still sleeping peacefully when we crossed the drawing room on tiptoes to reach the exit to the zaguán.

The Torment of Tantalus

At dawn we were already quite far from the hacienda of Ojo de la Parida, although still on Don Anú's lands, which on that side reached almost to Socorro. The sun's rays were still breaking through the mist over the cottonwoods. Drawing near the river to water the horses, we heard what sounded like the bellowing of an ox, accompanied by the slapping noise of the scoops of a water mill lifting the water from the main current to fill an acequia.

Arriving near the waterwheel, I was surprised not to hear the neigh of the beast that should be pulling the heavy wooden wheel. But looking closely through the mist, I could see that the waterwheel was being dragged, not by an animal, but a man. Bound by the neck with a leather collar to the wheel, the poor wretch had his hands tied behind his back with a rope so that he couldn't get loose from his pillory.

"Water, for the love of God, water!" The man was calling out to us, but in such a hoarse voice that I'd taken it for an animal moan.

"My God!" exclaimed Lieutenant Loring, waking up suddenly from the hangover that had kept him half asleep since we left the hacienda. "How is it possible that someone could tie a man as if he were a beast of burden?"

It might seem strange that, being submerged to the knees in the current and with the water that overflowed the wooden buckets running over his back, the poor devil could still be thirsty. But in fact the way the halter tied his neck to the wheel did not permit one single drop of the water that was spilling to reach the lips of this Tantalus.

I jumped off my horse, brought the waterwheel to a halt with one arm, and with the other offered the man a swallow from my canteen, which the poor soul drank eagerly. His clothing, tattered from the rubbing of the wheel, emitted a filthy smell, as he was forced to answer nature's call without getting out of his pillory, as if he were tied to the bench of a galley.

Taking pity on his condition, the lieutenant dismounted and, with a single blow of his sabre, cut the rope that tied the man's hands behind his back. On seeing his hands freed, the face of the forced laborer showed first a grin of happiness, but it changed immediately into a grimace of terror; and, looking around him as though fearing that someone might have seen what had happened, he put his hands together again, crying out in his hoarse voice, "Tie me, for Christ's sake! Tie me again to the waterwheel! I asked you to give me a drink, not to untie me."

I translated the man's words for the lieutenant, explaining to him that most likely he had been tied there as some sort of punishment. I continued acting as interpreter between the two, although more than words would have been needed to allow those two very different worlds to understand each other.

"I don't know what offense you have committed, but not even the worst crime can merit tying you to this waterwheel like a beast of burden," said the lieutenant. "This territory is now part of a civilized country, and they cannot apply these barbarous punishments."

"The worst crime that you can commit in these regions," sobbed the poor wretch, "is to fall into disfavor with the Supreme Master of these lands."

"The Supreme Master of all this territory is the people of the United States! I am an officer of the American army, and you don't have anything to fear while you are under my protection," said the lieutenant, brandishing his sabre over the man's bare back as if he were about to knight him.

The forced laborer looked at us with feverish eyes, where you could read surprise and even incredulity, and when I translated the lieutenant's words into Spanish, on the man's parched lips appeared a painful grin that he probably intended as a sarcastic smile.

"I am a servant of Don Anú Baca; my parents were peons of Don Anú, and even my grandparents served on his lands. I must answer to the master of the Ojo de la Parida with my life and property, not to the American army. With that sabre you will be able to cut off my head or cut out my heart, but you will never cut the ties of several generations that join my family to my patrón."

I assured that man that it was not our intention to make him fall out of favor with his patrón, but to help him in his sad situation, and I promised to tie him to the waterwheel again if he would tell us the misdeed that he had committed to deserve such a hard penance.

"My only misdeed has been to not want to commit one," groaned the man, sitting down on the ground, "but to defend my innocence I would have to accuse someone too powerful."

Before he could go on talking, I offered him a piece of jerky and some bread that I had in my knapsack, and the poor wretch devoured that frugal grub as if it were a banquet. I used all my powers of persuasion to convince him to tell us his story, swearing by all the saints that we would not repeat it, even in a confessional.

The man finally agreed to tell us his misfortunes.

"My name is Donato, a name that the parish priest of Sabinal gave me in view of the gifts providence awarded me, although it is one of those very gifts that has reduced me to my present condition. I was born strong and robust from my mother's womb, and the midwife didn't have to look very hard to verify that a boy had just been born, for I came into this world well prepared for love. And ever since I was a young man, I have always been happy to let anyone inspired by a healthy curiosity see the unusual virility that nature has blessed me with.

"I have never used my endowment, which many could have envied, for lewd purposes, although at times I was tempted by the mischievous maidens who, during the fiestas to bless the acequias, would hide among the canebrakes in order to see me naked while bathing myself. I was already engaged to be married to a virtuous young girl from San Acacia whenever the priest would come, and then I would be able to make good use of the abundance with which Christ our redeemer had endowed me from my birth. That's when this misfortune struck me.

"It all began during the grape harvest, when I was doing some work in the vineyards of the patrón. Don Anú's daughter cast her eye on me, and asked her father to employ me as gardener for his hacienda, pretending that she had heard of my skills at tending fruit trees and all kinds of grafting. Cursed be the day that I accepted that work, although there was very little I could have done to refuse the wishes of the patrón! For several months I worked in the master's orchard. I made sure his table was always well supplied with the sweetest grapes, the reddest apples, the juiciest peaches, and every day I entered the room of the master's daughter to leave her a basket with the first fruits from the garden. All went well until, just two weeks ago, I took her some purple figs which were oozing honey, recently harvested and wrapped in a willow basket with leaves from the same tree the fruit had been picked from so the figs wouldn't lose the freshness of the early morning dew.

"I was already going down the stairs of the torreón where the patrón's daughter has her quarters when I heard the voice of the beautiful Esther calling me. When I entered the room again, I blushed to see that the master's daughter had come out to the antechamber wearing only a filmy camisole, whose openings revealed the flower of her charms.

'Come over here, don't be shy!' Don Anú's daughter called to me, and when I got near, she caught my hand while she asked in a throaty voice, 'Donato, haven't I asked you to bring me only ripe fruit? What is this that you have brought me?'

"And when I picked from the basket one of the figs so ripe that it was exploding, showing her the granules of seed distilling sugar, she took my hand that she had a hold of to her belly until I felt the dampness of her desire.

'Don't be foolish—stretch out your hand and touch my ripe fruit! This purple fig will give you more pleasure than those tasteless fruits!' And while she was saying that, with the other hand she was searching among my inner clothing until she found the hardness of my virile member and squeezed my testicles between her fingers, as if they were ripe purple figs. 'Come and let me enjoy the sap from your virility!' the woman said to me, while her avid lips sought to sip the sinful honey.

"As you can imagine, my body did not remain insensitive to such provocation, but a scapulary of the Santo Niño de Atocha that I was wearing around my neck gave me the energy to react to those lewd propositions and not without difficulty I pulled the woman away from my mast, where the sap of my fruit was already spilling in her mouth like milk from ripe figs.

'What do you want from me, woman?' I asked, pulling my torch away from her lips, which were still drooling with desire. 'Did my mother not warm the oven for me? Did they not feed me at home with the bread of honor and fidelity to the patrón? Why then do you want me to eat from the dish of bad faith and dishonor?'

"I wish I'd never said any of it. Seeing herself rejected, the shrew began to scream and call for help. And when the other servants and maids came to help, she threw herself on the floor and accused me of having broken into her room and tried to rape her, swearing by all that was sacred that she had not done anything to provoke me. She was a wily one! It was difficult to defend myself because it looked as though I were obviously guilty, the principal witness being my own virility, poking out of its cage like a fighting cock. The bitch showed her clothes reddened by the fig pulp to prove that I had used force, and showed the rips in her camisole, which she had made with her own fingernails.

"I had no way to defend my innocence, nor was it advisable to do so, because if I told the truth, I was accusing the master's daughter of lust and deception. Taking justice in their own hands, the other peones took me to the corrals and castrated me with the same knife they use to castrate the bull-calves, while the maids, some of them Indians, avenged themselves for the abuses that others had committed on them, covering me with blows and scratches. They were going to hang me from the same fig tree where I had picked the sinful figs, when Don Anú appeared, attracted by the shouting. When he saw me castrated, bleeding half to death, and converted into an *ecce homo*, a flogged Christ, he had compassion for me and decided that I should not be killed, but rather spend the rest of my life half submerged in this water so that my evil desires might cool off. And here I am, turning this wheel of shame, condemned for life because of a sinful love!

"Now that I've told you my story, I beg you to fulfill your promise and tie me again to the waterwheel. Let's not play with fire; someone may just pass by and tell the patrón that I was trying to escape his punishment!"

It didn't seem necessary to translate Donato's story in full for Lieutenant Loring (although I thought that perhaps after his misfortune, instead of Donato, it would have been more appropriate to call him Castrato). I gave an abridged and slightly altered version, fearing that the officer might feel offended to hear his lover of the previous night described as a scheming, lustful woman.

I promptly fulfilled my promise, tying the unfortunate fellow again to his pillory, with his hands bound behind his back, using the same hemp rope we used to hobble the mules. And after having returned the wretched soul to his animal condition, we continued on the road toward Fort Conrad, where we arrived at dusk.

The Spider Woman

After giving the peones from the Rancho de la Parida the slip, the twins took hidden trails through brush in the Manzano Mountains and traveled all night under cover of darkness. When dawn came, they saw to the south the extension of the Jornada del Muerto, bordered on the east by mountain ranges that formed a natural barrier in the direction of the Sierra Blanca. To cross the Jornada, they had no choice but to take to open country, confident they had put enough distance between them and their pursuers.

As Narbona had taught him, Decoy led the way, his eyes fixed on the ears of his horse; he couldn't suddenly turn his head around and glance back, and least of all could he look up into the sky, because doing so could immediately unleash a thunderstorm. But as the red ball of the sun started to rise above the monotonous wastelands, peppered only with chamisa plants, Cimarrón began showing his fatigue and lost his composure. He lowered his eyes toward the horse's hooves when the animal stumbled over a molehill, looked up in the direction of the sky to follow the trail of a few clouds that the wind was pushing from the southwest, and even turned his head around to say something to Gil Gómez, who was riding behind him, until his friend had to remind him, "If you wish to comply thoroughly with what Narbona told you, you must not look up into the sky, because that could bring a downpour on us; you also can't look around to see what's behind you, since it could attract the enemy in our direction."

But Cimarrón, in no mood for sermons, answered defiantly, "Surely you don't think that because I look up into the sky I'm going attract rain and hail!"

"Be careful. In the altered language hail is *that which throws several objects at the earth.* If I were you, I wouldn't defy Narbona's instructions."

"Very well, whatever may be the right way of saying it, but just because I raise my eyes toward the sky, on a clear day like today, I don't think that it's going to unleash a storm." And to show his disbelief, Cimarrón let go of his horse's reins and looked up into the sky, opening his arms and offering his chest to the sun's rays.

"Well, look at *those which one wishes would move about on the surface of the sky;* it wouldn't surprise me if at any moment they release a downpour over the plains."

"Bah, don't tell me you believe all those stories! Do you really think that just by turning my head I can cause an enemy attack?" And suiting the action to the word, he quickly turned his head toward the horse's hindquarters instead of looking slowly over his shoulder sunwise as his mentor had told him to do.

Decoy had barely made this gesture when, from the bottom of the valley, they could hear the thundering hooves of the posse that Esther had sent after them.

"Maybe next time you'll pay more attention to my advice!" exclaimed Gil Gómez, galloping off.

The cuates dug their spurs into their horses and struck the mules with the reata, trying to gain ground on their pursuers, although this time the other riders were quite close. All at once the sky grew dark and a torrential rain began to fall. The dry gully suddenly became a powerful arroyo running with muddy water.

Fortunately, the downpour was so intense that it made it impossible to see three steps ahead and wiped out any trace of a trail. The twins branched off to one side of the cañada and hid among some rock formations, succeeding once again in giving the slip to their pursuers. After waiting for a while in the rain, they peeked cautiously out at the ravine. They could hear the rumbling of the current, which, a few hundred meters down, emptied into a subterranean channel that turned into a drainage of mud and rock.

Not even a trace could be seen of the posse; the earth seemed to have swallowed the horses along with their riders. Perhaps they had to turn back to avoid being washed away by the current. As quickly as the sun had disappeared, it came back.

"Now I understand why they call this place Chupadera Mesa (Drainpipe Mesa)," said Gil Gómez.

The danger was over. When they climbed back up the steep bank of the cañada, they saw the red stone walls of the Gran Quivira mission shining under the glaze of the recent rain as if it had been built the day before. It was one of the oldest missions that the Franciscan fathers had founded to convert the Jumano Indians at the northern end of the Jornada del Muerto. Two other missions in the region, Quarai and Abó, had also been abandoned several centuries ago because of the drought and the effect of the plague among the Indians but above all because of the continuous onslaught of the Apaches. That is why those settlements of Christianized Indians were called "the missions that died from fear."

Looking for a cool place, because the midday sun was beating fiercely on the plains, the twins entered the mission church, whose thick stone walls were virtually intact although it had lost part of its roof. Half closing one's eyes, it wasn't difficult to imagine a procession of neophytes walking toward the altar singing a religious hymn, under the guidance of a missionary with a long beard and a coarse sackcloth. However, what the travelers heard as they crossed the threshold of the church was not celestial music, but rather the cawing of the big black bird, which was perched on top of the stone cross on the altar.

"Do you see what I see?" Gil Gómez asked Decoy in a low voice, as he began to unsheathe his rifle silently, avoiding a sudden movement that could scare the bird away.

"It seems as though *he who spreads his wings* doesn't want to leave us alone," said Decoy, also in a whisper while the genízaro shouldered his weapon. "But I don't believe it's worth wasting a bullet on that varmint."

"That dirty carrion eater alerted the peones when we came close to the hacienda at La Parida and it looks as if it has been following us since then."

"Remember what Narbona said, that using *that which discharges wind* could deter the Sacred Beings from protecting us, and especially in a church!" warned Decoy.

And picking up a rock, he threw it at the bird with all his might; but when the projectile was about to reach its target, the bird took off flying. He managed only to hit one of its legs, tearing away a black feather that whirled up in the air for a few moments above the apse of the church.

While they followed the bird's flight with their eyes, outside the church they noticed a column of whitish smoke coming from behind a bush in the direction of an abandoned Indian settlement near the mission ruins. They thought it must be their pursuers, who had come to camp in that spot; but then the genízaro remembered what Ninsaba had told them just as they were about to depart. "My mother told us about an old lady who lives alone; she knows the region well and could give us some good advice."

"Quite honestly, one can't find a more lonely place for a human being. On the other hand, among the rocks there is enough company," said Decoy, referring to the rattlesnakes that were basking in the afternoon sun on the rocks.

"Careful not to step on *he who is moving a hoop along,* who at this hour is taking a siesta," said Gil Gómez, showing once again his command of the war language.

Moving silently through the bushes, the cuates went toward the smoke. It was coming out of one of those circular rooms that the Spaniards called *estufas,* but whose original name was kiva, as the Pueblo Indians still call the subterranean rooms that they use for their council meetings and prayers. Almost completely covered with bramble bushes and tumbleweeds, the stone and sand structure protruded a few spans above the ground, and from the underbrush emerged a wooden ladder, one of the poles longer than the other.

The cuates climbed down the ladder with care, because several of the rungs were loose or rotten, and besides, there was more steam than light coming from the fire burning at the bottom of the hovel. When they reached the floor and attempted to take a few steps stretching their arms out in the darkness to feel their way, the young men felt on their faces and arms the smooth and sticky spider webs that covered the walls and ceiling of the cave.

When their eyes got used to the semi-darkness, they were able to make out at the back of the underground room a shape that barely resembled a human being. It was an old woman with a small head and thin hair, a very wrinkled face, a fat round body covered with a frayed blanket like a spider web, and long, thin arms that stretched out in an enveloping gesture to greet the visitors.

"Welcome strangers, *cackle, cackle . . .* whoever you are. What brings you to this lonely place, the two of you traveling together? *Cackle, cackle . . .*"

The old lady's toothless gums made a curious clicking sound as she spoke, and her eyes reflected the glow of the fire with multiple reddish sparkles, like the multifaceted eyes of an insect. The cuates were so surprised by the creature's strange appearance that they didn't find the right words to answer. The old woman repeated the question. "Where are these two handsome young men headed together?"

"Really we're not bound for any place in particular. We were just passing through, and not knowing where to go, we decided to come into this hole," Gil Gómez finally answered.

His friend added, "The truth is, we don't have a better place to go to, and since the sun is so hot in the heat of the day, we have been looking for shelter among these ruins."

"Can you two be the ones who are in search of your father?" asked the old lady.

That question took the cuates by surprise, and they started babbling the first thing that came to mind. "We don't know this region very well, and we were following the route of the Sun, but if you know the way to the Sierra Blanca, perhaps you could show it to us," said the genízaro.

"I'm glad you're not the ones looking for your father. I had been told that two young warriors would be passing through here who were also following the Sun's route. Then you are not the famous Twin Warriors?"

"How can we be the Twin Warriors! We don't even look like one another!" this time Decoy answered. "Notice that my friend is taller than I, and I'm bulkier and more robust."

"It's funny, *cackle, cackle,*" said the old lady, scratching the only spot on her head where she had a few thin hairs. "I would have attempted to dissuade the twins from taking such a long and perilous road, but if you're not the ones, so much the better. I wonder if they would have paid attention to me, because all young people are the same when it comes to being reckless! *Cackle, cackle.*"

Gil Gómez didn't want to lose the opportunity to get information from the old lady. "Even though we're not the ones you expected, since we're not acquainted with this area, perhaps you could give us a few suggestions to help us in our journey. Your advice could be very useful to us!" he said, winking at his friend.

"The twins are going to need a lot of help in order to survive the dangers of this route: there are too many enemies between here and the place where their father dwells. It is a narrow barranca, at the bottom of which runs a spring that cascades from the top of the Sierra Blanca," said the old lady. And she added with a deep sigh: "If I could just talk with them, it is possible that I would be able to offer them some advice to escape those obstacles unhurt. *Cackle, cackle . . .*"

"You can tell us those things, as if we were the Twin Warriors," Decoy suggested, joining the game that his friend had begun.

"On the road to the Sun," said the old lady, who puckered up her lips as she talked, chewing her words the way the spider does when she eats a fly. "The travelers will have to cross at least four dangerous spots: the Canyon that Spreads and Closes Up until Crushing the Traveler, the Arroyo That Turns into a Torrent, the Canebrake Whose Sharp Canes Destroy the Traveler, and the Burning Sand Dunes That Bury Those Who Step on Them."

While she was describing those dangers, the old lady's long, bony arms moved and cracked, imitating the waving of canes, the turbulent movement of the water, or the whistling of the wind above the sand. She continued, "These obstacles are practically insurmountable, but there is a magical formula to calm the fury of those places, which in reality are live enemies in disguise." The old lady stopped for a moment to see how the cuates would react: "But perhaps you will not need it, *cackle, cackle . . .*"

The cuates exclaimed in unison, "Tell us just in case!"

"Very well. This is what you have to say when you come to one of the four obstacles which I mentioned to you:

> *Put your feet down with pollen.*
> *Put your hands down with pollen.*
> *Put your head down with pollen.*
> *Your feet are now pollen.*
> *Your hands are pollen*
> *All of your body is pollen.*
> *Your mind is made of pollen.*
> *Your voice is pollen.*
> *The pathway is beautiful (biké hozóni).*
> *Go in peace!"*

The old lady remained quiet for a moment so that the cuates could memorize the magic spell, and then warned them, "To reach the Sierra Blanca you will have to cross four mountain ranges: the Sierra Oscura, Sierra Soledad, Sierra de San Andrés, and Sierra de los Órganos. The mountains will serve as points of reference so that you don't lose your bearing when the noon sun makes the horizon waver. Your course is due southeast, so if the mountain ranges, which lie to the west, are too close to you, it is because you have lost your way, and you have come too close to the river."

The old lady marked the location of the mountains on the floor of the cave with the same stick that she used to poke the fire, showing how the Río Grande curved like a taut bow whose bowstring was the Jornada del Muerto.

The Magic Atole

"By the way, I haven't even offered you anything to eat; you're going to think I'm a very unfriendly old lady. In fact, I had prepared something to eat thinking that the Twin Warriors would come famished, after such a long trip," said the old woman, taking a small clay pot from a corner. "But I suppose that you too have an appetite."

The cuates nodded their heads yes, while the old lady tried to rekindle the fire, with some difficulty because the wood was still damp.

"The weather is strange: this morning there was radiant sunshine, so I went looking for a load of firewood, and when I least expected it a downpour came as though out of nowhere, *cackle, cackle* . . ."

"It's true that the weather is somewhat unsettled," said Gil Gómez, kneeling on the ground and blowing on the ashes to revive the flames of the fire. "But don't worry, we'll help you rekindle *that which tells a story.*"

On hearing the stranger use the war language, the old lady examined him more closely with her small intense eyes, but she made no comment. She placed near the fire a tiny earthenware vessel with some *atole* in the bottom and set about stirring the paste with the same stick she was using to poke the fire. When the corn paste began to warm up, she added a handful of dry seeds that she carried in a leather pouch in her shredded clothing. "I hope this will be enough for you. I don't want you still to be hungry when you have a long journey yet ahead of you." Noticing that Decoy had the drinking tube and the scratcher hanging from his neck, she told him ironically, "Don't worry. We'll wait a bit until the atole cools down; I suppose you wouldn't like your food too warm. We'll remove the bowl from the fire before eating, because we're not in any hurry."

The cuates looked with some apprehension at the size of the vessel, which didn't seem big enough, but when they began to serve themselves they found that they could eat until they were full, and the contents of the bowl never seemed to diminish. Neither one had noticed that, while she was serving the food on the clay plates, the old lady had poured over it some special ingredients: turquoise powder on Decoy's plate and jade powder on the genízaro's, to strengthen their spirit and make their bodies invincible.

After they finished eating, the twins lay down by the fire. The old lady gave a toothless smile when she noticed that Decoy didn't lie face down, nor on his back, but rather on his side curled up in a ball, avoiding stretching out his legs. Before lying down, the two friends put their weapons and moccasins nearby, where they could reach them if they had to leave in a hurry.

"Don't get your feet too close to *that which tells a story* because you could burn *those by means of which one would dance about*," Decoy said to his friend, seeing that he was getting his moccasins close to the fire.

The genízaro, in turn, handed Decoy his blanket and said to him, "You can wrap yourself with *that by means of which one becomes warm*. I'm not going to use it because it's hot down here."

"It seems obvious that you are well prepared to cross Apache territory, *cackle, cackle,*" said the old lady, and asked, "Are you by chance waiting for a party of riders? Because right before the storm I heard the galloping of many horses in the direction of Chupadera Mesa."

Gil Gómez and his friend exchanged a knowing wink, and the genízaro replied, "Nonsense, we're traveling alone! Maybe you heard the rumble of thunder during the storm, but we haven't seen or heard anything."

The old lady shook her head, making her characteristic cackle. "So much the better, so much the better; because I could also recommend to you something that will keep those who go after you from being able to reach you. It's a trick that never fails."

Once again the two young men answered in unison. "Tell us just in case, because you never know!"

The old lady smoothed the floor of the cave with the backs of her bony hands. She whispered, "When you realize that someone is chasing you, with this formula you will be able to stop your enemies dead in their tracks. Even if they are about to catch you, you must stop a moment, and trace in the ground four lines with the point of a flint arrow: the first line will be marking four angles and will represent the zigzag lightning; the second one will be straight, and will represent the straight lightning bolt; the third is a zigzag and will represent the sun; and, the fourth one, straight, the rainbow." As she was talking, the woman drew the corresponding signs in the sand with her stick. She added, "But be sure that the zigzag lines are drawn by the older of you and the straight lines by the younger. And while you are drawing these lines you will sing this song.

I will make a mark that they will not cross.

☩

I am Nayénézgani, and they will not cross it.
With my leggings of black obsidian, they will not cross
it.
With my tunic of black obsidian, they will not cross it.
By my sides hang four capes of black obsidian.
My plume is of black obsidian.
Four lightning bolts of black obsidian sprout from me.
There where they go, they'll release deadly missiles.

☩

I am Tobadzístsíni, and I will make a mark that
   they will not cross.
And I will return with lighting bolts bursting from
   four places of my body.
Now, I'll return shooting, sending mortal objects
   here and there
And missiles that shoot from me."

The cuates made an effort to memorize the chant, although they could hardly keep their eyes open. But before letting them sleep, the old lady searched through her skirts, frayed almost translucent, and taking out some shiny objects with her bony hands, showed them to the cuates.

"Before you fall sleep, I want to give each of you a little gift, the same ones that I was keeping for the Twin Warriors. But considering how late it has gotten, I don't believe they are coming any longer," said the old lady. And she took from her rags a small ring of shiny obsidian, with two eagle feathers tied to it with silver threads, and handed it to Gil Gómez. "This one was for the older brother; this amulet is called *nayéatsos,* feather of the foreign gods, and it will let you rise above turbulent waters and calm the fury of the sharp reeds and the devouring sands."

Then the old lady searched through the web of her tunic until she found a tiny little box made of willow, which, when she moved it, produced a strange hum—as if inside there were a bee or a bottlefly— which she handed to Decoy with a ceremonious gesture. "This little box contains a great treasure; it is the Big Bottlefly, who will whisper advice and warnings in your ear during the trip; never doubt what he tells you, because he is always right. He will indicate the best way to get to your destination. But never try to see him or open the box, because he will escape and you will not see him again. Biké Hozóni!"

The cuates were so tired that they were barely able to mumble a few words of thanks, and they slept until the following morning when a ray of sun entered the mouth of the kiva and woke them. When they looked around for the old lady, she was no longer there; nor did they find the earthenware pot in which she had cooked the atole that they had eaten until they had their fill.

Intrigued, they began searching the back of the chamber, where the old lady had been seated when they entered her lair, but they didn't find even a trace of her presence. The only thing they saw in the farthest corner of the kiva was a large spider web with a black spider at the back, the kind with a small head and a fat body called *black widow,* because it produces very painful bites that can be fatal.

When they touched the place where the fire had been, the ground was cold and the charcoal turned to dust between their fingers, as if it were very old.

But they did see the marks of the four lines drawn in the ground, two straight and two zigzag, but they were already so faint and blurred that they looked as though they had been there since the beginning of time.

Back Home

Coming through the large cottonwood gate of Fort Conrad and embracing my friends—among them the remarkable Timothy Baltasar—I felt once again that those adobe barracks I had helped build with my own hands were the closest thing to my home in that inhospitable place of exile, the captivity of Babylon.

After I had read two letters from my family that had arrived while I was wandering in the desert, I told Baltasar in full detail the conversation I had heard that night in the camp next to the Río Grande when Colonel Washington had compared New Mexico to the land of the Flood. The soldier felt very proud that the colonel had perceived the similarities between the Southwest desert and the wastelands of Babylon, even though, to tease him, I told him that for me it only proved the mediocrity of an army where the commander-in-chief and a humble soldier could share the same whimsical ideas.

In any case, they didn't give me much time to enjoy the relative comfort of the barracks; the afternoon of our arrival, an arms inspection took place, followed by the selection of those who would accompany Lieutenant Loring across the desert to try to catch up with the cuates before they could arrive at the Sierra Blanca . . . that is, if our bones were not left to bleach in some spot along the way.

The new garrison commander, Captain Morone, didn't choose those soldiers who seemed best suited for that mission, but rather the ones whose presence he judged least necessary in the fort. He also took into account Sergeant Sweeny's opinion, which consisted simply of pointing out those of us he disliked most. Timothy Baltasar and I knew that we had many chances to win that raffle.

The sergeant didn't disappoint us, because we were the first to be selected. Clearly someone thought our scalps could add a cozy touch to the tent of a Mescalero chief, hanging from the center post. *Morituri te salutant.* . . . But he who laughs last, laughs best, and when Captain Morone designated the sergeant to accompany Loring as second in command for the mission, the soldiers enjoyed seeing how Sweeny's nasty smile turned into a grimace of disgust. He had no choice, however, but to stand at attention and obey.

The experience of the previous excursion to the Sierra Blanca was certainly not an encouraging precedent, and several of the soldiers who had been chosen for this expedition used the remaining hours before leaving the fort to write letters to their families and entrust their belongings to a friend "in case something might happen."

Even Timothy Baltasar, who was usually hard to discourage, confessed to me that night when the rest of the company was sleeping or pretending to sleep, that he was feeling beset by the darkest of premonitions. While I was bringing my diary up to date, he stayed up late putting in order the famous trunk that he kept under his cot. After that he handed me its key, which I must admit left me quite pensive.

Not being able to sleep, I went out to the courtyard and found Hilario Tafoya smoking one of his corn-husk cigars next to the embers. He didn't seem surprised that I'd be walking about at that hour, but he extended his blanket so I could sit down beside him. He almost seemed to *know* that I'd be coming out to talk to him.

"Aren't you going to get ready for tomorrow's expedition?" I asked him.

"I will not go on that expedition. I was only waiting to say good-bye."

"What, you're going to abandon the trail of the cuates now that we have the company of dragoons to cross the desert?"

"Although I have already betrayed some of my people's beliefs, there are things I would not dare to do. And one of them is cross beyond the four rivers that form our world: in this journey we have already crossed the San Juan, San José, and Puerco rivers and now if I also cross the Río Grande, which is the eastern limit of our territory, I would not have enough strength to counteract the evil influence of enemy territory. Besides, you have already learned everything you need to know to make that crossing. Biké Hozóni!"

By the tone of his voice, I could tell this farewell was serious. "Perhaps you don't plan to see me again?"

Just seeing the helpless expression that I must have had at that moment, the Indian gave me a small pat on the back, an unusual thing for him since he usually avoided all physical contact with whites. He added, "Besides, you know that this column of soldiers will never catch up with Gil Gómez and his friend. Although at times you may come close to them, and may see the tracks of their horses in the sand, you know that they are protected by powers that make them invincible."

"Was that why you refused to cut them off when we left Cabezón?"

"Perhaps you would have been able to catch up with them before crossing the river, but now that they are in enemy territory they will have put in action all the powers of the war ritual. Now they are going on the path of the Twin Warriors!"

"You never wanted us to catch up to them, did you?" I asked again.

Tafoya's face adopted an expression so serious that it almost frightened me. It was the first time I saw a flash of fear in his eyes. "I would never have dared to lay a hand on them." After a pause, he said, "Tomorrow, when the detail leaves the garrison, I will not be with you. But before I go, I want to give you a gift."

From the buckskin bag he always wore around his neck, the Indian took a small feather with some of the down still on the shank. He handed it to me with great ceremony, resting it on his open palms; with the cool morning breeze, the feather seemed to spin on his hands as if it had a life of its own and might take off flying.

"This is *hyiná bíltsós,* a feather from a live eagle, pulled from its body, and it has great properties for one who knows how to use it in a tight corner. This feather will clear the obstacles and traps that you will find in your path in enemy territory, but you can only use it when you really need it. When you encounter an insurmountable barrier, take out the feather from inside your chest and sing this song:

> *Put your feet down with pollen.*
> *Put your hands down with pollen.*
> *Put your head down with pollen.*
> *Your feet are now pollen.*
> *Your hands are pollen*
> *All of your body is pollen.*
> *Your mind is made of pollen.*
> *Your voice is pollen.*
> *The pathway is beautiful (biké hozóni).*
> *Go in peace!"*

Tafoya repeated the song twice, and when he thought I had memorized it, he got up from beside me, picked up his blanket, and disappeared in the dark.

It was still as dark as Egypt when we trotted out toward the Río Grande. The place where we usually forded the river was swollen by some fierce downpour in the headwaters. As a farewell gift, perhaps to clear his conscience for letting us head into an uncertain situation, Captain Morone had let us take a light cannon that rolled on its limber, although we almost lost it when the mules that were pulling the carriage sank up to their necks in the turbulent waters.

We were fifty, counting Lieutenant Loring, Sweeny, the three artillery men who had joined our company, and half a dozen Apache auxiliaries. The detail that crossed that fateful river was embarking on a journey from which few would return.

Fortunately, as the light of a new day broke over the outline of the mountains, Timothy seemed to recover his good humor, and at the back of the file you could hear him humming his famous song:

> *How many miles to Babylon?*
> *Three score and ten.*
> *Can I get there by candle light?*
> *Yes, and back again.*

Jornada del Muerto

The cuates took the route that had been marked by the old lady at Gran Quivira, and riding toward the south, at the end of the first day's journey, they made out the silhouette of the Sierra Oscura above the hazy heat waves of the desert. Before evening fell, they thought they could see from a rise the metallic reflection of an artillery cannon and soon spied the detail that was rapidly crossing the desert in their direction.

"It looks like the American soldiers have finally caught up with us," commented Gil Gómez, pointing out the dust cloud the column was raising toward the west.

"According to what Narbona taught us, it's the moment to say *'the enemy's horses have been here,'"* Decoy said, adding with a slight smile, "and if they haven't been yet, they soon will be, because they are breathing down our necks."

"To the east we have the barrier of the malpaís, and to the north the men from the Ojo de la Parida may still be following us," answered the genízaro. "I'm afraid this time we are trapped."

The reddish sunset was lighting up the malpaís as if the blood of the giant slain by the Twin Warriors had started running again.

"If we need to, we'll trace in the ground the lines the old lady showed us to stop their coming," said Decoy.

The genízaro stared at him with a perplexed grin.

"Do you really think that spell is going to work?"

"I have learned to drink water in a cane tube, I have to wait until food cools down, and I speak an ungodly language. I hope all this is good for something!"

"We're going to need all the power in the world to get out of this tight spot!"

"If what we've been doing up to now has only been a game, let's keep playing it to the end." Dismounting, Decoy looked for a flint point and traced on the sand two straight lines while he murmured,

> *"I am Tobadzístsíni, and I will make a mark that*
> *they will not cross.*
> *And I will return with lightning erupting from*
> *four places of my body.*
> *Now I return, sending mortal objects.*
> *And projectiles that come from me."*

He handed the stone to his friend, who traced two serrated lines while he sang,

> *I will make a mark that they will not cross.*
> *I am Nayénézgani, and they will not cross it.*
> *With my moccasins of black obsidian, they will not cross it.*
> *With my leggings of black obsidian, they will not cross it.*
> *With my tunic of black obsidian, they will not cross it.*

Scarcely had they stopped reciting the chant when large whirlwinds of dust began to rise on the plains. The American troops were coming on the double. Looking for shelter from the hurricane-force wind, the dragoons dismounted; the mules that were pulling the limber became frightened and took off running with the cannon.

When the sandstorm calmed down and the detachment regrouped and was able to continue the march, the fugitives had disappeared into the foothills of the Sierra Oscura. They continued riding until well into the night and camped on the eastern slope of the mountain without lighting a fire so that the soldiers wouldn't spot them. Gil Gómez went up the slope of the mountain the way Narbona had recommended, and taking from his breast the little bag of sand from the Four Mountains, he scattered particles of the sacred dust to the four cardinal points and made an offering to the mountain, saying, "Mountain, bring me a suitable dream, a favorable message from the god Sun."

Returning to the place where they had made camp, he dug a little well in the sandy ground until water sprung up. They ate a bit of their supply of dried yucca and jerky and lay down to sleep under their blankets. Decoy used the tube that Narbona had given him to drink the water from the bottom of the well, and for the first time he could understand that it was a very useful tool in the desert.

Gil Gómez took a long time to fall asleep because of the relentless cold that went up the bed of the gully. Finally, he curled up with his face between his knees, and he managed to fall asleep. But at around midnight, the genízaro woke up shivering with cold. Frightened, he spoke to Decoy. "Hey, my friend, did you call me?"

Decoy didn't answer; he was sleeping soundly.

"Then why did I wake up?" the genízaro asked again. "Truly, you didn't touch me?"

His friend continued sleeping like a log.

"Why am I so restless, then? It seems as if a ghost passed through here and shocked me with its icy flight. Can't you see how I'm trembling all over?"

"What's happened, why have you wakened me?" Decoy finally said, rubbing his eyes still heavy with sleep. "Are the soldiers approaching?"

"My friend, I have had a very strange dream. We found ourselves in the middle of a canyon we were going to cross, and suddenly the mountain fell on top of me, crushing me; the rocks fell on us, but we got out, flying from there like flies."

It took Decoy a long time to realize what he was being told, but when he understood that it was a dream, he gave it a favorable interpretation. "The dream you have had is a good omen, and I believe it has a positive meaning for our trip. The mountain that you have seen in your dreams I believe represents Humbaba, and dreaming that it collapsed means we will beat him. We will cut off his head and we will dump his body in the desert."

The Canyon That Widened and Narrowed

After rounding up the horses that had bolted scared during the sandstorm, we camped at the foot of the western slope of the Sierra Oscura, where there was no watering hole within ten miles. Sergeant Sweeny did not allow anyone to get close to the canteens after curfew, warning that he would shoot at anyone caught trying to drink at night. The horses neighed from thirst, and they were restless all night long, trying to break loose from their pickets. We were also forbidden to light fires so as not to alert the cuates, who, according to Lieutenant Loring, couldn't be too far away.

"We were at the point of catching up with them, if it hadn't been for that unfortunate sandstorm," said the lieutenant in a very loud voice, no doubt to encourage his troops.

But morale was low, and that same night, five men deserted. The following day, when Sergeant Sweeny called roll, we learned that of the fifty men who had left Fort Conrad, only forty-five of us were left. The fact that Tafoya and the other Navajo auxiliaries had refused to accompany us had left us in the hands of a few Mimbreño Apaches, first cousins of the Mescaleros; one couldn't be sure whether they had come along to help or to spy on our movements.

As soon as we left the campsite, Timothy Baltasar immediately got by my side and started to make comparisons between our crossing and the exodus of the Jews across the desert, pursued by the army of the Pharaoh. The problem was that we, the American army, were now to play the unpleasant role of being the pursuers. But I reminded Baltasar that, according to Don Anú Baca, the Spaniards had also called the Mescalero Apaches Pharaohs.

That same morning, Lieutenant Loring regained hope when we saw shining in the distance the armor of the genízaro and his companion, as we entered a narrow pass of the Sierra Oscura.

"This time it won't be so easy for them to elude us," said Loring as he ordered us to pick up the pace.

At the risk of running the horses to death under the scourge of the sun, we were able to shorten the distance to the small cloud of dust being raised by the adventurers. The troops cheered up when they saw that the cuates had entered a canyon that seemed to get narrower and narrower. But when we got halfway through it, we realized that the trail was intersected by an impassable gully. Of the fugitives and their horses not a trace could be seen; perhaps they had used the Rainbow Bridge to cross over the abyss.

Lieutenant Loring stood at the edge of the fault, trying to figure out what engineering device could be used to overcome this obstacle, but as nothing came to mind, the typical military philosophy prevailed, and we fell back on Sergeant Sweeny's peculiar logic. "If those ruffians have passed by here, so too can the dragoons of the Army of the West," said the fool, leaning forward on the stirrups of his terrified horse, which contemplated the precipice with much better judgment than its rider.

On one wall of the ravine rocks stuck out at regular intervals and could be used to facilitate the descent . . . as long as they did not collapse under the weight of the horses and equipment, which was the likeliest outcome.

Fortunately for me, the lieutenant sent me scouting at the other end of the fault, so I was excused from performing a balancing act on the bare rock; but from the other end of the cliff I was able to hear the unmistakable echo of the equipment smashing at the bottom of the gully. The deafening sound of the bodies of the steeds as they hit bottom froze my blood; I feared that some of the animals had dragged their riders down with them as they fell.

On my way back along the edge of the ravine, I found a place where the fault narrowed enough that a good rider could jump across to the other side. A few shreds of mist still hung about the edge of the gorge, making it difficult to judge the width of the chasm; at times it seemed to narrow and at others it apparently widened. I was tempted to try to jump with the horse, but I remained indecisive, since if I miscalculated the distance, I could well end up with my bones at the bottom of the deep gully.

All of a sudden I recalled my conversation with Tafoya the night before our departure, and I remembered the verses that I was supposed to sing whenever I found myself facing an insurmountable obstacle.

> *Put your feet down with pollen.*
> *Put your hands down with pollen.*
> *Put your head down with pollen.*
> *Your feet are now pollen.*
> *Your hands are pollen.*
> *All of your body is pollen. . . .*

I remembered also to take out the eagle feather that Tafoya had given me, and half closing my eyes the way the Navajo did, I recited the rest of the song.

I felt then as if a mysterious force was lifting me in the air, and when I opened my eyes, I found myself with my horse on the other side of the precipice, looking at the frightful pit that opened up at my feet, which I had cleared without knowing how I had done it. I was still overcome with vertigo from this experience when I heard the voice of Lieutenant Loring calling me. I saw his silhouette on the other side of the chasm, enveloped by shreds of fog that had drifted up from the bottom of the precipice. "Burdette, where are you? Come back, come back to the formation immediately! We have had a terrible accident! Four of our companions have fallen with their horses to the bottom of the ravine. Come back to avoid further disasters!"

A gust of wind cleared the fog that covered the rough edge of the gully. I was able to see the lieutenant clearly on the other side of the chasm, and he saw me. When he realized where I was, the officer stared incredulously, first at me and then at the gap, several yards wide, between the two sides of the ravine.

"May I ask what you're doing on the other side of the ravine? I sent you to find a safer path, not to risk your life with circus stunts. Please return to your place in the detail immediately!"

I could not jump again, as the chasm seemed to have grown even wider. And it was impossible to recover the bodies of the soldiers from the bottom of the precipice. But thanks to the signals that I gave them from the other side of the gully, the rest of the column was able to cross the ravine by means of a small bridge that Lieutenant Loring ingeniously constructed using the wagon poles of the carretas. That night, wrapped in my blanket but not yet asleep, I received an unpleasant visit from Sergeant Sweeny, who whispered in my ear, exhaling his foul-smelling breath in my face, "Burdette, I still don't know how you did it, but I know that you jumped the gully to make me look like a fool, and to make yourself look good in the eyes of the lieutenant. I want you to know that from now on I'm not going to leave you alone for a second. Instead of being in the vanguard, you'll be at the rear of the column, so if there is a difficult crossing, you'll be the last one to cross! Is that clear? Because I don't intend to say it again!"

What was clear was that of the fifty men with whom we had departed Fort Conrad, now there were only forty-one of us.

The Torrent That Swelled When the Traveler Passed

After clearing the canyon that widened and narrowed, at dawn the cuates headed south, emerging from the Sierra Oscura and heading for the Sierra Soledad. They crossed a canyon where a creek ran along the bottom. The sun came out as they were nearing a spot where the stream bounced along in small cascades, forming a rainbow of intense colors.

"Look how the rainbow is showing us the way through the mountains!" said Decoy. "This is truly a good omen. Biké Hozóni!"

"Well, what I'm seeing flying in front of me is not exactly a good omen," said Gil Gómez, pointing to the black bird that was hovering above the arroyo.

"I believe that you are seeing everywhere *he who spreads his wings,*" answered Decoy. "Perhaps it's not the same one we saw before."

"I know the way it flies. Besides, do you see that it's got a foot hanging? Probably when you threw the stone at it you broke its leg. All we need is for it to attract the Americans here with its cawing," muttered the genízaro.

"Wait. I believe *he who spreads his wings* wants to tell us something," said Decoy, pulling on the horse's bridle as he saw that the black bird was flapping its wings in circles above their heads and cawing as if to catch their attention. "It seems as though he would like us to avoid crossing *a rope-like object of specular iron ore lies.*"

"I'm beginning to get fed up with all these silly stupid omens and sorcery," said Gil Gómez, as he spurred his horse to cross the stream.

But at that moment they heard a rumbling like thunder, and the genízaro barely had time to move a few meters away from the arroyo, where the stream had suddenly swelled, turning into a powerful torrent that carried rocks and bushes in its path.

"Now you see that I wasn't mistaken," said Decoy. "On this occasion *he who spread his wings* was trying to warn us of the danger."

"Evidently. In any case, the flood has calmed down and we can get across," said Gil Gómez, climbing down from the small hill where he had sought safety.

In fact, as quickly as the stream had swollen, it returned to its normal level, and if not for some broken branches and overturned rocks, it would have seemed as though the water had never overflowed its banks.

"If I were you, I would wait to see what happens," said Decoy insistently. "It could be that this is another one of those obstacles the old lady mentioned, and it would be good for us to recite the incantation that she taught us." Suddenly he extended his hand. "Wait!"

This time the flood surprised the genízaro and his mount in the middle of the riverbed, where the mass of water was of such volume that it lifted the rider and his horse in the air and submerged them in the swirl of mud, rocks, and bushes uprooted by the flood. Seeing that his friend was being swept away, Decoy galloped downstream, and untying the horsehair rope from the pommel of his saddle, he managed to lasso him around the waist and pull him out. The horse, on the other hand, disappeared, as if sucked up by the flood.

When Gil Gómez climbed to the edge of the riverbank, mud oozing through the joints of his armor, he threw himself on the grass to catch his breath.

"I don't know why you insist on wearing that armor," said Decoy. "If it had filled up with water, you would have sunk to the bottom like a rock."

"If it hadn't been for this breastplate, the boulders and the tree trunks would have squashed my ribs," answered the genízaro, still shaking water from every part of his body.

When he stopped shivering, they climbed up the canyon to a place where the arroyo narrowed and its waters still ran with some force. But when Decoy recited the song that the old lady had taught them to overcome obstacles of this kind, the current subsided and the flow of the water decreased so sharply that the cuates and their horses crossed to the other side on a bed of almost dry sand.

While they were crossing, Cimarrón thought he heard a strange humming keeping time with the murmuring of the water: *"Go on,"* it said. *"Go on, continue the path toward the home of your father."* But he decided it was only his imagination.

As night fell, the twins camped in the deepest part of the valley, and they searched for a shelter among the rocks that would protect them from the chill of the night air from the nearby desert. Gil Gómez went up the mountain until he found a suitable place to dig a waterhole and spread sacred pollen in the direction of all four cardinal points as an offering to the Sun.

Afterward he descended to the bottom of the valley where they had camped, and he lay down in a rock crevice, curled up in a ball to conserve his body heat, since he had lost the blanket that was tied to his horse saddle, along with other possessions. Soon he fell asleep, but around midnight a gust of cold wind awakened him and he thought his friend was calling him. "My friend. Were you calling me? Why have I woken up?"

Decoy was sound asleep and didn't even answer him.

"I would have sworn that someone touched me! I wonder why I find myself so restless? Why is it that all of my muscles are trembling as if I had a fever? It seems as though somebody is trying to rob me of my sleep."

Eventually the genízaro was able to wake up his friend and tell him the dream that was bothering him. He described it to Decoy. "I ran into a wild bull in the middle of the desert, and as he saw me he bellowed and scratched the ground, digging up so much dust that it obscured the sun. Seeing that he was about to charge me, I took off running, but he caught up with me and with a terrible force he gored me on the side, tearing up my clothing and knocking me on the ground. Then he squeezed me with an enormous force, pressing my abdomen until I lost my breath and blood was beating with force in my temples. But when I thought that the bull was going to finish me, he turned me loose and he offered me food and fresh water from his canteen."

After reflecting for a moment, Decoy offered this explanation for the dream. "Surely the character you saw was not a wild bull but Narbona's spirit, which has protected us during our journey, and has helped us find watering holes of fresh water all along the road.

After that positive interpretation of his dream, the genízaro calmed down and a refreshing sleep overcame him.

The Flight to Egypt

After making our way through the ravine where we had lost our companions, we once again found the trail of the adventurers, who were crossing sandy terrain where it was difficult to hide their tracks. All went well until we had to cross the bed of an arroyo where there were signs of recent flooding. Large stones were turned over and the mud still damp, even though the desert air dried everything in an instant.

Since the channel of the arroyo cut through a deep cañada, in order to avoid an ambush the lieutenant ordered the other officers to split the column in two: a vanguard and a rear guard. I was assigned to the latter, according to Sergeant Sweeny's recent order. To make sure I didn't get ahead again, the sergeant had ordered me to oversee the progress of the artillery limber and the two wagons of provisions at the rear of the column. On this occasion Sweeny's grudge against me may have saved my life.

The vanguard had barely begun to cross the ravine, three abreast, when, coming from the top of the mountain, we heard a sound like thunder, and through the bed of the ravine, which a moment before had been dry, a wall of water descended with such force that it dragged stones and tree trunks in its path. Those who were lucky enough to be near the other side of the ravine spurred their horses and escaped the flood, but the poor fellows who were caught in the middle of the arroyo were lifted in the air by the force of the water. In a few seconds they were dragged off by the whirlpool of stones and mud.

Those of us who had remained dry tried in vain to help our companions, but the strength of the current was such that when we tried to get near them, the torrent had already swallowed them like a giant drain. Fortunately, Lieutenant Loring had been one of the first ones to cross to the other side of the gully. Nor was Timothy Baltasar among the group of the missing men.

After a few moments of confusion, the flood seemed to subside. Those of us who had not crossed the gully were ordered to try to get to the other side. Since I was in charge of the rear guard platoon, responsible for the cannon and provisions, I decided to use my head. First I waited until the torrent had slowed. When it returned to a stream of normal proportions, I neared the edge of the water and recited that prayer that I had heard from Tafoya:

> *Put your feet down with pollen.*
> *Put your hands down with pollen.*
> *Put your head down with pollen.*
> *Your feet are now pollen.*
> *Your hands are now pollen.*
> *All of your body is pollen.*
> *Your mind is made of pollen.*
> *Your voice is pollen.*
> *The pathway is beautiful (biké hozóni).*
> *Go in peace!*

When they heard me murmuring that song, the soldiers beside me must have thought I was terrified literally out of my wits; but be that as it may, after I recited that prayer, the waters continued to subside and we were able to cross the arroyo undisturbed. The wheels of the artillery limber left their mark on the mud, which in the warm northeast breeze was drying rapidly.

A few hundred yards downstream, we once again found the trail of the cuates, who had passed by there a few hours before. I noticed that the tracks no longer showed two horses and two mules; now they seemed to be missing a horse. I thought perhaps they had lost it crossing the arroyo.

We found the bodies of our companions—six of them, rather, because two more were missing—downstream, where the flood poured out into a wide canebrake between two mountains. Remembering what had happened to the bodies of our companions during a similar flood in Dog Canyon, I recommended digging the graves of the drowning victims far from the streambed, so that another new flood would not uncover the bodies.

As on the other occasion, Timothy Baltasar was in charge of reading the "last prayer," since he was the only one who had a Bible in hand and knew how to read what was relevant:

> The Lord is a man of war: the Lord is his name.
> Pharaoh's chariots and his host hath he cast into the sea:
>   his chosen captains also are drowned in the sea of Reeds.
> The depths have covered them:
> They sank into the bottom as a stone.

The soldiers were touched by hearing the funeral prayer that Moses had recited over the remains of the Pharaoh's army, without thinking that in those circumstances it was our cavalry that had been swept away. But when Lieutenant Loring had poured the last shovel of dirt into the grave and the bugler sounded retreat over the burials of those poor souls, the soldiers repeated one of the verses that Baltasar had read:

> Is it that there are not enough graves in Egypt
>   that you bring us to die in the desert?

After that, the soldiers exchanged looks of understanding and, just after sunset, they congregated in small groups around the campfire. The clothing that they had put on the bushes to dry was fluttering in the evening breeze, projecting eerie shadows. And in the depths of the soldiers' eyes, illuminated by the glow of the fire, you could clearly read the word *desertion*.

To avoid being accused of taking part in the mutiny that was brewing, I moved away from the group of my fellow soldiers, approaching the place where the officers were gathered. On seeing me arrive, Lieutenant Loring came up to me. "Your friend Baltasar is very knowledgeable about the Bible."

"Before joining the army he studied to be a minister, Lieutenant."

"In fact, many of us who end up as soldiers have been frustrated in our true vocation. But what's certain is that each one of us feels God in our own way," said Loring, looking at me in a peculiar fashion.

Could the officer have been told that I had recited Tafoya's prayer before crossing the flooded gully? Later on, while I was trying to update my diary by the light of the fire's embers, Timothy Baltasar came to me with his Bible in his hand.

"Look what I've found: 'And it came to pass, when Pharaoh had let the people go, that God led them not through the way of the land of the Philistines, although that was near . . . but God led the people about, through the way of the desert, near the Sea of Reeds.'"

"Well, and what do you think?" I asked him, impatient to get to sleep.

"It's clear! The cuates have chosen the way of the desert, the longest and most difficult route, to reach their destination, according to the scriptures. So it is they who will be protected under the arm of our Lord, and if we insist on following them, only more bad things will happen to us, as happened to Pharaoh's army."

"Don't you think enough bad things have already happened to us in two days of travel?" I asked Baltasar, wrapping my blanket around me and trying to find sleep.

"More could happen, if we insist on continuing in pursuit of those adventurers. I sense that some mysterious force protects them, because they keep going forward over the same obstacles where we stumble."

"Well I think you have good instincts. I believe that the twins have performed certain rituals that protect them against the adverse forces of enemy territory."

"Don't tell me you believe in that Indian witchcraft? You could condemn yourself!"

"Perhaps it works for them. As Lieutenant Loring says, each one feels God in his own way."

When Baltasar finally went to sleep, and I drew near the fire to put out the last coals, I found written in the dust the same words that the soldiers had murmured at the end of his prayer.

Is it that there are not enough graves in Egypt
that you bring us to die in the desert?

That same night nine men deserted, the very ones who had been plotting around the fire. Between the deserters and the eight we had lost the day before in the flood, plus the previous losses, of the fifty men who had left the fort, only twenty-four remained.

Fire in the Canebrake

At dawn the next day, Sweeny woke me by kicking me in the back, and I was still half swollen with sleep when I mounted my horse and accompanied the column's march. In fact, it didn't really matter whether I was asleep or awake, because there wasn't much to think about or talk about while we rode alongside the dense canebrake that spread out at the foot of Sierra Soledad.

Perhaps for lack of anything more interesting to talk about, the rumor that I had succeeded in calming the furious waters of the torrent by reciting certain native chants ran throughout the detail . . . or, rather, what remained of it. I noticed that my companions began to look at me with a mixture of curiosity and mistrust, the way the common folk usually treat the prophets and visionaries, the same way the people of Israel had treated poor Moses.

News of my supposed magic powers even reached the ears of Sergeant Sweeny, who spurred his horse to the rear of the column where I was riding.

"Burdette, rumor has it that you have learned some witchcraft from your friend the Navajo renegade. I want you to tell me if there's some truth to that gossip."

"I assure you that if I had magic powers the first thing I would do is to turn this torrid air into a cool breeze. The only things Tafoya taught me were a few songs of his tribe, which I sometimes sing for fun."

"You think you're pretty smart, don't you?" replied the sergeant, who was always annoyed by my respectful answers. "Just remember one thing: if I hear you recite any of those devil spells again, I'll hang you from the nearest tree!" And when he noticed that in the middle of that plain there wasn't even a bush to hang your hat on, he roared: "Or whatever looks like a tree in this wasteland!"

Fortunately, Baltasar and I had agreed never to lose sight of each other so that the sergeant couldn't play a foul trick on us without witnesses. Seeing that Sweeny was giving me a hard time, from the other end of the column Timothy began to sing. He knew it got on the sergeant's nerves, and the fool fell into the trap, spurring his horse back to the vanguard to make him shut up.

We tried to detour in order to avoid crossing the dense canebrake that spread out to the very foot of the mountain range, but the scouts returned from the reconnaissance saying that from this side, the mountain slope rose vertically. Lieutenant Loring had to give orders for the formation to go through the midst of the canebrake, where the reeds grew mixed with thickets of cattail, the kind that have hard leaves as sharp as razorblades.

Digging their spurs, the officers forced their horses to enter the thicket, hoping it might open up farther along. But the stalks of the cattails were growing even closer together, and blood began to flow from the horses' flanks. To make things worse, the wind whipped the thicket with such force that even the points of the cattails pricked the horses, and when the poor beasts tried to protect themselves from the cruel points, bucking and kicking, they got deeper cuts. Neighs of pain began to be heard everywhere, and several horses reared up, throwing their riders to the ground.

Reaching a small clearing crossed by the stream that flooded the canebrake, the lieutenant gave the order to halt and dismount for a few moments' rest so that we could check the horses' wounds. Some animals had their chests covered in blood, and although most of the cuts were superficial, we couldn't cross that broad thicket at the cost of the hides of our mounts, already weak from the heat and the hard march.

While trying to find a way out, Loring permitted the men and horses to drink in the arroyo, and someone had the bright idea of building a fire to make some coffee. As dry as the canebrake was, it was almost inevitable that a spark would set fire to the rushes. In a matter of seconds the wind spread the fire so rapidly that the flames soon licked at our feet and at the hooves of the horses, which started neighing and rearing back. A couple of frightened animals succeeded in escaping from their riders and entered the thicket kicking and bucking until the smoke and flames enveloped them completely. Poor beasts!

To make the situation even worse, at that moment a rifle volley was fired, or at least that's what we believed, and all the men threw themselves to the ground, thinking that the Apaches had taken advantage of the fire to ambush us. Some sought refuge by jumping into the stream, although its turbulent waters were still rushing down. In spite of the gravity of the situation, it was comical to see the dragoons with their heads covered with water plants sticking out of the current like fat frogs.

As it turned out, the Apaches had nothing to do with the detonations we had heard: the flames had reached the wagon with the ammunition, and the cartridges started to explode because of the heat, although fortunately the random bullets hadn't wounded anyone. But in fact, even without an Indian attack, we were not in a comfortable situation, trapped in the middle of a burning canebrake.

In the midst of the general confusion and the cloud of smoke, which grew denser by the minute, I noticed that someone was pulling on my sleeve, and turning around, I saw the child-like face, covered with soot, of the company bugler, who whispered in my ear, "For God's sake, Burdette, I'm too young to be burned alive!"

His blue eyes looked at me with an expression of unbounded faith and confidence whose like I had never seen nor will I ever see again. No doubt the boy wanted me to recite the same prayer that had helped us the day before to cross the torrent in flood. Struggling to concentrate in the midst of that commotion, I succeeded in remembering the verses that I had heard from Tafoya:

> *Put your feet down with pollen.*
> *Put your hands down with pollen . . .*

As on the previous occasion, suddenly everything seemed to quiet down. The wind subsided and some clouds that appeared unexpectedly in the sky released a gentle shower on the canebrake, which gradually stopped burning, although it continued to smolder a long time. The fire had even helped to open a kind of path through the thickets of cattails through which we could pass without hurting the horses.

After picking up the arms and equipment that were scattered through the canebrake, the column marched out again, and by nightfall we had arrived at the southern slope of the Sierra Soledad. However, when Lieutenant Loring authorized us to light a fire and distributed a demijohn of whiskey among the troops to try to raise morale, the faces around the campfire were so covered with soot that we looked more like an assembly of chimney sweeps than a decimated company of soldiers.

When Sergeant Sweeny called roll before we retired to sleep, three more men were missing. We never found out if they had burned in the canebrake, drowned in the swamp, or if they had made use of the prevailing confusion to desert, which was the most likely.

Of the fifty of us who had left Fort Conrad four days before, only twenty-one men were left, including the Apache scouts, who, to our great surprise, had not yet deserted.

He Who Is Moving a Hoop Along

After having cleared without any problem the first three obstacles that the old lady from Gran Quivira had prophesied—the Canyon That Spreads and Closes Up, the Arroyo That Turns Into a Torrent, and the Canebrake Whose Sharp Canes Destroy the Traveler—the cuates headed east. At dawn they could make out the bluish profile of the Sierra Blanca above the horizon.

For several hours the cuates rode slowly, since Gil Gómez had to ride one of the mules. The desert was becoming increasingly arid and bare, and by noon they found themselves in an area of fine, whitish sand that formed dunes the size of hills.

"This is the last of the obstacles pointed out by *she who became wrinkled,*" said Decoy, stopping his horse. "The Desert of White Sands."

The black bird that had followed them since they crossed the Río Grande had appeared again and traced concentric circles far above, using the warm air currents that rose toward the incandescent disc of the sun. Gil Gómez put his hand over his eyes to be able to follow the bird's flight without being blinded.

"I wonder what new misfortune *he who spreads his wings* is bringing us?" the genízaro asked himself. "Now it seems as if these godforsaken white dunes are moving, as if underneath the sand there were *he who drags a hoop!*"

In fact, the intense noon light falling across the dunes made them shimmer like the body of a reptile.

"It must just be a mirage caused by the sun," answered Decoy. "Let's go on and see what happens!"

They started to climb one of the giant dunes, leading the horse and the two mules by the bridle. The sand was so fine that the pack mules sank up to their hocks and the cuates' feet slipped on the slope without being able to advance. When they were close to the summit, the crest of sand suddenly fell on them like a wave breaking, enveloping them in a torrent of white dust that rolled them down to the bottom of the slope. They were still shaking off their clothing when the black bird swooped above their heads, and suddenly a warm, hurricane-like wind hurled sand particles against their eyes, turning the surface of the desert into a dusty breakwater.

The pack mule, which was halfway up the slope, neighed, terrified, as it felt the sand giving way under its hooves, and the cuates saw it slowly sinking into the sand, as though sucked down by a mysterious force. Gil Gómez tried to get close to the mule to cut the leather straps of the packs, but the sand shifted under his feet as if a monster were digging in the entrails of the Earth. He was barely able to grab for the reins of the animal that was trying to keep its snout out of the sand, but he didn't succeed in saving the pack mule from that dry flood.

Then, Decoy recalled a prayer that he had heard Narbona recite at dawn on the last day of the ceremony. Protecting his mouth with his hand from the blowing dust, he managed to recite it.

> *I am the son of the Sun*
> *When I go out to walk.*
> *I am walking beyond the White Sands!*
> *I am walking beyond the hill of the crow's tail!*
> *I am walking beyond the range of everlasting life.*
> *I am walking beyond the frontier of happiness.*
> *Biké Hozóni.*

No sooner had he finished reciting those stanzas than the wind subsided and a gentle rain commenced to fall on the desert. In a few minutes it formed a solid crust on the surface of the dunes, which prevented the wind from blowing the sand particles. The evaporation of the rain had formed a protective mist above the incandescent ball of the sun, and the horizon ceased to waver with that dizzying glare. The scorching wind gave way to a cool breeze that groomed the crests of the dunes with a light whisper. *"Go on, go on, to the house of your father,"* murmured the strange little voice, but Decoy once again thought that it was only the whisper of the wind.

The cuates were able to get up from where they were lying, half buried, and they shook off the grains of sand that were embedded under their fingernails and had gone through the joints of the genízaro's breastplate.

When they came close to where the mule was lying down, they saw that the animal had suffocated, unable to keep its snout out of the sand. They cut the ropes of the pack and loaded it on the only mule they had left. From then on, the two of them would have to ride the same horse.

By nightfall they had left the desert sand behind and were already in the environs of the Sierra Sacramento. They camped in a spot where they would be protected from the mountain wind. As he had done on other nights, Gil Gómez climbed to the side of the mountain and dug a small well for drinking water. He filled his canteen and around the waterhole spread pinches of sacred pollen and earth from the Four Sacred Mountains, asking the Sun to bring him a favorable dream.

When he descended, Decoy had prepared a place where he could rest, covering a crevice between two rocks with desert grass, since they had lost their blankets during the storm.

Before going to sleep, Gil Gómez noticed a volcanic rock that had been decorated with the silhouette of a monumental head, with the eyebrows, eyes, and open mouth of a giant. There were other paintings on the rock, but the one that stuck in the genízaro's mind was that of the giant warrior, and for a good while he was unable to fall asleep. Finally he curled up in the nest that his friend had prepared, and, resting his chin on his knees, he fell into a refreshing sleep.

But he woke up in the middle of the night and called his friend:

"My friend! Did you call me? Why did I wake up?"

But Decoy went on sleeping.

"Seriously. Didn't you touch me? Why do I feel so restless? It seems as though a spirit passed by, for I felt a chill throughout my body. I have had a terrible dream, even worse than the previous ones."

When he was finally able to awaken Decoy, he told him the dream. "I was watching the Sun move across the sky, and it glided above us with its wings open like a dark cloud. It frightened me. Its appearance was horrible, with wings like an eagle and the claws of a lion, but it had a human head and its breath was deadly; fire came out of its mouth. I grabbed hold of its wings and was transported through the air until I flew over a deep canyon, but on reaching the abyss, it let go of me and I was crashing against the rocks, shattering into pieces. I don't know what interpretation you can give this dream," added Gil Gómez, still trembling with anxiety, "but remember that Narbona told us that if we should have a dream in which we died, on the following day we would have to kill an animal so that it would replace us in our destiny."

"Don't worry," said Decoy. "The old man also told us that oftentimes bad dreams can bring good luck, if one gives them a positive interpretation."

Those words of encouragement brought comfort to the genízaro, and curling up in a ball again to protect himself from the chill of the night air that came down from the mountain, he was able to fall asleep once more.

The Sandstorm

Each day that passed without our being able to catch up with the fugitives made Lieutenant Loring more nervous and the troops more discouraged. The soldiers had lost all sense of discipline, and only the threat of punishment kept them in marching order. We all knew that Sweeny was ready to use the pistol or sabre at the least sign of insubordination.

If there had been no more desertions after the fire in the canebrake, it was only because we all knew that fleeing across the desert meant certain death. On the other hand, if we didn't catch up with the cuates before they entered the Sierra Blanca, the Apaches would most likely find us before we found the two fugitives.

That morning we left very early following the trail of the wanderers, whose tracks appeared clearly in the sand going due east. The wheels of the artillery limber sank two spans deep in the white sand under the weight of the cannon, and the wagon that had survived the fire didn't roll easily either, so in half a day we didn't get far.

Toward noon, near some sand dunes as high as hills, the flight of the carrion eaters led us to discover the body of one of the cuates' mules; the carcass was almost covered by the sand and we thought that a desert storm had taken them by surprise. Lieutenant Loring cheered up when he saw the vultures flying over the dead mule, thinking that relying on only two horses would slow their progress through the sand. But in fact they still had a day's advantage on us, and our horses also were beginning to weaken, sinking into the sand up to their hocks.

Toward the end of the afternoon a hot hurricane-force wind began to blow, hurling sand particles in our faces with the force of missiles. The sun was covered with a kind of vermilion veil of desert sand suspended in the air, and, as the sandstorm advanced in our direction, we saw the profile of the dunes undulate like the waves of an angry sea.

We all looked around for a place to take shelter, but we were in the midst of the most desolate wasteland where there wasn't even a small rock outcrop or the flimsiest bush under which to hide from the blizzard of sand. Suddenly I felt as if the sand were shifting under my soles, and the horses neighed in terror, noticing that the earth was giving way. In the midst of the sandstorm, the soldiers turned toward me with an anguished plea, and from those throats hoarse from fear and fatigue one voice burst forth. "Sing, Burdette, sing one of the chants that the Indian taught you!"

With the dust entering my gullet, I could barely pronounce the words that Tafoya had taught me. But I managed to overcome my own anxiety and, closing my eyes, I recited the song.

> *Put your feet down with pollen.*
> *Put your hands down with pollen.*
> *Put your head down with pollen.*

I will never forget the image of those dragoons half buried in the sand, with their faces still sooty from the ashes of the canebrake fire, like warriors painted for a sacred ritual, repeating with me the refrain, in rough, out-of-tune voices:

> *All of your body is pollen,*
> *Your mind is made of pollen,*
> *Your voice is made of pollen.*
> *The path is beautiful.*
> *Go in peace!*

To the tune of that chant the wind seemed to calm down, and suddenly a gentle shower fell over the desert, forming a small crust of humidity where our boots and horseshoes found firm ground. At dusk, on the far horizon, one could see a brilliant rainbow whose curve faded out in the snowy peaks of the Sierra Blanca.

That night we camped beside the Tularosa River, and we were able to bathe by the light of the moon in a pool of fresh, clear water that flowed down from the mountains. For the first time since we had left the fort, both we and the horses had abundant water, and not in the form of a devastating torrent or a pestilent swamp. For a while we forgot not only about the threat of the Apaches but also about hunting the fugitives, and the unfamiliar sounds of laughter and jokes were heard again around the fire.

While a festive atmosphere prevailed among the men, Lieutenant Loring distanced himself from the gaiety, lying on a blanket on the riverbank with a damp cloth on his forehead. During the sandstorm, the officer had lost his hat, and the blistering sun had given him a bad heat stroke. All night long several soldiers took turns putting damp cloths on his head to relieve the headache; and I could hear him moaning in his sleep.

Sergeant Sweeny was also not in a good mood. He had not been able to prevent the other soldiers from joining in my song to fight against the storm and the worst thing was that the entreaty had apparently worked! I knew that Sweeny would not forgive me for that last trick; but that didn't change anything, since for some time the sergeant had had it in for us, Timothy Baltasar as well as me. He was only waiting for the right moment to settle accounts.

As the senior soldiers were busy with the sick officer, the Apache auxiliaries disappeared during the night, further reducing the number of our decimated column; although some of us would rather be alone than in such poor company.

Sweeny's Sabre

At dawn the next day, we broke camp, even though the lieutenant had not improved during the night. When he woke before dawn, he complained of a strong glare, although not a speck of light had come over the mountains. They put a damp bandage over his forehead and eyes, and we arranged a kind of litter for the sick man in an empty supply wagon. Those of us who still had a horse to ride did so, and those who didn't started walking, one foot in front of the other. And thus we set out up the mountain.

All the soldiers, including myself, were praying for the speedy recovery of Lieutenant Loring, not so much out of sympathy for him as to avoid reporting to Sergeant Sweeny, who had taken over as head of the expedition, being second in the line of command.

When the sun rose we could see where the Sacramentos joined the Sierra Blanca. The orange glow illuminated a barren plain bristling with dark rocks and some giant cacti, whose arms projected menacing shadows in the clarity of dawn.

Sweeny decided to go up the mountain in a northeasterly direction, avoiding Dog Canyon, which seemed the right idea to those of us who had suffered the Apache ambush in that cul-de-sac. The sergeant was so puffed up at riding at the front of the detachment that he didn't seem to fit in his dusty tunic. He had ordered the wagon with the sick lieutenant to the rear, in theory so that Loring would be safer in case of a possible attack, but in fact he wanted to stress that for the time being he was in sole command.

The journey was extremely hard, and before noon two more horses fell dead, overridden, and several of the men who were on foot also fell to the ground, exhausted; but Sweeny forced them to go on, threatening them with his unsheathed sword. That braggart surely wanted to show that under his command the detail could cover more distance, even if we left a trail of corpses.

Suddenly, when the sun was beating down mercilessly, and the horses' hooves struck sparks on the flint rock, from the rear of the file a voice was heard softly singing that famous song.

> *How many miles to Babylon?*
> *Three score miles and ten.*
> *Can I get there by candlelight?*
> *Yes, and back again.*

Even though our tongues were swollen with dust and thirst, some of us soldiers started repeating the refrain.

> *If your heels are nimble and light*
> *You may get there by candlelight.*

That nursery rhyme, echoing back and forth among the basaltic monoliths, must have sounded to the sergeant like a cry of rebellion; and in a certain sense it was. Sweeny spurred his horse down the hill until he reached the one who, according to him, was always the culprit, Timothy Baltasar. Even though the scene unfolded some hundred yards from where I was, I could hear the dialogue perfectly, as the voices echoed against the rocky hillside.

"I see that you still have energy to spare, soldier," said the sergeant to Baltasar in a menacing tone. "Perhaps you'd like to give your horse to one of the dragoons on foot?"

"On the contrary, sergeant. I only try to cheer myself with this song," answered the soldier with the tone of polite indifference that so angered Sweeny; and he added: "I guess at this pace we'll soon arrive before the walls of Babylon."

"You'll arrive at the gates of hell before that," answered Sweeny while lashing him across the face with his whip.

"Damned tyrant!" exclaimed Baltasar, contracting his body and arms under the violence of the blow.

But Sweeny thought Baltasar had reached for the belt where he wore his pistol. Or at least that's what he said later. It's difficult to know whether Baltasar would have had the guts to draw his revolver to defend himself; but in any case, Sweeny didn't give him the chance, since he was only waiting for an excuse.

With a speed unimaginable in such a fat man, he took his sabre out of its sheath and without further warning, stuck the blade with all his might into Baltasar's shoulder. From where I was I saw the metal flashing under the sun's stroke. I heard the muffled blow when the steel cut to the shoulder bone through clothing and flesh, and immediately I saw Timothy's body fall from the horse like a sack.

In the face of such a cruel and cowardly deed, I dug my spurs in the flanks of the horse, which responded reluctantly, and when I reached the spot where my friend had just fallen I jumped to the ground and tried to lift Baltasar's body, bent double with pain. The deep gash across his shoulder was rapidly soaking his tunic with blood. I unfastened the buttons of his clothes and, reaching for my canteen, I poured into his cracked lips the few drops of water that remained in it.

"Come on, Baltasar, don't let yourself be frightened by a scratch!" I murmured in my friend's ear.

Timothy must have recognized the contact of my hands or the whisper of my voice, because he opened his eyes, which were already covered with the same opaque veil that had blurred the eyes of that poor white woman in He-Mule Swamp, when the Apache arrow pierced her heart.

"Burdette, don't lose the key to the chest that I gave you . . . don't forget that that is my treasure . . ." murmured Baltasar in a faint voice.

"Rest assured, I won't forget," I told him, squeezing his hand, which had suddenly become cold in spite of the torrid temperature.

No sooner had he said that than his head rested on his chest, and he fell unconscious because of the loss of blood.

"Burdette, can you tell me why you have abandoned your post, disobeying my orders?"

The sergeant's voice sounded very far away, and perhaps he had called me more than once before I heard him and turned, without letting loose of Baltasar's body.

"Don't you hear me? I'm telling you to stop nursing that insolent wretch and return to your place in the column!" shouted the sergeant again.

I stayed crouched where I was, staring at Sweeny with an expression of the deepest hate and scorn with which one could look at a human being.

"Burdette, for the third and final time, I order you to leave here and take your place in the rearguard. You're committing a serious act of disobedience that I am not willing to tolerate!"

"You can do what you wish with me, but I don't intend to leave my friend alone in this condition!"

"You will do as I say or suffer the consequences!" said the sergeant, starting to raise the still bloody sabre.

"By God, I will not move from here!"

"By God, I'll send you to hell with your friend!"

The sabre was raised again, projecting its curved shadow on the stone. With the body of my wounded friend in my arms, and my back against the basalt rock, I couldn't budge. But at that very moment a shot rang out, and when we looked in the direction of the report we saw Lieutenant Loring with a smoking gun in one hand, his forehead still bandaged, using his sabre as a cane to stand upright. No one had noticed that the officer had risen from his cot and stumbled to where the action was taking place; by shooting in the air he surely saved my life, because nothing else could have stopped Sergeant Sweeny, ready to strike.

"Sergeant Sweeny, take your place in the rear guard and call the assistant surgeon to attend the wounded man. Until the circumstances of this incident are clarified, you are hereby relieved of your command," said the lieutenant in a faint but firm voice, and he added to the bugler, "Sound the order to dismount, and half an hour's rest for the company! Burdette, take command of a squad and go look for water. But don't go farther than two miles from here."

Scarcely had he finished giving those orders when the lieutenant dropped the revolver, his legs doubled up, and he fell full length next to the carreta. I released the body of my friend for a moment and helped the other soldiers place Loring in the wagon again. When I returned to Baltasar, who was lying unconscious at the foot of a stone monolith, I noticed that on the face of the basalt there were several marks similar to those I had found carved in the rock of El Morro: the symbols of the taut bow and the hourglass.

Book Seven

Friend, you have not called me,

    why have I wakened up?

If you have not touched me, why do I feel restless?

If no angel has passed by, why are my limbs numb?

Friend, I have had a third dream, and it was

    very frightening.

The heavens thundered, and the earth shook.

Daylight disappeared and darkness set in.

Lightning flashed and fires sprang up,

the clouds burst, and it showered death.

The glow went away, and the fires went out,

and everything that had fallen turned to ashes.

Let us journey to the plains and reflect on all this.

POEM OF GILGAMESH
Tablet V, Column iv

Sun Horse

In the last stretch of their journey, the only mule they had left was exhausted, so the cuates were forced to put it out of its misery. They were left with only one horse for the two of them. Before proceeding, they buried whatever was not essential in a deep hole in the sand. They took with them only a couple of small bags of food, two rifles, the cedar bow Narbona had helped them make, and two monumental axes tempered by the blacksmith from Cabezón.

For the rest of the morning the cuates continued climbing the arid high plateau that led into the sierra, always followed by the big black bird that sometimes would fly low over their route and then let itself be lifted by a gust of warm air until it was blurred against the glaring sun.

Upon arriving at the foothills, they consulted Dawson's map to find the narrow pass to the top of the sierra that in the Spanish map appeared as Quebrada de los Mesteños. But the mouth of the canyon was so well hidden between the recesses of the rock and the vegetation that they almost passed by the entrance. Suddenly Decoy heard a little whisper that almost became blurred with the murmuring of the wind. "Xec, Xec! Behind those rocks is the path you must take to reach the home of your father!" said the same tiny voice that he had heard before.

Decoy then recalled the gift that the Spider Woman had given him. Searching his clothes, he found the little willow box that the old lady had given him, and then he was able to hear very clearly. "You're taking the wrong road. Take a look to the right. Behind those large cacti the entrance to the gorge can be found!" The voice came through the slits of the tiny box, but recalling what the old lady told him, Decoy chose not to open the case, lest the Big Bottlefly escape.

"I believe we're overshooting it!" he warned the genízaro. "Just look! Hidden behind those cacti is the entrance to the gorge."

"It's true. I was distracted observing the flight of *he who spreads his wings,*" said Gil Gómez. "It seems as though that damned bird has done everything possible to sidetrack us."

Following the course of the ravine, in the late afternoon they came to a stream that ran peacefully through a small grove of walnut trees. At some point, though, the arroyo must have flooded, because the debris of bushes uprooted by the torrent could be seen on the banks, and the marks of the dried mud reached the foot of the cliff. On the highest point of a Spanish bayonet, they recognized the cap of an American soldier, waving like a banner in the evening breeze. At the bottom of the canyon, the walls were covered with vegetation: cacti, thickets of palo verde, and tall agave plants.

"Here's where the Mescalero Apaches must have laid the ambush in which the officer in charge of the expedition was killed," said Gil Gómez. "This is what the Americans call Dog Canyon."

Decoy lifted his nose, sniffing like an animal recognizing a familiar odor. *"'The enemies' horses have been here.'* I can smell the Apaches' wild ponies."

As they rounded the bend of the gorge, they came upon a larger valley where the stream formed a pool, surrounded by a small canebrake. On the other side of the swamp, they could see the pointed tipis of an Apache village outlined against the sky. The twins dismounted, and, tying their horse to a stump, they crawled to the very edge of the pool, observing the village from behind a thicket. Apparently their presence had not been detected: the women came and went, busy with their chores; the children splashed at the banks of the swamp; and the old ladies approached the arroyo with oiled willow baskets to collect water. Since they could not see a single adult man, they concluded that the warriors of the tribe had gone out on some hunting or war expedition, leaving only the women and children. Everything was calm.

Right at that moment the black bird landed on the tip of the bush behind which they were hidden and started to give out such caws that it caught the attention of the group of old ladies who had come close to the bank of the stream with their baskets. "There's that damned bird again!" exclaimed the genízaro, ducking his head in the bushes.

Moving the underbrush to try to hide better, they betrayed their presence, and the old ladies threw their vessels to the ground and took off screaming and running in the direction of the village. All this attracted the attention of a band of boys who, not knowing what the fuss was all about, launched a volley of rocks where the underbrush had moved, forcing the cuates out of their hiding place. "Let's seek refuge in one of the tipis before they smash us with rocks," said the genízaro.

According to the rules of Apache hospitality, if a stranger voluntarily entered one of the rancherías, no one could hurt him as long as he was within the confines of the village. Trusting in that custom, the cuates dashed across the swamp to the tipis as fast as they could run. The boys, evidently not so well acquainted with tribal etiquette, didn't miss the opportunity to shower them with insults and rocks.

To avoid that painful barrage, the twins dived through the opening of the first tent they encountered, which was set a certain distance from the others in the village. On its side was painted a yellow sun surrounded by red rays. Inside they saw a middle-aged woman with a bone awl in her hand, and toward the back of the tipi were two younger women who resembled her. The three of them were mending a large blanket that covered practically the entire floor. In spite of her fright, the oldest woman faced up to the intruders. "What are you doing here?" she screamed. "My husband will return soon, and when he does, he's going to weave this blanket with your scalps!"

"We were told that we could find our father around here," said Gil Gómez, somewhat taken aback by their reception.

"What nonsense are you talking?" responded the woman, even angrier. "How are you going to find your father here? This is the tipi of the Sun Horse!"

"The truth is that we didn't have very specific directions, but an old woman told us that we should look for him around these parts," said Decoy, also somewhat puzzled.

"It seems to me that you have totally lost your way, but I fear you could pay dearly for this mistake. Sun Horse does not permit strangers in his territories, and I prefer not to think what he'll do with you if he finds you here. If I were in your shoes, I would get out of here before he returns. He has left the village on a war raid, but surely he'll return by nightfall, and he's got a very short temper. Leave while you still can!"

"The problem is that we don't know where to go; we came across the desert and we have lost our horses and provisions. It makes no difference to us whether we wait here for your husband to kill us or return to die in the desert where a column of American soldiers awaits us!" said Gil Gómez, looking truly desperate.

The woman was touched by the helplessness of the strangers, and the two young women let out sighs of understanding as they saw the predicament in which the handsome young men found themselves.

"Here comes the Sun Horse!" said one of the girls, peering out the entrance of the tipi. "You must hide immediately!"

Through the slit in the tent, the cuates saw a band of Mescalero riders crossing the pond at full gallop, headed for the village and being welcomed by the women and children with lots of shouting. The one who appeared to be the leader was riding a spirited sorrel pony and wearing a cap made of beaver skin in the shape of a fez; his shield was painted with a yellow and red sun. As soon as the chief dismounted, the old women and children who had seen the cuates coming went up to him and all started talking at the same time with great excitement, pointing in the direction of the tent, where the two strangers had sought refuge.

Through all of this, the black bird that had previously alerted the old women came to perch on the top of the tipi and began to make loud caws to attract the attention of the warrior, who stuck in the ground the lance that he was carrying in his hand and headed for the tipi brandishing a huge war mace.

As they saw him come closer, the two young women quickly got up, while the middle-aged woman remained motionless, seated in the center of the room. The women wrapped the cuates in the blanket they were mending, so that Gil Gómez and Decoy were rolled up in a huge bundle in a corner of the tent.

"I have been told that while I was away two strangers came into the tipi. May I ask who these intruders are and what on earth they are looking for?" said Sun Horse as he entered the tent, brandishing his mace.

Although the warrior's tone of voice showed his anger, and the war paint on his face was fearsome, the way he talked with a swollen and stuttering tongue revealed that he had just had an intimate conversation with a bottle of liquor. The older woman looked him up and down and replied sarcastically, "I suspect that once again you have celebrated your war exploits by drinking too much *tiswin;* I recommend that you take a bath in the pond to clear your head. And put that mace away before you hurt somebody."

Sun Horse turned red with rage and crossed the tent in a rolling gait, looking in every corner, but it didn't dawn on him to search under the blanket that was rolled up in a corner. "Where in the hell have you hidden them? It seems incredible that while a man goes out to defend his village against a band of American soldiers, his own wife and daughters take advantage of his absence to let a couple of strangers come into their tent. You should be ashamed of yourselves!"

"I think you're the one who should explain himself, Sun Horse!" hissed the woman. "You have always insisted that you were never unfaithful on your trips to faraway lands. So how can you explain the arrival of two handsome young men at our tipi saying that they're searching for their father?"

"How dare they say such a lie, those two shameless scoundrels! If I find them I will kill them with my own hands!" shouted the warrior. As he raised the mace, he stumbled and grasped at the center post of the tipi, which almost collapsed.

"If you wish to know why they say that they have come looking for their father, all you have to do is ask them: right there, underneath that blanket, are the boys who claim to be your sons," said the woman, adding in a sarcastic tone, "If it's true that you have never cheated on me, then please explain where they have come from."

As he saw the bundle where the twins were hidden, the warrior rushed at them brandishing his mace, but halfway there he lost his balance, fell flat on his face, banging his head against a stone *metate,* and remained unconscious for several minutes.

The cuates had stuck their heads out from under the blanket, but when they saw that Sun Horse was heading for them, they ducked undercover again. But the woman took advantage of the warrior's dazed state to drag him out of the tipi, still unsteady, and with the help of her daughters to toss him into the pond. The man emerged with his buckskin tunic dripping wet and war paint running down his face.

When he had dried off and calmed down, Sun Horse returned to the tipi and sat down with his legs crossed close to the fire. He gestured to the cuates to come close. When they came out from under the blanket, despite his hangover, the warrior noticed the contrast between the colonial breastplate and the symbols of a bear and a serpent on the chest and arms of the strangers. But he pretended not to pay attention to their strange appearance and addressed them in a conciliatory tone:

"I regret not having treated you before according to the laws of our hospitality, but the truth is that in this remote place we are not accustomed to visits from strangers. Besides, we are concerned because we have learned that a column of American soldiers is crossing the desert headed toward these mountains."

Gil Gómez was on the point of saying that those soldiers were following them, but he quickly realized that the Mescalero chief might not be pleased to know that it was they who had attracted the military detachment to the area, so he held his tongue. On second thought, he told the warrior only about the adventures that he and his friend had had on their trip, and how they had lost three animals. He finished by asking permission to stay in the village for at least a couple of days, until they were able to regain strength and perhaps procure fresh horses.

Sun Horse seemed satisfied when he heard that the strangers had come to the village only to procure mounts and provisions to continue their journey, but he shook his head once again. "On any other occasion I would have been pleased to provide what you need to continue on your journey, but you have arrived at a bad moment. At this time we're preparing the puberty ceremony for those two young maidens you see there, who are my two daughters. Surely you're acquainted with the preparations needed for that ritual. We must cut down trees to construct the ceremonial cabin, sew the dresses from white buckskin so that they are dressed like the White Painted Woman, gather the food for the guests, and a host of other things. I'm afraid you've come at the worst possible time, boys, so I can't do much for you under the circumstances."

The cuates were disappointed in his response, but the woman stepped in, saying to her husband, "To hear you talk, anybody would think you were going to sew the buckskin dresses and knead the dough with your own hands. But in fact it will be me and the other women of the tribe who sew and cook for our families and friends and provide what's necessary for the ritual. I don't believe it would be good to drive these strangers away from the village when we're about to celebrate life and the generosity of nature. And besides, I believe such selfishness could well attract the disapproval of the Sacred Beings. Let these two young men stay in the village while the ceremony takes place, and you can tend later to gathering whatever they need to continue their trip."

The Maidens Who Had Never Been Touched by the Sun's Light

Not daring to expel the strangers for fear of offending his wife, Sun Horse set about making their lives unbearable by subjecting them to a series of trials to test their stamina. He hoped that the intruders wouldn't be able to withstand these ordeals and would decide to leave the settlement of their own free will.

But the warrior did not suspect that they had been warned about what was in store for them by the old woman of Gran Quivira, who had given them several protective amulets, as well as the Big Bottlefly, who always alerted them to what he was up to. In addition, the cuates relied on the help and complicity of the warrior's own daughters. Their father had kept them so isolated that they had never seen an adult male up close, and so, being near puberty, the young maidens were very taken with the handsome strangers.

The first thing Sun Horse did was send the travelers out of the tent, under the pretext that it would not be proper for them to spend the night under the same roof as the maidens. The temperature dropped sharply after the sun went down in the canyon, and the cuates would have had a hard time if they had spent the night in the open air near the pond with only a fistful of rushes for shelter. But as soon as the warrior fell into the deep slumber brought on by alcohol and strong emotions, the girls picked up the big blanket they had been mending when the strangers arrived and took it to the place where they were already shivering from the cold under the stars. So the cuates spent a warm and comfortable night. And before dawn the girls picked up the blanket so their father wouldn't suspect anything.

When Sun Horse woke up and peeked over the canebrake, expecting to find the cuates frozen stiff, he was very surprised to see them sleeping peacefully. But the warrior wasn't discouraged that his first ploy had failed. He ordered the maidens to prepare a sweat hut so the young men could warm up after having spent the night in the open air.

"Come on, girls, don't you see that these men are numb with cold?" said the crafty fellow to his daughters. "One of you prepare the hut and the other one go heat up the rocks; they must be four stones of clear quartz, the kind that reflect the sunlight with different colors. After their difficult journey, these boys deserve to rest!"

But beneath these outward signs of hospitality, Sun Horse was plotting another mean trick, and the Big Bottlefly warned Decoy with its little voice, "Xec, xec. You must not trust that friendliness one tiny bit! Your father intends to kill you! He's going to make the stones in the sweat hut explode by pouring cold water on them while they're red hot."

While the girls were building the sweat lodge against the canyon wall, the Big Bottlefly gave them more advice. "Xec, Xec, dig a hole in the stone wall to protect yourselves from the explosion!"

Following the instructions of their invisible ally, the twins set about digging like badgers into the chalky wall of the escarpment. In a few minutes they had made a hole in which they curled up in a ball, covering the entrance of the opening with the pieces of a whiskey demijohn and other objects that had been left behind by soldiers who had camped at the foot of this same cliff. When Sun Horse poured a pitcher of cold water through the hole at the top of the hut and the hot quartz stones exploded like grenades, the incandescent fragments of rock didn't even touch the cuates.

After waiting for the warrior to ask them three times if they were hot enough—really expecting them to be scorched to death—the young men answered on the fourth time, "Yes, now we're warm enough. Can we come out?" And they left the hut intact, leaving Sun Horse scratching his head. For the first time he muttered to himself, " I have to admit that these young men are extraordinarily strong and resilient. Could they actually be sons of mine?"

While he was thinking of a new ordeal for the strangers, he ordered them to take a dip in the pool to wash off the sweat. He ordered the girls to accompany them so they could dry them off and give them a massage with aromatic herbs when they emerged from the water. But since the devil never rests, after taking a short dip in the pool, the young men came out with their manhood erect from the mere contact with cool water. The girls didn't stop observing with great interest how their rigging had raised up, and moved by curiosity, the older of the maidens asked Gil Gómez, "Does that cane in your belly always grow when you bathe? My mother has already explained the differences in bodies of male and female, but she didn't tell me that the man's appendage swells in the water like the roots of bulrushes."

"Some parts of women also swell with cold water," answered the genízaro, and gently pulling the maiden toward the arroyo, he showed her how her nipples became hard when they came in contact with the water.

The girl blushed at the pleasure she got from the tickling at the points of her breasts, but she tried to resist when the playful hand of the man began to caress the silky moss between her legs.

"The plant that grows in my abdomen likes the moist dark openings as the eels do. We can hide in the canebrake so no one can disturb our play," said Gil Gómez, taking the girl's hand. "You will see that in a short time with me you can learn more than during the four nights of the puberty ceremony."

"I don't know if Sun Horse would like us to go frolicking about near the water with these strangers," said one sister to the other.

"Aké, aké!" came the little voice of the Big Bottlefly, who had been half smothered in the folds of clothing when Decoy had removed his tunic to get in the water with the other maiden. "Remember that you are not permitted to have sex with women while you are on the Enemyway. Besides, enjoying these maidens who are going to be initiated soon into the puberty ceremony would displease the Sacred Beings and the Sun himself!"

Decoy faintly heard what his tiny conscience was telling him, but the call of the flesh was more powerful than the voice of reason. The genízaro was already going into the deep thicket with the other maiden, and he began to follow, pulling the other sister by the hand. The two couples emerged a while later, the young men with their shafts limber and the girls with rosy cheeks, their curiosity satisfied.

"They can no longer call us the girls 'who were never touched by the Sun's light,'" said the older one, remembering the tale their godmother had told them about the origins of mankind.

When they were still busy enjoying themselves, the black bird began to caw on the canebrake, directly above where the twins were lying with the chief's daughters. But since all the villagers were occupied building the pine lodge that would be used for the puberty ceremony, no one noticed that the strangers had had their way with the maidens before they could run toward the Sun.

Sun Horse became somewhat pensive when he saw his two daughters return from the pool with their cheeks aflame and the hems of their tunics muddy. But, without bothering to ask what had happened inside the canebrake, he decided to make one last attempt to get rid of the strangers.

"While you dress in clean clothes," he told the twins, "I'm going to prepare a little tobacco for us to smoke around the fire—a very special tobacco!"

Decoy noticed again the buzzing that was coming from the little box Spider Woman had given him, and he bent his head to hear the Big Bottlefly's message: "Aké, aké, now your father wants to kill you using a poisoned pipe. That tobacco is very special! But if you swallow a blue-colored secretion that the Giant Caterpillar vomits, the poison won't work."

Cimarrón was asking himself where he could find this blue vomit when on the path that went toward the chief's tent he saw a velvety caterpillar crossing, the kind that secretes a stinging liquid. He was going to pick it up with a stick when the creature defended itself by spitting two squirts, each about two inches long. Decoy took the two blue globs in the palms of his hands and showed them to his friend.

"What do you plan to do with that?" asked Gil Gómez.

"We have to eat it," said Decoy. He brought his hand to his tongue and swallowed one of the globules, which had a bitter flavor.

The genízaro saw his grimace. "You seriously want me to eat that stuff? Have you lost your mind?"

"Trust me for once! Lick this liquid from my hand and try not to make a fuss!" said Decoy, pointing to Sun Horse with a wink.

Gil Gómez swallowed the liquid. It made him want to vomit, but he managed to overcome the nausea and sat down next to his friend to smoke the turquoise pipe that the warrior had just taken down from a nail on the tipi's central post. A few minutes earlier the warrior's daughters had dressed the cuates in buckskin tunics with fringes hanging from the sleeves, and the two ex-maidens, still warm from the roll in the reeds, laughed with pleasure when they saw how handsome their lovers looked dressed in clean clothes. But this time their giggles and knowing glances didn't go unnoticed by the warrior, who admonished them harshly. "Why are you laughing like two fools? It's better for you to go rest and prepare yourselves for the ceremony that will begin this very night. You know very well that you have to watch your behavior especially in the days preceding the ritual, because the way you behave in these days will mold your character and behavior in the future. So you should make an effort to be discreet, hardworking, and chaste—especially chaste! Remember that all the problems of humanity began when the daughters of the first chiefs made use of their bodies prematurely."

In fact, the restrictions that the novices had to observe during the days before the ceremony were similar to those imposed on the young warriors on their first expeditions: the maidens had to refrain from all excesses. They could not change clothing, and their godmothers gave them a scratcher to scratch themselves and a cane to drink water so that the liquid would not touch their lips. And, of course, they couldn't have any contact with a male so they would still be virgins when they ran toward the Sun.

In other aspects, the puberty ceremony of Apache girls was different from that practiced by the Navajos. The Mescalero Apaches built a large conical cabin, cutting four pine trees some forty feet tall, which were secured in the ground to the beat of a ritual song. The structure was then completed with the trunks of other, smaller firs and covered with oak branches.

When Sun Horse had filled the bowl of the pipe with tobacco, he lit it with a stick from the fire and took a deep puff, pretending to inhale the smoke but not taking it into his lungs. Afterward he passed it to the cuates, who really inhaled, blowing out a large mouthful.

"*That with which I would like to smoke!*" said Gil Gómez, since that's the way one said pipe in war talk.

The warrior was surprised to hear the Apache war language from the mouth of a stranger, but more so to see the cuates passing the pipe back and forth, inhaling deeply and exhaling the smoke with every appearance of satisfaction. The tobacco was almost gone and the cuates had not fallen down. He looked at the empty bowl and sighed heavily. "All right.

I give up! You are strong and resistant and have passed all the tests I have subjected you to. I even admit that I would be proud to have sons like you! But now tell me, what do you want from me?"

The Weapons of the Sun

The cuates looked at each other, understanding that the moment to tell the truth had arrived. Gil Gómez spoke first. "My friend and I have come to the Sierra Blanca to kill Humbaba and to free humanity from his curse. But we know that whoever enters the Cedar Forest is overcome by a strange weakness, and we know that we will need very powerful arms to fight the power of its guardian. Several people have told us that you would be able to help us procure those special weapons."

The warrior stood up and put his hands to his head. He covered his ears with the palms of his hands as if refusing to listen to any more nonsense. "Who could have misled you like that? Where do you expect me to keep those weapons if I don't even use them for my own benefit? Do you believe that if I had access to them I would be fighting the American soldiers with a hide shield and a stone mace?"

"The person who sang the ritual of war over us told us that someone more powerful than he would provide us with the arrows with which we would be able to kill the fierce Humbaba. Although we will also need flint armor, flint knives, flint axes."

"In the first place, I don't have those weapons nor do I know where you will be able to find them," interrupted the warrior. "And even if I had them, I don't believe that I would give them to you to attack Huwawa, who is in charge of defending the sanctuary of this mountain range and preventing the enemy from desecrating the forest where the spirits of our ancestors live."

"All we want is to have the same weapons that the Sun gave to the Twin Warriors when they went to fight against the giant Yeitsó at the top of San Mateo Mountain," said Decoy.

"At last! Now I understand that someone has been getting you all worked up with those stories about invincible heroes who travel on top of the rainbow, and about wicked monsters who in years gone by went around devouring humanity," said the warrior, shaking his head. "Haven't you two also been told that those things occurred many, many years ago, and that there are no longer any colossal giants or heroes dressed in shining armor?"

"We believe that those ancient stories can give you power to fight the enemy," said Gil Gómez.

"In my tribe, not even suckling babies believe those fabrications; we are too busy trying to save this last redoubt by tooth and nail from the white man's greed."

"If you wish to preserve this territory," said Gil Gómez emphatically, "you will have to sacrifice Humbaba. The great white chief knows all his misdeeds and wants to erase that plague on humanity from the face of the earth."

"If you don't help us destroy Humbaba, the American soldiers will come with their horses and cannons and will chase all of you from the Sierra Blanca. They will build a fort in the middle of your mountains," added Decoy.

"The day Huwawa dies," Sun Horse answered, "the soldiers will enter the sacred forest and the Mescalero Apaches will have to go live in the desert among the snakes and scorpions."

"You're mistaken: if we liquidate Humbaba, you will be left in peace," lied Gil Gómez with aplomb.

"But for us to defeat him, we need special weapons: lightning arrows, flint machetes, flint armor, and all those old weapons," said Decoy.

Sun Horse paced up and down like a lion in a cage. Finally he seemed to make a decision. "By sheer persistence you will succeed in getting everything you want!" he exclaimed, adding in a confidential voice, "Close by here there's a cave where we Apaches have been saving things from past generations. We don't visit that site very much because we don't like the things that have belonged to the dead, but it's possible that there you'll find what you're looking for."

"If you tell us where we can find what we're looking for, we will go there alone. We don't need you to come with us. We're not afraid of the spirits of the dead!" answered Decoy firmly.

"I shall go with you, because you would never be able to find the entrance to the cave. But it seems preposterous that you're looking for those old relics when you have two good rifles like the ones you have buried under the bushes. Not even our children play war games with that old junk, but it's your call!"

"Someone told us that it would be useless to try to defeat the keeper of the Cedar Forest with firearms, because Humbaba is protected by seven shining layers, and that utilizing *that which discharges wind* would only succeed in making the Sacred Beings angry."

"Doubtless you have fallen into the hands of some unscrupulous person who has taken advantage of your credulity. I've also noticed that at times you use our war language, but you must know that we no longer utilize the secret language among ourselves on our raids. It's too hard to remember those terms in the heat of battle, and it leads to confusion."

"As for us, it has helped us get this far, overcoming many obstacles," answered Decoy, who refused to be intimidated by the warrior's skepticism.

"All right, if you believe in those things, I won't be the one to break the bad news to you. Follow me!"

Leaving the village, Sun Horse led them up the cliff on a path so narrow that they could only walk by putting one foot in front of the other. When they reached the top, they could see the tipis in the village looking like little paper cones planted at the bottom of the canyon. The warrior led them into a narrow crevice that turned into a deep cave.

Following the warrior's steps in the semi-darkness, the twins reached a spacious gallery, its ceiling pierced by light from the west, illuminating the entrance to various other galleries. Farther on, the principal path opened on a steep ravine. At the bottom was a forest where the brilliant coats of herds of deer and elk shone. Their antlers seemed varnished with the twilight.

"In that ravine there's game to supply my entire tribe with meat and hides for several winters," said Sun Horse. "Is that what you were looking for?"

Gil Gómez and Decoy stood looking in amazement at the vast herd. They had never seen anything like it in all their hunting expeditions. But a little voice said to Decoy, "Tell him no, that's not what you were looking for!"

"It's not those animals that we want; in just one hunting outing, Gil Gómez and I supplied meat to all the rancherías of the Río Puerco Valley," he said with such aplomb that he thoroughly squelched the warrior.

They kept on walking through the galleries of the grotto until they came into a branch of the previous ravine. At the bottom of this one swarmed herds of wild horses and mares with coats and manes of all colors imaginable, from jet black to the most blinding white: dapple-gray, roan, dark gray, pure black, palomino, chestnut, sorrel, dun, deer color, and wolf gray. It was difficult to guess the size of that herd, but neither Gil Gómez nor his friend had ever seen a similar string, not even when Decoy roamed among the mustangs on the plains.

"Is this what you were looking for?" asked Sun Horse in a proud voice, while noticing the admiration on the cuates' faces.

Again Decoy heard the little voice whispering to him, "No, say that

that's not it!" and again answered decisively, "We haven't come here looking for horses. With the herds we steal from the Navajos we have enough for us and we even have some left over to sell to the American soldiers!"

"I believe that you are wrong to turn down this wealth of horseflesh, but it's your loss," responded the warrior without hiding his annoyance.

They continued walking down a narrow passageway where they stumbled in the semi-darkness upon some rusted iron utensils that must have been used to pierce the bowels of the earth. The cuates recalled that Dawson's map showed an old mine in that region; at the back of this man-made tunnel one could hear the dripping of a subterranean vein. A while later they emerged into a spacious cavern, barely lit by a thread of light coming through a crack in the ceiling. When their eyes adjusted to the semi-darkness, they saw that in small cavities in the rock were more utensils and an assortment of art pieces, from little figurines made of jade, shell, and turquoise representing birds, horses, bears, and serpents, to huge stacks of deer and bison hides and headdresses made of eagle and owl feathers.

In one of the compartments the cuates saw gold chalices and silver plates, embossed missals and richly adorned censers, as well as chasubles and sacerdotal vestments embroidered exquisitely in gold and silk with biblical scenes. The garments were spotted with orifices surrounded by dark ochre spots: arrow wounds. The cuates thought they must be seeing the treasures from the missions of Gran Quivira. Nearby was a heap of armor from the colonial period, and some swords and armor with gold inlay encrusted with precious stones.

"Neither the prayers of their priests nor the armor of their warriors could protect them from the strength and the precision of our arrows," said Sun Horse, pointing to the niche where those relics were piling up. Then he added: "If you need any of those arms, you may take them; our people don't like the things that have belonged to our dead enemies."

"Those won't work against our powerful rival. We want flint armor, a flint mace, flint machetes, flint wristbands, and flint gaiters. That's what we need," said Decoy.

"I repeat, I cannot furnish you those arms. Weapons made of flint haven't been worn here in a while. Craftsmen no longer have the patience to model and polish those stone weapons, and besides they are not practical in battle because they are too heavy. If you fancy yourself wearing a breastplate, I recommend that you get one of the old Spanish ones, because it's more like what you're looking for, and they'll always be more resistant than your dented brass breastplate."

The twins took a gold-inlaid breastplate and a coat of mail that, with a good polishing, would look like new. But Decoy insisted, "Above all we need the magical arrows: a *Lightning Arrow,* another *Straight Lightning Arrow,* a *Sunray Arrow,* and a *Rainbow Arrow.* That's what we came looking for!"

"Well, in that case, please tell me where to find them. Perhaps you think that I'm some kind of magician or witch doctor," answered the warrior, at the limit of his patience. "If I had those magic arrows I would already have used them against the American soldiers."

Then Decoy heard the voice of his tiny advisor. "Tell him to go to the deepest part of the cave, behind that stone pillar!" Decoy followed the direction indicated by the buzzing sound that rang in his ears, and they found, behind a stalactite, a small cavity at the bottom of which they saw several objects covered with a thick layer of dust.

One was a quiver made of mountain lion's hide, which had shrunk with the passing of time to the sad condition of a moth-eaten skin and whose ears had been eaten away by insects so that it had lost its elegance. But when they got close, they noticed four arrows with eagle feathers protruding from the quiver; something inside the quiver seemed to be moving and making a rattling sound similar to the noise of a rattlesnake.

The warrior had come close reluctantly, and when Decoy stretched his hand to grab the quiver, he warned him, "If I were you, I'd be careful. It wouldn't surprise me to find a serpent or a scorpion in there."

Decoy half closed his eyes and sang one of the songs that Narbona had sung during the ceremony of the sand painting:

> *The rays shoot from my feet, I'm in the Sun.*
> *The rays shoot from my palms, I'm in the Sun.*
> *Four ray arrows shoot from my body, I'm in the Sun.*
> *When the rays leave my body and fall upon the enemy,*
> *The latter moans and collapses, I'm in the Sun,*
> > *I'm in the Sun.*

After that he plunged his hand into the deepest part of the niche in the rock. When he seized the lionskin quiver he felt a strange sensation, as happens when you hit a funnybone and feel a shiver that runs through your whole body.

Then it was Gil Gómez's turn to approach the crevice in the rock, and out of the dust he retrieved a flint machete and a flint ax.

"This is what we came looking for. Whenever you want, we can get out of here!" said the cuates in unison.

When Sun Horse and the twins came out of the cavern, the Ruidoso Valley was completely in the dark. The firmament was crowded with stars that were mirrored in the shining wall of the cliff, and below, in the village, they could see the great bonfire that had been lit in front of the cabin where the puberty ceremony for the two maidens was to be celebrated.

In order to have their hands free, the twins had put on their armor and the coat of mail that they had found in the cave. From the lionskin quiver that Decoy had hung over his shoulder came a diffused glow, as if phorescent objects were inside.

The Bells of La Luz

Once Loring had relieved Sergeant Sweeny of his command, the leadership of the detail fell on me, since I was the most senior soldier. Under other circumstances I would have been proud to lead the men, but our column had been reduced to a handful of pitiful soldiers and a string of footsore horses escorting a cart with two sick passengers—one wounded by the harshness of nature and the other by the cruelty of a fiendish human.

Under the circumstances, I decided to make a detour to the village of La Luz, where I knew we would at least find some adobe walls, wood to build a fire, and some water in the neighboring arroyo.

When we arrived at the abandoned settlement, I gave orders to have the sick men placed in the church, whose thick walls were quite well preserved. The lieutenant continued to suffer from sunstroke, and Timothy Baltasar had lost more blood because of the rattling of the wagon; his face was white as snow. Only his tremendous physical strength kept him alive after having received that brutal wound.

As evening fell over the purple crest of the mountain range, a cold breeze that came down from the mountain made the church bells move and they began to ring with a sad tone, as if an invisible hand were trying to foretell our gloomy future in that ghost town.

Seeing the tense, worn-out faces of the soldiers in the light of the campfires, I could predict that that night all those who still had the strength to follow the Tularosa River toward the south, and reach the Mexican border, might well desert. What I couldn't imagine was that, in the midst of that predicament, the seed of greed could still grow in the human soul. Several of the men from the fort had heard references to a rich placer in the headwaters of the Ruidoso, and knowing that they were in those environs—instead of remembering the fate that other greedy men had met right there, including Dawson himself—in the eyes of those foolish men I could easily detect the lust for gold.

Making the rounds of the camp, to be able to report to the lieutenant, I realized that small cliques were forming; whispering animatedly, they became quiet when they saw me coming. I even caught one of the dragoons drawing a map on the ground, probably an attempt to reproduce Dawson's map, although the other soldiers rubbed it out with their feet when I approached. I wouldn't have been surprised if Sergeant Sweeny, resentful that Lieutenant Loring had admonished him for his horrible action, had been encouraging the other soldiers to desert.

Having figured out what was going on, I went toward the church where the sick men were in order to inform the lieutenant of the situation, even though I knew we could do very little to confront the mutineers; we were only a half-blind officer, the dying Baltasar, the assistant surgeon who attended to both of them, and myself.

Arriving back at the church, converted into an infirmary, I found Loring sleeping so soundly that I preferred not to bother him. Baltasar, on the other hand, had regained consciousness and called me to his side. On reaching his cot, I found more life in his eyes, although only a faint whisper came out of his throat. He grasped one of my hands between his large paws to draw me closer to him.

"While we were crossing the desert in the cart, it occurred to me the only way in which we can defeat these Bedouins of the desert . . ." he said in an agitated voice that I attributed to the fever. I tried not to show my perplexity. Noticing that I had put my ear closer to his lips, the wounded man added in a whisper, "Camels! The answer to all the problems we have in these dry regions lies in the formation of a camel detail. The Camel Corps of the United States Army!"

I thought my friend was hallucinating as a consequence of the fever; but when he saw my expression, Baltasar reacted immediately. "Don't think I'm delirious. I know most people take me for a crank, but you know better than anyone that sometimes mirages become a reality. The chants of the Indian Tafoya, which none of us took seriously, have probably saved our lives . . ."

I feared that speaking to me might use up the little strength that remained in him, but I realized at the same time that it was very important to him to finish telling me what he was thinking, so I squeezed his big hand with both of mine and indicated with a sign that he could go on:

"Count the days that have passed since we left the fort, count them . . ." I tried to remember the dates, but my head was spinning, and the wounded man had already made the count. "Although it may seem like an eternity, only a little over a week has passed; and in those seven days we've lost half the horses, by accident or exhaustion. And if we hadn't found water here today, tomorrow the rest of the animals could have died of thirst. Isn't that right?"

Seeing me nod my head yes, the wounded man continued speaking, although in a weaker and weaker voice. "Do you know how long an Arabian camel can go without eating or drinking? Up to a week, because of the energy that it stores in its hump. Thanks to that, camel caravans have been able to cross the vast desert sands of the East, and they call these animals *ships of the desert* . . ."

Seeing that his strength was failing, I interrupted him. "Don't you think you should try to rest? You will have time to think about those things when you get better."

Baltasar gave me a familiar mocking smile. "You know very well that the sergeant's sabre has given me a one-way passage to the green fields of Eden, but if you want you can take charge of converting my dream into reality. This idea might have occurred to me before, but until I crossed the desert of White Sands, which is exactly like the sandy deserts of the Middle East, I hadn't taken into account that the only beast capable of crossing these dry barren regions is the *ship of the desert*. With a camel corps, in a few months we could liquidate the Apaches . . ."

Typical of Baltasar's ideas, it was difficult to know if this one was superb nonsense or a brilliant inspiration. In either case, the only way to calm the wounded man was to let him talk. He went on, "You must not forget that in the trunk I keep under my cot, whose key I gave you before we left, I have a collection of books on the East, and in one of those books you will find how the colonial armies in Afghanistan and Egypt used the camel."

When I finally succeeded in getting him to sleep, I was the one who stayed awake a long time, and when sleep got the best of me, my exhausted mind tortured me with dreadful nightmares. I saw Baltasar crossing a desert with very high white dunes atop the hump of a huge camel, richly harnessed in the eastern style. My friend Timothy was not dressed in the tunic and hat of a dragoon, but rather he looked like a soldier in some colonial European corps, sporting a long, white jellaba with gold trim and a kepi with a large red tassel that swung in front of his face to the swaying rhythm of the camel's stride. He carried in his hand, unsheathed, a sabre as curved as a scimitar from whose bloody blade were falling thick drops of blood that left a red trail on the white sand. But suddenly the sand was stirred up like a tidal wave under a sudden strong wind, and the silhouette of my friend and his exotic mount disappeared from my sight, enveloped in a dust devil. The sensation of reality in the dream made me wake up in a cold sweat, and I then heard the weak voice of Baltasar asking for water. When I got near to give him water from my canteen, I touched his forehead and could tell that his fever had risen since the previous evening.

When I woke up the next day, the sun was coming through a crack in the tottering wall, and I noticed around me an unusual silence for an army encampment. With the revolver in my hand, I ran toward the ruined houses where the other soldiers had spent the night, but they were empty. Of the fifteen men in camp the previous night, ten had deserted, including the infamous Sweeny.

Aside from the assistant surgeon, who was still drowsy in a corner, the deserters had left behind only the young bugler, who was so frightened that he was unable to tell me what had happened the night before. When he stopped stuttering, we found out that the mutineers, before leaving for the mine in the Sierra Blanca, had considered slitting the throats of the lieutenant, Baltasar, and me. The only thing that had stopped them was knowing that I usually slept with my revolver cocked under the pillow, and I was a light sleeper.

The deserters had carried with them everything that could be of any use to them, leaving behind only half a dozen footsore mules, the empty provision wagon, and the howitzer, after having hidden the ammunition. Of the fifty men who had left Fort Conrad a week before, without counting the two sick ones, only three of us remained: an assistant surgeon who had the reputation of spending more time drunk than sober, although at that moment he was sober for lack of alcohol, a young terrified bugler, and myself. The only thing we could count on to fend off an Apache attack was a crumbling adobe parapet and a cannon without ammunition.

When the morning wind made the bronze bells peal in the church tower, it seemed to me that even the toll had a mocking sound.

From that moment on, the time in that ghost town began to pass so slowly that I thought I was going to go crazy. Suddenly an uncontrollable desire to leave that hole overcame me, the wish to escape even if it meant death. But there was only one way to leave with dignity, so I asked the lieutenant's permission to go in pursuit of Sweeny and the other fugitives.

"Are you sure you want to go follow the trail of those cutthroats?" said the lieutenant, looking at me through the slit in his bandage. "Even if you bump into them in the mountains, you know that the probability of them giving up without a fight is slim."

But the officer knew that it was our duty to try to capture the deserters. There was little he could do but agree to my request.

"Burdette, be careful, and see that the Apaches don't catch up with you before you can catch up with the deserters," Loring urged me, clasping my hands.

I chose the mule that seemed the least crippled, and loading a bag of rations, munitions, and a canteen on the animal, I took off for the Sierra Blanca with a certain sensation of relief in my heart. There's something in my character that makes me react in tense situations with an urge to flee toward the unknown.

Something similar happened to me the night they brought my father home badly wounded, after having been robbed and knifed by two thugs in a dark alley in New Rochelle. I couldn't bear my mother's tears or the frightened doe eyes of my sisters. Instead of remaining where I was needed most, I wandered the streets aimlessly. When I returned at dawn the following day, my father was already dead, and I would never forgive myself for that desertion.

I must say, I had scarcely gotten a couple of miles away from the camp when I began to feel remorse for having abandoned my companions in the ghost town. But it was already too late to return. As Timothy Baltasar would have said, he who looks back at Sodom and Gomorrah can turn into a pillar of salt.

The Dance of the Devil

When Sun Horse and the cuates returned from the abandoned mine, all the people were gathered around the cabin where the girls' puberty ceremony was being celebrated. The strangers would have liked to have a chance to say good-bye in private to the warrior's daughters, but they couldn't even get near the novices. The girls were constantly guarded and instructed by the women attendants who were preparing them for the ceremony, until dawn when they would run toward the Sun.

The attendant was called *she who trots them off*, since she was the one who gave the signal for the girls to come out running toward the rising sun. These attendants had painted the bodies of the girls with yellow pollen, the color considered a symbol of fertility, and also red, which represented blood and life. They had been dressed in white buckskin tunics, adorned with fringes of the same material, and embroidered with strings of multicolored beads in the shape of a cross and small brass bells that tinkled at the slightest movement. The maidens' hair was unbraided, but on the back part of the mane they wore a small tail with a tuft of hair to which two eagle feathers were secured.

On the first night of the ritual the *gan* would come down to bless the young novices and would dance before the big cedar bonfire that was burning in front of the ceremonial cabin. The gan represented benevolent spirits who had helped the Apaches in difficult times, and they were said to inhabit some caves below the line of the horizon, at each of the four cardinal points.

As the sun dropped behind the ravine, the gan came down from the top of the gorge and, shouting and jumping acrobatically, they burst into the esplanade in front of the ceremonial cabin. Each one of the four dancers wore a large headpiece in the form of a cross made of three branches of the so-called Spanish bayonet with vertical pieces like the horns of a deer, but with much greater span.

Their faces were covered with black cloths, and in place of openings at eye level, they wore brass buttons hanging on the mask, which shone brightly when they reflected the light of the flames. Their bare torsos were painted black, but with designs of lightning, stars, and multicolored butterflies on their chests and backs. They wore ankle-length buckskin skirts tied at the waist, with long tassels and little bells, and sharply pointed moccasins with the design of a serpent on the instep.

All night the mountain spirits danced to the syncopated chants of the singers, gyrating around the fire in a dizzying manner. One minute they bent over at the waist until the antlers of the headpiece scraped the ground, and the next they raised themselves with an animal-like agility. The dancers' feet followed the vibrating rhythm of the drums and their arms made chopping motions in the air with wooden scimitars that they brandished in both hands.

The first white men who had contemplated that dance, without knowing its meaning, had called it the *Dance of the Devil* because the image that the dancers projected against the firelight, with reptilian contortions and the furious onslaught of the monumental headpiece, had a somewhat diabolic appearance. But for the Apaches the gan represented very powerful but benevolent forces.

Upon sensing the first sign of light on the horizon, the novices, who had rested on the hide of an unwounded deer where their footprints were outlined with sacred pollen, got up and began to dance to the rhythm of a chant in which the principal singer wished them a long life full of satisfactions and fertility while he shook a rattle made with the hooves of a young stag. The beat that the maidens marked with their feet was undulant and gentle, so as not to leave the perimeter of the hide, but the swaying of the long tassels on the tunics gave their steps a sensual rhythm.

Seated in the circle the onlookers had formed around the cabin, the cuates watched the novices dance, their mouths watering to think that those young girls had been theirs, even though they were aware that enjoying their bodies before having celebrated the puberty rite had violated an important taboo.

Just before sunrise, the singer painted the maidens' faces, arms, and legs with white clay, and on the palm of the left hand a yellow and red disc, symbol of the sacred marriage of White Painted Woman with the Sun. And when the orange disc of the sun finally peeked over the edge of the ravine, the singer stepped up the beat of his chant. The attendants gave shouts of joy, and the four gan stopped dancing around the fire, signaling with their wooden wands at the sun's disc and getting ready to disappear to their hiding places, since they were creatures of darkness.

At that moment, when all those present were waiting for the first of the maidens to start running toward the sun, Decoy heard the little voice of the Big Bottlefly whisper urgently in his ear, "Aké, aké! There is your enemy! The gan who is fourth in line, the one who wears the headdress with a star on top and a lightning bolt painted on the arms is Huwawa himself! Don't let him escape!"

The dancer with a star headpiece must have suspected something. Suddenly letting the wooden sabre fall to the ground, he jumped over the logs in the bonfire, which showered a torrent of sparks as he passed, and, without waiting for the other dancers, began to climb like a buck through the path that led to the top of the canyon.

Again Decoy listened to the voice that was telling him, "Don't let him escape to the sacred forest; he has not yet put on his armor of seven layers that make him invincible."

"Let's go get him!" shouted Decoy to his friend. "That dancer is the keeper of the Cedar Forest, Humbaba himself!"

"How can you know that?" asked the genízaro.

"A little bird just told me!" answered Cimarrón, pulling him up from the ground.

Hastily snatching the bag of weapons and armor that they had hidden under a tree, the twins took off in pursuit of the enemy along the steep path that went up almost to the top of the escarpment wall. At that very moment the maidens had started running toward the Sun.

The Cedar Forest

After I rode all morning without stopping, the sun, which had been hidden since dawn behind a cover of gray clouds, peeked above the mountain range, making the snowy cone of the Sierra Blanca shine. Behind me, at the bottom of the valley, I had left the village of La Luz and its sinister bells.

While I crossed the trail of dry lava that shot from the top of the slope, I thought that the landscape of that mountain range resembled the scenery that Tafoya had shown me as the place of battle between the Twin Warriors and Yeitsó. I asked myself if this stretch of the malpaís might not be the trail of petrified blood of another Cyclopean giant. I recalled then that the last time I had seen the signs of the twins—the taut bow and the hourglass—had been at the foot of the rock where Timothy Baltasar had fallen, and that memory momentarily made my heart skip a beat.

But I must admit that the excitement of the adventure outweighed the anxiety I felt about the fate of the companions I had left behind. As I climbed the mountain slope, however, I began to worry more for the safety of my own skin. As I approached the threshold of the Cedar Forest, whose tall crowns began to blend into the purple light of the evening, my excited imagination began to see strange forms in the tree trunks. And the whistling of the wind between the branches reminded me of what Dawson had told us about the fate of the miners who were crucified on the tree forks with their own tools, even though I had never heard the noise that the wind makes as it blows between the ribs of dead people.

I knew that this was not the time to let myself be carried away by my imagination, but rather to keep my good judgment and a cool head. After all, I was a soldier of the United States armed with a Springfield rifle and a good ordnance sabre, and not an Indian healer or one of those gullible Mexicans, prone to fall for any kind of superstition. Only if I kept cool could I succeed in my mission. If I allowed myself to be influenced by stories of magic and sorcery, I could end up leaving my bones among those cliffs.

Despite my good intentions, as I entered the forest I felt a profound chill that had nothing to do with the cold breeze coming down from the mountain. A strange weakness overtook me, with a tingling sensation in my limbs and my back. Even my mule must have felt something; I could feel a shiver run through its bones from the tip of its hooves all the way to the beginning of the tail. Unfolding the blanket that I had rolled up behind the saddle, I covered my shoulders and the animal's hindquarters with it. The mule continued dragging its hooves along a path that led to the heart of the forest.

When I came to a small clearing in the forest, I stopped to rest and to eat a bite of bacon and biscuit ration that I had stuck in the provision bag. Although the darkness around me was as thick as India ink, I didn't dare build a fire for fear of being detected and, after unsaddling and hobbling the mule, I curled up in the hollow of a dead tree trunk, trying to fall asleep. But I still felt the restless sensation that I had upon entering the forest and even the little bit I had eaten had not set well.

I found myself lying in the dark with my eyes wide open, alert to each rustle of the branches, holding my breath every time an owl hooted in the forest, and scrutinizing cedar trunks, which gave off a blue-green glow, as if the last rays of twilight had stuck to their bark. I stayed awake for a good long while, listening to strange whispers that seemed to come from the branches and observing the flashes that ran from one trunk to another, like will-o'-the-wisps. But in spite of those visions, the fatigue of the journey overcame me. Resting my head in the saddle seat, I curled into a ball between the roots of the dead cedar and fell asleep.

Around midnight, I was awakened by one of those tremendous mountain downpours that would have reminded my friend Baltasar of the Deluge. My only protection was my army-issue blanket, and the dirt it had accumulated during the trip had almost made it waterproof. But I moved away from the shelter of the tree because lightning had begun to flash, flooding the forest with whitish light, and I feared that the long trunk might attract a lightning bolt.

Suddenly the rumble of the storm subsided and the forest turned dead silent. It was then that I heard a voice that echoed in the forest like thunder: "Who has come to defile the trees on my mountain? Who has dared to touch the cedars that grow in the heart of the forest?"

I pinched my arm, hoping that that frightful scream was a product of my imagination, but unfortunately I could tell it wasn't a nightmare because the mule, whose reins I had taken lest the lightning scare it, let out a neigh of terror and rearing up wildly, broke the bridle and ran off into the darkness in spite of the hobble, bucking and kicking against an invisible enemy. I tried to follow her for a short stretch but it was useless; the night seemed to have swallowed her up. I curled up once again under the dead tree trunk and in spite of my terror, sleep got the best of me.

On the Trail of Humbaba

The cuates followed the track of the gan with the star headpiece who had rushed into the mouth of the cave. For a while they could follow the sound of his footsteps in the galleries of the old mine, but after a while the echo distorted the sounds of their own steps in the labyrinth of passages and they lost the trail of the fugitive. They found themselves in a dark maze, unable to find an exit because the light of dawn had not yet penetrated the cracks of the rock.

Finally they saw some light filtering through a narrow gallery that looked as though it had been dug by an animal, and, dragging themselves like ferrets through that burrow, they came out the other side of the Quebrada de los Mesteños at the edge of a forest so thick that the sun's rays couldn't penetrate to the underbrush. They had reached the threshold of the Cedar Forest.

The cuates stopped at the edge of the woods, admiring the thickness of the tree trunks whose upper crowns were barely visible. Although the trail that entered the forest was clean and clear of brush, as if inviting you to tread on it, an impressive silence reigned in that place and a strange glow emanated from the rugged bark of the trees. They were indeed in the Cedar Forest; its aroma floated on the pure mountain air with an intoxicating intensity. And beneath the shelter of the branches, flowery and thorny shrubs intertwined, forming dense thickets.

The two friends finally took a few steps on the path, but as soon as they crossed the threshold of the forest, a sudden paralysis overtook them, especially attacking Decoy, who sat down on the ground, dropping the sack of weapons and the lion skin quiver.

"Go on if you like," he said to the genízaro, covering his face with his hands. "Each step I take is as hard as if I had lead in my legs. I warned you that this forest was bewitched!"

"I too noticed a pins-and-needles feeling in my limbs. Perhaps the aroma of some exotic plant is causing this feeling of weakness, but if we go on walking, surely it will pass," answered Gil Gómez, and, holding his hand out to Decoy, he tried to help him up. But Decoy buried his face deeper between his arms, so that his friend wouldn't see that he was sobbing.

"After having overcome so many obstacles and dangers," said Gil Gómez, "now that we can almost taste victory, we must not let ourselves be defeated by discouragement and weakness."

Decoy kept staring at his friend and wiped the tears from his face with the back of his hand. He stood up and took the bag of weapons in his hand, exclaiming, "We have come to battle the guardian of the Cedar Forest, and we will not leave here without his head. Brother, take my hand, and let us run together toward what fortune wants to give us!"

The cuates took off running along the trail, crashing into clumps of boxwood and thorns that scratched their limbs and faces, and singing while they ran.

> *You were born to destroy the evil monsters.*
> *My son, you must run.*
> *You have shoes of black flint, you must run.*
> *You have leggings of black flint, you must run.*
> *You have armor of black flint, you must run.*
> *You have a heart of black flint inside you, you must run.*

They went running down a steep trail that ended in a forest clearing carpeted by a thick layer of grass, where they rolled around with the momentum of the run, breathing in deeply the powerful aroma of the grass and crushed flowers. Exhausted from exertion and lack of sleep, the two friends fell asleep on the grass.

When Gil Gómez woke up, darkness had already fallen over the mountains. An icy breeze blowing through the thicket chilled his limbs. "My friend, if you didn't call me, why am I awake?" he asked Decoy, who continued sleeping like a log and didn't answer him. Gil Gómez persisted: "You really didn't touch me? Then why am I so restless? I believe a spirit must have passed by, because my limbs are trembling. My friend, I have had another dream, and this one has really been frightening."

At last Cimarrón woke up, and Gil Gómez could tell him his dream. "The heavens thundered and the ground shook; suddenly everything was still and darkness spread. A thunderclap sounded and a conflagration spread with devastating fire; it began to rain death, and the darkness became denser. Then the incandescent flame was consumed and the fire went out, and all the matter that had been falling turned into ashes. I must find out what this terrible dream means."

But Gil Gómez didn't get an answer. His friend had fallen asleep again. "Decoy, wake up. A strange feeling of gloom has come over me. Don't you hear a strange cry in the murmur of the wind?"

"I don't hear anything special; it's only the whisper of the breeze moving the branches," answered Decoy, rubbing his eyes.

"I wonder if it's the sound of Humbaba prowling in the mountain. For the first time since we left Cabezón, I realize that it's crazy to challenge the keeper of the forest in his sanctuary."

"It's too late now to think of those things," answered Cimarrón. "If we join forces, nothing will be able to beat us. We must find Humbaba and defeat him."

"If I weren't even more frightened to cross this gloomy forest at night, I swear to you that I would go back the way we came!"

"Would you dare to return to Cabezón now? The old and young of the village would laugh at us and call us cowards!"

"There is something in this cursed mountain that drains one's spirit and paralyzes the blood. I believe the icy breeze coming down the mountain has frozen my heart," said Gil Gómez, finally standing up. "I don't think the forest keeper will mind if we use our axes to cut a few branches from the trees so we can build a fire and warm up."

"You want to say for us to cut *that good round object which lies,* using *that by means of which I customarily chop,* to build *that which tells a story,*" Decoy corrected him.

"I said what I said. Besides, you heard Sun Horse: even the Apaches no longer use the war language, because it's inefficient," answered Gil Gómez.

The genízaro then reached into the bag of weapons and withdrew the huge axes that the blacksmith from Cabezón had forged for them.

Approaching the closest tree, he set about cutting off some cedar branches, which he quickly piled up in a heap. The sap from the trunks made the fire catch rapidly with a lively sputtering, and soon a dense cloud of smoke merged with the darkness of the night. But the first cedar branches had scarcely caught fire when a mighty wind gathered some storm clouds in the sky, and such a heavy downpour fell on the forest that in only a few seconds it put out the fire, leaving the smoldering logs hissing like rattlesnakes.

At that moment a raucous voice thundered through the forest. "Who has come to defile the trees on my mountain? Who has dared to touch the cedars that grow in the heart of the forest?"

When the cuates turned around with the axes in their hands ready to face their enemy, they saw only the trunks of the cedars, which had begun to glow with a greenish light that flooded the forest.

"It's the trees themselves that are speaking!" exclaimed Gil Gómez, raising his axe against the nearest trunk. "It's the cedars that are bewitched, and if we cut them down, we'll break the spell of this cursed forest."

But when he tried to chop at the tree, the blade didn't make a dent in the trunk, and the giant axe rebounded as if the bark of the cedars were made of layers of iron. The stronger the blow and the harder he tried to get the steel to bite into the wood, the stronger shone the protective halo around the trees, and the trunks spit out the axe blade with such force that the rebound almost wounded the twins.

Again the voice thundered the same phrase through the heart of the forest. The sound seemed to come from everywhere and nowhere. "Who has dared to touch the cedars that grow in the heart of the forest?"

Then the cuates saw emerging from the half light of the forest the silhouettes of the hooded dancers who had performed the Dance of the Devil. They did the same frenetic steps, with the pirouettes and contortions that made their headpieces sway. No sooner did the headpieces rise to touch the tree trunks than they bent down and swept the very roots of the trees.

The brass buttons that the gan wore on their masks reflecting the greenish light with an intense brightness, the rattling of their skirts blending with the hiss of the wind in the branches, all produced a dizzying effect. The twins ran from one place to another pursuing the shadows of the dancers, who would appear one moment behind the trunk of a tree only to disappear the next moment. They seemed no more solid than the fireflies that swarmed in the dense thicket.

Finally the silhouettes of the dancers began moving away, dissipating in the wake of the green brightness until once again the forest remained deserted and silent. The only sound in the clearing was the crackle of the embers where some drops of sap still burned.

The two friends huddled together, and in spite of their nervousness and fear, sleep soon overcame them.

Duel in the Sierra Blanca

When the cuates woke up, sunlight was already filtering through the treetops, and the remains of the fire emitted a faint aroma of resin. Afraid of seeing more of the visions that had terrified him the night before, Decoy hadn't yet dared to open his eyes when he heard a tenuous little voice from the bag where he was carrying his weapons. "Aké! aké! How can you even think of putting me aside when you need me most?" He remembered that while they were in pursuit of the gan through the maze of the cave, he had put the little willow box with the Big Bottlefly in the bag. When he brought it out from among the odds and ends, he noticed a tone of indignation in the voice. "You shouldn't have attacked the trees with your steel axes; that irritates the mountain spirits, who protect the tree trunks with a shining halo! Why didn't you use the flint machetes that Sun Horse gave you?"

Decoy kept the small willow box next to his chest, and he told Gil Gómez, "We can't let ourselves be defeated by a few crude tricks; next time the keeper of the forest tries his sorcery on us, we're going to use the special weapons that Sun Horse gave us."

"You're right! Next time we'll put aside these dull axes and use the flint machetes, the cedar bow that Narbona prepared, and the arrows from the quiver made of lion's skin. That ghost can't scare us in broad daylight the way it could in the dark!"

"Yes, but remember that machete is *that which is helpful to oneself in cutting,* and bow *that which is good for one;* the arrows are *those with which one throws first.* And ghost in war language is expressed by *that which is not visible.*"

"You're right," agreed the genízaro. "When I'm excited I forget to use the war language. Let's take a swim in the Ruidoso. The cold water will clear our heads!"

While they were swimming a ray of sun broke through the canopy of the forest and hit the cascade, forming a small rainbow. Later, the genízaro put on the breastplate embossed in gold that he had found in the cave, and

Decoy the coat of mail, whose links sparkled in the green light that flooded the underbrush. Gil Gómez grabbed hold of the cedar bow and, using all his strength, he stretched across it the bowstring made from deer tendon that their mentor had given them. He stuck the flint axe in his waist. Decoy seized his own flint axe and threw the lionskin quiver across his shoulder. Its eagle-feather arrows shone in the sun.

When the twins took off walking through the dense underbrush, the thicket seemed to open up before them. Decoy was their guide, taking his instructions from the Big Bottlefly.

"Follow the riverbed until it becomes a small lake!" said the insect. "The keeper of the forest customarily stops at that place to drink water at noon, whenever he finishes making the rounds of the cedars. Hurry, because while he's drinking he usually puts aside his weapons, and it's a perfect time to attack him!"

Decoy said to his friend, "Let's pick up the pace. I believe I know where we can surprise our foe!"

"And how do you know?" asked the genízaro.

"Just follow me and trust me," said Decoy.

After following the Ruidoso and topping a steep slope, they came to a gully where the river turned into a small swamp.

"Aké! aké!" whispered the Big Bottlefly. "This is it. Go down the slope quickly and hide in the canebrake that surrounds the pool, because Huwawa can show up at any moment."

They had barely hidden in the canebrake when they heard strong footsteps that made the ground tremble and saw two huge buffalo horns looming above the hill. Even though Humbaba had the sun to his back, the twins were able to make out the silhouette of a warrior of gigantic proportions, its head covered with a buffalo head with skin and horns. The animal's snout hanging down in front covered the warrior's face. His torso was crammed into a large tunic covered with scales of flint that shone like a steel breastplate. In his right hand the giant was carrying a bunch of huge darts.

Following the instructions of their invisible advisor, the cuates hid in the canebrake so that the warrior wouldn't see them when he came close to the edge of the pool. Leaving his lances within reach, he knelt to drink.

"What are you waiting for? Now's the time for you to get close to him, while his face is submerged in the water," whispered the Big Bottlefly in Decoy's ear. Decoy in turn gestured to his friend to get close to their prey.

The warrior had his face in the water and was swallowing the liquid, making a terrible noise that echoed through the gully. The cuates' blood froze. *K-ol, k-ol, k-ol,* was the noise he made as he drank, a sound like drainage. The cuates crept stealthily within a few yards of where the giant was kneeling with his enormous abdomen hanging over the pond and for a few instants had him at their mercy.

But they hesitated, and the Big Bottlefly had to encourage them again. "Let's go! Let's go! Now's the time to shoot an arrow into his loins. What are you waiting for?"

But at that moment the big black ugly bird appeared in the sky, dove to the edge of the pond, and fluttering its wings over the place where Humbaba was drinking, began to make terrible cawing noises. Alerted, the warrior began to stand up, and he saw the cuates' reflection on the surface of the water. Seizing the darts that he had left on the grass, he confronted the genízaro, saying, "How is it possible for a man of courage to come all the way here in the company of an idiot? This one here who doesn't even know who his father is and has never drunk his mother's milk, like a young tortoise!"

Seeing that the cuates didn't dare to respond, the giant continued, "I had that tadpole at my mercy, Gil Gómez, but I refused to kill him. I should have cut out his throat and fed it to the vultures. Now I regret not having done it."

Facing Decoy, he said, "Why do you return now, you worm, to this place from which you fled long ago, bringing Gil Gómez with you as your protector?"

The warrior paused and pulled off his mask, exposing a face deformed by a monstrous scar. As he continued to speak, the flesh turned into a repugnant grimace. Gil Gómez and Decoy felt a chill of terror and instinctively squeezed the handles of their weapons.

"Look at how your hands contract, ready to attack. But don't forget, I must be the one who shoots first."

While the warrior spoke, his featureless face contorted itself like a jumble of intestines. Gil Gómez turned around, whispering in Decoy's ear, "Humbaba's face moves and twists like the viscera of an animal! I can't stand the sight of those horrible grimaces. You'll have to shoot! Grab *that which is good for one* and aim at *that which one throws first!*" He extended his bow toward Decoy, not daring even to look at the giant.

But at that moment the Big Bottlefly intervened. "He's using those grimaces to intimidate you, but you don't have to look at his face! You can judge your aim by the reflection of his body in the water. I will let you know when he's going to attack!"

"We will not be intimidated by the grimaces of a sorcerer!" declared Decoy in a loud voice that trembled with panic and determination. "We have the weapons that Sun Horse has given us, and we're going to use them against this braggart. We'll see if Humbaba is capable of stopping the arrows of lightning!" And following the advice of their invisible ally, he whispered in his friend's ear, "You don't need to look at his face. Aim at the reflection of Humbaba in the lake! I'll tell you when we'll have to dodge *that by means of which one is quickly killed.*"

The giant already had the first dart in his hand, ready to throw, but he was taking his time, prolonging the moment and trying to distract his adversaries.

"Aké! aké! Get ready to duck—he's about to shoot! The first dart is aimed high!" warned the Big Bottlefly.

And so, with an extremely rapid movement of his arm, the giant shot a dart that passed by, whistling above the heads of the twins, who had ducked just in time. As it missed the target, the missile left an incandescent trail, grazing the tops of the trees. Finally it buried itself in the embankment on the lowest part of the gully, making a hole as deep as a badger's lair.

Seeing that he had missed, the giant roared and aimed a second projectile at the legs of the cuates, who were warned again. "Aké! aké! He has aimed low: this time you must jump up."

That's what the two friends did, and so the dart went by, burning the grass under their soles and felling bushes until it hit a thick cedar trunk, which it split in half.

Humbaba fired two more darts, one to the right and another to the left, but the cuates dodged both of them by twisting their waists after having been warned by their invisible advisor. When they saw that the giant was left without any weapons, the cuates got ready to shoot, but the Big Bottlefly warned them, "Wait for an instant because someone very powerful is going to help you! Before you attack him you have to wait for the giant to lose the seven flint capes which make him invulnerable."

The sun was reaching its zenith, and when the horns of the giant's forehead were silhouetted like a half moon against it, the burning disc seemed to open up, and from it descended a ray that illuminated the warrior's scales of flint with a blinding glare.

A deafening crack sounded, and twelve hurricane winds struck the bosom of the valley: the North Wind, the Hot Stifling Wind, the Warm Breeze, the East Wind, the Wind that Can Take the Horns off Goats, the Sharp Cold Breeze, the Strong Wind, the Rainstorm, the Blizzard, the Downpour, the Typhoon, and the Whirlwind. All the winds whirled around the huge body of Humbaba, spinning him like a top and peeling away one by one the layers of flint that served him as armor.

When the winds died down, the shadow of the giant swayed from side to side. His hideous face had lost its color, as when the blood is cleansed from the viscera of an animal. Without the protection of its seven tunics, the warrior's silhouette shrank as if someone had peeled away several layers of skin, and he remained motionless at the edge of the pond, whose waters had turned choppy from the strong wind's turbulence.

"Your time has come! Prepare the bow and arrows, and aim the first arrow at the instep of the foot, so as to make him stagger," said the Big Bottlefly's tiny voice to Decoy, who in turn transmitted the instruction to Gil Gómez, who put the first arrow from the quiver on the bowstring and got ready to shoot.

When his fingers let go of the tip of the arrow, it produced a zing that sounded like the hiss when the fuse of a rocket is lit. The shaft whizzed by the genízaro's fist that held the bow, leaving him with a burnt spot on his skin. The cuates couldn't see the arrow hit its target, but the giant felt the impact and stumbled forward heavily. One after the other, the four arrows went from the lionskin quiver to Narbona's bow: the second struck the waistline, and the powerful abdomen doubled over under the impact; the third was aimed at the scrotum, and when the giant's head was brought down with pain, the fourth arrow was aimed at the nape of his neck.

Then Humbaba spun around and, bending his knees, he slowly toppled forward, sinking his terrifying face in the mud at the edge of the lake.

"Let's go! Don't stand there like a rock! He's still breathing. Now you must put him out of his misery: use the flint machete to cut off his head!" came the tiny, cruel voice.

The Man Who Killed Humbaba

After spending that night in the middle of the forest, hearing mysterious voices and seeing will-o-the-wisps floating among the trees, at the first light of morning I set about finding the mule that had been frightened during the storm. But following the animal's trail wasn't an easy task, because its tracks had been partly erased in the downpour. The underbrush had been torn up by the strong wind, and the sunlight had not yet burned through the thick blanket of fog that nestled on the forest floor. Several times I fell into deep ruts full of water, and other times I got tangled up in brambles so thick that I left shreds of skin from my face and hands in the underbrush.

To be able to walk faster, I decided to leave my saddle, the blanket, and the rest of the equipment hidden in some bushes. I only took with me the rifle in its holster and my canteen. It was already near midday when, reaching the top of a steep incline that overlooked a deep wash, I thought I heard voices.

My pulse beat more rapidly when, listening carefully, I recognized the voices of Gil Gómez and his friend Decoy. They sounded very close, just on the other side of the slope. Leaving the canteen on the ground so that it wouldn't make a noise scraping a branch, I cautiously withdrew the rifle from its holster and crawled slowly beneath the underbrush until I could look down at the other side. Following Tafoya's teachings, I hid my head in a tuft of grass and I left the rifle flat on the ground, so that the barrel wouldn't reflect the sunlight that had begun to break through the cloud cover.

On the other side of the embankment, the terrain flattened out in a riverbed, where the arroyo fed a small lake, surrounded by canebrakes and cattails. And down below, barely twenty yards from my hiding place, were the adventurers we had been following for close to two weeks. But they weren't alone. On the other side of the pond stood a menacing Apache warrior of gigantic proportions with a handful of darts in his right hand. My heart skipped a beat when I recognized on his head the helmet with buffalo horns that I had seen on the Apache horseman in the He-Mule Swamp, the one who had fled with the white hostage!

From where I was hiding, you couldn't see the Apache's face well, but I had the impression that it was deformed by some wound or sickness. His corpulence was accentuated by a long tunic embedded with brilliant stones that sparkled in the sunlight that now fell on the gully.

The cuates were dressed again in armor, but they didn't have either a rifle or firearm of any kind; the cacique carried only a bow and some arrows and his friend was armed only with a quiver made from animal skin and a stone machete. For all I had cursed those braggarts when I was following their trail through the wilderness, I couldn't avoid a chill thinking that they were going to face the terrible keeper of the Cedar Forest virtually unarmed. But it was too late to do anything, for the fight was beginning.

The giant shot the first dart, with Cyclopean force, but the projectile passed over the heads of the cuates, who ducked from the waist with incredible agility. The dart struck the earth with such force that I felt the ground shake under my body. The second dart also missed its target; it passed beneath the feet of the cuates and struck the root of a large tree, which it sliced in half. The next two arrows also missed, one to the left and the other to the right. I was surprised to see the skill with which the cuates dodged those projectiles, thrown with superhuman strength and deadly precision, as if they could guess where their enemy was going to aim before he shot.

The warrior was left empty handed, and he was waiting for the cuates to use their weapons. But at that moment the sun reached its zenith, and the contestants turned to look at the sky, where a large black storm cloud covered the face of the sun.

Only then did I realize that there was a fourth person in the scene whom I hadn't seen before. Hidden in the shrubbery that surrounded the ravine, on the other side of the gully, was a Mescalero Apache mounted on a spirited sorrel colt, wearing a fur bonnet like a Turk and a round shield painted with a large yellow and red sun. He wore a long tunic painted with symbols of serpents and carried a huge bow in his hand.

Just as the black cloud crossed the path of the sun, the rider reached behind and pulled from his quiver a very long arrow, which he placed in position to shoot. I thought he was going to aim at one of the contestants in the ravine, but the warrior drew his bow in the direction of the sky and fired the arrow. As it went up, it produced the whistling sound that an artillery shell makes before hitting its target; and upon reaching high in the sky it exploded like a grenade!

At that same instant, from the center of the black cloud a powerful whirlwind shot forth, yanking the bushes out by the roots and even rocking the trunks of the cedars. Even though I was lying face down, the force of the storm was such that I had to grasp the strap of my cap with my teeth to keep it from flying off my head. I also had to half close my eyes for a few moments to protect them against the particles raised by the whirlwind.

When I opened them again, the fierce turbulence had calmed down, although it had destroyed the bulrushes that surrounded the lake. The water in the pool was still making waves as though in the midst of a storm. The strong wind had stripped the flint tunic off the warrior with the buffalo headdress! His silhouette was sadly diminished.

Seeing that their powerful enemy was lying half-naked on the bank of the pool with his armor shattered by the force of the gale, the cuates prepared to attack him. Before he drew the bow, I saw the genízaro spit on the palm of his hand and rub the wood of the bow and the cord with his own saliva. Decoy gave him an arrow, taking it from the quiver, and pulled the bowstring until the muscles of his forearm seemed on the point of bursting.

"Remember not to look at his face," Decoy said to him while he aimed. "Go by the reflection of his body on the lake!"

But the surface of the water was still agitated by the storm, and the giant's silhouette oscillated on the surface with the waves, so that it was difficult to take good aim by that distorted reflection. In fact, the arrow buried itself in the mud bank instead of in the body of the giant. Moved by an uncontrollable impulse, I cocked the firing pin of my rifle and, without thinking twice, I fired. The report of the weapon was carried by the wind, but the bullet reached its target, although because of the rush I only wounded the Apache on the instep of his foot, making him stumble.

The genízaro's next arrow also landed in the water, but I had had time to reload, and this time I hit the warrior in the abdomen, making him double over at the waist. The archer also failed with the third and fourth arrows, but by then I had gotten in a better position from which to shoot, and I placed a bullet in the lower belly. When the buffalo mask dropped under the impact of that shot, I sent the fourth and last bullet to the nape of the Apache's neck. Fortunately, in the heat of battle, the cuates hadn't even noticed the shots from my rifle, since the wind carried the report in another direction, so my intervention went unnoticed.

I thought my last shot had broken his neck, but the giant seemed made of iron. He took two or three steps before his knees buckled and he fell face down, burying the horns of his devilish helmet in the mud. The cuates had come close to where the giant fell when he lifted his face from the mud and got halfway up, rising to his knees before his executioners.

Gil Gómez had a stone axe in his hand and Decoy a long flint machete, and they were ready to aim the final blow, but standing face to face with the enemy, they seemed to hesitate. Indeed the giant's demonic face, stained with mud and blood, inspired more pity than fear: the wounded enemy raised his hands in an imploring gesture. "Gil Gómez, don't kill me, be generous and let me live! I'll teach you the secrets of the forest, I'll show you the different kinds of bushes and aromatic plants, we'll walk around together under the branches and I'll cut you the healthiest trees . . ."

"Don't pay any attention to him!" Decoy shouted at his friend. "Don't ever think of listening to his words; don't accept his pleas. We have come here to kill him!"

The giant then turned to Decoy. "You know that I've had you at my mercy for a long time. I could have killed you before you entered the forest and dragged you to the deepest part of the underbrush to feed your body to the carrion eaters. Take advantage of your victory and be magnanimous! Convince Gil Gómez to spare my life!"

"Absolutely not!" howled Decoy, beside himself. "Brother, finish off the guardian of the Cedar Forest. Kill him, smash him, pulverize him! Let's end our task before the mountain spirits come to help him. Let's finish with Humbaba so that what you wrote on the rock of El Morro becomes reality."

Again the warrior spoke to Decoy, trying to earn his compassion. "Remember when you would walk through these forests like a cub, and you would drink the water of the springs of these sierras. Now it's in your power to spare me from death; speak to Gil Gómez so that he will let me live!"

But Decoy remained insistent. "Come on," he told his companion, "don't let yourself weaken! Give him the coup de grace and let everyone know that it was you who killed the fierce guardian of the Sierra Blanca."

When he heard this Humbaba emitted a roar of fury and cursed Cimarrón. "I hope you never get to grow old alongside your friend and that neither of you succeeds in safely navigating the river of life! And when you do die, I hope no one remembers you and that you leave no trace of your existence."

Then Decoy turned impatiently to his friend. "It seems that you don't listen to me when I speak to you, and that you only have ears for the cries of Humbaba. If you don't strike him, I'll do it myself!"

Gil Gómez then raised his stone axe and landed a terrible blow on Humbaba's neck; the giant's head remained attached to the body only by a thread of flesh and tendons, but Decoy grabbed it by the hair and, using the machete like a saw, cut the last filament that joined it to life, afterward throwing the head far away. It rolled through the mud until it landed at the edge of the lake. Dark blood began to shoot from the slit throat of the giant, forming a rivulet of blood that ran toward the place where the head had landed.

The two killers hurried to the place where the blood was flowing down the mountain, and before it reached the water, the genízaro drew a zigzag sign deep in the mud with his stone axe. Immediately Decoy thrust his flint machete in the ground and drew a straight line. They repeated the operation, drawing four parallel marks, two straight and two zigzag-ging. The blood flowed away from where the giant's head was lying and spread out in the meadow. Then Decoy took the head and put it in a buckskin bag.

The cuates tried to drag the huge body of the giant into the underbrush to hide it, but not even by pulling with all their strength, each tugging on a foot, could they move it even an inch. They approached the edge of the forest and with the flint axe began to cut large branches of cedar, placing them on top of the giant until they had completely covered him. Later they made a fire to light the pyre, and soon a dense aromatic smoke rose toward the sky.

Whether it was the reflection of the light from the bonfire or another strange phenomenon like the others I had witnessed, the trunks of the cedars began to glow in full daylight as if with their own light, throwing beams of the same blue-green radiance that I had noticed the night before in the forest clearing. A gentle and abundant rain began to fall over the forest, washing the giant's blood flow toward the riverbed, and the water began falling among the tree trunks in fat drops, as if the cedars were saying farewell to the keeper of the sacred forest.

I took advantage of the curtain of water that enveloped the mountain to get out of my hiding place without being seen, and grabbing my canteen and rifle, I slipped away on all fours down the other side of the embankment. I was afraid that the Apache rider with the sun design on his shield might still be prowling around, but he had also disappeared under the mantle of the rain. As soon as I felt sure no one was following me, I started running as if the devil were after me, trying to orient myself in the midst of the underbrush, to the place where I had left the saddle and the rest of my belongings.

Only when it stopped raining could I find the path that took me near the clearing where I had spent the previous night, and some yards from there I saw the backside of my mule, wet and shining. After spending the night lost in the forest, she had returned to exactly the same place and was grazing quietly among the bushes. When I found the saddle and the rest of my belongings, I placed the bridle and headstall over the mule's snout and put on the saddle, tightening the cinch. Before leaving, it occurred to me to take a look around the place where I had spent the night to make sure I had left nothing behind. I had never seen a setting more beautiful and idyllic than that forest clearing when the afternoon sun penetrated the double protection of clouds and canopy of green and shone on the carpet of thick grass crowded with flowers. After the rain, the cedar branches gave off a sweet aroma, and even the thorn bushes had a sweet and pungent perfume. I wondered if my hallucinations of the night before had been due only to fatigue and nerves.

And that's when I saw them, hanging high up on the same dead cedar at whose roots I had spent the previous night. There were the soldiers who had deserted the camp, but I wasn't going to need handcuffs or shackles to detain them, nor would it be necessary to court martial them. About twenty feet off the ground, in the tree forks, were hanging the corpses cut down the middle, top to bottom—pinned to the branches with their own sabres—of the men who left the ghost town planning to steal the treasure of the Sierra Blanca.

The obese body of Sweeny occupied the place of honor in that panoply. Although the swollen face was already half eaten by the carrion birds, I recognized him by the tassels of the sabre whose handle stuck out between his ribs, the same sabre with which he had tried to send my friend Baltasar to hell.

Resting on nearby branches of the dead tree, a silent group of eagles, hawks, and vultures were waiting for me to leave so they could continue their greedy banquet in peace. Unable to hold back, I let out a cry whose echo resounded all across the mountains, and digging my spurs into the flanks of the poor animal, I left at a gallop through the underbrush, jumping over arroyos and deep gullies, and didn't stop until I was out of that bewitched forest.

The Ninth Life of Baltasar

For two days and two nights I was lost in the maze of the mountain range, and at dawn of the third day I came out at the Río Tularosa, whose water was running at full capacity due to the downpours at the headwaters in the mountains. Even though we were still in the dry season—the first days of July, according to the dates in my diary—those rainstorms had turned the desert green; the arroyos were covered with masses of flowery oleander, and even the fierce stems of the Spanish bayonets shone with white flowers. As I approached the river bed, I saw that the water had overflowed, inundating the rushes and tules that at sunset took on a bright red color—hence the name Tularosa *(tule rosa)* that the Spaniards had given the river.

As evening fell, when sunset inflamed the canebrakes and the huge bulk of the Sierra Blanca seemed to hover above the horizon, I came within sight of the ghost town. And my heart sank, not knowing what had happened to my companions, whom I had abandoned in the midst of those ruins while I followed the trail of the deserters. Like writing on the wall, at that very moment the wind carried the gloomy sound of the church bells, and I knew that a tragedy had occurred. Under the weight of that premonition, I spurred my half-lame mount, which used its homing instinct and last breath to gallop down the steep slope to the town of La Luz.

As I rode at breakneck speed toward the village, episodes from the life that I had shared with Timothy Baltasar ran through my mind in rapid sequence, from the time I saw him arrive at the barracks as a recruit with his gawky figure and his knapsack hanging from his wide back, the scene of his first discussion with Sweeny because he refused to get on horseback, and the second discussion when he scolded him for his ignoble deed with the Indian child, up to the tragic outcome of his confrontation with the sergeant. But the thing that was freshest and clearest in my mind was the deathly expression on Timothy's face when I went to help him after he was struck with the sabre. His eyes were covered with an opaque veil, the same one that I had noted on the white woman who fell at my feet at the Ciénaga del Macho. As I recalled all these memories, I had the cruel hunch that my friend had died.

But someone was still alive in that ruined bastion! As I got close to the village I saw that the flag of our company still flew atop the church tower, and it became clear to me that the sentinel was also on the alert when I heard the whistling of a bullet above my head, followed by a rifle report. Before I was able to react, another shot went off, and this time I felt the ground coming toward me when my mule collapsed between my legs, struck by the projectile.

Protecting myself with the body of my poor animal, which was still kicking with indignation at its unfair fate, I tied to the tip of my sabre a kerchief of doubtful white, which I waved vigorously, hoping that my companions would be able to recognize that universal sign of peace. At the same time I was hollering my name, company, and rank as loudly as I could. Later, when I had occasion to look at myself in the mirror, I understood why my companions could well have mistaken me for the enemy. During my entrada in the sierra, not only had I lost all trace of military clothing—my tunic had been torn apart by the underbrush, which had also kept my dragoon cap as a souvenir—but even my face, marked with deep scratches and stained with mud, looked more like the face of a Mescalero Indian painted for war than that of a United States soldier.

Despite my disreputable appearance, when they finally recognized me and I was able to approach them in a wobbly stride, the assistant surgeon and the bugler embraced me the way you hug a dear friend who has been given up for lost. Just behind them was Lieutenant Loring, and I didn't need to ask him what had become of my friend, because he was carrying Baltasar's Bible, and he handed me the well-worn book with a sorrowful expression. "Your friend told me that you would take charge of all his personal effects. A little before the end, Baltasar spoke of a trunk that he had left at the fort for safekeeping; he insisted that you had the key to it. While he was delirious, he spoke a lot about camels, about some ships of the desert. . . ."

It's when I heard him talk about Timothy Baltasar's camels that I collapsed. The fatigue and tension of recent days caused my emotions to overflow upon hearing the confirmation of that tragedy. I started to cry like a child, resting my head on the officer's shirtfront, which I left soaked with tears and mud.

When I had calmed down, having regained my spirits with the help of a flask of liquor that the lieutenant kept in a leather case, my companions asked me to tell them what had happened in the mountains. They had been sure that either the Indians or the deserters would polish me off within two days of my departure. In the most objective and succinct way, but glossing over some details of my adventures that they would not have believed, I recounted the events of my expedition, and how I had found the bodies of the deserters hanging from a thousand-year-old cedar. I described the sensation of weakness and even paralysis that overcame me upon entering the bewitched forest, and the storm in which thunder and lightning made me see visions and hear supernatural voices. Lastly, I told them how I had witnessed the battle between the twins and the huge giant Humbaba, although I opted to omit my participation in the death of the guardian of the Cedar Forest. I thought that my part in the deed would have humiliated Lieutenant Loring, compelled to stay back at the camp to recover from his sunstroke while a modest soldier fulfilled the mission with which he had been entrusted.

Neither the news of Baltasar's death nor the horrible fate that the other comrades had suffered kept the survivors from celebrating our reunion with a banquet of mule meat—from the same mule that they had just shot by mistake—since the poor souls hadn't had a decent meal in several days. Even I had to admit that the mountain air and the emotions had whetted my appetite.

While we were eating supper next to the bonfire, I asked them how they had been able to prevent an attack by the Apaches who infested the area, for whom that reduced detail would have been easy and tempting prey. In fact, it was no more miraculous for me to have returned alive from the Sierra Blanca than it was for those wretched souls to have survived the dangers that lay in wait outside the ghost town where they were camped.

But, according to what they told me, Lieutenant Loring, with an astuteness worthy of the most experienced Indian fighter, had conjured up the idea of lighting several fires at night inside the ruins and organizing a guard shift in which the few defenders of that bastion rotated positions periodically. This gave the impression to any enemy who might have been observing from afar that the troop garrison was much larger and stronger. At dawn he had the bugle play, which could be heard many leagues throughout the valley, and they also moved the unloaded cannon around, so that its bronze barrel sparkled to each of the four cardinal points.

Compared to the clearing in the forest where I had spent the night during my visit to the Sierra Blanca, the adobe house crowded with scorpions and salamanders in the ghost town seemed as safe and comfortable to me as the best suite at the Astor Hotel in New York. But in spite of my fatigue, it took me a long time to fall asleep that night, because those same ruined adobe walls had been witness to my last conversation with Timothy Baltasar, that conversation in which—probably due to the effect of a high fever—he had spoken to me with such passion about the camels, a topic that he had also discussed with the lieutenant.

It still seemed incredible to me that that mind, so alive and imaginative, had ceased its fabulous schemes and that I would never again hear the sarcastic tone of his remarks, nor the melody of his famous song about Babylon. Precisely because of having been in real life a totally improbable character, he seemed destined to be immortal, as proved by his luck up to that point, since he had managed to survive his own carelessness and distractions, for which he was famous in the company. In fact, his companions believed that Timothy had more lives than a cat, as he proved by surviving almost unhurt in the Apache ambush at Dog Canyon.

But perhaps Baltasar had already used up his ninth life, and now his name could be added to the long list of casualties from that mad expedition. Of the fifty soldiers who had left Fort Conrad, only four of us remained alive, including myself, a convalescent officer, an old drunkard doctor, and a bugler, barely an adolescent.

The Navigators of the Flood

Once I was able to fall asleep, I would probably have slept like a log until well into the next morning, but the assistant surgeon, who stood the last watch, woke me at dawn to tell me that he had seen a suspicious movement by the river. Putting the spyglass in my pocket and a revolver in my belt, I went to the embankment that overlooked the riverbed, over which floated a thick cover of mist. At first I didn't see anything unusual, and I would have thought our sentry had drunk one too many during guard duty except that I knew not a drop of alcohol remained amongst our depleted provisions.

But as soon as the sunlight broke through the mist, through the reeds and cattails that grew on the bank I saw a strange vessel coming down the swollen river. It was a raft made from thick cedar logs, navigated by the two friends who had killed the keeper of the Cedar Forest, who were pushing it along with a long pole. The keeper's head, stuck in a buckskin bag, was resting on the prow of the vessel; and the horns of the buffalo headpiece that stuck out of the bundle were leading the way through the canebrake like the figurehead of an ancient galley. The sun glinted on the metallic armor and flint weapons of the cuates, lending them the appearance of legendary heroes returning from their exploits with a minotaur's head as a trophy.

The cuates knew that there was an encampment of soldiers in the abandoned village, and, far from trying to elude us as they had done until then, they were looking for us to propose a deal. As soon as the raft had run aground on the bank, they disembarked and came toward me, saying that they wanted to speak with the head of our detail, and as soon as I took them before Lieutenant Loring, we learned the purpose of their mission.

"We need your carreta to transport some tree trunks that we're going to take to the church in Cabezón, and in exchange for letting us have it, we will bring you the horses and provisions that you need to get back to the fort. We will also be your guides and escorts until you arrive at the Río

Grande," said the genízaro, sitting cross-legged in front of the officer on the floor of the ruined church.

As I was still acting as interpreter between the Río Puerco cacique and Lieutenant Loring, I was able to smooth out the terms of that proposal. Being acquainted with the officer, I knew his pride would not let him acknowledge that the cuates had triumphed where the army had failed. Consequently, I took the liberty of interpreting the genízaro's words in a way that would make us appear to be doing them a favor.

"These rogues need our wagon in order to get some tree trunks to the Río Grande; apparently they promised them to the villagers of Cabezón. In exchange for letting them take their trunks in our carreta they are offering to get us the horses we need to return to the fort."

"Ask them where they expect to find fresh horses in the desert," said Loring, trying not to lose his dignity by immediately accepting the deal.

In order to facilitate the agreement, a small deception occurred to me that would let the officer save his honor.

"Lieutenant Loring gladly accepts your proposal," I said to the genízaro without consulting my commander, "but only on the condition that you hand over the map of the Sierra Blanca that you won gambling in Bernalillo. He thinks you no longer need it, but it may be useful to the army."

The cacique searched in the tunic that he was wearing under his armor, withdrew the map in the oilcloth wrapping that I knew so well, and without saying a word, handed it to me. I didn't have to explain much to the officer, because as soon as he saw the map, I noticed that his eyes shone with a spark quite distinct from that of the fever he had suffered from the sunstroke. That's when I told Loring the rest of their request.

"The twins are also asking our permission to accompany us on the return trip, and in exchange for the army's protection, they offer this map that they know will be of interest to you."

Loring nodded his bandaged head in agreement and extended his hand toward the map; but his answer showed that it wasn't so easy to deceive him. "Tell him that we accept his proposal, because in our situation, we have no other alternative. As for the army's protection, I know very well that a handful of sick and wounded men wouldn't be able to guide even a gaggle of geese. Nevertheless, I demand that when we reach the Río Grande Valley and enter a settlement, we soldiers will march in first, and they will go behind, as if they were our auxiliaries."

When I translated his words, the cuates shrugged their shoulders, and then got up and extended their hands to the officer to close the deal. The way Lieutenant Loring pressed their big rough hands between his confirmed my impression that behind the fragile constitution of the officer were the makings of a good soldier.

Decoy's Secret

Although it seemed almost impossible to find a good string of horses in that wasteland, before nightfall the twins had returned to camp with more than twenty horses, most of them mustangs. Others bore the army brand, and they must have joined the herds of wild ones after having lost their riders during some of the previous expeditions to the Sierra Blanca. Decoy was riding a magnificent bay stallion with an almost white mane and tail that obeyed the orders of its rider as if it had been broken after a long training. He knew those herds and their haunts like the back of his hand, having spent part of his life roaming those lands in the company of mustangs.

The cuates also brought the carcass of an enormous elk, laid across the back of one of the horses with its antlers dragging the ground. Immediately volunteers appeared to skin the elk, and the assistant surgeon employed his anatomical knowledge to quarter and season the animal, whose ribs were put to roast slowly in the embers of the bonfire. As big as the animal was, it turned out to be small for the accumulated hunger of that group who for two weeks hadn't tasted any meat except for horses and mules that died of fatigue or by accident.

Although we invited the cuates to share in the party, they only agreed to eat when the rest of us had finished. And even then I noticed that Decoy waited until the roasted meat cooled off before sinking his teeth in it. I could tell they were following a special ritual for eating and drinking, for I also saw that Cimarrón was using a kind of little tube to suck the water from the canteen, and he scratched his back with a little rod. They even spoke to each other in a peculiar language; I heard the genízaro say something like *that which tells a story* to refer to the fire.

That same night, when the rest of my companions were already asleep, I had a chance to listen to an interesting conversation between Gil Gómez and Decoy. The cuates were camping in a house next to the one I occupied, so that you could hear perfectly what they said on the other side of the cracked adobe walls. Although I'm not in the habit of eavesdropping, I confess that on that occasion my curiosity was stronger than my respect for privacy. And in any case, it would have been difficult not to listen to what they were saying, since their voices could be clearly heard from the other side of the wall.

"What's wrong with you?" I heard Decoy say to Gil Gómez. "You seem to be having trouble falling asleep."

"Yes, in all that business of the bewitched forest there's something that, no matter how many times I turn it over in my mind, I just can't figure out," answered the Cabezón cacique.

"Can it be what Humbaba said about me?"

"Why did he speak as if he had met you before? You told me that the only time you were in the Cedar Forest was when you were lost with your herd in the storm."

"What I told you while we were returning from the Bernalillo Fonda wasn't the truth, or at least, not all the truth: I had been in the Sierra Blanca before."

"And why didn't you tell me then? Now I understand why you didn't want to go back there."

"The way I met the keeper of the forest is part of a terrible nightmare that I would have preferred to forget."

"You don't have to speak about it if you don't want to," the genízaro said.

"No, I can't flee from those memories forever, although they seem to me already as distant and foreign as if they had happened to somebody else."

Here is the story that Decoy told his friend.

"Some time ago, at least three years before I ended up in Cabezón, a family of farmers from Missouri decided to abandon their lands and join one of the caravans that was going to California, hoping to find the Promised Land they had heard about from others as naïve as themselves. Besides a married couple, the family consisted of a boy twelve years old who seemed older because of his robust build and another boy only a few months old who was in the care of a Negro servant.

"But like many other Argonauts, they never found their golden fleece. When they reached the banks of the Pecos, which was swollen by a flood, the guides detoured the caravan to the north, leaving the Sierra Blanca to the south. Near an arroyo that opened out into a pond surrounded by a thick canebrake, the caravan stopped, and the father sent the boy to fetch water while he unhitched the mules and the mother prepared supper.

"After collecting the water, the boy stayed a few moments at the edge of the swamp listening to the noises of waterfowl and contemplating the reflection of the first stars in the calm water. He was thinking about the mountain springs in California, where he was hoping to find gold nuggets as brilliant as those stars.

"Suddenly the silence of the swamp was broken. A flock of ducks flew out of the canebrake, frightened by some unusual movement. When the boy turned in that direction, he saw the silhouette of an Apache warrior who wore on his head a buffalo headpiece; across his face was a monstrous scar. The boy was so petrified by that vision that he couldn't even let out a cry, and before he could react, the warrior had struck a blow on his head with his war mace, which left him lying face down in the mud.

"Like snatches of a nightmare, the boy heard afterward the reports of firearms mixed with the war whoops of the Indians and screams of terror from the women in camp. Still half-conscious, he realized that his body was draped across the withers of a horse, with his head hanging and blood from the wound dripping by his nose.

"The Apaches had demolished the camp and slain all the men, including the boy's father. They had taken as prisoners the boy's mother and the Negro servant who was carrying the baby. The boy knew that his mother was still alive when he heard the moans of a woman forced by her captors to run barefoot on the desert stones.

"Two days after the massacre, the boy noticed that the Indians had picked up their march, and he guessed that they were fleeing from a party of soldiers that was pursuing them. The Apaches forced the captives to run faster, and anyone who couldn't keep up was eliminated without pity. When the Negro servant carrying the baby lagged behind, the Indians ran her through with a lance and smashed the baby's head against a rock.

"Upon approaching a small stream that ran through a valley, the Apaches let their hostages rest, perhaps thinking they had evaded their pursuers. But early that morning the hill that overlooked the gully shook under the gallop of a column of cavalry, and in the valley shots and cries of pain resounded. In the boy's mind, the echo of the soldiers' shots and the laments of the wounded Apaches blended with the shouts that he had heard a couple of days before when the Indians attacked their camp: the clamor of firearms and the cries of the terrified women and children were the same, and he felt the same fear that he had experienced then—to the point that when the warrior with the buffalo headdress tied his hands again and put him over the withers of his horse, riding off at a gallop, the boy felt almost relieved at escaping another massacre. His mother had been left behind, and the boy had the feeling that he would never again see her alive."

Although I couldn't see their faces, I imagined Decoy's expression when he choked up and had to pause. Then he continued.

"I don't know how long I was held captive in the Cedar Forest, under the tyranny of Humbaba. Perhaps it was only a few months or even weeks, but I know that in that time I went crazy, as much for the pain of having lost my family as for the loneliness of that cursed forest. The cruel witch treated me like a slave. He would beat me whenever he pleased, and at night he tied me to a tree with a horsehair cord so I wouldn't try to escape. I still have the mark of that noose on my neck.

"But one night during a storm he had to turn me loose so I could help him control the horses, who were frightened by the thunder, and I took advantage of that occasion to climb on the back of a colt and break away.

"All night long I galloped through the forest, and when the horse fell in a hole and broke his back, I continued running on foot as though the devil were after me. I crossed the desert, trying to get as far as possible from Humbaba's territory, until I fell down exhausted. I believe that my instinct had taken me to the same spot where the Apache attack on my camp had taken place, or some place similar, because when I woke up I found myself on the bank of an arroyo surrounded by a thick canebrake, face down in the mud.

"I was so weak that I wouldn't have been able to drag myself even to drink water from the spring, but then a doe antelope came near me and rubbed the milk from her udder on my lips. Thanks to the company of antelopes and horses that gathered to drink at that swamp, I was able to survive. And the memory that stayed in my mind of the cruelty of human beings, the natives as well as the white man, made me avoid the company of my peers until the drought in the plains took me to the Gila Mountains, where for the first time I felt the attraction of a woman.

"You know the rest of the story. You know which woman I'm referring to and how I appeared at a later date in Cabezón."

The voices quieted behind the adobe wall, but I stayed awake for a while, watching the dying embers in the campfire. I remembered when they told me in Fort Conrad that the strapping youth had appeared in the plains and how the villagers of Cabezón had contracted the services of an old witch who would make a double of Gil Gómez, creating a rival for his impetuous heart. And I recalled Sweeny throwing the Indian baby in the water with his willow cradle, and what the Indian Tafoya had told me when I commented on that terrible incident:

"If the Coyote had not kidnapped Water Monster's son, the human race would not have ascended to the Fourth World fleeing from the deluge; and if the maidens had not given birth to the monsters, surely Changing Woman would not have given birth to the Twin Warriors to free humanity from that plague. Perhaps the spirit of the Apache boy whom they threw in the water will reincarnate in the body of a great warrior, like Born From the Waters."

The Last Tablet

When I woke up at dawn the following day, intending to enter in my diary the latest news—including the confidences I had overheard the night before—I realized that I had no paper left to write on. What in almost any other place in the world would have been an easily solved problem, was hopeless in the middle of that wasteland since it would not be possible for me to obtain even a single sheet of paper until we were back at Fort Conrad. Paraphrasing the eternal song of Timothy Baltasar, it was about "three score miles . . . and ten" from the half-ruined Babylon that was the ghost town of La Luz to the Río Grande Valley.

The shortage of writing material made me very nervous, since after being away from camp for a few days, I felt a pressing need to write down the experiences of my excursion into the Sierra Blanca lest my brain, shaken by so many emotions, begin to confuse reality with fantasy. I also needed to express on paper my sorrow at the death of my friend, to put in black and white the epitaph that would help me convince myself that I would never again see the person who had shared so many of my hardships and joys.

I searched in vain for some scrap of paper among the empty sacks of provisions and in the leather saddlebags of my dead or missing companions. I used to write on the backs of company reports, but even those tablets were used up. On this fateful expedition so many incidents had occurred that the lieutenant had used up his stock. Later I learned that those who had remained in camp had utilized any scrap of paper that fell into their hands to start the fire so they would not have to leave the relative safety of the village to look for dry branches.

Something that kept bothering me was why Timothy Baltasar should have died precisely during the days that I was away from camp. But I didn't have the courage to ask the lieutenant how his last moments had been, or if he had left some message or legacy apart from the Bible that Loring had handed me in such a laconic way the day I returned from the mountain range. In my walks around the ghost town and its environs I didn't run across any mound of earth or wooden cross that would mark my friend's grave. Nor did I wish to find out where he was buried; it seemed I preferred to cling to the fantasy that, turning the corner of one of those ruined walls, I might bump into Timothy Baltasar. While I wandered aimlessly, as if sleepwalking, among the ruined houses, I realized that one of the healthy effects of keeping a diary is that, as one puts on paper one's experiences and feelings, one is clearing out those memories, avoiding turning them into obsessions.

Fortunately the need to help gather the belongings of the camp and to prepare provisions for the return trip kept me busy the rest of the day. With everything we had lost on the journey, there wasn't a lot of equipment to pick up, and the provisions were reduced to a few strips of elk meat that we had set out to dry in the sun. But we had to fill the water barrels, because as soon as we entered the desert we would be far from any water hole, and we had to help the cuates to get out of the river and lift onto the carreta the enormous cedar logs that had floated down in the flood. Having to struggle with those oversized logs, splashing in waist-high water, and other physical efforts that were required to organize the transfer served to take my mind off other things. That night I collapsed on the camp cot and slept like a log.

The next day we left before dawn, and the early wind made the bells of the ruined church toll a musical epilogue to the adventure that had begun only a few weeks before, when Gil Gómez and Decoy had decided to go to the Sierra Blanca—although perhaps my superiors had showed a greater folly by sending me and the Indian Tafoya to try to intercept them on their journey. With the entrada of the cuates into the Cedar Forest, and their victory over the fierce Humbaba, one could consider the first chapter of that saga closed. But I had a feeling the story didn't end there.

We started the return trip in the half light of dawn, sticking close to the Tularosa River so that we could easily obtain drinking water though we knew that eventually we would have to cross the White Sands Desert. Lieutenant Loring rode in the vanguard, still wearing a wet bandage on his head to lessen the effects of sunstroke but sitting upright on his mount as though he wanted to show that, in spite of what anybody might think, he was still the commander of the expedition. After him came the assistant surgeon, on the only mule with an army brand that had survived the adventure, and by his side the bugler on a pinto pony, one of those that Gil Gómez had brought from the mountain; and right in front of me were the two chieftains, taking turns driving the six pairs of wild stallions that pulled the cart. I brought up the rear of that handful of ragged souls.

Our retinue was a silent one. Even the cuates managed to be quiet, turning around now and then to look at the spoils of the conquered adversary. The head of Humbaba, half concealed in a buckskin bag, was swaying with the carreta, leaving a trickle of seepage and drops of blood in the ruts. Certainly the sorcerer's head, with its bonnet of buffalo horns poking out of the torn leather, was not very good company to cheer the way, especially when the hot desert wind began to blow and the horns of the animal head emitted a whining sound that seemed to come from the very mouth of hell.

As if it wished to give an even sadder and more ill-omened appearance to our silent march, every now and then a big black bird would pass low over the convoy. At times it had the impudence to land on the witch's head, where it began to emit mournful caws, the way a dog howls on the grave of its owner, until one of the cuates galloped up to it and scared it from its gloomy perch with a crack of his reata. I wanted to think that perhaps different birds were attracted by the carrion smell, but I soon noticed that it was always the same bird, because it had a white crest and one foot was hanging down. I began to suspect that the remains of the witch still had an evil power of attraction, a hunch that would soon be confirmed.

While I was riding in the rear of the retinue, observing how our shadows stretched out over the sand dunes when the incandescent ball of the sun rose over the crest of the mountain, I was mulling over the incidents of the journey and giving thanks to God that our hides had not been left hanging from the branches of the thousand-year-old cedars, as had been the fate of our companions. Lured by the rumor of gold and taking bad advice from the infamous Sweeny, they had dared to desecrate the sanctuary of that mountain range.

I wish I could believe that the dramatic outcome I witnessed in the heart of the haunted forest had put an end to that odyssey, but I remembered that the gravest problems began for Ulysses when he undertook the return to his beloved Ithaca. And although it would have been presumptuous to compare our miseries with the glorious deeds of that immortal hero, what is certain is that we still had a long way to go and a lot of yarn to untangle. What would happen to Lieutenant Loring when he was back at the fort, having lost by death or desertion more than ninety percent of the soldiers in his column? How would the witch Esther react when she saw the adventurers, who had scorned her spells and had escaped the pursuit of her peones, return triumphantly from their expedition? Even the villagers of Cabezón—the same villagers who had encouraged their young caciques to undertake that risky adventure, perhaps with the secret hope that the twins would leave their hides hanging in the mountain range—would they welcome the cuates home?

Although I refuse to put at the end of the last tablet the words *to be continued* the way the authors of dime novels do to attract the reader's interest to the sequel, there was an incident on the return journey that I don't want to leave untold here, since it foreshadows what was bound to happen later. In the same way, the last strophes of an epic poem end with a linking verse that serves as the prelude to the following stanza.

Colophon

They met each other at the market place;

Enkudú blocked the gate with his foot, not

allowing Gilgamesh to go through.

They wrestled one another, entangled

like two fierce bulls.

They smashed the door post to smithereens,

causing the wall to shake.

When Gilgamesh bent his knee,

touching the ground with his foot,

his anger diminished and they

untangled from each other.

POEM OF GILGAMESH
Tablet II, Column iii

The Vigil of the Gods

The incident happened, I seem to recollect, the night before we undertook the crossing of the White Sands Desert when we established our camp along the edge of the river, using the corrals of an abandoned ranch to fence the mustangs, who were still longing to go back to the freedom of the plains. While my companions were setting up our reduced equipment among the half-destroyed sheds of the ranch, I had stayed close to the river, watering the horses and helping the cuates unhitch the team.

While I was busy with that task, I heard a muffled cry coming from the back of the carreta, where the cuates were lowering the bag containing Humbaba's remains. Turning around, I saw that Gil Gómez was staggering under the weight of the sinister trophy; he stumbled and ended by dropping his prize and falling down the embankment, flat in the mud. Decoy tried to help his friend, but he bumped into the head of the witch, and showing the effects of a sudden dizziness, he also fell on his knees near the genízaro, swearing, "Damned Humbaba, his curse seems to catch us, even after his death!"

"Remember that something like this happened to us entering the bewitched forest, when we suddenly felt paralyzed," said Gil Gómez in a thin voice.

"I swear I was overcome by a sudden weakness when I lifted that sack," said Decoy, trying to kick away the witch's forehead, whose horns seemed to have stuck in the sand.

"Be careful that the head doesn't roll as far as the river! If the blood of the giant meets the water, Humbaba will live again," warned the genízaro, trying to move the giant's head but falling again face down in the mud.

Seeing them in this predicament, I covered my nose with my sleeve and with the toe of my boot pushed the pestilent bundle, which rolled down the slope until some bushes kept it from falling into the water. As soon as I separated Humbaba's head from them, the twins seemed to recover and, holding each other up, they climbed to the edge of the embankment, where they stayed lying down for a while, gasping as if they lacked oxygen.

"Remember what Narbona told us about the scalps of dead enemies?" Gil Gómez said to his friend, once he had caught his breath. "After a battle, the Navajo warriors always perform a cleansing ritual to avoid being affected by the bad vapors of the dead, and we haven't done it."

Decoy could not stop rolling his head from side to side, as if he had just gotten off a merry-go-round, and Gil Gómez continued, "When the Twin Warriors returned to Changing Woman's house after having defeated the giant Yeitsó and hung his head on a post near their cabin, they felt a sudden weakness. According to what they told me when I was a child, the Twins then pulled off a cedar branch and sucked on the bark, which had an antidote for the spell."

The cuates looked at each other and then around them, until a few yards away they found a small juniper bush, the kind the Spanish called sabino. Cimarrón dragged himself to the foot of the bush and pulled off a couple of green branches, giving one to his friend. Raising themselves up on their elbows, without further ado they began sucking on the resinous bark as eagerly as a couple of schoolboys chewing on sugarcane. The remedy seemed to work since in a short while the robust lads regained their powers completely, including the desire to eat and drink. Decoy spread their blankets at the foot of the cedar bush while the genízaro went to find a sack of provisions that he had dug up that morning from where he had hidden it on the way to the Sierra Blanca after their pack mule was lost in a sand storm.

Soon he returned with a small carafe of whiskey, and sitting down under the juniper, he pulled the cork out with his teeth and took a big swallow. Then he offered the bottle to his friend, who didn't turn up his nose at that medicine, perhaps not as healthy as the cedar sap but certainly tastier. Possibly because the alcohol had become stronger after having spent several days buried under the burning desert sands, or as a consequence of their recent faintness, the contents of the bottle had an immediate effect on its avid consumers.

As they repeated their swigs, I noticed that the cuates began to speak louder; later they began to let out guffaws, and finally they started singing some of the chants of the war ritual, the same ones I had heard from Tafoya when the Indian explained his traditions by firelight. I was not concerned until I heard the genízaro sing one of the chants of the Enemyway changing the content of some of the phrases and words, making a parody of the original song. According to what Tafoya had explained to me, an intentional distortion could bring down serious consequences on anyone who dared to take lightly the powers that were invoked in that ritual:

*I am the son of the **moon** when I go walking.*
*Beyond the **Black Dunes** I go!*
*Beyond the tail of the **cursed crow** I go!*
*Beyond the mountain range of the **wicked life** I go,*
*Beyond the frontier of the **misfortune** I go.*

Decoy went along with his friend's joke until he seemed to realize that this parody could bring about the hostility of the same forces that had helped them during their expedition. Grabbing Gil Gómez by the arm with which he was tipping the carafe, he tried to prevent him from drinking more, telling him, "Remember that Narbona warned us that while were on the path of the enemy we must avoid drinking alcohol, saying obscenities or changing the words of the ritual, because that could provoke the anger of the Sacred Beings . . ."

"Do you intend for us to spend the rest of our lives observing the ridiculous rituals that old crank taught us?" said the genízaro, struggling to recover the carafe of whisky.

"Well, thanks to that old crank we've been able to overcome obstacles on the way and defeat the spells of Humbaba," answered Decoy.

"Hold it, hold it!" said the genízaro, struggling to raise the neck of the carafe to his lips again. "Fortunately, we've arrived at the end of our journey, and I assure you I don't plan to spend one more minute respecting those stupid routines, like calling things backwards or having to turn my head like an owl over my shoulder in order to look behind. Do you by chance plan to spend the rest of your life waiting for your food to get cold and eating only the toughest pieces of meat?"

"Narbona told us that until we were out of enemy territory we would have to continue practicing the war rituals. We could only lift those restrictions when we reached the border of the Río Grande and we had left the mountains at our backs."

"Narbona also told us that during our expedition we could not go near a woman, and nevertheless we enjoyed the daughters of Sun Horse and we deflowered them almost right in the puberty ceremony. Perhaps you don't remember that?"

"Yes, of course I remember, but that's all the more reason not to further provoke the powers that have helped us during our expedition. They could still turn against us!"

"You can do as you wish, but as for me, starting now, I will call things by their names, and I believe that you should do the same. In any case, give me back the bottle because I still haven't finished . . ."

The genízaro tried to snatch the container of alcohol from his friend's hands, but Decoy had a good hold on it and, half joking, half serious, they began to struggle while rolling on the sandy slope going into the river, each holding one of the handles of the demijohn, until on one of their tumbles the bottle struck a stone on the bank. In the silence of the dusk, the clay container burst with the thunder of a firearm, and the echo of the explosion rolled through the valley for a few seconds.

For a moment I thought Gil Gómez was going to react violently to the loss of the precious liquor, but after remaining a few seconds helplessly watching the contents of the bottle—the few drops remaining—spread on the sand, he decided to make fun of it. Grasping the largest piece of the carafe, he threw it in the air, saying, "All that remains of the whisky I offer to the gods who have helped us in our enterprise, although I don't know if there will be enough for all," and he punctuated his own joke with a loud guffaw.

Adding insult to injury, the genízaro bent toward Decoy, and before he could react, yanked off the leather string that the strapping youth was wearing around his neck and with all his strength threw it up in the air with the scratcher and the drinking tube, shouting, "Here is the drinking tube, too, so you don't choke on the liquid, and just in case, the scratcher to scratch your stomach after a drunken spree. . . . Lest you take our jokes the wrong way and get angry with us!"

The genízaro had hardly finished his sentence when a tremendous bolt of lighting streaked through the darkness of the heavens, illuminating the river valley with blinding brightness. And in the twinkling of an eye, in the same sky where a moment before the stars had been shining, a storm cloud formed, unleashing an intense downpour, with hail as well as rain.

I had noticed with curiosity the object that Cimarrón wore around his neck, the kind worn by novices on war expeditions. They could not let water touch their lips or scratch themselves with their hands. But when I was ready to leave my hiding place to look for that interesting amulet, I saw that Decoy was ahead of me. Ignoring the hail that peppered his back, he crawled between the willows that grew along the river until he recovered his talisman and returned to sit next to Gil Gómez, who was dumbfounded by the sudden explosion in the heavens.

Although the storm passed quickly, I sought refuge from the downpour under the wooden planks of the carreta, because I knew that in that wilderness one could go to bed with a clear sky and wake up under a real deluge. That night I slept soundly again, but just before dawn I was awakened by a murmur of voices from the brush where the cuates had fallen in a drunken stupor.

Still half asleep, I recognized Cimarrón's hoarse voice. He was trying to tell his friend something, but Gil Gómez didn't seem to pay too much attention to him and only answered with grunts and yawns.

"My friend, do you know why the gods have held council?" asked Decoy.

"What are you talking about? Please let me sleep," replied Gil Gómez, his voice still a bit hoarse.

"Please, listen to me," begged Decoy. "Tonight I had a very strange dream, and I would like to see if you can come up with an explanation for it. I saw a grotto in the heart of the mountain, and in the middle of the cave there was a fire, and around the fire, the Sacred Beings had gathered to talk about us."

"You say they were talking about us?"

"Yes, they were discussing the episodes of our trip to the Sierra Blanca, how we had obtained the weapons to kill Humbaba and everything else. It seems they were annoyed with Narbona and Spider Woman for having helped us overcome the obstacles along the road. But more than anything they were discussing what our fate should be."

"What can the gods possibly care about our fate?"

"They were angry at us for having killed the keeper of the Cedar Forest, and because we had felled the sacred trees. Some of them were furious that we had enjoyed the maidens before the puberty ceremony. All of them agreed that we should be punished, although they couldn't come to an agreement as to who should pay for our sins."

"And what is it that they decided?" I heard the genízaro ask, in an impatient voice.

"Some of the gods thought that both of us must die, but others thought that only killing me would be enough. And that's what they finally decided," concluded Decoy, a ring of anxiety in his voice.

"Why were they going to kill you and not me, if we both went hand in hand in this adventure?"

"The gods claimed that it was I who had convinced you not to spare Humbaba's life and the one who also had cut off his head . . . they referred to me with a strange name: *he-who-cuts-around*.

"But it was you who in the beginning didn't want to come along, and it was I who persuaded you to accompany me. If someone must pay for our mistakes, that somebody has to be me!"

"They seemed to know that you were the son of Ninsaba, and they appeared to be more inclined to condone your mistakes than mine."

"So they were willing to spare my life at the expense of yours?"

"Yes, that was the council's verdict, and I can assure you that in my dream those voices sounded terribly real, although I was never able to see their faces. I woke up covered in a cold sweat!"

A long silence followed, which Gil Gómez finally broke. "You already know what you have to do to keep the dream from coming true: you must take the flint knife and kill your horse right now, so that the horse can take your place in destiny."

"I don't plan to slaughter my horse or any other, just because of that absurd nightmare," answered Decoy resolutely.

"If it were only a nightmare, I don't believe that you would have wakened me up to tell me. Besides, if you don't dare to kill the bay stallion, I myself will do it."

"I was the one who caught that horse in the Sierra Blanca, and I will be the one to decide what I want to do with it," answered Decoy in a sharp voice. "And I warn you that I will not allow for that animal's life to pay for our whims."

"You know very well that that is the only way to prevent the gods from carrying out their sentence. Where's the flint knife?"

"I won't let you kill that horse!" exclaimed Decoy in a threatening tone. "Leave that knife alone!"

Although the light of dawn was still breaking through the mist over the riverbed, I was able to catch a glimpse of the shapes of the cuates wrestling at the edge of the slope like two immense reptiles intertwined in mortal combat. Then I could hear the muffled impact of a body hitting the ground, and by climbing up the embankment, I was able to make out Gil Gómez's silhouette while he ran with his stone machete toward the corral where we had locked up the mustangs. But just as he had climbed over the corral posts, Decoy jumped the fence like a cat, knocking down the genízaro with the momentum of his body, and they rolled on the ground grasping each other while the horses made way, neighing with terror.

Quietly approaching the spot where the fight was taking place, I saw how Decoy struggled to wrest from his friend's hands the flint knife, which in the haze of the early morning shone with its own light. The genízaro resisted with all his might, and I wouldn't have been surprised if, in the course of the violent struggle, the sharp knife had injured one of the fighters. Despite his efforts, the genízaro was losing ground to the sheer strength of Decoy, who managed to straddle his opponent and began to twist his wrist to make him drop the weapon.

Sensing he was losing, the crafty Gil Gómez resorted to a trick, and feigning loss of resistance in the arm that had a grip on Decoy, with his free hand he grabbed a big clod of dirt and struck his opponent on the head. Decoy's parietal bone cracked like an anvil under the blacksmith's mallet, and the body of the strapping youth doubled over and rolled on the ground, while Gil Gómez hurried toward the herd of horses with the flint machete in his hand.

The mustangs had witnessed the fight with their ears pricked and their muzzles flaring, and seeing the genízaro coming close to them with a threatening attitude, the animals stretched their necks, backed into the posts at the rear of the corral, and kicked in the air like sheep when a wolf enters the fold.

It didn't take long for the genízaro to locate the horse that he was looking for. The yellowish coat and the whitish mane of the bay horse shone among the dark backs of the other animals. As if frozen by fear, the mustang remained alone in the center of the ring, its front legs spread apart and head raised up, looking at its executioner approaching. The other animals moved aside as the man stepped forward brandishing the flint knife, its blade flashing in the first ray of sun.

Thanks to the hypnotic effect of the flint blade, which mesmerized the mustang, Gil Gómez could come so close to him that the point of the machete almost touched the stallion's shoulder. But just as he was about to strike the mortal blow, Decoy jumped on him again, using his powerful forearms to grab his neck like a tourniquet. For a moment I thought that the vertebrae in Gil Gómez's neck were going to break, but once Decoy had control of him and the genízaro let go of his weapon, he loosened the hold and turned his adversary's body free. Gil Gómez fell to the ground like a rag.

Then I saw Decoy approaching the mustang, which had remained immobile as if its hooves had been nailed to the dirt. He softly caressed its neck, rubbing its mane until the animal quit shaking. Next he led the horse to the gate of the corral, and patting its rump, he set it free. The mustang hesitated for a moment, looking back toward the corral, smelling the herd, but when Decoy gave it a good slap whose echo reverberated through the ruins of the hacienda, the animal threw back its ears and took off like a shot. It crossed the river in two jumps and continued galloping toward the mountains until the waving of its white mane blended with the sunlight above the snowy crest of the mountain.

When the silhouette of the horse disappeared from sight, Decoy returned to the corral and helped his friend to his feet. Gil Gómez was still gasping for air, and putting an arm under his shoulder, Decoy half carried him to the bank of the river, where Gil Gómez stuck his head in and drank for a long time. Hidden in the branches of mesquite, I had not missed a single detail of their encounter, and I believe I was the only one from the camp who witnessed that spectacular fight, which had the same ending as the famous duel in the plaza of Cabezón. Once again the sheer strength of the man raised in the plains had prevailed over the craftiness of the cacique from Cabezón.

When I came close to the corral to see if the fence had been properly closed, I saw an object shining in the dust, and I bent to pick it up. I recognized immediately the cane tube and the scratcher that Gil Gómez had thrown up in the air the night before, and which Decoy had recovered, losing it again during the fight. As I observed them closely, I saw that the two small cane sticks had engraved in the edge the marks of the Twin Warriors: the taut bow and the hourglass. The leather band that connected them was broken.

I was going toward the cuates, to return that object to Decoy, when all of a sudden it dawned on me that perhaps he no longer needed them, since he had triumphed in his expedition and in addition had just taught his robust friend a lesson. My mother used to say that the most insignificant objects could have their usefulness when you least expected it. Thus, I kept the drinking tube and the scratcher with its cord in a fold of my tunic and I must say that I felt a warm sensation when that amulet came in contact with my chest.

Glossary

Abuelo grandfather

Acequia irrigation ditch or canal

Adelantado leader of a land or sea expedition, who was given governship of the lands to be discovered or conquered

Alabado a traditional religious hymn; common among the Brotherhood of the Penitentes

Alcalde mayor

Apachería area not conquered by the Spanish Crown, subject to raids by hostile Indians, including the Apaches

Arriero a muleteer, often thought of as being Mexican

Atole cornmeal mush or gruel usually made from blue corn

Barranca a steep-sided ravine

Berrendo (adj.) mottled; (n) antelope

Bizcochitos anise-flavored sugar cookie

Cacique an Indian chieftain; by extension, a political boss; someone who submits a group of people to his absolute power

Cañada a dry riverbed, small canyon, or narrow valley; originally applied in Spain to a cattle trail with ancient rights of passage

Cañada de ganado cattle trail or path

Carreta an oxcart, a wagon with wooden wheels

Chamizo sagebrush

Chaparral a place abounding in scrub oak, sometimes of vast extent and impenetrable

Cíbolo buffalo; applied for the first time while Vásquez Coronado and his party were crossing the western prairies, in search of the Seven Cities of Cíbola

Cibolero buffalo hunter

Cimarrón a stray animal living in the wild; term also applied to intractable cattle or men who stayed away from the rest of their kind

Compadre in the Southwest this referred to godfathers of the same child, or to a close friend

Concha shell; by extension, a disc or knobs of silver used to decorate horse gear or, by Navajos, on belts

Conducta a trade caravan or a military expedition; in colonial times, a conducta traveled twice a year from Santa Fe to trade with Chihuahua and Mexico City

Cuate twin and, by extension, friend or pal

Descargaderas sluice gates or floodgates in an acequia

Despoblado depopulated, abandoned; also applied to a vast expanse in the wilderness, never inhabited before

Dikohé young Apache warrior

Diné or dineh the Navajo Indians' word for themselves, literally, "the People"

Disciplina a whip used once upon a time by the Penitentes for self-flagellation, often made of yucca fibers

Doña Sebastiana figure of death

Entrada a military mission of exploration or reconnaissance

Estufa an adobe fireplace or furnace, and, because of the similar shape, a kiva

Fandango a lively dance, with castanets and triple measure; also used to describe a party or celebration

Flauta a flute

Fonda an inn

Gan an Apache ritual dance and the dancers who perform it

Genízaro a non-Pueblo Indian captive rescued by the Spanish settlers from various nomadic tribes and living in more or less Spanish fashion: derived from old term janissary

Gente de razon people who follow Spanish custom

Hacienda a ranch or estate of a large landowner; the main house where the landowner lives

Hermano mayor presiding officer of Penitente group

Hidalgo a member of the Spanish blood nobility; applies also to someone with a generous and noble soul

Hogan round or polygonal Navajo dwelling

Horno in the Southwest, a beehive-shaped outdoor oven

Iikáála Navajo sand painting

Jacal a small hut with walls comprising poles chinked with mud

Jerga a coarse woolen cloth

Kinaálda Navajo girls' puberty ceremony

Kiva a Pueblo Indian ceremonial room, sometimes underground

Machete a large, heavy knife

Malpaís lava beds, badlands

Mayordomo ditch boss

Meseta plateau or tableland

Mesteño a wild, unbranded, or stray horse (mustang); term originally used to describe the stock belonging to the Mesta, a Spanish stockman's corporation, with no specific individual owner

Mestizo a person of mixed European and American Indian blood

Metate a flat stone with a concave surface on which grain is ground

Mescal an intoxicating drink made from the agave plant

Monte country heavily thicketed; and a card game introduced from Spain and Mexico

Morada a chapel or meeting place of the local Brotherhood of Penitentes

Natán, natanes from a Navajo word, *naat'áanii,* meaning chief, leader, or headman

Palo verde a small, spiny tree or shrub native to the Southwest and Mexico

Patrón master

Penitente a lay Roman Catholic Brotherhood of Indo-Hispanic origin that observes certain rites related to the Passion of Christ

Peón a member of the landless laboring class; in some cases, the economic dependence on the landowner was such that he was close to being a slave

Placer a location of sand or gravel in which gold was found, also used of deposits of other rich minerals

Potrero pasture land; a narrow ridge between canyons

Presidio a fort, as built in Spanish colonial time

Ranchería an Indian settlement

Reata a rope; also a string of horses

Rebozo a shawl

Remuda a herd of horses; term applied to the spare horses taken on a trip or roundup: remounts

Reredos an altar screen

Sabino juniper tree or bush

Santero a woodcarver who makes images of saints

Santo a statue of a saint

Seguidilla a Spanish popular song, and the dance that goes with it

Serape woolen shawl worn by men

Spanish bayonet a yucca with sharp leaves and a long stem

Tiswin, tisgüín corn liquor

Torreón a round tower built for defense; frequently built as part of an hacienda

Trastero cupboard

Vara a Spanish unit of length slightly less than a yard. Also a cane that is a symbol of authority

Viga roof beam

Zaguán an entrance or entrance hall to a building